DUKES TO THE LEFT OF ME, PRINCES TO THE RIGHT

Kieran Kramer

St. Martin's Paperbacks

DUKES TO THE LEFT OF ME, PRINCES TO THE RIGHT

Copyright © 2010 by Kieran Kramer.

Cover photograph of couple © Shirley Green

For information address St. Martin's Press, 175 Fifth Avenue, New York, NY 10010.

ISBN: 978-0-312-37402-0

Printed in the United States of America

St. Martin's Paperbacks edition / December 2010

St. Martin's Paperbacks are published by St. Martin's Press, 175 Fifth Avenue, New York, NY 10010.

10 9 8 7 6 5 4 3 2 1

Praise for
WHEN HARRY MET MOLLY

"A delectable debut...I simply adored it!" —Julia Quinn,
New York Times bestselling author of *What Happens in London*

"At once frothy and heartfelt, *When Harry Met Molly*
satisfies! This book is better than dessert!"
—Celeste Bradley,
New York Times bestselling author of *Rogue in My Arms*

"Kieran Kramer pens a delightful regency confection...a
wonderfully bright debut." —Julia London,
New York Times bestselling author of *A Courtesan's Scandal*

"A delicious romp that will keep you laughing. A fun
heroine and a sexy hero make this a delightful read."
—Sabrina Jeffries,
New York Times bestselling author of
The Truth About Lord Stoneville

"I couldn't put it down...a charming delight!"
—Lynsay Sands,
New York Times bestselling author of
The Hellion and the Highlander

"A wickedly witty treat...an exquisite debut!"
—Kathryn Caskie,
USA Today bestselling author of *The Most Wicked of Sins*

"*When Harry Met Molly* is a delightful, page-turning
read! New author Kieran Kramer will capture both your

To Mom and Dad

And to Jeannie

Thanks for all the love.

ACKNOWLEDGMENTS

Once again, I have to thank Jen and Jenny for seeing me through—I couldn't have done it without either one of you!

And a big thanks to my sister Devon, who's always there to encourage me and make me laugh.

I'd also like to thank Herbert Ames. He's a NASCAR man (and secret angel) who was wearing a white suit and a huge grin the day I met him on a plane. I was flying with Devon, and we couldn't get seats together, which was a bad thing as my sister doesn't like to fly. Herbert, who's never met a stranger, said he couldn't move as he was squashed in, but he promised to take very good care of Devon for me.

A minute later, he called up the aisle in a big, booming Southern drawl, "Kieran Kramer, are you a book writer?"

I was in a middle seat six rows ahead, so I had to stand up, turn around, and answer Herbert in front of a bunch of bored-looking people waiting for the plane to take off.

I dared myself to say, "Yes, Herbert, I am," even though I hadn't found a publisher yet.

And I *was* a book writer! I had the thousands of pages to show for it.

Well, Herbert whipped out his cell phone and called his good friend Janet, who was a writer, too, and urged her to read my book.

"Kieran Kramer's gonna make it, I just know it!" he shouted into the phone. And then he passed it six rows up to me (everyone on the plane looked a lot less bored by this point), and I had a few words with his friend.

Janet was kind enough to read the first chapter of one of my manuscripts. She wrote me a note about it—said it had some good things and also some things that needed work but that, overall, she thought I had a wonderful voice and to hang in there.

Well, I read those encouraging words from Janet Evanovich over and over again as I wrote another story that sold months later, my first book, *When Harry Met Molly*. So thanks very much to you, too, Janet. You and Herbert both helped out a stranger—lucky me!—and for that I will be eternally grateful.

CHAPTER 1

In a proper English drawing room on Clifford Street in London's Mayfair district, Lady Poppy Smith-Barnes, daughter of the widowed Earl of Derby, threw down the newspaper and stood up on shaky legs. Finally, the secret passion she'd been carrying around with her for almost six years would have its day in the sun.

"He's here," she announced to Aunt Charlotte. "Sergei's in England."

She could hardly believe it. She'd resigned herself to being a Spinster—she was in good company, after all. But now . . . in a matter of a moment, everything had changed.

Her prince had arrived.

Aunt Charlotte, tiny in her voluminous, outmoded gown, stopped her knitting. "Are you sure?"

Poppy found the paper again and put it under her aunt's nose. "He and his sister are touring with their uncle's last portrait and unveiling it for the very first time here in London."

"Oh, Poppy!" Aunt Charlotte's eyes were a bright,

mischievous blue above her spectacles, and her powdered white wig sat slightly askew on her head. "He's
the only man on earth who could coax you out of the
Spinsters Club."

"Indeed, he is." She hurried to the front window and
looked out, expecting *something* to be different. But the
day appeared like any other day. She knew, however,
that it wasn't. It was special.

Sergei—the perfect boy, and now the perfect man—
was in Town.

She spun around to her aunt. "Do you think he'll remember me? It's been six long years. I was fifteen. We
had only a week. It seems a lifetime ago."

"How could he forget you?"

She shrugged. "So much has happened to him. He's
been traveling, he was in the military—I kept up with
him as best I could through the papers. I'm afraid he'll
see me at a ball and walk right by me."

Aunt Charlotte laughed. "No one walks right by
you, dear. Not with that fiery hair and impudent air."

"*Aunt.*" Poppy's cheeks colored. "This is a fine time
to remind me I'm not the malleable sort."

Aunt Charlotte calmly resumed her knitting. "Eversly
will survive the turndown, and so will you. It's not as
if you haven't had a great deal of practice."

Eversly was due to arrive within the hour, and his
would be the twelfth marriage proposal Poppy had rejected in the three years she'd been out. Two of those
offers had rather predictably taken place during the fire-
works at Vauxhall. Another two had transpired at Rotten
Row in Hyde Park at the fashionable hour, both times

while she'd sat astride docile mares (Papa wouldn't let her take out the prime-goers). One proposal had taken place in front of a portrait of a spouting whale at the British Museum at eleven in the morning and two more at the conclusion of routs that had dragged on until dawn. One had transpired in the buffet line at a Venetian breakfast after she'd overfilled her plate with wedges of lemon tart to make up for the dull company, two had occurred in her drawing room over cold cups of tea—tepid because her suitors had prosed on so long about themselves—and one had taken place, inexplicably, at a haberdashery, where she'd gone to buy buttons for Papa's favorite hunting coat.

Two barons, a baronet, three viscounts, four earls (one of them only nine years old at the time), and one marquess had proposed to her. Two had had large ears. Four had had small eyes. Three had smelled of brandy, and one had lost his breeches in a fountain. One had been missing his front teeth (and it hadn't been the boy).

Stay calm, she told herself. *More than ever, you have a reason to say* no *to Eversly.*

As the clock ticked closer toward the earl's arrival, Aunt Charlotte kissed her on the cheek and left the room. Poppy waited another agonizing twenty minutes. Finally, there was a knock at the front door, and she put her newspaper under a pillow. Kettle, Lord Derby's elderly butler, greeted the visitor in his usual sober way.

Poppy stood.

Then she sat.

And then she stood.

Finally, the earl, a veritable Adonis, entered the room.

He had gleaming blue eyes, a golden curl on his fore-head, and shoulders so broad she should feel weak in the knees.

But her knees stayed firm.

"You're alone." Eversly's eyes were warm. She could tell he had genuine affection for her, and she did for him, actually. He was sporting, congenial company, but she couldn't help thinking of him only as a friend. It was always that way with her suitors, as if there were a big NO stamped on all their foreheads.

Thanks to Sergei.

"Yes," she told Eversly, swallowing hard. "I *am* alone."

They both knew what *that* meant. Without her father or Aunt Charlotte by her side, she was unchaperoned. Only an engaged or married woman could meet a man alone in a room.

But she wasn't quite alone, was she? There was her mother—sedate, mature—smiling down at her from her portrait, her wedding rings sparkling on her pale, slender hand. Her hair was the same shining copper color as Poppy's own wavy locks; her eyes, the identical emerald green.

The earl moved toward Poppy, skirting a small table and rounding a chair. He lifted her hand to his lips and brushed a soft kiss against her knuckles. "We shall do well together," he said, in a low-timbred voice that should have sent shivers up Poppy's spine.

But it didn't.

She stole a glance at his perfect lips. She'd heard from her aunt's maid, who'd heard from the maid of a widow who'd had an affair with him, that he was a splendid kisser.

"We should," she said with a little intake of breath, "were we to marry."

Lord Eversly arched an eyebrow. "Aren't we?"

"No, we aren't," she said in a small voice.

"What?" The earl's voice became a mere squeak.

Poppy bit her lip. It was always at this point she reminded herself of the Spinsters Club and the vow she'd made with her two very best friends, Lady Eleanor Gibbs and Lady Beatrice Bentley. None of them would marry except for love.

And then, to inspire herself further, she imagined herself kissing Sergei.

"I can't marry you," she said to Lord Eversly, feeling braver now. "I'm so sorry."

And she did feel sorry. He was such a dear.

He winced. "But your father said—"

Poppy blinked. "He doesn't know."

"Doesn't know what?"

She was reluctant to hurt him, but she told her usual story. "I'm to be engaged," she said. "And it's a love match. Surely you understand."

"I demand to know his name," the earl said rather breathlessly.

Sergei, she wanted to say. But instead she said, "The Duke of Drummond." Her tone was firm but gentle. She'd been through this scenario many times before.

Her other suitors believed she'd met the Duke of Drummond on a walking tour she'd taken in the Cotswolds, but he was totally fictitious, actually, a product of Cook's lurid imagination. Cook enjoyed making up tales as she stirred her pots and chopped her vegetables, but that was part of her charm (if a floury-faced, wild-haired harridan in the kitchen who tippled occasionally could be called charming).

Indeed, just this morning, Cook told Poppy another outlandish tale about the duke. Poppy already knew he was the mightiest, fiercest duke ever to have walked the earth. And she knew as well that his ancestral castle jutted out over a cliff above the swirling waters of the North Sea. According to Cook, he'd murdered his brother so he could become duke, and to forget his guilt, he regularly plunged off this cliff for a swim. Occasionally, he came back up from the depths with a writhing sea creature under his arm, usually one with large, snapping teeth.

Today, Poppy learned the dreaded duke had even fought an octopus the size of a Royal Mail coach—and won.

"Did you say the Duke of Drummond?" the earl demanded.

Poppy yawned. "Yes, he rusticates somewhere far away."

Eversly drew in his chin. "Never heard of him."

"He's quite wicked."

"Wicked?" The earl raised his brow.

"Wickedly handsome, that is," Poppy recovered. She thought again of Sergei. "We met three years ago. Remember the year I missed that impromptu boat race on the Thames?"

"Oh, yes. I do recall. My side won, actually. I had a prime spot at the front of the boat, and Miles Fosberry fell in the river. We couldn't fish him out until we'd finished."

"Right." She gave him a sheepish smile. "Well, while you and your team were rowing past your less-favored acquaintances, I was on a walking tour of the Cotswolds. The duke was on one, too. We met at a village fair."

"But your father—" The earl's brow puckered. "Lord Derby never mentioned it. He said you were free to accept my offer."

"Drummond hasn't exactly *offered* for me yet," she explained. "But he's"—she paused—"on the verge."

She'd been quite clever to have come up with that phrase—*on the verge*. Her previous suitors had found it suitably vague, so that when they saw her dancing for weeks and months—and some, for *years* after her rejection of them—they didn't think to question her story.

"It's simply a matter of time," she said. "I've never told my father. It's my secret"—she laid a hand on her heart—"my secret of the heart." She allowed her voice to go a bit trembly. "And I'm not willing to reveal it yet, even to Papa."

Lord Derby would be furious, of course, that she'd turned down the earl's suit. But surely he'd recover. He was far too busy toiling away for England to waste time being angry at her for long, especially if she cried and told him she was waiting for a true love match, like his and Mama's.

The earl looked down at his well-polished Hessian boots, and when he looked up again, his gaze was both besotted and disappointed.

"I still like you," Poppy protested. "As a friend. This little . . . engagement thing between us—let's forget it, shall we? I'll see you throughout the Season, won't I? We can share a waltz." Although her dream was to share her next waltz with Sergei.

She dared to lean forward and give Eversly a small kiss on his cheek. She wasn't one to dispense her kisses lightly, and the whole *ton* knew this of her.

"I shall hold you to that waltz," the earl said, a little gruff. She could tell he genuinely cared for her. Nevertheless, his old good cheer sneaked back into his tone.

"I look forward to it." She smiled. "Meanwhile, I know I can count on you to be discreet. Please don't say a word to anyone about our . . . conversation."

"I wouldn't dream of it." The earl bowed and left the drawing room without another word.

She waited a few seconds for Kettle to open the front door, then she ran to the window and looked out. Lord Eversly descended the front steps rather slowly. Poppy recognized that walk. It was the gait of a jilted bachelor. She'd induced it in many men.

But by the time he ascended the steps of his fine carriage waiting on the street, the earl's pace had picked up to his regular jolly one. And why shouldn't it? He was a wealthy, handsome peer of the realm with tremendous charm. Plenty of women would accept his suit. Why, she'd put a bug in several girls' ears this very week.

She turned around to see Aunt Charlotte standing in

the door, a loose curl from her wig hanging in her eye and making her look quite the scamp. "I heard every word," she whispered loudly. "I'm *so* proud of you for following your heart. But—"

"But what?"

"We're doomed. I hope your emergency suitcase is packed."

"It is," Poppy said in a thin voice.

"You know the procedure. Now that Waterloo is behind us, Spinsters in untenable situations no longer retreat to the north of Scotland. We're forced to go to Paris!"

Aunt Charlotte appeared delighted at the prospect.

"Poppy?" It was her father's voice. She could hear him in his boots, clomping down the hall toward the drawing room. "That wasn't the earl leaving, was it? I've brandy and cigars in the library to celebrate your betrothal."

Outside, Lord Eversly's coachman cracked his whip, and he was gone.

But Poppy's problems had only begun.

CHAPTER 2

Nicholas Staunton had always been a light sleeper—
growing up in a drafty castle that took the brunt of
howling North Sea storms had seen to that—so when he
felt someone shaking him, saying, "Wake up, Nicholas,"
he knew, wherever he was in the ether of his mind, that
something was wrong. No one should have to shake him
to wake him up.

Especially when he knew he had something to do.
He couldn't remember *what,* but it was something
rather urgent and distasteful.

He opened an eye. A shaft of morning sunlight
pierced the edge of his vision, blinding him.

And then he smelled something.

Lilies.

God, he hated lilies. They reminded him of his parents' funerals. But someone he knew—someone he'd
bedded—wore a lily scent. And he seemed to recall
that he endured the cloying odor because she was very
good at—

Yes. At *that*. What she was doing now.

He closed his eye again and sank back into that hazy, sublime world, where he basked in hot, carnal sensation and forgot all about the distasteful, urgent thing.

But then the hot, carnal sensation suddenly stopped. He groaned and wished with all his might for it to come back.

"Nicky, wake up," a feminine voice insisted.

He winced and ignored it.

"I don't *do* things like this in the daylight," the heavily accented voice went on, "and I have no intention of going further. I'm only trying to wake you up. So *wake up*."

He felt a light slap on his right cheek, and with a great deal of will and a tremendous amount of reluctance, he managed to open his right eye and confront the pest jarring him awake.

Good God. Now he remembered who wore the lily scent. She lay a mere inch from his face, her hard brown eyes glinting with impatience and her ebony curls falling around her face.

The way a witch's would, he had the incongruous thought.

"Natasha," he muttered.

The Russian princess.

She rested her cheek on her hands and smiled at him—a slow, heated smile. He'd a vague recollection of sipping brandy from her navel sometime after midnight, but he couldn't remember anything after that.

His limbs were sore and he had a pounding head and he'd really like to go back to sleep, to tell the truth.

Back to a *deep* sleep.

"Nicky," she hissed in his ear, "the Howells come

back from Sussex this afternoon." She placed the flat of her palm on his bare chest. "If they find you here, they'll make me pack my bags and return to St. Petersburg. Don't doze off again! It's almost eleven."

Eleven?

Eleven wasn't good. Eleven was bad, in fact.

He felt confused. Why had he stayed?

He never stayed.

Morning sunlight, he'd come to discover, was like a splash of cold water on a man and an excuse for clinging in a woman. "You're right," he muttered as he rolled out of bed. "I've got to go."

Natasha's eyebrows lowered over her small, elegant nose. "You don't have to agree so readily. Many men crave to wake up in my bed."

Nicholas didn't mind annoyed females—their pique gave him an opportunity to appease them with his special "I-know-you're-angry-but-you'll-forget-after-I-do-this-to-you" restorative (something he'd picked up from an Indian text), but today he didn't have time.

Today—

Ah. Now he remembered. Today was the day he was to find Frank before the big cockfight to be held at noon in Cheapside, which he was sure his brother would attend, and remind him (last time it was by holding him upside down out a second-floor window) that he really mustn't gamble away his allowance anymore, nor steal spoons from White's.

Yes, that was Nicholas's plan, to reform his recalcitrant brother.

And snow would fall in London in July—

But it was still his plan. He wasn't allowed to give up hope on Frank. It was one of the self-imposed rules he'd established for himself after their father had died.

"Nicholas." The princess slapped the coverlet. "Are you even listening to me?"

He found his dove-colored breeches and pulled them on. "Yes, and it's a good thing you woke me," he soothed her. "I've got a meeting with my lead attorney. He tells me it's important."

It was his standard line, but come to think of it, Groop *had* called him into his office last week. Nicholas had been too involved, however, to bother showing up. Young widowed Russian princesses with voluptuous figures, bewitching accents, and superior connections made for quite a good reason for ignoring obligations. He'd go see Groop straight after he'd rattled Frank's teeth.

That is—he amended, and pulled his shirt over his head—after he'd calmly talked sense into his brother.

He strode to a small mirror above Natasha's bureau, willed his own dissolute reflection to be noble, and made quick work of his cravat, ignoring the fact that he needed to shave. Then ran his fingers through his hair once, and gave his head a shake, like a dog.

There. The look served him well enough, judging by the number of women who batted their lashes at him in the street and the number of men who crossed to the other side to avoid him.

"Prinny was right." Natasha compressed her lips. "You *are* an Impossible Bachelor, and I'm a fool to share my bed with you."

He wouldn't deny it. Being selected an Impossible Bachelor last year with his good friends Harry, Lumley, and Arrow had only given him *more* reason to kick up his heels while he could. While the weeklong wager had been vastly amusing—who wouldn't love entering one's mistress in the Most Delectable Companion contest?— he'd come *this* close to legshackles. One of the losing mistresses' consorts had been forced to marry. Luckily, that sad fate hadn't fallen to him or any of his friends but to a weasel who'd been seducing young virgins for years and getting away with it—until Prinny's scandalous bet, that is.

Which reminded Nicholas—he *was* a Bachelor, known for his skill at evading the parson's mousetrap— so what was he still doing here? And where was his damned coat?

He bent low, sending a crashing pain through his head. But there the rumpled garment lay, under the bed, a comfortable nest for two snoozing corgis.

Natasha lifted her feet, and he nudged the dogs awake long enough to pull the coat from under them with the least amount of disturbance to their slumber.

When he stood, a slant of that dreaded morning sunlight hit him square in the eye.

As if on cue, Natasha bounded from the bed and took his arm. "Imagine the children we could have if we married." Her expression was more determined than dreamy. "*My* hair. *Your* blue eyes. And the boys with that sweet cleft in their chins, like you."

She pulled him closer, and he paused in his dressing,

one arm inside his coat sleeve. "I'm sure I mentioned I've no intention of marrying and having children of whom I'm aware for at least another decade, possibly two."

He was an expert at seduction and was damned sure she wasn't in danger of producing any ebony-haired, blue-eyed children any time soon—ones fathered by him, that is. The women he bedded never seemed to notice how disciplined he was, how carefully he kept a wall up between them, even in the throes of passion—

Especially in the throes of passion.

He looked around the room for his hat and found it next to another corgi—Boris, the one with the missing eye—and a small, empty bottle of brandy on the floor by the bed. Of the two glasses nearby, one had a golden puddle in the bottom. The other—he picked it up and sniffed it—had never been used.

Natasha laughed, but he caught an uneasiness in her tone. "Men and their brandy. It turns them into—" She gave him a smoldering look then, and he knew she was thinking of their sensual play of the evening before. Or attempting to get *him* to think of it.

She bit her lip.

He sat down on the bed next to her and shackled her slender wrists with his fingers. "Tell me truthfully what happened," he said. His voice was firm. But fairly gentle, for a man with a sore head, a growing suspicion, and an unfulfilled, hot carnal need.

She lowered her eyes.

"Natasha?"

"All right." She looked up, her tone defiant. "I took liberties last night. I added something to the brandy because I wanted you to *stay*. Is that too much to ask?"

Bloody well it was too much to ask. "Do you often drug men who take you home?"

She refused to answer.

He turned her chin toward him. "Tell me."

She shrugged. "It's a habit of mine. I find it rather titillating."

Looking into her lovely face, marred by a petulant expression, Nicholas saw how stupid he'd been to give in to temptation. He rarely made such careless mistakes. In fact, he wondered if he was losing his touch.

He'd known after one conversation with her at Gunter's, where he'd followed her one day last week, that she'd no political *on-dits* of any import to offer, not even a morsel or two about her famous uncle Revnik or her twin brother, Prince Sergei.

Yet when Nicholas had run into her at a musicale later that evening, he'd come back with her afterward to Lord and Lady Howell's residence, sneaking into her bedchamber through her balcony—out of sheer boredom.

He'd been back twice, which said a great deal about his mindset these days. He was in a rut, well before he should have sunk into one, by his appraisal. Ruts were for men over thirty.

He released Natasha's wrists and stood. "Today we say good-bye."

She sniffed. "You've no heart, Nicholas."

"Consider yourself lucky for having found out so

quickly." He arched a warning brow. "You could've killed me, you know—me or one of your precious corgis. A few licks out of a tipped-over glass might be enough to do a doggie in."

He could tell by the way the young widow's eyes widened that she hadn't thought *that* far. She was impulsive and, for all her sophistication, not very bright.

"Don't worry," he assured her. "Boris and company appear none the worse for wear this morning. But here's a bit of advice: don't drug the men you bring back to your bed. It's bad form. And in your case, bad politics."

He'd learned through experience that no woman likes a man to leave her bed whistling, so he closed the door with his usual somber expression on his face. This time it wasn't faked. He *did* feel somber. It had been a near miss.

But when his champagne-buffed boots hit the pavement outside Lord and Lady Howell's Mayfair town home, Nicholas couldn't help but be restored to good humor. It was a gorgeous day, and he already knew just the expensive bauble he'd buy to soothe Natasha's wounded pride, a bracelet she'd admired at an exclusive shop yesterday.

It was a small price to pay for his folly.

A few hours later, his pockets considerably lightened, Nicholas went to a meeting with Groop.

But he wasn't his attorney. Far from it. The man was actually a spy chief in the clandestine branch of the government fondly known by its employees as the Service.

"Your IF is long overdue," Groop told Nicholas in his

thin, reedy voice. His cravats were always perfectly folded and his coats cut by Weston. His natural sartorial elegance called attention away from his long face and beady eyes. "You shall marry for King and country."

"The King is quite mad, thank you," said Nicholas. "And I still don't see why marriage has to be my *Inevitable Fate* any time soon."

The Service was fond of abbreviating terms. It lent an air of elitism to the whole profession, but certain codes—especially the more melodramatic ones—drove Nicholas a bit mad himself.

Groop arched a brow. "The higher-ups believe your new title will thrust you into a whole new realm of desirability among the *ton*'s matchmaking population."

"I haven't told anyone my new title, save for three very close friends. They and a few government hacks at Whitehall are aware of it, but men don't tend to talk, especially about little-known dukedoms that carry no influence."

"Nevertheless, everyone in the social world will soon know, and no one will care that your father made no ripples in Town. A duke's a duke."

"But—"

Groop put up a hand. "Prinny's come out with a new directive. He's cut short your year of mourning and has included you in his new crop of Impossible Bachelors. The list comes out any day, and you and your new title are on it."

"Good God. Nothing's as desirable as the unattainable. Every girl and her mother will be trying to win me over—damn Prinny's hide."

"It's entirely too much attention you don't need," Groop agreed smoothly. "Therefore, you must slide into a dull, proper, entirely respectable engagement immediately. You'll make your first contact this evening at the Grangerford ball."

"This *evening*?" Nicholas sputtered. "With whom, may I ask? You know I avoid anyplace young, insipid debutantes tend to gather. Finding a bride will take some time in a gambling den. Or at Madame Boingo's Palladium Show. I'll have to take you, Groop. She dresses in nothing but feathers."

"Not to worry, Your Grace. We've already chosen you a suitable candidate in a satisfactory quid pro quo arrangement. The girl's father unknowingly hired one of our own Service employees who does private detective work. It seems this particular earl was looking for *you*."

"Me?"

"Every one of his daughter's rejected suitors has said she claims she's on the verge of a betrothal to you. Of course, until she mentioned your title, not a one of them had ever heard of it, nor are they aware you're in current possession of it. As far as they're concerned, Lady Poppy has been carrying a torch for a wicked, mysterious, faraway lover for three years."

Nicholas gave a short bark of laughter. "Absurd."

"Your esteemed colleague discovered that you and the subject of his search were one and the same person. I've put the information to great use, as you will soon see. Here's the girl's name."

He shoved a scrap of paper across the desk.

Nicholas almost swallowed his cheroot, but he leaned forward anyway, feeling a faint curiosity about this so-called candidate. "Lord Derby's daughter?" he said after a quick glance. "He's a high stickler, and no doubt she's a milk-and-water miss. I prefer a red-cheeked hussy or no one."

"We could find no red-cheeked hussies among London's Upper Ten Thousand, Your Grace."

"God knows you tried." One of his small joys in life was teasing Groop.

"Your goal is to become an afterthought in the minds of the *ton*," Groop reminded him, as usual ignoring all of Nicholas's attempts to bait him. "Lady Poppy Smith-Barnes is almost on the shelf. We took a gamble, brought Lord Derby in, and told him of your connections to the Service."

"I *hate* when you do that. I want to work a long time, not be a flash in the pan. I'm aiming for the wall of unsung heroes, you see. I plan to be front and center."

"Right," Groop said dryly.

Groop had one serious shortcoming. He still couldn't tell when Nicholas was being serious—and Nicholas was very serious about that wall.

Of course, Nicholas liked keeping Groop guessing. He didn't need anyone to get close.

Close was reserved for his favorite horse, Fritz (who was now twenty-five and stabled at Seaward Hall), and his good friends, Lord and Lady Harry Traemore, Viscount Charles Lumley, and Captain Stephen Arrow of the British Royal Navy.

Everyone else could jump in a lake. Or go about their business. He didn't care which.

"Lord Derby is a loyal subject," Groop was saying. "Nothing to fear there. We told him he'd be doing a great service to his country and alleviating his own problems in the bargain if he would agree to your marrying his daughter, under certain conditions."

"What conditions?"

"He has to help expedite the betrothal if you run into snags. And he must agree to pay off your brother's debts and help get your family estate back on its feet. We can't have any financially insolvent dukes, you know. Leaves you open to blackmail."

Nicholas propped his feet up on his employer's desk. "My God, Groop, that's brilliant. The government can keep paying me a pittance and let a private citizen award me the compensation I deserve for marrying a silly debutante who just might be off in the head. Why didn't I think of that?"

Groop didn't blink an eye. "The fact of the matter is, starting right now, you're off assignment until your betrothal takes place."

"That's ridiculous."

"We've a particularly intriguing assignment coming up, too," said Groop, "Operation Pink Lady. It comes with an MR, a rarity in our profession."

Monetary reward, and Groop was right—they were hard to come by. Operation Pink Lady must be very important, which made Nicholas want to work on it all the more.

"How large is the MR?" he asked.

"Substantial. But you won't need it if you align yourself with the house of Derby."

"True, but—"

"But you want the assignment anyway."

"Of course. Luscious assignments don't come along as often as I'd wish. I want the monetary reward, too. The bigger the pile, the better. Seaward Hall requires a great deal of work, and in case Lord Derby's tight-fisted, that MR will be good insurance."

"We should make a decision in the next day who shall handle it. If you want to be considered for it and if you care to continue working with the Service at all, you'll betroth yourself to Lady Poppy tonight."

Nicholas rose from his chair. "You dry-lipped devil. Why couldn't you have told me this sooner?"

Groop shook out his cuffs. "I called you in a week ago. But you were too busy bedding Russian princesses to come in."

"Oh, yes . . . right." Nicholas sank back into his chair.

"This ultimatum should come as no surprise," Groop said, steepling his hands under his chin. "On the first day of your training, you were told your IF."

"Yes, but I thought I had several decades' leeway."

Groop's gaze was unwavering. "Spoken like a true Impossible Bachelor. If you'd remained Earl Maxwell longer, you might have had another five years' grace period. But the fact is, you're now a duke. A duke should be married. Especially a duke who dabbles in clandestine work for His Royal Highness's government."

Nicholas scoffed. "I do much more than dabble."

"We're aware of that, Your Grace."

"You know how I feel about marriage."

"I do. If a brilliant, generous man like your father could be so deceived—"

"Then so could I."

"Not all women are like your stepmother, draining away entire fortunes."

"Yes," Nicholas said, "but which ones aren't? That's the question."

Groop sucked in his cheeks. "As you've no fortune to drain away at the moment, you've no need for concern in that regard."

"Damn your cold, clear grasp of the situation, Groop."

"Yes, you're between a rock and a hard place, Your Grace. Your brother is currently in debt to Lord Wendell for a thousand pounds."

"I know that," Nicholas sputtered. "The half-shiner I'm sporting right now is what happens when an empty wooden keg thrown by one's fleeing sibling meets with one's eye."

Groop steepled his hands. "Let me be blunt, Your Grace."

"It's your favorite thing to be."

"Money *and* adventure. You and I both know you need them in equal measure. If you refuse to marry this girl, you'll have neither."

"I could go out on my own," Nicholas said. "I could find my own wealthy bride, and I could certainly have my own adventures outside of the Service."

"I've no doubt you could find that wealthy bride, Your Grace, but adventure? Where shall you find that adventure outside of the Service? At Seaward Hall?" He gave a bitter little laugh. "You'd slowly give up the idea that adventure exists, and you know it. You need *me* to seek it out for you, to put it in your lap, and to remind you that you're more than a duke." Groop drew himself up tall. "You're a clandestine agent for His Royal Highness's government," he concluded dramatically, which for Groop meant his facial muscles twitched.

Nevertheless, Nicholas was shaken. Groop was right. Again.

Frank's problems . . . Seaward Hall's decay . . . to forget his personal troubles, he was foolishly indulging in too much brandy and too many women—sly women like Natasha, for example, who could have killed him if she'd wanted to.

He'd allowed himself to be vulnerable—was acting like a dilettante, as a matter of fact—and it was now time to shore up his defenses. A discreet mountain of money to dispense as needed, a meek bride, and a boring title would help restore some stability to his otherwise topsy-turvy life.

"Fine, then," he said, never afraid to admit he was wrong. "But I'll do the thing on *my* terms."

The Service and his obligation to it always won out in the end, but he had to throw in a bit of rebellious rhetoric to keep things amusing.

"You're wise not to waste time lamenting the current state of affairs," his imperious advisor said over his spectacles. "Lord Derby will meet you at White's at eight o'clock so he can make his own assessment of you, as any good father would. If you pass muster—

which I'm sure you will—you'll go to the Grangerford ball on your own and do your duty. If all goes well, by the end of the evening, you'll be betrothed."

"God help me."

Groop tossed Nicholas something.

He caught it handily and looked down. It was a ring. A lovely one.

"It belonged to your mother," Mr. Groop said.

"How'd you—"

"We have our ways."

"Of course."

Mr. Groop gave him an odd smile—half paternal, half wistful. "Might as well get used to the look of it."

Yes, he might as well, Nicholas mused as he left Groop's office in search of a bride. But he didn't have to like it, did he?

CHAPTER 3

"*You*—the young lady with the chamomiles in her hair!" The heavy Russian accent coming from behind Poppy at the Grangerford ball almost made her jump.

She inhaled a shallow breath and turned around to see a sturdy gentleman with broad shoulders and a large mustache who wore the uniform of a Russian army officer.

"Take those off," he said, lifting his chin at her head.

My, he was rude!

But Poppy kept her head high and her demeanor cool. "Why?" she asked calmly. Inside, she was flummoxed—

And hurt on her mother's behalf.

Every time Poppy went out, she tried to wear one thing she used to see her mother wear when she went out to parties. Some nights, she'd put Mama's special mother-of-pearl bracelet on her wrist or wear Mama's rings on her fingers. Other nights, she'd don her mother's favorite kid slippers, the ones with the embroidered peacocks on the toes that she'd had resoled twice now.

Still other nights, she'd wear one of her mother's favorite fringed shawls or put fresh flowers in her hair, as she had tonight.

A beautiful young woman with glossy ebony hair knotted in a fanciful twist appeared from behind the man. She wore an exquisite gown in bold scarlet silk adorned with intricate black beading, a heavy diamond necklace, and many rings on her fingers.

It was Natasha, Sergei's sister.

Poppy forgot her pique and was thrilled to see the princess in person for the first time. She had the same dark beauty as her twin brother.

Was Sergei right behind her? Poppy had been on pins and needles all week hoping to see him, but they'd yet to cross paths.

Now the princess stared at Poppy's face, her hair, and her gown—and gave her a slightly bemused smile.

"Introduce us, please," she said to one of her escorts. Several had appeared around her in the last few seconds, two of whom Poppy recognized as her father's cronies from Parliament.

The uniformed man, probably serving as the princess's bodyguard, moved back. One of the Englishmen, Lord Wyatt, stepped forward and cleared his throat. "Princess Natasha, this is Lady Poppy Smith-Barnes, daughter of the widowed Earl of Derby."

Poppy inclined her head. "Honored to meet you, Princess."

Lady Natasha inclined her head, as well. "I see Russian flowers in your hair," she said in flawless, honey-thick English. "Chamomiles. I saw them from the top of the stairs, in fact."

"Yes." Poppy smiled, pleased the princess had noticed. She'd decided that if she were to wear flowers tonight, she would choose the national flower of Russia in honor of Sergei.

"Remove them," Natasha said curtly.

Poppy felt an immediate stab of alarm in her middle, and her face flamed. "Wh-why?" she asked again.

But Natasha moved on without explaining. Lord Wyatt turned around, his brow lowered, and whispered impatiently, "Do as she says, Lady Poppy. We don't want any friction between our countries."

Friction? Between England and Russia?

Because of her *flowers*?

Poppy didn't see how wearing flowers in her hair constituted a diplomatic gaffe. But as the daughter of a member of the House of Lords, she dared not take any chances. With shaky hands and without leaving the ballroom floor, she pulled the flowers out of her curls and stuffed them in her reticule.

Everyone around her stared.

"Look at someone else, please," she blurted out, and made a beeline for Eleanor and Beatrice.

Before she could open her mouth to tell them what had transpired between her and the princess, Beatrice said, "We saw."

"She's wicked," Eleanor added.

"But Sergei's not," Poppy insisted. "Every family has its bad apples, don't they?"

But Beatrice and Eleanor had stopped listening. They were looking over her shoulder.

"There he is." Eleanor gasped.

"Good heavens," said Beatrice. "I see what you mean. He's—"

"Perfect," breathed Eleanor. "No wonder you've been fobbing off all your suitors."

Poppy turned and looked at the man standing at the top of the stairs. Her heart swelled with happiness.

Sergei!

He was older, of course. But he'd only grown handsomer. The memories of her romantic week with him in St. Petersburg came flooding back.

"Gracious, he's staring right at you," said petite Eleanor, her masses of strawberry-blonde hair highlighted by the glow of hundreds of candles in the double chandeliers overhead.

Beatrice, gorgeous as always with her luminous brown eyes and her rich, dark hair pulled back in a sleek knot, squeezed Poppy's hand. "He'd be lucky to have you," she said firmly. "Remember that."

"If you're meant to be, we'll find out together," added Eleanor.

"Thanks." Poppy felt a lump in her throat. "I'm so glad I have you two."

Without another word, the three of them overlapped their hands. "Hell will freeze over," they recited in whispers, "before we—"

"Give up our passions," said Beatrice.

"And give in to our parents," murmured Poppy.

"To marry men we don't love," added Eleanor.

Whereupon they released their hands and said together, "The Spinsters Club? Never heard of it," as Eleanor gave a delicate yawn, Beatrice sipped from a glass of ratafia, and Poppy fiddled with a curl on her shoulder.

She usually felt exhilarated after saying the pledge. Stronger and braver, too. Because no matter what Papa said about women knowing their places and marriage being a business arrangement, she wasn't going to marry a man who didn't have her heart in his full possession. She'd far rather be a Spinster—a Spinster with very good friends in the same predicament—than succumb to such a fate.

The prince made eye contact with her and grinned, and Poppy felt her whole insides light up. She couldn't help it—she grinned back.

He remembered her.

He headed her way with a small entourage. Poppy schooled herself to be calm, and she prayed she'd say the right thing.

Once in front of her, the prince raised her hand and kissed it, just as he had the first time he'd met her six years ago.

"Poppy. It *is* you." He stared deep into her eyes, and her knees trembled. "What a fantastic surprise to see my little English friend all grown up."

"H-hello, Sergei." She drew in a breath. "I mean, Your Highness."

He threw back his head and laughed. "Don't dare call me that. I am always Sergei to you, and I would like you to introduce me to your friends as Sergei."

What a gracious royal he is, Poppy thought, as he paid his respects to Beatrice and Eleanor. They were charming, witty, and sincere in their enthusiasm about the prince's visit to London. She couldn't have been more proud to call them her best friends.

The prince was impressed by them, as well. "I see, Lady Poppy, you've been in delightful company since I saw you last. My own friends would be honored to dance with them." Indeed, two very distinguished Russian aristocrats had already bent low over the other Spinsters' hands.

Which meant Poppy could abandon herself to the enjoyment of the evening. She did just that when Sergei took her hand and wrapped it under his arm.

"There are few things in the world more intimidating than a roomful of curious people," he said. "Best to face them down first and let the other gentlemen in the room know what's what. And then we shall dance."

What's what?

Poppy couldn't help thinking the prince was using strong language. Was he implying she was *his*? That all the other men ought to steer clear?

Oh, if so, he was simply adorable, even after all these years. So effortlessly charming. And so . . . kissable.

Poppy's schoolgirl crush came roaring back, stronger than ever.

Of course, if any one of her old suitors noticed her affinity for the prince and cared to ask about her Duke of Drummond tonight, she already had an easy reply. The duke had asked her to marry him, and she'd declined.

Who could blame her?

Prince Sergei was obviously a worthy distraction.

While they paraded about the room, Sergei deigned to stop and converse with only two important members of Parliament—although at least five more Very Important People attempted to capture his attention—and then he took Poppy out to the dance floor and swept her into a waltz.

She released a happy sigh. Hadn't she waited six years for this moment?

Sergei squeezed her hand. "You are pleased, I think, that I've arrived. In fact, I see from your expression you feel it has been too long since we've last met."

"It *has* been too long," she dared to say.

"Tell me about your life." He was gorgeous when he arched his brow.

She shook her head. "I've been quite busy since I saw you last. In between my studies and my social and charitable obligations, I run the household, planning the menus, conferring with the staff. I only wish I could serve as my father's hostess, but he won't entertain, not even his stuffy government colleagues."

Prince Sergei's expression was sympathetic. "I'm sorry to hear the news about Lady Derby. She made quite an impression on St. Petersburg society."

Poppy's heart warmed to hear the kind words about her cherished mother. "Thank you for saying so."

"Oh, but it's true." He gave her an endearing grin. "I'm equally sure your father can't have had a better helpmate than you these last six years. He's a lucky man, although you're meant for more than serving as the mistress of your father's household. So much more."

His voice was warm. The look in his eye promised something. And although she wasn't sure what, it left her breathless.

"Thank you," she whispered shyly.

Her dream was happening too fast. Then again, she'd waited for a moment like this for a long time. She'd endured how many insipid conversations? Patiently danced with how many men who didn't make her heart speed up? Bought how many ball gowns for parties where she spent half the night yawning behind her fan?

No doubt tomorrow all of London would be talking about how the prince had arrived at the Grangerford ball and had come directly to *her*. They would wonder what he meant by his attentions.

So would she.

When the waltz ended, a Russian envoy came running over with a glass of lemonade and handed it to Poppy.

"Why, thank you." She smiled and took a sip. It was quite nice to be spoiled so.

"And find me a beautiful flower," Sergei said to the man.

"Yes, Your Highness. But your sister will be unhappy. She likes no one to wear flowers except her."

"My sister is intolerable," the prince said in a tight voice.

Poppy couldn't agree more, but she was shocked to hear the prince say so out loud.

But his face softened when he looked at Poppy. "This pretty lady should always wear flowers in her hair."

She felt a blush rise up her cheeks. The realization

that the prince was here and lavishing her with attention was such a shock that she couldn't think of a response. She sent him a quick smile, but she felt as if she were watching something extraordinary happening to someone else.

Marrying Sergei had been her dream ever since she'd met him. She dared not think that it could possibly come true. But it might. It just might. She was no green girl—she'd had a dozen proposals already, and she recognized the signs.

Sergei was interested in her.

Perhaps their flirtation which had ended so abruptly in St. Petersburg would resume at an entirely new, more sophisticated level.

But she had no precious seconds to cherish the hopeful feelings welling up inside her. The butler announced some late arrivals from the top of the stairs.

"Lord and Lady Harry Traemore!" he cried.

Poppy watched the Traemores descend the stairs slowly, whispering to each other, oblivious to the stares of envy and admiration from the crowd below. They'd been married less than a year and seemed divinely happy. Lord Harry clung to his wife's hand, and she looked up at him with adoring eyes.

They were perfect for each other.

"They are a fine-looking husband and wife," said Sergei.

"Aren't they?" Poppy replied, knowing every girl in the room was wishing the same for herself—

A love match.

And then she noticed someone else at the top of the

stairs. Under the blazing candles, he was wild-looking. Not in his dress. That was perfectly presentable. But even from this distance, she could see his eyes were a stormy gray and his mouth forbidding. His dark blond hair was longer than was fashionable and brushed straight back from his rather commanding forehead.

The way he stood was different from the other men of her acquaintance, too. He stood as if he owned the room. As if he owned the Grangerfords' house and all the company in it.

And didn't care for it *or* them.

Sergei studied him. "He looks a heathen, doesn't he? Even though his coat is of superb cut."

Poppy said nothing in return, unable to look away from the brazen-eyed gentleman.

And then he made eye contact with her.

She felt a jolt down to her toes. Her breath grew shallow, and a buzzing began in her ears. Who was he? And why did he gaze at her as if he knew her?

She abruptly looked away—disconcerted by his boldness—and instead watched the butler thrust out his chest, clench his fists at his sides, and boom, *"The Duke . . . of Drummond!"*

Poppy stopped breathing. And then somehow, very slowly, the room began to spin.

CHAPTER 4

Which one was Lady Poppy?

Nicholas looked around the room and spied her immediately next to the Russian prince, Natasha's brother. He'd never met Sergei, but Natasha had told him her brother always got what he wanted.

He'd just better damned well not want Poppy.

She was already taken.

"You won't be able to miss her, of course," Lord Derby had told him at White's earlier that evening. "She's got titian hair, and she's beautiful, but she won't look demure. As much as I love her, I'm often baffled at how many suitors have offered for her hand. She's most unbiddable. Let that serve as a warning to you. Oh, and for years she's been besotted with that Russian prince, whom we met several years ago in St. Petersburg. She speaks a bit of Russian and will no doubt be attempting to converse with him."

Sure enough, the girl in the seductive pale blue gown at the prince's elbow had shimmering red-gold hair and a direct gaze that took no enemies. Nicholas felt a twist of lust in his belly when he caught the wink of a diamond-shaped pendant at her breasts, but he was actually far more intrigued by the shocked expression on her face, which was quickly followed by a determined tug on the prince's arm.

There was nothing docile about *her*.

No matter. He'd marry her, ship her off to Seaward Hall, and give her what every woman wanted—babies and the occasional bauble to keep her happy. He'd even bring her to Town once a year to satisfy that yearning every woman seemed to have to socialize.

But then he'd send her back to Seaward Hall again—to write letters, entertain the neighbors, arrange flowers, rear their children, and whatever else it was that women liked to do—while he went back to London and worked for the Service.

Being married wouldn't have to change his life much at all.

The music started up again, people converged on the dance floor once more, and Nicholas strode down the stairs. He caught Lord Derby's eye and then moved straightaway toward the copper-haired goddess, ignoring all attempts to snag his attention along the way.

As he approached Lady Poppy, her eyes, a dazzling emerald color, grew larger and larger. Prince Sergei cast a careless glance at him, as if he were nothing more than a fly to be swatted away once he came close enough to be a genuine nuisance.

Nicholas felt an instant dislike for the man.

"Nicky!" A feminine arm reached out from the crowd of dancers and stopped him.

Blast. It was Natasha. He saw the bracelet he'd bought for her dangling from her wrist.

"Do you always ignore royalty?" she asked him peevishly.

He suppressed his impatience and kissed her fingers. "Hello, Your Highness. I'm sorry I missed you."

"I'm thirsty," she said, like a small child.

Right. He was meant to get her a drink, but she was surrounded by perfectly respectable gentlemen who'd be willing to get her some lemonade.

"I'm sure Lord Crowley or Sir Benjamin would be happy to oblige." He moved on, ignoring the princess's loud sigh.

But his efforts to disentangle himself came too late. Lady Poppy had disappeared.

CHAPTER 5

Poppy thanked God she had a strong constitution. Her momentary dizziness had been almost instantly replaced by a strong survival instinct—

To flee.

She gave Prince Sergei a flimsy excuse—her hem had come down—and left him before he'd had a chance to reply.

"Lady Poppy!" Lord Cranston called to her. He'd been the first suitor to have proposed to her at Vauxhall. "Your duke is here."

"Yes, we shall finally meet him," said the gentleman next to him, Sir Gordon, who'd proposed to her at the haberdasher's.

And straight ahead she saw Lord Winsbury and Lord Beech, the Corinthians who'd proposed to her on horseback. And to their left was the pompous Marquess of Stansbury, who'd proposed to her over tea in her drawing room.

She pretended not to hear either Lord Cranston or Sir Gordon, and she must steer clear of Lords Winsbury

and Beech and the Marquess of Stansbury. In fact, she
must leave the ball immediately.

But the stairs to the front hall were blocked by a clus-
ter of four more of her old suitors—Lord Greenwood,
Sir Jared, Baron Hall, and Lord Nottingham—all of
whom were staring avidly at the Duke of Drummond
and searching the ballroom—

For her, no doubt.

Fear was a new thing for Poppy. She despised it. It
took all enjoyment away. She was tempted to cry, but
she threw off that idea and put on her most neutral expression instead.

Beatrice and Eleanor came up to her, their brows
smooth but their eyes alight with surprise and concern.

Eleanor laid a hand on Poppy's arm. "We don't understand what's going on with this duke who calls himself
Drummond. We thought he wasn't real."

"I thought so, too," Poppy said in an anguished whisper. "I'm done listening to Cook. She tells tales—tales
that are supposed to be tales but they're true."

"*Too* true," said Beatrice with a shudder, looking
over her shoulder, presumably for the Duke of Drummond. "So they're not tales, after all."

"But Cook pretends they are." Eleanor nodded.

"Which *is* telling tales, isn't it?" Poppy hissed.

"No matter," said Beatrice, all business. "Let's get
you out of here."

"The only way out without attracting notice is through
the gardens," Eleanor whispered.

"So I've surmised," Poppy said. "I was heading there
now."

She'd sneak round to the front of the house and call a hackney, or if she were unable to, walk home. It was only two streets over.

"I'll clear a way." Beatrice did her best to find the path of least resistance toward the terrace.

They were almost to the double doors to the garden, which were flung wide open, when a large figure planted itself in front of the trio and blocked their way.

Lord Washburn. He'd been the one to have no breeches on when he'd proposed to her. He'd lost them in a drunken fight that had taken place in the basin of a fountain.

"We must talk, you and I," he said to Poppy.

"I can't." She didn't like the look in his eyes. He appeared drunk. Angry. Worthy of the reputation he had of being rather volatile.

"No, she can't, Washburn," said Beatrice breezily. "She's ill."

Eleanor gave him a stern look. "Please get out of our way."

"I must ask a burning question first," Washburn insisted. "The Duke of Drummond is here tonight, Lady Poppy. Yet you're nowhere near him."

She hesitated but a moment, not sure what to say, but it was enough of a pause for Lord Washburn.

"Ah." He nodded his head sagely. "I see how it is."

"No, you can't possibly," Poppy said.

He gripped her wrist. "He's dishonored you. Cast you off." His face was beet red. "How *dare* he."

"You've got it all wrong, Washburn," said Beatrice.

"And let go of her wrist." Eleanor hit his arm with her reticule.

"Yes, Washburn," Poppy said, "I'm not a child."

"Fine, then." Washburn glowered and dropped Poppy's arm. "But you're hiding something, my lady."

Poppy inched closer to him. "My personal affairs are none of your concern," she whispered, "but as you're being quite vocal in your curiosity, I shall give you a short explanation. Drummond is simply busy this evening. As am I. We'll meet on another day to discuss, um, our impending nuptials." She made a move to the left, but Washburn cut her off again, his eyes blazing.

"You're too good for him," he said. "Duke or no duke, how could any man of breeding ignore *you*?"

She forced herself to smile, although she would have preferred to push past him and run. "That's very kind of you to say, but my friends and I really must be going."

He ignored her, turned, and called, "Drummond!"

Unfortunately into a lull. One of those rare lulls at a ball where the musicians are in the process of lifting their violins once more to their chins, when the women are taking another breath to gossip, and the men, to share information about their latest equine purchase at Tattersall's.

The moment of stillness passed as quickly as it came, but there was no time to lose. Beatrice and Eleanor both elbowed Washburn in the side. Poppy managed to get in front of him, but he grabbed her arm. She twisted hard, kicked his ankle—"Ow!" he cried—and escaped.

Right into the path of the Duke of Drummond, who

now stood before her, his face set in hard, unyielding lines, although she caught a glimmer of curiosity, and perhaps even amusement, in his eye.

"I'll be glad to take you where you want to go, Lady Poppy," he said in a dangerous voice that made her heart slam against her chest.

"I'm not going anywhere," she responded, her chin in the air.

He knew, didn't he? He knew she'd been pretending to be engaged to him for three years . . . that she'd been pretending to be madly in love with him, as a matter of fact.

Blast.

Whatever was about to happen next couldn't possibly be good.

CHAPTER 6

Nicholas's first thought when Lady Poppy stumbled into him was that he was a very lucky man. His future wife was gorgeous *and* ready for battle, her eyes snapping emerald fire and her breasts rising and falling above that low bodice with its winking diamond pendant.

Nothing like a worthy opponent with an abundance of sensual allure to make a man's blood run hot.

She was flanked by two striking friends with the same confident look about them. He saw he'd have to force his agenda upon Lady Poppy quickly if he was to get anywhere at all.

Without preamble, he raised her hand to his lips and left a lingering kiss upon it. And why not? They were supposed to know each other very well. In fact, almost a dozen men at the ball thought they were on the verge of an engagement.

Her eyes flew open, and she appeared to be grappling for words, but nothing came out of her mouth. And no wonder. She was caught between a rock and a hard place, just as he was.

She was supposed to be in love with him.

He saw how much it cost her, that she couldn't tell him to leave her alone.

Without preamble, he got down on one knee and pulled out his mother's ring. The position felt as awkward as he'd imagined it.

"Wait." The object of his quest laid a shaky hand over her heart. "What are you doing?"

"Yes, what *is* he doing?" Prince Sergei strode up with Lord Derby at his elbow. "Call him off, Derby. Your daughter looks none too pleased."

"Not necessary, Your Highness," Lord Derby said equably. "The Duke of Drummond has held the key to my daughter's heart for three years now, and I'm most pleased he's coming up to scratch."

Sergei stared at Lady Poppy. "Is this true?"

She bit her lip. "Actually . . ." She gave a delicate snort. "It's amusing, really. And quite a long story. Shall I . . . shall I tell it?"

"Go ahead," Sergei urged her.

"Don't torture yourself, Your Highness," called someone in the crowd gathered behind Nicholas to watch the spectacle. He recognized the voice of Lord Eversly. "She told me the story herself just last week. Sadly for me, she's in love with the fellow."

"Not anymore," Sergei said with a confident air. "Surely."

And he looked at Poppy for confirmation that he was the culmination of any woman's dreams.

Nicholas was tempted to roll his eyes.

Lady Poppy, meanwhile, stared at the prince, her

strawberry lips parted. "Um, well, the duke and I," she choked out. "We . . ."

She trailed off and looked back at Nicholas.

"We're madly in love," he said, taking her hand in his own. Then he gazed into her eyes and put on his best besotted grin. "Why, she's my sunrise. And my sunset. She's my everything." He let out a long sigh. "And what am I to you, dearest darling?"

"I can think of no words," she gritted out. "None at all."

"That's quite all right," he said, with an understanding smile. "Love has made you speechless." He grabbed Lady Poppy's hand and winked.

"Just nod at the appropriate moment," he whispered to her, then cleared his throat and said the words he had hoped he wouldn't have to say for years to come. "Lady Poppy Smith-Barnes, will you be my wife?"

Poppy took in the large crowd gathered around her, Princess Natasha and Aunt Charlotte among them. She could hear everything, too—a tiny gasp from Beatrice, the random screech of a violin bow accidentally rubbed against a violin string, the cough of a gentleman behind her—and especially the pounding of her own heart in her ears.

The Duke of Drummond was proposing to *her*—after mouthing all sorts of sweet nothings to her?.

Sweet nothings that had made her want to gag, incidentally, and box his ears—because they'd been entirely false. Somehow—

He'd found out.

She wished she were dreaming. She wished she could go back to her waltz with Sergei, where everything had seemed perfect. Surreptitiously, she pinched her thigh through her gown to make sure she wasn't dreaming.

Her heart sank. Nothing changed. Drummond was still there on bended knee, staring at her with that smarmy look that made her want to slap him across that freshly shaven cheek of his.

Papa (how had he found out?), Sergei, her best friends, Aunt Charlotte, even Natasha . . . all of them were waiting.

This was really happening. But Poppy had no idea how. Or why. Cook had made those stories up. Hadn't she? And even if the duke were real—why would he be proposing? She had no time to think on the matter. He needed an answer, obviously.

Right now.

"I—" She knew she should say yes. All her suitors would not only *not* scoff at her—they would commend her for staying faithful to her supposedly one true love, who happened to be extremely eligible. She'd be a duchess and married to a man so handsome that just looking at him sideways took her breath away. She couldn't even *describe* what happened to her when she looked at him head-on, when her eyes locked on to his unfathomable gray ones.

But she was a Spinster. She would marry only for love.

She straightened her spine, prepared to say no as graciously as possible—no matter the consequences. Eleanor, Beatrice, and Aunt Charlotte would support her.

"Yes!" shouted someone from the stairs.

Poppy looked up.

It was Prinny—he'd arrived late, and was carrying his usual open bottle of wine. "Is that Drummond on bended knee?" he cried.

"Yes, Your Highness," the wily duke called up to him. "I'm proposing to a young lady."

Prinny laughed. "She says yes, yes, *yes*! She'll have you, Drummond, and it shall be the wedding of the Season! Shan't it, everyone?"

"Yes!" replied the crowd. And broke into wild applause. "Yes, yes!"

Poppy blinked.

Drummond stood and tugged her close.

And then he kissed her. Thoroughly. A possessive, sensual kiss that sent shocking tingles to her toes. She had no time to think when she finally managed to pull her head back. She could only feel. And what she felt was rage.

Hot, burning rage.

Her hand itched to slap him. But she couldn't. She was supposed to be in love with him.

Damn the man.

"You never said yes," he said into her ear. "But don't get any ideas. I'll be one step ahead of you."

That was exactly the kind of rude statement the wicked, unscrupulous Duke of Drummond would make to an unsuspecting girl.

And then he had the temerity to raise her fingers to his lips for another kiss. The crowd went wild; everyone, that is, except Sergei, Natasha, and of course, Eleanor,

Beatrice, and Aunt Charlotte. She swung around to see them, to gain strength from their indignation.

Sure enough, her dear friends and aunt stood frozen like statues and staring at her and Drummond together—

With silly grins on their faces.

What were they thinking?

The Spinsters were in crisis. One of them had been entrapped!

Poppy had never felt so alone in her life. She pretended to smile graciously at the duke. "I don't know what you're about," she murmured for his ears only. "But hell will freeze over before I marry *you*."

"I shall explain the situation further tomorrow"— his voice was unperturbed—"when I arrive at your house for dinner at seven o'clock."

"But I'll be out tomorrow night. I've a musicale to attend—"

"You won't be attending any musicale," he said. "You'll be waiting in your drawing room for me, *if* you know what's best for you," he added silkily, and held her hand up high, to the crowd's delight.

She almost gasped. How dare he tell her what to do? And hold her hand aloft as if she were a trophy?

He left her side to accept congratulations from Prinny and all her former suitors, and she simpered for the company, accepting her own felicitations—but inside, she was livid. Absolutely livid.

This man was *not* going to get the best of her.

She was saving *that* for Sergei.

CHAPTER 7

Victory.

Nicholas tried not to savor it too much, as his prize despised him, but he couldn't help feeling a little bit triumphant.

He'd never had his hand wrung so hard—never heard so many men say in awed tones, "You must be something extraordinary," or "How did you manage it?" or from one fellow, a tear trickling down his cheek and a mumbled, "Take good care of her, will you?"

He felt as if he'd won Helen of Troy—and perhaps he had.

He looked over at Lady Poppy and she was glorious in her suppressed fury, so untouchable and fierce that if someone had brought him enough wood to build a gargantuan wooden horse for her at that moment, he might just have done it.

"Take her home, Drummond," Lord Derby told him after the hubbub had died down slightly, which meant only that Nicholas was receiving a slap on the back or a cheroot stuffed in his pocket on an average of every twenty seconds versus every ten.

"But Papa!" Lady Poppy grabbed her father's arm.

He gently but firmly pushed her hand off. "No ifs, ands, or buts, my dear. You're an engaged woman now, and your fiancé shall escort you home with my permission, which I give freely."

"No," she interrupted.

"And if you don't marry him," Lord Derby went on as if she hadn't spoken, "I'll cut you off without a farthing." He speared her with a look. "Don't think I don't mean it because I do. I swear upon your mother's grave."

"Ssssh, Papa!" Poppy looked around them. "How could you say such a thing? That's not like you!"

He shook his head. "I don't feel a bit guilty. When you turned down a perfectly acceptable match like Eversly, it was the straw that broke the camel's back. You're fortunate Drummond is willing to take you on. As far as I'm concerned, your days as a spinster are *over*."

Lord Derby calmly kissed Poppy's brow. She was apparently so incensed and shocked, she let him.

Nicholas held out his arm, and slowly, reluctantly, she took it.

"Don't say a word," she muttered, as he escorted her through the crowds.

He was doing his best to be a gracious winner, so he had no trouble complying. She'd had a severe shock, coupled with a blistering scold from her father. He'd be happy to grant her a few moments of silence.

But a few minutes later, ensconced in his comfortable carriage, she was ready to spar. She sat opposite him, her eyes flashing. "What was that proposal about?" she demanded. "You don't even *know* me."

"You're the one who's been using my name for three years to fob off your other suitors," he said, refusing to be ruffled. "Isn't this marriage what you want?"

"Huh," was all she said.

The vehicle turned a corner sharply, and she shifted her gaze away from his to the window. He studied the curve of her jaw and the white planes of her shoulders, exposed in the folds of her shawl. She was gorgeous. And oblivious to the danger she presented to him and every other man who encountered her.

Perhaps he'd enjoy begetting those children with her.

She turned to look at him, her mouth pursed in an attractive pout. "You're up to something havey-cavey. No doubt you need money, and I'm a convenient source. But I sense you've other reasons for proposing. I've good instincts."

"Not as good as mine."

"You can't know that."

"My instincts tell me they are."

"How can your instincts tell you your instincts are better?"

"Easily," he said. "Anyone with good instincts would understand." He gave her his best diabolical smile. "But as for your assessment, dukes always need wealthy wives to prop up the properties and to beget future dukes. Why not choose a wife who's been pining after you?"

"I have not been pining. Besides, even if I had been—which I repeat I have *not*—your reasons go beyond that."

"Your instincts are good."

She sucked in a breath. "I knew it."

"I do need a wife quickly, and for more than financial security," he said, not apologetic in the least. "I'm not at liberty to explain why. But it certainly doesn't reflect poorly on you that you are my choice."

She crossed her arms. "I might be your choice, but *you* aren't mine."

"A dozen rejected suitors would say otherwise, but who is he, this man who has your heart?"

She pursed her lips. "There's only one man who can tempt me to give up my Spinster status—"

"You're not a spinster—quite yet."

"But I'm close," she said, "and I have no desire to marry anyone but—" She hesitated. "I can't say."

"Why not?"

"Because it's private."

He sighed. "You have no desire to marry anyone but Prince Sergei."

She felt her face pale. "How did you guess?"

"It's easy to see you have a *tendre* for him. And he's besotted with you—that is, you or your father's money. I can't tell which one yet."

"How dare you."

He gave a small chuckle. "Are you sure you want him? You know nothing of him."

"I know this," she said, leaning forward and poking him in the chest with a finger. "I know that I have my *own* plans for my future, and they don't include marrying a smug, insufferable man. It will suit my purposes to remain betrothed to you for one month, which will ensure that I may stay in Town. But then I plan to break it off, no matter how angry it makes Papa." She nodded firmly. "You can take my offer or leave it—and find yourself another fiancée. I refuse to budge."

"Even though your father will cut you off without a farthing?"

She crossed her arms and made a face. "He didn't mean it."

"I assure you, he does. He told me so. And remember, he vowed upon your mother's—"

"*Don't* bring my mother into this." She inhaled a deep breath. "All right," she conceded, "perhaps he really meant it."

He didn't say a word.

"But I refuse to marry you. Even if I'm cut off without a penny. No one tells me whom to marry."

"But you said you wanted the Duke of Drummond." Over and over again, apparently.

She made an exasperated face. "That was a mistake. Of course I don't want *you*. I was referring to a fictitious duke, one that Cook tells stories about. As for Papa, I'm not some piece of meat to be bartered, and if he condemns you for backing out of your agreement, I'll be sure to tell him I forced your hand." She arched a brow. "Which I've just now managed. Haven't I?"

"No. You haven't." He heard the resolve in his voice and hoped it was having an effect. "I intend to adhere to the agreement I made with your father. We shall marry, whether you like it or not. Even if it means I have to drag you kicking and screaming up to Gretna."

"You wouldn't dare."

Her bravado was rather intoxicating.

"Yes, as a matter of fact, I would. And your father would do nothing to save you. You see, he believes we'll make a fine match. I happen to agree. You're a pleasure to look at, an adequate kisser—"

"*Adequate?*"

"So far."

"I'm far more than adequate for any man! You'd be lucky to get another kiss from me, but you won't. Oh, no." She gave a breathy chuckle. "I'll get out of this. Just you wait and see."

"Believe me, it will be a long wait." He wondered if his fascination with her was evident and hoped it wasn't. Cool. Calm. Detached. That's what he needed to be in his Service work, and that's what he'd be with her. Even though something in him was responding to her like a dog to the scent of a fox.

"I'm committed to my IF," he said, "and I've no desire to turn back now, especially as you'll bring me a hefty dowry. Our betrothal leaves me open to receiving a massive MR to boot. That is, of course"—he let out a satisfied sigh—"if OPL comes through. Which it should."

"I have no idea what you just said."

"Good." He moved to her seat and wrapped an arm around her shoulders and squeezed just hard enough that she couldn't get away without a struggle. "As much as you seem to despise me, I'm not a beast. I'll give you one month to get used to this betrothal, and if you manage to play at being a docile fiancée during that time, I'll kindly delay the wedding three months to accommodate your—ahem—timidity."

She rolled her eyes.

"But in the next thirty days," he went on, "you'll make our attachment clear to polite society, or I'll explain to your father in vivid terms why we need to marry immediately." He reached into his coat pocket, pulled out a stocking, and held it up for her examination.

"Why, that's one of my stockings! It even has my initials on it. Where did you get that?"

"I have my connections."

"What?"

"Don't bother firing your scullery maid. She's probably in Portsmouth by now. I gave her a ticket on a packet to America."

She tried to slap him, but he grabbed her wrist. "And don't *you* try to run away, either. When I find you—and I will—we'll marry that day. Or perhaps we'll simply live in sin at Seaward Hall, my family's estate, until the special license comes through."

Her lips thinned and she yanked her wrist back. "You're a beast."

He put the stocking back in his pocket and patted it. "Seaward Hall is lovely this time of year. The freezing winds off the North Sea in the spring aren't nearly as bad as the polar ones in the winter. And there's a dungeon."

She shuddered. "All right. I'll act *truly* engaged to you for a month—whatever that involves."

"Don't look so despondent. Men want women who are unavailable. I assure you, Sergei will find you more desirable than ever now that you're engaged. Not that you have a future with him."

"So *you* think. It's either with him or no one. I'd rather live alone than marry a man I don't love."

"I admire your stubbornness. To an extent." He yawned. "I'm the same way. But there does come a point when it's best to see the forest for the trees. And that time is *now*."

CHAPTER 8

Poppy felt her heart thumping fast against her chest when the Duke of Drummond slung an arm about her waist. "Exactly what are you doing?" she demanded to know.

"Kissing my fiancée," he murmured, and lowered his mouth to hers.

She refused to think the kiss might be on a par with the sweet, yearning kiss Sergei had given her in St. Petersburg six years ago, even though it was definitely doing something to her insides, something shocking.

"You can't do that," she insisted, yet she couldn't help but continue kissing him. "I never said yes to our betrothal. I pinched your arm. That was meant to be a distinct *no*."

"But we're betrothed anyway." His mouth, warm and teasing, nuzzled her neck.

She was furious. His lips were doing outrageous things to her. And he smelled like a man, all woodsy and lineny and something indefinable that made her want to put her hands to his shirt and rip both left and right at the same time.

Drummond laughed, and twirled one of her curls about his finger. "So . . . you won't call my driver to your rescue?"

"No, you ridiculous man," she said. "I can handle you myself."

His eyes gleamed. "I believe you can," he said, and kissed the column of her neck, lingering on her pulse point. Then he pulled her onto his lap in one deft swoop of his arms.

Oddly enough, she felt cozy. Comfortable. *Aroused.* Confound him.

"Perhaps I'll scream," she said.

"Don't bother." He kissed her ear.

She lifted her head. "What happened to your brother? Or was it your uncle?"

He stunned her by taking one of her fingers in his mouth and sucking on it. Good God, it felt impossibly rapturous, and she felt a sharp, sudden urge to—

She didn't know. But he had better stop sucking. *Now.*

She pulled her finger out, quite rudely, she thought, but he didn't seem to care. He went right to rubbing her bottom with the flat of his hand.

It was shocking of him.

And she didn't want him to stop.

"My brother—blast his hide—is still here in London," the duke murmured, still rubbing away at her bottom, "but my uncle disappeared. He was only thirteen when he ran away. We think he became a sailor and was lost at sea."

She let him kiss her again. Perhaps he wasn't the wicked duke of Cook's tales, after all. Perhaps he was even an amiable, kind, patient man. As harmless as a—

She blinked. He was none of those things. He was like a cobra in a basket, waiting to strike. A vampire who wanted to suck blood out of her neck. A Venus fly-trap—and she was the fly.

"Wait a moment." She sat up a fraction. "I still don't trust you. I'm only kissing you to prove I'm more than an adequate kisser. Far more."

"How many times have you practiced?"

"None of your business."

"I thought so." He looked back down at her and caressed her temple with a scratchy thumb. "You *are* a spinster, through and through. Don't you believe in having fun?"

"Not with scoundrels," she said, feeling prim and prudish even as she insulted him.

But he didn't seem to care. He laid her out on the seat, and now his mouth was on hers and she couldn't get enough of him.

Never, *ever* had she felt this way when she'd been kissed. She felt greedy, insatiable.

So what did it mean?

She forgot to wonder as he lifted her leg and slipped his hand underneath her gown. He ran that hand over her knee and down her calf. And then he ran his hand almost all the way up her thigh and let it linger there as he kissed her, teasing her mouth open so he could explore her with his tongue in a most intimate, daring fashion.

Please keep doing what you're doing, she thought, and it was as if he read her mind. He kept kissing her mouth and caressing her thigh, but then he kneaded her breasts through her bodice with his other hand, running his thumb over her nipples as if they were buttons to play with.

And then he moved his mouth to the cleft between her breasts. And then—

And then he did more.

He nudged aside one side of her bodice with his mouth, moved his lips lower and lower . . .

And suckled her breast.

She had no words for what it felt like. All she knew was that she felt the sharpest twinge of pleasure between her legs the instant his mouth and tongue touched her nipple.

He was the devil himself to make her feel this way.

But she wanted it to go on forever, especially when the hand on her thigh began to move closer and closer to her most intimate flesh.

But he didn't touch her there. Of course he wouldn't. That would be shameful, wicked, and altogether—

Please. Please *touch me there,* she had the insane thought.

She clung to him and moaned and ran her fingers through his hair—it was silky and springy and oh-so-thick—and she was dying for him to suckle the other breast.

And move past her thigh with his nimble fingers.

Her list of wishes was getting longer, and all because he was the most maddening, tempting man she'd ever encountered.

But instead he drew back, gently lifting her bodice into place again.

"We can't do any more than that at the moment," he said, his voice low and his pupils dark. "You're livid with me."

"I am?"

"Yes." He pulled her up to a sitting position. "It will hit you in"—he paused—"three, two, one—"

"*Don't* condescend to me." The sweet pleasure she'd experienced only moments before evaporated, although her breast still tingled. And so did the vulnerable spot between her legs.

"See? I'm right."

She refused to answer. Discreetly, she straightened her spine so as to push out her chest in the hope he'd lean down, pull down her bodice, and kiss her that way again.

Or brush the tips of her breasts with his hand, at the very least.

He gave her a lazy smile. "I know what you're thinking."

"Of course you don't."

"Yes I do." He had a certain gleam in his eye that made her breathless. But then he chucked her under the chin. "We're here. In fact, we've been sitting outside your home for over five minutes."

She blushed. "I—I didn't notice."

"Now go inside before your household dies of curiosity. Especially Cook. I'm sure she's anxious to meet me. Is she ginger-haired?"

"Yes."

"Freckle-faced and snub-nosed?"

"Yes."

"Voice like a foghorn?"

"Yes."

"Tendency to embellish stories . . . and add too much salt to soups?"

"Yes, on both counts."

"She must be my cook's twin sister. She told me her twin cooks for a widower and his daughter in London, both of whom are sly, murderous types."

"Oh." Poppy felt vaguely guilty, as if she really *had* killed someone.

The duke gave her a stern look. "I saved your precious reputation tonight."

She stared at him. "You're no gentleman to say so."

He laughed. "I'm merely the first gentleman who's dared encourage you to be yourself—a nice girl who longs to be naughty. It's why you've been telling your suitors fanciful stories. You'll soon find that nothing is boring anymore. Not when you're with me."

He threw open the carriage door, leaped out, and offered her his hand. She narrowed her eyes to convey her disapproval of him as he swung her down, which meant she wasn't really looking at what she was doing and landed against his chest.

"I'm sure it was the shock of that ridiculous betrothal that accounted for my behavior in the carriage," she said in her most proper voice.

"Indeed." He bowed, a glint of wry amusement in his eye.

She climbed the stairs, opened the door, and refused to look back at him, even though she sensed he was watching her.

He was right about her being bored. And he knew *she* knew he was right.

It annoyed her no end.

CHAPTER 9

It was a little-known fact about Nicholas that he always practiced archery when he was sexually frustrated. Of course, that meant he rarely did. He was usually a sexually sated male who preferred to spend his sporting hours boxing at Gentleman Jackson's or fencing at Angelo's.

But in his view nothing beat piercing sandbags with arrows when it came to releasing tension caused by a craving for a female. In fact, he was bound to get a lot of good archery practice in until he wedded and bedded Lady Poppy Smith-Barnes. Even the thought of her pert little chin or those endearingly bony elbows drove him mad with lust.

Which was why he was in Hyde Park much too early in the morning the day after his betrothal. He'd even managed to locate his brother at a dreary hotel in Cheapside and drag him along.

"I can't believe it." Frank was breathing down Nicholas's neck (in quite the literal sense) when he bent down to pick up the arrow he'd dropped. "You missed the bull's-eye by a good half inch."

Nicholas ignored his unsporting behavior. "It's been known to happen. Must you stand so close?"

"Must you be my brother?" Frank scowled, his bantam-rooster chest pushed up to Nicholas's stomach.

Nicholas refrained from rolling his eyes. "You should take to the stage. Your gift for melodrama is wearing anywhere else." He pulled back on the bow and focused on the sandbag target once more.

Frank scoffed. "I might have to. Especially since I'm down to my last farthing."

"That's not my fault."

"Oh, yes, it is. You hold the purse strings."

"And you've been given a generous allowance. But you gamble it all away."

"That's what a gentleman of leisure does. *Stupid.*"

Nicholas tossed the bow and arrow aside. Frank had always gotten away with calling him names at home. Mother had intervened every time, and after she'd died, his stepmother had actually encouraged Frank's insults. But both of them were gone.

Nicholas grabbed his baby brother by the cravat and hauled him close to his face. "Grow up."

"No." Frank's eyes narrowed. "Big *dummy.*"

Nicholas forced himself to remember that Frank was, quite simply, an ass. The last ass in the family had been Great-uncle Hesperus, who'd fathered six children among three housemaids.

Nicholas supposed the family was due another ass now. Which gave him the wherewithal to drop his brother to the ground without killing him. "And your speaking like a two-year-old is somehow going to convince me to give you additional funds?"

Frank stood up and wiped off his bottom. "It should. If you were a *good* brother." He broke an arrow over his knee for emphasis.

Nicholas bit his cheek and picked up the bow again. "Listen. If you'd stop gambling, which you're not terribly good at, you might notice you can do other things better."

"Like what?"

Nicholas thought. "Like, um—"

He thought some more, poised the arrow, and then shot it directly into the bull's-eye.

"See?" Frank let his hands drop to his thighs. "You do everything right. Which makes it so I can't. So why should I try?"

Nicholas handed him the bow and arrow, stood behind him, and twisted him toward the target. "Because you were gifted with a brain, and a healthy body, and devoted parents who gave you many opportunities to prove your worth. Until Mother died, of course, and then Father became quite useless."

Blast. He hadn't meant to add that last bit.

There was a beat of silence.

Frank shot the arrow ten feet to the left of the target. "If you'd let me shoot barrels with a blunderbuss, I guarantee I'd do better than you."

"We have no barrels—"

"I do. I've loads of them."

"Nor blunderbusses."

"You could get one."

Nicholas clenched his jaw. "Well, it's clear that to-day, we *don't* have them. So let's go again, and this time pretend the target is me."

"I hate archery *and* you."

"Very well, Frank." Nicholas strove to keep his anger in check. "I won't dwell on the fact that if you had any integrity whatsoever, you'd try to be a decent brother because that's the right thing to do. But if you want your allowance to continue, you *will* stop stealing spoons from White's or any other establishment and you *will* alert me if you get into any scrapes."

"You always were a nosy bastard," Frank said.

"Yes, I suppose I am. The Drummond name's at stake."

"I think you're jealous. You want to know what I'm up to because my life's much more exciting than yours. That's it. You can't let me have any fun because you're the boring older brother."

It was the same old story.

Nicholas gathered up his things. "I'll see you around." He began to walk away, then turned. "Are you staying at that hotel for long?"

Frank's lower lip stuck out. "None of your bloody business. But you saw—my bed is no better than a pile of straw. And I'm down to two waistcoats."

Nicholas felt a war being waged within him, but then he reached into his pocket. "Here." He threw Frank a leather pouch filled with gold coins. "An advance on your next allowance."

Frank sneered, but he grabbed the bag. "I'm not going to thank you, you old miser."

"Then don't." Nicholas turned away and refused to look back.

"Hey."

Very reluctantly, Nicholas stopped. Turned around.

"Is it true you're marrying Lady Poppy Smith-Barnes?" Frank asked sullenly.

Nicholas hesitated but a moment. "Yes."

"She's a morsel I'd like to pluck."

"No, you wouldn't, Frank, because if you did I'd kill you. And I'll maim you if you ever say something rude about her again."

Frank narrowed his eyes, then he whipped around and took off at a run. He held the leather pouch up in the air and said, "The first thing I'm doing with this is bed a whore, and I'm going to imagine it's Lady Poppy Smith-Barnes when I do."

Nicholas stopped and inhaled a deep breath.

You will not kill your own brother. His parents' words echoed in his head.

But when he walked back to the Albany, he was angry. Angry that he was saddled with an immature idiot as his brother. The only thing that kept him trying to help Frank was the memory of his father's face whenever he'd talk about his big brother, Uncle Tradd.

His father James had needed his brother.

Near the end of his life, the duke had asked Nicholas to carry him that morning to the shore—which, of course, Nicholas had done.

"We try to deny it," James told him while they watched the waves pound the sand, "but blood is thicker than any grievance or separation. No matter how irreversible—or in your case with Frank, how sensible—the parting, at the core of your being is a silent mourning. For me it has never gone away. Learn from my story, Nicholas, so that you may have a modicum of peace."

And so Nicholas knew he couldn't—and wouldn't—abandon Frank the way Uncle Tradd had abandoned his own father.

Just in case Frank needed him.

But once a year Nicholas *would* sit him backward on a horse and make it go—Frank would never know the time or place, but God, it brought Nicholas such joy, such unbridled delight, to see his brother bobbing madly on that horse, yelling for help. Nicholas deserved that, didn't he? After all, the other 364 days of the year, Frank brought him nothing but misery.

Oh, and he called him Frank the Farter every once in a while. But that's because Frank called him Nick the Nutsack.

That's what brothers did.

"I could do so much worse, Father," Nicholas said to a passing cloud.

So much worse.

He was practically a saint.

CHAPTER 10

Poppy had been caught. She was officially betrothed. Her engagement to the Duke of Drummond had made it into the morning papers. Every ounce of her being protested because it was so obvious—

I should be marrying Prince Sergei.

Dumbfounded, she cast the paper aside. She'd *always* been able to wrangle out of an engagement.

Until now.

Last night she'd slept so poorly that she'd given up when the moon was still high in the sky and sat at her window, listening to the sounds of London and taking sips from a restoring punch Aunt Charlotte had left outside her door.

Oh, who was she fooling? She'd taken no sips. She'd downed the entire thing in twenty minutes and gotten sodden drunk, flung open her windows, and yelled into the night, "Damn you, Drummond! Damn you to bloody hell!" at least twice before her father himself strode into her room and locked the window.

Now in Lord Derby's drawing room, she sat with

her two best friends, both of whom wouldn't quite look her in the eye.

She was rather wincing at them herself. That cursed punch, after all.

"I can't believe you two were *grinning* when he proposed," Poppy said, treading lightly because of her poor head, but attempting to pace in front of the fireplace. "Aunt Charlotte, too. She explained it away by claiming stomach pains."

"I couldn't help it," Eleanor replied, her head low. "You two looked *adorable*. It must have been the light. The candles put a certain glow on you that was, um, a bit magical."

Beatrice shook her head. "I don't know what came over me, either. In that moment, when he kissed you, it was as if all the fairy tales came true. And then I became sensible again. I realized he'd . . . he'd forced you into a metaphorical—and actual—corner."

Beatrice was a stickler for details.

"As for the metaphorical corner, you had no idea it existed!" Eleanor huffed. "Who ever knew the Duke of Drummond wasn't a legend?"

"Exactly." Poppy threw up her hands. "He battles large sea monsters. He's crazy, murderous, wicked, and—"

She'd kissed him. She'd kissed him to distraction.

She licked her lips and bit the inside of her cheek. She was in a nightmare. And she only wanted to wake up.

"Don't worry," Beatrice reassured her. "Despite the awful announcement in the newspaper, we members of the Spinsters Club will help you out of this somehow."

"We know if you choose anyone to marry, it will be Sergei," Eleanor added stoutly.

"But how?" Poppy said. "How can I possibly save myself?"

"Paris is out." Aunt Charlotte popped into the room, and took the best seat by ordering Eleanor cheerfully out of it. "Your father caught on. He's paid all the servants extra wages to report to him any havey-cavey packing of suitcases. In fact, we no longer have trunks of any kind. He's donated them to charity. He's confiscated our pin money, too, and even put all our jewels in his safe. We have to ask to use them when we go out, and we'll be escorted by footmen at all times, unless we're with Drummond, of course."

"That's not the worst of it." Poppy sank onto a chair by her aunt. "Drummond says if I run and he catches me, we'll marry that day—or live in sin until the special license comes through."

"Did he now?" Aunt Charlotte drawled. And then gave a little laugh. A wicked little laugh.

"Aunt," Poppy remonstrated with her.

The Spinsters' mentor sat up. "Oh, yes, that would be *dreadful.*"

Poppy shook her head. "Something's wrong. Something's come over each one of you—"

"I assure you, niece," Aunt Charlotte said in her haughtiest tones. "I've not forgotten Sergei's the only man who comes even *close* to fulfilling the requirements for you to receive dispensation from the Spinsters Club rules." She blinked. "It's just that Drummond falls into the category that should make every Spinster wary: he's dangerous. A dangerous man can make a Spinster forget like that"—she snapped her fingers—"every tenet of the Spinster way of life."

God, she was right. Poppy simply had to think about the duke kissing her, and her Spinster knees almost buckled. Not that she would admit it out loud.

Eleanor raised her teacup. "Never fear, Lady Charlotte. We can recite those tenets backward and forward."

"Our standards are so high, we're bound to be Spinsters forever." Beatrice clashed cups merrily with Eleanor.

Poppy felt guilty, terribly guilty. *If they only knew the truth,* she thought. Dangerous men were—

Well, they were dangerous.

Aunt Charlotte chuckled. "I'm proud to say I had the devil of a time drawing up the latest edition of the Spinster bylaws. Lord Bimmington was blowing in my ear the whole time. And Sam-the-footman was quite leering at me. No wonder—I was wearing my teeth, of course. And that recklessly red silk gown from Milan."

Poppy knew the very one. It really *was* reckless.

She gave her aunt a hug. "You're the best chaperone a girl could ever wish for," she whispered in her ear.

And it was true, but part of Poppy felt rather wistful for a shrew of a chaperone, one who might tell her all the naughty things she'd done with the Duke of Drummond the night before would come back to haunt her—and put her plan to win Sergei in jeopardy.

She needed reminding, and an embittered battle-ax might restore her to the lofty daydreams she'd harbored for six years about Sergei.

"Do you think the duke really did have his uncle murdered?" Beatrice asked her in hopeful tones—and no wonder, she wrote shocking novels with an occasional dead body in them.

"Whether he did or not," said Eleanor, "there's absolutely no chance he's ever fought an octopus as large as a Royal Mail coach." She was the artist, so her sense of proportion was impeccable.

"Heavens, of course not, on both counts." Although a perfectly silly part of Poppy still wondered.

But thankfully for her fanciful imagination, not for long.

There was a loud commotion outside and a forceful knock on the front door, followed by a demanding exotic voice and much yapping.

Kettle came into the drawing room. "Princess Natasha and her dogs to see you, Lady Poppy," he announced.

She shared a surprised look with her aunt and Spinsters Club sisters. "Show them in, Kettle," she said, not sure what to think.

Natasha strode in, strikingly elegant in a pale green morning dress with a sheer overlay and a high, frothy collar framing her long, slender neck. Her only accessories were the two panting corgis she carried, one of whom was missing an eye.

Poppy stood, her knees a bit wobbly. "This is indeed, um, an honor, Princess."

"Yes, an honor," Eleanor echoed.

Beatrice surreptitiously hit Eleanor's thigh.

Poppy moved in front of the two of them while Natasha looked about the room as if no one else were in it, even though Aunt Charlotte was staring goggle-eyed at her.

"I had hoped for a private audience," the princess said in a honey-thick Russian accent.

"Oh, we'll oblige," Aunt Charlotte said, picked up her teacup, and left.

Beatrice and Eleanor, too, picked up their cups and exited the room right behind her.

"Wait!" Poppy called to them.

But they shut the drawing room door, and she was alone with the princess and her two dogs.

Natasha sat on the settee with them. "So," she said, "you're doing it again."

"What?"

"What you did last night with those chamomiles in your hair. Calling attention to yourself, when really, you are better served blending in."

"I am?"

"Only a rare few of us are meant to shine, Lady Poppy, and you are not one of them. But don't despair. Yes, you're to marry the Duke of Drummond, but no doubt he shall remove you to his estate in the north, where you can be a docile, almost invisible wife, which is your duty."

Poppy cringed inside. She did not want to be a docile, almost invisible wife to anyone. She must explain that she was *not* to marry the duke. But how could she?

She'd no idea.

"Yes," she said vaguely. "We're, um, betrothed, but you know how those things go. Can't look too deeply into the future. Would you care for some tea?"

"It's much too early," Natasha returned abruptly, and eyed the painting of St. Petersburg over the pianoforte. "My English contacts tell me you have a passion for my country, and now I see for myself that you do."

"I do my best," Poppy said, "to learn about *all* the world's cultures, although, yes, I have a special place in my heart for Russia."

And Sergei.

Natasha leaned forward. "Tell me, when did this courtship between you and Drummond take place?"

What a shame she'd changed the subject. Her courtship with Drummond was hardly Natasha's business, but Poppy dared not tell her so. "I recently purchased a Russian icon that I've yet to hang on the wall," she said instead. "Would you like to see it?"

Natasha gave an impatient sigh. "I see icons in Russia all the time."

"Of course." Poppy swallowed hard.

Natasha appeared quite content to sit where she was. Forever, if need be, judging from the way she eased herself farther back into the settee. "You were about to tell me how you and Drummond came together."

Goodness gracious, Poppy thought, what was she to do? She'd have to make up a grand story, the way Cook did. She only wished she had a simmering pot to stir.

"We met at the circulating library. I'll never forget it." She laid a hand on her breast. "My heart—"

"I didn't ask for maudlin details." Natasha rolled her eyes. "Love has nothing to do with courtship, or at least it shouldn't." She stood, rather violently. "I came today to say that it's unfortunate you're involved with

Drummond. I was beginning to think you should serve as one of my attendants at the Lievens' ball, where my wretched brother and I are to unveil my uncle Revnik's last masterpiece."

Poppy's face flamed. *Wretched* was a strong word. And Sergei was her beloved. But she couldn't very well defend him. Family matters were family matters. And she wasn't in the family—yet.

Nevertheless, perhaps she could serve as a mediator of sorts, remind Natasha of her brother's good qualities. "Do you . . . do you and Sergei ride together?" she asked the princess. "Or play card games?"

"Shut up about him." Natasha curled her lip. "He makes me ill."

"W-why?"

The princess scowled. "Isn't it obvious?"

Poppy gave a nervous shake to her head. "No. Not really."

Natasha gave a short laugh. "He is a brother. Brothers *rot*."

"Oh." Poppy raised a shaky hand to her breast. "I'm an only child. I'd no idea."

Drummond apparently despised his brother, too.

The mere recollection of the duke's existence brought to her mind his captivating sneer and condescending manner. Both made her palms itch to wring his neck.

Natasha jutted her chin at her. "What's your answer?"

Poppy flinched. "I'm afraid I forgot the question."

She'd been thinking of Drummond, after all, and before that, all she'd heard had been the word *wretched* being used to describe Sergei. It had been like a knife through her heart.

"I asked if you will accept the great honor of serving as one of my attendants. You will be privileged to hold my gown and adjust my tiara, a gift of the czar himself. The ball shall be the event of the Season. But now you're too busy preparing for your wedding. What a shame."

Natasha raised her shoulders the tiniest fraction and let them fall.

"Oh, yes, I'll be much too busy preparing for my wedding," Poppy assured her. If she didn't play the happy bride-to-be, the princess would report it all over Town, and then every suitor she'd ever had would call her a fraud. "And I wouldn't be a very good attendant, I'm afraid."

"Why is that?"

"I don't want to blend in, as much as you believe I need to." Now she let *her* shoulders rise and fall a fraction of an inch. "I plan to attend the event at the side of my future husband. I shall waltz with him and perhaps even kiss him in front of all the company."

Oh, God. She didn't want Drummond. And she wasn't a hoyden. Why had she said all that?

Natasha gave her a glittering smile. "Good luck with your duke, Lady Poppy. Rumor has it he has no heart, but that's neither here nor there."

Poppy tried to be grateful for the remark. She'd been reared to think the best of people, so there was the slightest chance it had been made with friendly concern.

But she doubted it. If the princess felt anything like she did now, she was hoping Poppy would trip over her hem and fall down. Poppy was wishing the very same for Natasha.

But the princess strode smoothly out the front door, down the steps—her corgis' ears like little flags—and was swept up by a footman into her carriage, which went rollicking away with much yapping from its interior and at an unnecessarily high speed.

When Poppy turned back to the drawing room and sank into her seat, she couldn't help releasing a wistful sigh. A royal from Russia had come to visit this morning. And not just any royal. Sergei's sister.

How exciting such an event would have been even a day ago. But now that she'd met Natasha, Poppy was the opposite of excited, which was unfortunate. She'd had such hopes they'd be good friends.

Even more lowering was the fact that she was trapped in an engagement to the wrong man and he was to come to dinner tonight. Her temples grew damp at the thought. She had no idea what she'd say to him. She was beside herself that he'd interfered in her life without her permission.

She stood and looked at herself in the mirror. "If he's not going to play fair, then I shan't, either," she told herself out loud.

If he could be like a vampire or a snake, she'd be like a spider in a web, and she'd wrap him up in a little threaded ball at the soonest opportunity. Or perhaps she'd be more like a governess and torture him with boring lectures so that he'd fall asleep, whereupon she'd write nasty things on his forehead, words like GO AWAY, RUDE MAN.

She strode out of the drawing room to Papa's library and then to her bedchamber, where she lay on her quilt and searched through a text on agricultural tools, vowing to find the perfect tedious lecture.

But as she was reading about chaff cutters, dibbers, and flails, she fell asleep.

CHAPTER 11

When Nicholas knocked on the door at 17 Clifford Street at precisely seven o'clock, he was rather irritated and deflated, having waited all day to see if Groop would contact him to tell him Operation Pink Lady would be his.

He hadn't. And it wasn't.

Which was why he was scowling when the door was opened by the butler.

"Good evening, Your Grace. I am Kettle, at your service. Do come in."

With his protruding ears and round face, he certainly matched his name. No doubt Lady Poppy set him to boil often.

"Thank you, Kettle." Nicholas handed over his cape, gloves, and hat, a wad of cash tastefully hidden under the brim. "I presume you mean Lord Derby is expecting me. He received my note about security measures?"

"You presume correctly, Your Grace." Kettle discreetly pocketed the bills. "He made sure Lady Poppy's bedchamber window is locked, and we've a servant guarding every exit from the house. Regrettably, the earl was called away with Lord Wyatt on emergency Parliamentary business and is still not back. He begs you to be patient as he'll be a trifle late for dinner."

"I'm happy to wait." Nicholas had dreamed about Lady Poppy's snapping emerald eyes and coppery mane. And now he'd see her again. He felt exhilarated at the thought, especially because he already knew she wouldn't be easy.

Not easy at all.

He wondered if a good night's sleep and almost a full day to reflect upon the advantages of a connection to him had softened her outrage into something more . . . tamable.

And almost hoped it hadn't.

"By the by, Lady Charlotte is out for the evening," Kettle said. "But Lady Poppy awaits you in the drawing room." He gave Nicholas a meaningful stare. "I know you've been approved by Lord Derby, but Cook has told us all about you and your scandalous exploits, Your Grace. And let me assure you, I shall be on the lookout myself, on Lady Poppy's behalf. Yes, indeed."

"Shall you?"

"I most certainly shall."

"Very good, then." Nicholas patted the butler on the shoulder, and they walked in comfortable silence to the first door on the left.

He waited for Kettle to announce him and heard Poppy bid that he enter. He braced himself and walked into the room.

She was posed by the pianoforte, her back ramrod

straight, looking like a diamond of the first water, a large ruby necklace snuggled between her breasts.

Drummond raised her hand to his mouth, turned it over, and kissed her palm, sending a distinct pattern of gooseflesh racing up her arm.

"I'm sorry to have missed your aunt," he said. "She seems a lively sort of chaperone." Lady Charlotte had even winked at him last night, after he'd proposed.

Poppy lifted her shoulders and let them drop. "Yes, she's that way because she's a Spinster."

"What has that to do with anything?"

"She can do *what* she wants with *whom* she wants *whenever* she wants," Poppy said.

"Spinsters are to be envied, then."

She lifted her chin. "I somehow doubt your sincerity."

"You should, perhaps," he agreed. "Except when I'm complimenting you. You're exquisite tonight."

"Thank you." She flushed.

There was the sound of a carriage rattling to a stop in front of the house.

Drummond inclined his head. "Is that your father?"

"Yes. He's often grouchy. Aren't you afraid?"

"No, of course not," he said. "We see eye to eye. I've told you."

She bristled. "Don't remind me. I demand to know something before he arrives. What does IF mean? And MR? And OPL?"

"You *are* curious, aren't you?" He gave her what he hoped was an enigmatic smile. "But I won't tell you. You have no need to know."

"So? I know many things I've no need to know."

"Well, this will be one less thing. And even if you did need to know, I'd think twice before telling you. Sorry, but my instincts tell me you're not good at keeping secrets."

"Your instincts are wrong. Why should you have secrets anyway?"

"Because often the most exciting, most pleasurable things in the world *are* done in secret." He pulled her closer and kissed the tender hollow at the base of her neck. Her scent was sweet and seductive.

She arched her neck, then seemed to recall herself. "My goodness." She gasped and pushed him away. "You *are* a scoundrel."

"You think so?"

"Of course." She gasped again, but he was determined to be completely unmoved by her outrage and shock.

She drew her brows together. "No one should have secrets. And no one should be invisible. Don't ever think you shall whisk me away to the north and make me a docile, dutiful wife."

Nicholas laughed. That was exactly what he intended.

"What's so funny?" she asked him.

But Lord Derby arrived before he could answer.

"Let's tuck into our dinners right away," Poppy's father urged them. "Lord Wyatt is a demanding colleague. He's called another meeting." He took a rather hasty gulp of wine.

Nicholas saw Poppy wince.

"Again, Papa?" she asked in a thin voice.

"You know I have duties at Whitehall, my dear, and Wyatt has the country's best interests at heart." Lord Derby looked over his spectacles at Nicholas. "So, when will the marriage take place? Sooner is better than later."

Nicholas slowed the sawing of the piece of beef on his plate. "I'd say after a month we could start having the banns read." He kept his tone jaunty. "Until then, we'll have a getting-to-know-you period."

Poppy appeared to be seething, but she didn't disagree.

"Excellent idea." Lord Derby speared a potato. "Poppy will have plenty to tell you."

"I was actually referring to getting to know you both, sir," Drummond said immediately. "I know very little of your political beliefs. I'm sorry to say my father never took his seat in Parliament, so if I'm to become up to snuff, I really must become better informed. Unless it's too much trouble, that is."

"Not at all." Lord Derby's eyes lit up. "Where shall we start?"

"The economy," Nicholas replied.

Poppy nudged him with an elbow and narrowed her eyes at him.

And no wonder. Nicholas was sure no subject could be larger, or nearer and dearer to Lord Derby's heart— outside his affection for his daughter, of course—than the state of the English economy.

Sure enough, a quarter of an hour later, Kettle had to appear at the dining room door with Lord Derby's hat before he seemed to break loose of his political theorizing and return to the present moment.

"The time has flown," said Lord Derby.

Poppy appeared shocked by his pleasant manner.

"But before I go," her father went on, "I must make mention of an unsavory topic. According to an impeccable source I heard from today, there is a missing uncle in your family tree, Drummond, an uncle who should have been duke. I'm not quite sure I approve of mysteries. Especially as they relate to titles."

"So you spoke to Cook, Papa?" Poppy intervened.

"No." He glared sternly at her. "She dared speak to me when she brought me my coddled eggs this morning. I gather her twin is your cook, Duke."

"That she is." Nicholas nodded soberly. "Marvelous with the roast beef, the two of them, I must say. But as for the mystery about my uncle, you're right, Lord Derby. It exists. But what can one do with an uncle who's been missing forty years? Other than notice he's gone—and carry on."

Lord Derby stared at him for a good ten seconds, then shook his head. "You're very lucky I admire intelligent men with nerve. We need more of those types in Parliament." He stood from the table. Drummond rose, too. "I must go. My daughter shall see you out in a few minutes."

"But Papa!" Poppy's cheeks pinkened. "We haven't even served the fruit and cheese."

Nicholas felt the awkwardness of the moment. He understood her concern. She was probably thinking

they should linger over this getting-to-know-you meal.
And afterward, Lord Derby should lead him to the library for a brandy and a cheroot and shoo Lady Poppy
off to bed because they'd be ensconced in those big
brown leather club chairs for *hours*.

Drummond guessed that Lord Derby viewed his
daughter's engagement like a bill to be passed before
Parliament rather than as a milestone in her life—the
biggest milestone she'd probably yet encountered.

Unfortunate as the situation was, Nicholas could do
nothing but bow and say, "Thank you, sir, for a most
enlightening evening."

Lord Derby merely grunted, then turned to Poppy.
"You'll need a trousseau."

"Yes, Papa," she said in a bland tone.

Nicholas assumed most young ladies would look
ecstatic at the thought of a trousseau. But Lady Poppy
apparently felt no joy.

He supposed he should feel humiliated or concerned, as he was the man she was to marry, but their
mutual die was cast. Regrets could serve no purpose.

With Papa gone and the servants plainly lingering,
Poppy knew Drummond had no choice but to go himself. She rose from her seat, and he took her hand. Leaning over it, he left a lingering kiss on her knuckles.

If only he would leave a kiss elsewhere on my body,
she had the unwelcome thought.

"It's been a challenge meeting your father," he said,
"and a huge pleasure. I shall come round tomorrow
afternoon to take you up in my curricle. We shall cir-

cle Hyde Park at the fashionable hour. Remember, you'll be a proper fiancée. For one month."

He patted his pocket—the one with the stocking in it—then smiled.

The rat. She'd find a way to wipe the smug look off his face. Soon.

"Very well," she said.

The corner of his mouth tilted up. He'd won this round, and they both knew it.

His mouth was dangerously close to hers, but he looked over his shoulder at Kettle, who handed him his cape, gloves, and hat.

"On your way, Your Grace," the butler warned him.

Drummond put the hat on his head. "No need to worry, Kettle," he said with a grin, his eyes on Poppy. "I've no time to give her a proper kiss good night this evening anyway. I've a card game to get to—and I'm fifteen minutes late."

"A card game?" Poppy couldn't help saying in disbelief. She was furious her curiosity about what constituted a proper kiss would not be satisfied because of a *card game*.

He was already at the bottom of the steps, and he'd donned his cape and gloves. When he looked up at her, her heart pounded in an entirely unacceptable manner. A lady couldn't help thinking very bad thoughts about him. He didn't have to wear his hair so long, nor did he require that swagger. Or the obvious attention he paid to maintaining a superb physique.

"Good night, Drummond," she said primly.

"Good night, Poppy." He chuckled. "I know what

you're thinking again." And then he went walking merrily down the street.

"You don't," she cried after him.

He spun around, his cape swirling about his thighs. "Oh, but I do."

"Really?" She found she couldn't breathe.

"Really," he said, his square jaw lowered, his dark brow arched, and his eyes full of—

She didn't know, but it drove her mad with longing.

"Shut the door," he called to her as if she were a child.

"Don't tell me what to do." She was furious, but she did shut the door. Slowly.

He stood watching her the whole time. When the door was finally closed, she leaned her forehead against it, still furious but feeling rather weak in the knees again.

She knocked her head against the wooden panel. What was *wrong* with her? She didn't *like* the Duke of Drummond. He was smug, bossy, and rude.

Rather like her, actually.

"My lady," Kettle interrupted her thoughts.

She'd forgotten he was there. She pivoted her forehead slightly and peeked at him. "Yes, Kettle?"

"I forgot to give the duke his cane." He held it up.

"Oh." She stood up straight and sighed. "I suppose he can get it next time." She was about to walk upstairs to think about kissing him while she brushed her hair when she was struck by a thought. "Wait a moment, Kettle. He didn't come in with a cane. I was peeking around the door of the drawing room when he arrived. Are you sure it's his?"

Kettle pulled in his chin. "You're right, miss. Fancy my not being able to recall. But it must be his. It was sitting here in the corner by the door. And his name is carved on the side."

Sure enough, the name *Nicholas Staunton* was carved down its length. "How odd," she said. "I wonder who put it there?"

Kettle looked almost abashed. "I was away from the door for a few moments, um, delivering a message to the kitchen. I've no idea."

He had a crush on Cook, Poppy knew, but she never minded when he deserted his post to woo her.

"It's quite intricate, the carving, isn't it?" She ran a hand across the fine wood of the cane. It was a gorgeous thing. "Why would such a fascinating cane be left at my house? And with the duke's name on it? Could it be a prank?"

"But it's not amusing," Kettle said, staring at the cane in his hand.

"No, it's not," said Poppy. "It's merely baffling." She drew in a breath. "Perhaps his valet slipped it in the door. It might be the duke's favorite cane and he left it at home by accident. It could be the valet expected you to hand it to him upon his departure."

"Yes. Someone could have opened the door and left it for him while—while I wasn't minding my station." Kettle's face went red again.

And before Poppy could assure the butler that she didn't mind his being human and abandoning his post for love, the bottom of the cane popped open.

"Bloody hell," Kettle said, then put a hand over his

mouth. "A gadget cane! I'm sorry, my lady, but I've never seen one open from the bottom like that. I *knew* this duke was a most unusual sort of duke. He exudes danger. And mystery."

"From every pore?" Poppy asked, although it was really a rhetorical question. They both already knew the answer.

"Yes," Kettle said anyway. "From every pore." And shook the cane.

A tightly rolled piece of paper fell out.

She exchanged a wide-eyed look with the butler, then eagerly, they both bent to pick up the scrap.

Poppy got to it first. "Thank you, darling Kettle," she cried as she bounded up the stairs. "I don't think the valet left this cane, after all. I believe someone else did—and expected the duke to find this message. Perhaps this will tell me why he needs a wife."

"And whether he murdered his uncle!" Kettle called up to her.

Yes, and that, too.

CHAPTER 12

Nicholas took the gawking in stride when he drove Poppy along Rotten Row in Hyde Park the next afternoon. She was a pretty socialite renowned for rebuffing suitors, and since their engagement, he knew rumors were flying fast about him, the little-known Drummond line, and the mysterious, long-ago disappearance of his uncle. Together they were a London sensation, especially in his glossy black phaeton with yellow-trimmed wheels and a pair of matched grays.

Before he knew it, Poppy had taken the reins right from his hands. Her gaze as she maneuvered between other vehicles was shrewd and intelligent. She cast her eyes briefly his way and gifted him with a rather bewitching grin. "I do like to drive."

"What a surprise," he said mildly.

He wanted to relieve her of her clothing right then and there, but he wasn't particularly astounded. He was a man, after all, with a man's usual lustful thoughts, and she was a beautiful female extremely responsive to his attentions—when she forgot she disliked him.

Her driving so expertly was another reason to be sexually attracted to her. Helpless females bored him to tears.

She leaned closer. "Do you think we're fooling everyone?" she whispered in his ear.

"Of course," he replied. "Just look at them."

Everywhere, people stood turned to stone as they passed. And their eyes were filled with hope and softness and indulgence.

Let that darling couple enjoy themselves, their looks seemed to say. *He's even letting her take the reins.*

As if he'd had a choice.

From behind them, he heard the yapping of many small dogs. The next moment, Princess Natasha's brougham appeared alongside his phaeton, and Poppy pulled up on the reins.

Natasha was sultry and magnificent, dressed in the first stare of fashion, and her dogs were clean, fluffy, and spirited—except for the sullen one-eyed one, Boris, which showed him his teeth—but Nicholas felt nothing but annoyance at seeing the Russian beauty.

He'd hoped she'd moved on from their liaison. But the way she looked at him gave him the distinct impression she hadn't.

"Lady Poppy, Drummond," the princess called out to them in a tone demanding attention.

He inclined his head. "Good afternoon, Princess."

"It's a marvelous afternoon. That is"—she arched one brow and stared at him—"it is *now.*"

A cringeworthy remark if there ever was one, he

thought, and prayed Poppy didn't sense the undertone of sensual invitation in the princess's voice.

Poppy gazed around the park, then back at Natasha, and smiled. "Yes, since the sun has come out in the last few minutes, it *is* a marvelous afternoon, Princess. I'm glad you're enjoying your day."

Hmmm. Nicholas's fiancée was either a true innocent or as wily as Natasha and pretending to misunderstand her. He felt distinctly protective of Poppy either way. No doubt he was swayed in part by the fact that her delectable bosom was almost spilling out of her gown, although Natasha's was, too, come to think of it.

Yet he felt nothing but indifference for her charms.

The princess sucked in her cheeks and shot Poppy a displeased look. "I suppose I am enjoying myself, although when you spurned my invitation to go shopping today, Boris was most disappointed and refused to eat his morning partridge. However, I informed him it was best for newly betrothed couples to parade themselves before society as soon as possible, ere ill rumors spread about their lack of compatibility."

Poppy's brow puckered for only a moment. "How kind of you to keep Boris apprised."

"Yes, and it was an insightful observation, Princess," Nicholas added coolly. "Poppy shall indeed be very busy with nuptial preparations over the length of your stay in London."

Stay away, was what he meant, of course.

Natasha obviously understood. Her eyebrows gathered over her nose, and she opened her mouth to speak, but before she could say anything else, Nicholas took the reins from Poppy's hands.

"Good day, Princess," he said, and urged the horses forward.

"Yes, good-bye, Princess," Poppy called back to her. "Oh, and I've decided I *would* like to go shopping with you, after all. I'll be in tooouch!"

They passed her and her collection of dogs in mere seconds. Nicholas was grateful his horses were prime goers.

"Drummond," Poppy remonstrated with him when the yapping had faded. "How *could* you?"

"Here, take them back," he said, and handed her the reins.

She immediately accepted them. "Not that. I'm talking about the princess. You cut her off as she was about to speak."

"I didn't notice," he lied. "Feel free to maneuver where you wish. There's a flashy clump of flowers over there you might enjoy. As pink as a drunkard's eyes."

But Poppy ignored the clump and drove on. "You told her I'll be too involved in wedding details to see her."

"You *shall* be busy." He sighed inwardly.

"Not too busy for *her*. Not anymore, at any rate."

"You mean, you won't be too busy for *him*." He took the reins back without asking, feeling a sudden pique. "We both know it's Sergei's attention you desire."

"So? You should seek his attention, too. Natasha's, as well."

"I don't give a diamond-studded shoe buckle about

Russian royalty." He felt rather bitter about being passed over for Operation Pink Lady.

"But Mr. Groop says you *must* pay attention to them," Poppy said. "He said so in the note Kettle and I found in your cane."

Nicholas pulled the horses to an immediate stop. *"What did you say?"* Truly, he couldn't have heard her correctly.

"I said Mr. Groop. And it was really quite an easy code to decipher, especially if you're familiar with Hamlet's first soliloquy—"

"Not—another—word." He gripped her hand to make the seriousness of his intentions clear.

"But—"

"Poppy. I mean what I say. If you speak again, I shall kiss you senseless in front of Lady Jersey, who's approaching to our left."

"Go ahead." She tossed her head.

He sighed. "I was *threatening* you. If I kiss you senseless in front of Lady Jersey, you'll never make it into Almack's again."

"The lemonade is blasted weak," she asserted. "I don't think I should miss it."

He took a deep breath. "You won't say another word to me until we may speak in private."

She looked down her nose at him. "All right. But I'm not accustomed to people threatening me, staring down my bodice, baldly confessing they're after my money, and having secrets. I find the whole situation quite reprehensible." She leaned closer. "And in the oddest way . . . invigorating."

He threw her a look. "Invigorating, did you say?"

The damned lust was rising in him like sap.

The chit was driving him mad.

Mad.

And not just in an annoyed sort of way. It was spring. The sun was shining. She was flushed and sweet-smelling, and there was a quiet little shady spot nearby that no one ever seemed to bother with. He'd always wanted to use it for kissing a delectable girl.

A delectable, brazen girl with a brilliant mind was even better. Those codes took him all night to solve.

"I'm taking you home now," he said in neutral tones, to mask the covetous sensations burning through him.

She looked at him as if she were a bound-and-shackled prisoner—a bound-and-shackled prisoner with very kissable lips—but fortunately she said not a word.

Truth be told, Nicholas found threats and secrets invigorating, too, and if he understood the situation correctly, Operation Pink Lady—OPL—was now his.

His.

And the MR that went with it. Thank God, when it rained, it poured. A substantial monetary reward certainly couldn't hurt matters, even if he were marrying an heiress.

But he was also alarmed. How in bloody hell had Poppy found out about Groop? How much did she know?

And how would he keep her out of his business?

He turned the horses toward the east. She'd no idea what she'd stepped into, did she?

He stole a glance at her.

Apparently not.

The "tortured captive" look was gone. She had a self-satisfied "I've-got-a-secret" look. She should never play card games for money, he thought. And she most certainly would never make it in the Service. She wore too many emotions right there on her flimsy, puffed-up sleeve.

A shabby steed bearing a portly young man in an ill-fitting, stained coat pulled alongside the curricle just before they were to leave the park. Nicholas was disappointed to see that it was Frank.

He prayed for patience. "Yes, little brother?"

Frank ignored him and leaned close to Poppy. "I wouldn't marry my brother if I were you. He's only marrying you because the estate needs money. You're filthy rich, so you'll suit." He chuckled. "Not to mention I'll cost you a fortune. I'm an inveterate gambler, you know."

She stared at him for a cool few seconds, long enough that his horse grew restless and a pucker of uncertainty marred Frank's brow.

"You're not fooling me for a minute," she told him. "You're terribly excited I'm marrying your brother because you hope I'll be the big sister you never had. Well, you're right. I'll not tolerate your gambling for a minute. I'll box your ears if you misuse my fortune."

"Is that all?" Frank laughed.

"You've obviously never had a sister." She arched her brow at him. "We're capable of more. *So* much more."

Frank wheeled about on his horse and scowled at Nicholas. "You think you've got the best of me, aligning yourself with this Lady Poppy person, don't you?" He tried to laugh, but it was a poor imitation. "Well, think again."

He tore off on his horse.

They watched him wreak havoc among a party of picnickers, galloping over their blanket.

"My goodness," said Poppy. "What a brother."

"You're almost as provoking as *he* is." Nicholas shook his head and picked up the reins. He was amused by her just a tad, even though the amusement wasn't nearly as strong as the desire he had to peek down her bodice again.

She cast him an arch glance. "You're not my father, nor my employer. I do *what* I want *when* I want—"

"With *whom* you want. I know. You spinsters are quite a handful."

When they rode out of the park into the busy streets of London, he wondered how in hell he was ever going to explain her to Groop.

CHAPTER 13

"Five hundred thirty steps." Poppy stopped, took a deep breath, and wondered how many other young-ladies-turned-spy the gray-eyed duke had brought up here. "We're only on three hundred ten."

"It's worth it," Drummond said, and held tight to her hand.

They were climbing up to the Golden Gallery at the very top of St. Paul's Cathedral—at night. "No one can hear us up there," he said. "And no one can approach without our knowing. We can speak freely."

She withheld the comment that they could speak freely in her drawing room, too—if Cook or Kettle or one of the maids didn't eavesdrop, which would be a rarity. So perhaps she should grant that he knew best where to conduct a clandestine meeting.

She'd lied and told Papa they were off to see a play on Drury Lane, and she'd begged to be allowed to go un-chaperoned, claiming her advanced age and betrothal to a duke were sufficient protection against any gossip.

Besides, she'd said, the play in question was one Aunt Charlotte had already seen.

Aunt Charlotte had merely winked at her. She hadn't seen that play, but she knew, of course, that Poppy was doing all in her power to maintain her membership in the Spinsters Club, and sometimes that dedication required some creative thinking that went beyond the usual evasive techniques a Spinster employed with her suitors.

"As the betrothal is official, you must take Drummond head-on, I'm afraid," Aunt Charlotte had told her earlier in the day, sympathetically patting her hand. "Even if that means you have to be near his handsome personage quite frequently and devise as many moments as possible *alone* with him."

Although Poppy hoped their attachment would be temporary, her duty as a Spinster, according to her aunt, was to continue asserting her own interests and desires to the duke.

"Preferably at close range," Aunt Charlotte had clarified.

Poppy knew from her former governess's assessment of her that she was more sensible and astute than most young ladies. But the desire of her heart had nothing to do with books or rationality. Her primary desire, having been brought up on Cook's stories—and having lived her young life as the daughter of two people very much in love—was for adventure and romance herself.

She hadn't realized she could have either here in England, but Sergei was here now, so he'd take care of the romantic part, and she was climbing onward and upward with Nicholas to a secret place where they could discuss secret things, and at night, no less, which certainly counted as an adventure.

Although the adventure was dragging on rather a long time. Step after step she climbed. Finally, after many odd turns—with one brief rest so she could fix her slipper—and many more steps, they were there, at the top of St. Paul's.

When she walked outside and to the railing, her mouth almost dropped open.

"*This* is London?" She'd never seen it this way.

It was beautiful—even the drifting smoke that floated over portions of the city.

She looked out over a sweeping panorama of thousands of glowing lights, dignified architectural silhouettes, narrow streets, and the winding Thames, all encircled by a starry night sky and a waxing moon.

"It's magical," she choked out, nearly overwhelmed.

Drummond stood behind her, his hand lightly touching her waist. "Isn't it, though?" he said near her ear.

She was tempted to lean back in the circle of his arms and simply gaze at the glorious view . . . but she couldn't very well assert herself if he unleashed her recently discovered appetite for kissing. When they were kissing, all thoughts of defying him went out the window.

Besides, she was trying to save her kisses for Sergei.

"I can't see the stars like this from the street," she admitted. "And the city is . . . breathtaking." She'd never known it could be. Nothing in her experience had ever compared to St. Petersburg, but here she was—in the midst of a majestic scene—right at home.

She looked back at him. "Thank you for bringing me here."

His eyes were dark pools. "You're welcome."

Poppy couldn't breathe, he was so handsome. *But he's not Sergei,* she reminded herself. He was an arrogant Englishman with her silk stocking in his pocket, ever ready to force her hand. Who cared that when he kissed her, she longed to disrobe and have him run his hands all over her body?

"The paper, please," he said.

"Oh, yes." She pulled it out of her bodice—realizing a bit too late that hiding it there might not have been the best idea. She hoped he couldn't see her blushing. "Kettle and I enjoyed playing with that clever cane."

Drummond took the scrap from her, lit a match, and burned it without reading it.

She gasped.

"I already know what it says," he explained.

"We could have burned that at home."

"Yes, we could have, but it wouldn't have been nearly as much fun." He leaned on the railing next to her, his eyes on the city landscape. "Up here, you're much more likely to listen to what I have to say. There's something about this view that gives one clarity. Are you ready?"

"I suppose." She leaned next to him, elbow to elbow, and marveled at the incredible vista.

"You must stay out of my business while we're engaged," he said, staring straight ahead. "For your own good. I get involved in things that a proper young lady should know nothing about."

"Then I don't want to be a proper young lady," she blurted out.

"Of course you do," he said, censuring her with a look. "Proper young ladies don't create risk. Risk is part of my business. I must eliminate all unnecessary danger."

"Are you saying *I'm* a danger?" She backed away from him a step.

He was the Duke of Drummond, after all. Perhaps he'd planned to take her up here so he could throw her over the side of the gallery to her death.

"I'm not going to *eliminate* you," he told her with a chuckle. "Although I fear you could wreck the operation."

"What operation?"

"Operation Pink Lady. My assignment. My *secret* assignment. The one mentioned in that paper inside the cane."

Heavens.

For a moment, she could barely speak. "So that's what OPL means."

"Exactly."

"I want to help," she said. "And by the way, you're not the only one who deals with subterfuge. My friends and I have our own secret organization."

"Is that so? What's it about?"

"None of your business. It's *secret*."

"I'll bet it has to do with men. Women always have secrets about men. How to capture them, stifle them, and break their hearts."

She scoffed. "That's ridiculous. *Men* are the ones who

do that to women, and yes—that's a bit what our secret organization is about, protecting women's interests."

He gave a short laugh. "And you want me to entrust you with secrets? Look how easily you just told me yours."

"I was making a point. And I never told you any details."

"I got details enough." He lifted her chin. "The best way you can help *me* is to do nothing. Say nothing. And behave yourself, as any good fiancée would."

But she wasn't a good fiancée. She was a Spinster.

"No," she said. "I know too much now. Your employer shouldn't have left that cane at my house—"

"You shouldn't have been nosy."

"If you want my silence, you'll give me something to do."

"Why?"

"Because I'm having fun. And if you don't, I shall find a way to get involved anyway. You're right. I *am* a danger. I know just enough to wreak havoc. You'd best keep me close." She crossed her arms and raised her chin. "In case you haven't guessed, this is my way of paying you back for stealing my stocking."

She was asserting herself and her desires, wasn't she?

He stared at her a moment. "I wonder if I'm not insane to have brought you up here thinking you'd cooperate."

"You're not insane," she said, then wondered if she were wrong. All the stories Cook told almost made him out to be crazed. But surely he wasn't, she decided, even though she had no clue what had happened to his uncle.

Nobody did. It was still a mystery.

She cast a sideways glance at him.

"Very well," Nicholas said, his eyes boring into hers. "I'll keep you close. But this won't work if you don't trust me."

She bit her lip. "All right."

"I'm about to confide secrets to you, and I need a sign that you'll not go back on your word."

She drew in a deep breath. "Give me your pinky finger."

He laughed. "That won't do."

"Then what?"

The heated look he gave her made the hairs on the back of her neck stand up, and warmth spread through her limbs. "You're not suggesting—"

"I am."

"What?" she whispered. "A kiss?"

He shook his head. "Nothing so paltry."

She gulped. "You already have my stocking."

"That was to guarantee your adhering properly to your role as devoted fiancée. This is to get your pledge that you won't reveal secrets of another sort."

"What must I do?"

"What all my colleagues and I must do, those of us who work for Groop. Disrobe. And run around the gallery three times."

She gasped. Had he been reading her mind? She longed to disrobe . . . and have him run his hands all over her body.

"Don't worry," he said. "I won't touch you. No one ever gets touched. We do it to prove our mettle."

Blast.

She shook her head. "I can't."

"So much for your fun." He began to walk toward the door.

"All right," she cried.

He turned around, his expression serious. "Very well, then."

She rather liked the idea, if she were honest. She'd be disrobing for king and country. Even the martyrs buried at St. Paul's wouldn't fault her for doing her duty.

Slowly, she pulled at the ribbons of her bodice.

CHAPTER 14

One pull.

Two.

Nicholas saw the fabric on Poppy's gown loosen and kept his face impassive, but his body betrayed him. Heat spread from limb to limb. He could barely breathe, thinking of her disrobing in front of him.

Dear God, he wondered, would she do it? Would she run naked around the gallery—just so she could have secret adventures?

"Think of England," he told her. "That's what my colleagues and I do." It was a cheeky enough piece of advice from a cool, experienced bachelor, wasn't it? Even though his heart was hammering.

"I already thought of England," she said, her face implacable, and began to shrug out of one sleeve.

My, she was cool under pressure.

Nicholas rubbed a hand down his face. No way could he carry the ruse any further. He'd be a scoundrel to tease her out of her clothes, and she was a minx to look as if she were enjoying herself. The unruffled pleasure she took in wriggling out of that sleeve was enough to make the front of his breeches tighten to an embarrassing degree.

"That's enough," he said firmly, feeling the joke was on *him*.

"It is?"

"I wanted to make sure you were serious."

She sucked in a breath. "You mean, you and your colleagues *don't* disrobe and run around the gallery three times?"

"No. But congratulations. You passed the test."

"My goodness." Her hand froze on her sleeve. "You were lying." She let her hand drop to her side. "You're no gentleman."

"Perhaps I'm not." He pulled a cheroot out of his pocket and lit it. As usual, it was a fine distraction and he only wished he had some brandy to go with it. "But it was only a game. Nothing worth naming seconds over."

He puffed on the cheroot once, removed it, and let the smoke curl upward into the night.

"Game?" She flicked a wary glance at his breeches. "For whom? You or me? Being called an Impossible Bachelor shouldn't grant you leave to have boorish manners. Has no other female called you on them? I'm here to work with you—as your colleague. Not to be treated like one of your . . . your women."

"Yes, well, I *am* sorry." He couldn't believe it, but even though the cheroot was a fine one, he couldn't stave off a vague feeling of shame. He ground the smoky thing under his boot, then sprawled out on the stone floor of the gallery. "Sit." He patted the stones beside him. "We'll waste no more time on petty quarrels."

Deuce take it, he wished he could perform his sensual Indian maneuver on her, the one that calmed the angriest of females, but she wasn't naked, and that was a requirement for it to work properly.

"I won't sit." She arched a brow. "Not until you receive a comeuppance. Flimsy apologies won't do."

He heaved a sigh. "Come now. I already said I was sorry."

He tried to ignore the fact that her bodice was still unlaced, but he also didn't want to tell her. Glancing at it was like taking a sip from a hot buttered rum on a freezing cold day.

She pursed her lips. "Stay where you are, Drummond. I know the perfect punishment for a smug rogue like you."

"Is that so?" He couldn't resist a small chuckle.

Her.

Punishing him.

Ha.

"Remember," she ordered him. "Don't move." With slow fingers, she loosened her laces even further.

He lurched forward. "Wait a minute." He could really use that brandy now. His mouth was perfectly dry. "What's going on here?"

She sent him a well-satisfied look, then turned her back—and, much to his shock, shimmied out of the top of her gown and stays.

She looked at him over her bare shoulder. "I'm not

one of your jaded mistresses, nor am I a silly debutante. I'm a Spinster. You'd do well to remember."

He was mesmerized by her flirtatious stance, her
hands on her hips, and by the sight of the smooth plane
of her back tapering to a tiny waist. He could only imagine what her breasts looked like. She was beautiful and
strong—and he wanted her.

Badly.

"This is certainly an exquisite sort of punishment,"
he murmured. He was unsettled by her, to say the least,
and not only by her curvaceous form.

"Well, it's over," she said lightly. And with quick,
sure movements, she pulled her gown and stays back up,
laced herself in, and turned back around, delivering him
one last disapproving look. "Now, if you'd like to continue a discussion between equals, we may proceed."

And with a flounce, she sat down next to him.

He studied her, more intrigued than he'd been in
ages. He'd never met a female like her. "I'm supposed
to be able to recover from that?" He gave a small laugh
of disbelief. "Seeing a proper young lady reveal herself
in almost half her naked glory?"

She shrugged, adjusting her bodice. "You'll have
to." She tried to maintain a severe expression, but then
the corner of her mouth quirked up.

He grabbed her wrist. "I deserved every bit of that
torture." He was pleased to see she allowed herself a
small grin. "Just don't make me go through it again, will
you? Or maybe you should. But from the other side."

She slapped his hand. "Absolutely not," she said, then
wagged a finger at him. "You must promise me not to

tell any of your drinking friends what I did. It was only to prove a very important point. And if you have to ask what it is, you didn't learn a thing."

"Believe me, I learned." She'd brought him to his knees, at least figuratively. He couldn't remember the last person who'd managed that. He wasn't so sure he wanted any of his friends to know.

"Now," she said, her pique completely vanished, "we can get back to business." She gave him a warm smile, and he tried not to feel pleased about being back in her good graces.

"Very well," he said. "Here's the thing. I have to retrieve a painting for England."

It felt good to confide the details of his job with someone other than Groop.

"Tell me more." She leaned closer, her pupils sharpening and her lips parted like two pink rose petals.

Two very soft, supple rose petals.

Which he would ignore, he told himself. Duty must come first. *Always.*

And besides, she wanted him to treat her like a man.

No, not a man. As his partner. His colleague.

He could *do* that.

"We refer to the portrait as Pink Lady," he said. "It's said to be of a gorgeous woman in a pink gown dancing with her lover."

"It sounds lovely." Her eyes sparkled at the additional revelations.

"It might well be. But it's in the wrong hands."

"Whose hands?"

"Natasha and Sergei's, the Russian twins."

Poppy's eyebrows shot high. "You can't take anything from them. I'm sure they truly own the painting."

"Oh, but they don't. I can't say how I know, but I do. And the government has excellent reasons for wanting it. Somewhere in the background of the painting is a secret message. It reveals a mole in Parliament."

"A mole?"

"Someone on our side spying for another country."

"I do know what a mole is." She gave him a droll look. "I'm the daughter of a very active member of the House of Lords, remember. But what sort of person hides a message about someone as dastardly as a mole in a painting?"

"Someone who works for the Service. We tend to like drama. Besides, letters get intercepted. Messengers get killed. Who'd think to look at a painting? It's a clever method of communication."

She released a little huff of air. "So you have to steal it."

"Not steal. Retrieve. Big difference."

"Of course." Spoken like a true Service professional. She scooted closer to him. "Go on."

"The difficult part"—it was hard to think with her shoulder touching his—"is that Sergei and Natasha believe they own it."

"But they don't. Poor things. Why can't you just ask them to hand it over?"

"Two reasons. It's worth a great deal of money, and it brings them all sorts of attention. Their uncle Revnik painted it, after all. They don't know he worked for us and had every intention of getting that painting to his

English contacts in the Service. But he died rather suddenly of the smallpox, and the Service had no idea what happened to the painting."

"What drama!"

She was right.

"Now the twins are in England," he said, "cutting their swath through London society. They're bored, they're rich, and they crave constant amusement." Nicholas laid a hand on her knee. "We can't let them know we want the painting. It's a matter of national security."

"Oh, heavens," she whispered, putting her own hand over his and squeezing hard. "National security. Papa deals with that all the time. How do you plan to retrieve the portrait?"

"At the ball at the Russian ambassador's residence. We'll take it that night, before anyone sees it."

"With all of London society there?"

"It's the best time. Distractions will abound. And when they finally realize the portrait's missing, they'll have a long list of possible suspects to sift through."

"I see." Her eyes gleamed with shrewd understanding.

"Your job is—"

She drew even closer. "Please don't make it a sinecure. I want to do something substantive. It would make Papa proud."

"Very well." Nicholas liked her enthusiasm, her appealing grin, and her impressive vocabulary. And he must admit, her hand covering his. "Have you ever heard the expression 'Keep your enemies close?'"

She drew back with a happy sigh. "Of course. My

secret club says that all the time. 'Know your foe,' which I think is a bit strong as most of our suitors are perfectly lovely people. It's only those rude ones like Lord Washburn who drive us mad."

"All right, then. While you may not consider Natasha your enemy—and I know you don't believe Sergei is— you must realize they're our opponent at the moment, whether they know it or not. Your job is to help keep them happy while I figure out how to get the painting back."

"I'm thoroughly committed to that idea," she said breathlessly, which didn't surprise him, of course. "As for the painting, you'll retrieve it alone?"

"Yes. I've got a map of the interior of the Russian ambassador's residence. I've been inside once—but not far—and am familiar with their usual level of security. I'm assuming it will be stepped up. My task will be to locate the painting before they bring it to the ballroom. Count and Countess Lieven are excellent hosts and no doubt will want to build suspense, so I suspect they'll save the unveiling until the middle or end of the ball."

"I can also help steal the painting. I mean, *retrieve*."

Gad, she was becoming a little *too* enthusiastic. "No," he said firmly, "that's not a good idea."

"But—"

"There are no buts. Remind the twins you know the Russian language. Show them around London. Do whatever it takes to keep them content to be here—short of flirting with Sergei outright. Everyone must believe you and I are happily engaged, of course."

Her face fell. "How on earth will I *not* flirt with him?"

"You must find a way." He chuckled. "Think of him as your brother."

"Brother?" She crossed her arms. "That reminds me. He and Natasha hate each other."

"I know. We'll simply have to endure their squabbling—and prevent it if possible. The last thing we want is for them to leave the country in some sort of snit, taking the painting with them before the ball. And you have to understand—here and now, before we begin—that no matter how you're affected personally, you must do your job, despite what anyone else thinks about you. You must be strong and unwavering. Sometimes working for Groop can make you feel lonely. You won't be able to explain to your best friends or your family what you're doing. Occasionally, you might have to make up a bald-faced lie with no warning and be believable as you deliver it. Are you sure you're up to the task?"

"Of course I am," she said, a wrinkle on her brow.

"What are you thinking?" Drummond asked her.

"Of Sergei. You make him sound like a petulant child. I spent a week with him when I was fifteen," she said dreamily, "and he was nothing of the sort. He was *very* romantic."

Nicholas restrained himself from rolling his eyes. "Exactly what constitutes 'romantic' to a fifteen-year-old girl? Chaste kisses? Searing looks?"

She huffed. "If you'd only read the Russian poets, you'd know."

"Who says I haven't read the Russian poets?" He arched a brow.

"Have you?"

He'd read them all, although he wouldn't tell *her*. Instead, he grabbed her hand and pulled her so close, their noses almost touched. "I'm the dreaded Duke of Drummond, so it doesn't follow that I'd be a romantic who reads Russian poetry, does it?"

They stared at each other a moment, their mouths only inches apart. A sudden chill wind blew a strong gust that whistled around the gallery, lifting their hair and tugging at their clothes.

Despite the dropping temperature, Nicholas felt hot, unbridled lust.

"You're right," she agreed in a whisper, "it doesn't follow at all. However, Sergei has read them—in fact, he's memorized some of those poems and recited them to me—so no doubt he'll find a wealthy bride whom he also *loves*."

Nicholas dropped her hand. The girl was convinced Sergei had godlike qualities.

"You have your assignment," he said dryly. "And we've a façade to maintain. We're going to test the waters as a betrothed couple at a literary social to be held tomorrow at Lady Gastly's. I've already been to the Howell residence and invited Natasha. Sergei is in his own rented apartment several blocks away. Even though Natasha sulked about how we'd treated her in the park today, she eventually accepted for both of them."

Poppy gathered her skirt in folds. "I—I'm a bit nervous."

"Why?"

"I might have been good at making up tales about

being engaged to the Duke of Drummond, but I'm not a good liar in general. I'll stumble. I'll blurt something out, like, 'We're not really engaged.' At least in the park today, we had a sort of distance from everyone ogling us."

Nicholas sighed. "If you insist on having fun with me, as you say, you'll need to trust yourself."

"Of course." She appeared rather embarrassed at her show of nerves.

He stood and pulled her up by the hand. "By the way," he said, "you've established a long-running story that we're marrying for love. So don't forget to act the part."

"But—"

"I know you're bound and determined not to marry me. That's not the point. You've made your bed and you have to lie in it. You'll have to pretend to be in love with me, whether you like it or not."

"You'll have to help carry it off, as well," she insisted.

Somehow, beneath the gibbous moon and brilliant stars, Nicholas found it was easier to imagine they could.

CHAPTER 15

Poppy sat up in bed the next morning and had a stunning thought: she was doing clandestine work—for the Service. She could hardly believe it.

And she was completely over feeling sorry for her beloved Sergei and his rude sister. Yes, it was unfortunate that the painting wasn't really theirs. But if Sergei married *her,* she'd make sure he never missed it.

She climbed out of bed and eyed her reflection in the looking glass.

Love. That's what she saw. It was written all over her face. Her eyes were bright. Her mouth—well, she simply couldn't stop grinning.

It was her duty to keep Sergei happy.

Could Fate be any more kind?

All she had left to do was make sure he was as in love with her as she already was with him.

Oh, right—and then she'd have to get out of her engagement with the duke. She kept forgetting about that part. But once she showed Drummond the door—in a polite way, of course—it was all smooth sailing from there on out.

With that hopeful scenario in mind, that afternoon she accompanied Drummond, Sergei, and Natasha to Lady Gastly's literary salon, the latest social spectacle.

Lady Gastly took her arm as soon as she entered the vast drawing room filled with members of the *ton*. "I heard about your betrothal to that duke," she whispered in Poppy's ear.

Even though she'd ridden over in the carriage with Drummond, their thighs touching, Poppy had been trying very hard to forget about him. Especially because last night when they'd arrived at the bottom of St. Paul's again, he'd dragged her out into the street and kissed her senseless.

"I knew you wanted me to kiss you," he'd said halfway through the brazen encounter, "but not on top of a church." And he'd busied himself caressing her hips and bottom and teasing her mouth mercilessly with his own.

She'd abhorred that he was such a mind reader.

"It was shocking, absolutely shocking," Lady Gastly was saying now. "Do tell the details."

"I'm not sure what you mean," Poppy said awkwardly, still lost in her own kissing-outside-St. Paul's details.

"The murder," Lady Gastly explained. "Ducal intrigue. I'd never even heard of the Drummond line, and now I'm all agog, thanks to my cook."

"Your cook?"

"Yes, she's friends with another cook in Town who told her an uncle went missing."

"Right," said Poppy weakly. "That's just a silly rumor. He ran off to sea, is all." She vowed to go home and tell Cook to stop spreading tales about the Duke of Drummond, even if she suspected some of them might be true.

She had no idea if they were or not. She took a peek at him conversing with Natasha, his expression polite but cool. Drummond was a man of mystery. She certainly couldn't trust him, even though he was a most interesting companion. She'd gone to bed yesterday evening wishing she were thinking of Sergei, but she hadn't very well been able to do that when her spectacular evening with Drummond at St. Paul's had dominated her thoughts.

She couldn't think of Sergei until this morning, when she'd fortuitously rid herself of thoughts of the duke by dreaming about him all night.

But now, even though Sergei was sitting right next to her humming under his breath (she wasn't sure why), those dreams were coming back to her. And in them, Drummond was kissing her and running his hands all over her body again and—

"I hope they start the program soon," she whispered to Natasha.

Natasha arched a brow. "You look ill, Lady Poppy, and I believe Sergei should take you home. I'll need Drummond to stay with me in the event I'll require a translator. You're flushed redder than a pomegranate, I'll have you know."

"I am?"

Natasha nodded. "Sergei, stupid as he is, has a wonderful cure for the muck sweats he learned from his last mistress, a hag named Zoya. He has the worst possible taste in women." She eyed Poppy up and down with a scornful curl to her lip.

"I'm feeling fine," Poppy murmured, aghast at Natasha's personal revelations about Sergei and her tendency to insult him. She leaned down and petted the corgis in the princess's basket. One of the dogs growled at her, the one with the missing eye.

I'm just fine, she told herself, eyeing Nicholas's muscled calf out of the corner of her eye and ignoring the subsequent skittering of her heart. Nicholas's legs were, um, attractive, to say the least. She'd noticed them last night when he'd been sprawled on the floor of the Golden Gallery, his thighs tight in his breeches and his boots molded to his calves.

Sergei kept humming.

Hmm. She didn't remember him humming in St. Petersburg.

"What song is that?" Poppy asked him, really to make him aware that he was humming a bit loudly, not because she cared about the song.

"No song," he said with a shrug. "Just humming."

Poppy tried not to grit her teeth. He was her beloved, after all. If this were a new habit of his, she'd learn to love it. Humming would become one of those signature things that reminded her of him. Her heart would soften, and then she'd even start making requests—for different songs.

But definitely not this one.

"Perhaps you should hum a song everyone knows," she whispered.

Sergei shook his head. "I told you. This is not a song. I am humming, nothing more."

And went back to it.

Poppy put a discreet curl over her ear to mask the noise, and then she grew ashamed of herself. The poor man was nervous, no doubt, being in a new country. Humming must bring him a sort of comfort.

Thankfully, however, he stopped when Lady Gastly finally stood and called the room to attention. "Today we shall meet the former housemaid of a terribly shocking poet named John Keats," she announced.

The housemaid sat at the front of the room, her nose red and her mouth small and pinched.

"Very few know of his work," Lady Gastly went on. "And probably for good reason."

A trifle bored already, Poppy suppressed a yawn. This John Keats probably *would* be dull if no one had heard of him. And then she found herself stifling another yawn. Now that she thought about it, she'd slept very little last night, thanks to Drummond appearing in her dreams.

She took a peek at him sitting on the other side of Natasha and felt slightly annoyed.

He looked back.

"Yes?" he asked dryly.

She could hardly tell him the scandalous things he'd done to her in her dreams, but she *could* purse her mouth disapprovingly and return her attention to the front of the room.

Which was what she did, and somehow felt sad and lonely of a sudden. She *did* want to go home. Natasha had been right. Perhaps she was ill. She wondered if her face were still as red as a pomegranate and then determined it couldn't matter. She must stay and endure Drummond's handsome profile, as well as Natasha's sharp elbow in her side, and Sergei's humming if, God forbid, it started up again.

"Who *is* this John Keats?" Lady Gastly asked the housemaid. "And why have I never heard of him until you came knocking on my door?"

The housemaid scratched the side of her nose. "He's a poet," she said in a thick Cockney accent. "Most people never 'eard of him. It's because he's a bit of a rebel."

There were excited yet disapproving gasps from all around—but not from Poppy. She was too busy thinking about Drummond again and wondering what would have happened if she'd taken her gown all the way off at the Golden Gallery. For a moment there, she'd been *so* close.

Good thing she hadn't.

Yes, very good thing. Because then she would have possibly wrapped her arms about his neck and pressed her breasts against his chest and . . .

And moaned.

One didn't moan at the top of St. Paul's. Not unless one wanted to go to hell. Which was why she was so glad Drummond had kissed her in the street instead. When she'd moaned there, only two horses tied to a post had heard.

"I beg of you, Lady Poppy," Natasha leaned over and said, "please allow my recalcitrant brother to take you home. I could swear you just whimpered, and you're wriggling about like a small child. Boris is getting quite frantic."

Poppy gave Natasha a pinched smile. "I'm fine, thank you. I've simply a stitch in my side."

But she wasn't fine. She'd felt so *alive* last night! She wanted more of that feeling, and sitting here in this stuffy drawing room was doing nothing to help.

She only wished she could show Sergei the intensity of emotion she felt for *him*.

Somehow she would convey to him with her eyes that she adored him.

But he didn't look her way. He sniffed. She noticed his nostrils were quite large. Larger than . . . larger than she'd remembered.

He sniffed again.

"Have you a cold?" she whispered.

"No," he said, and gave a long, slow sniff.

"Of course you have one," she found herself insisting in a calm manner, just like a doctor.

But inside she was reeling. *Please, God*, she was thinking. *Please let it be a cold*. And not another annoying habit she'd never noticed in St. Petersburg.

She shifted in her seat and touched her hair, hoping no one thought *she* was sniffing so loudly and often. And then she felt terribly guilty. She should be thinking about making the prince a special punch to help him recover from his cold rather than be embarrassed about his sniffing.

What kind of true love took exception to a cold?

Because surely, that's what it was.

He sniffed again.

She almost giggled—a trifle hysterically. Natasha directed another scowl her way, but Poppy ignored her. The housemaid had pulled a piece of paper out of her pocket and was handing it to Lady Gastly.

"'Ere's Mr. Keats's poem," the housemaid said. "I dare you to read it."

"I suppose I will." Lady Gastly winced and held the paper by one corner. She cleared her throat and looked over her captive audience.

"'On First Looking into Chapman's Homer,'" she intoned. "'Much have I travell'd in the realms of gold. And many goodly states and kingdoms seen . . .'"

While her hostess ploddingly read the poem, Poppy sat up straighter. Miraculously, her annoyingly persistent thoughts of St. Paul's and Nicholas's kisses and Sergei's sniffing faded. The poem simply took over.

She was shocked.

And stunned.

Keats's poem was magnificent. It spoke of amazing discoveries and how life-changing they are. It affected her the same way her experience at the Golden Gallery had. Like the explorers in the poem who'd overlooked the Pacific, she'd overlooked London last night with the same "wild surmise," seeing possibilities she hadn't known existed.

Lady Gastly folded up the paper and handed it back to the housemaid. "Who here has a comment to make?"

Sergei sat stone-faced. Poppy wondered if he'd even understood the words in the poem, so she asked the prince in quiet Russian.

He yawned. "Yes, I like to ice-skate. Why do you ask?"

"Oh," Poppy replied, blushing. "I'm so sorry. I thought I asked if you understood the poem."

He gave a careless shrug. "It was boring."

Boring?

Poppy heartily disagreed, but perhaps because Lady Gastly hadn't read in the prince's native tongue, he couldn't appreciate it.

Natasha elbowed her hard. "Why don't they read a Russian poet?" she asked. "Someone should tell them so."

"I shall." Sergei stood, looking regal and commanding. His brow was firm, his chin was noble, and he wore many medals on his chest. "I would prefer to discuss a Russian work," he announced loudly. "Something by Aleksandr Pushkin will suit."

Poppy gulped and slid just a tad lower in her seat. She loved him, but she'd really have to talk to him about becoming "one of the people" when he was out socializing.

Lady Gastly laid her hand on her cheek. "Oh, dear. Perhaps we should forget about Keats, Your Highness. He *is* a shocking fellow."

There were murmurs of agreement.

But then a familiar voice spoke.

"I completely disagree." Poppy swung around and saw Nicholas standing. His voice was low but fervent. "Mr. Keats's poem is well worth discussing. He taps into man's intrinsic desire for adventure, something for which every soul yearns."

He made eye contact with Poppy, and she felt a rush of connection. He could tell she craved adventure, too, couldn't he?

"All of us can be grateful to have heard it," he concluded, and sat down.

One could have heard a pin drop.

Natasha drew herself up and sucked in her cheeks. Sergei directed a long, cold stare Nicholas's way. Even Lady Gastly appeared stunned into silence by the duke's outburst.

Poppy didn't know what to think. The Nicholas who'd just stood and spoken on behalf of Keats wasn't the callous rake she knew but someone entirely different. Someone who'd been moved by a poem.

His reaction shook her. Was he—could he possibly be . . . *sensitive*?

She dared to glance at him, and he winked.

The scoundrel.

He was as sensitive as a log. She should have known he was merely amusing himself. What did he know of poets and poetry? And what was he doing alienating Sergei and Natasha that way? Wasn't he supposed to make the Russian twins happy?

Poppy was so annoyed at his unapologetic air, she moved closer to the prince, who had resumed his seat. "Don't worry," she told him, "I shall discuss Pushkin with you."

Was he to be blamed for caring so very deeply about his country's poets?

"We have much to discuss," Sergei said, his eyes smoldering with *something*.

"We *do*?"

He leaned closer to her. "Be ready, Lady Poppy," he whispered in her ear. "Like the big Russian bear, soon I will roar at you with passion. The passion of Pushkin. And more. *Much* more."

He pulled back and smiled slowly.

"Oh," she said, and waited for that melty, shivery feeling to take over and for her heart to thump with wild abandon, but nothing happened.

Nothing at all.

CHAPTER 16

It was one of those moments when Nicholas wasn't sure his Service duty was worth it. The day after the literary salon, while Prince Sergei attended to business in Whitehall, Nicholas found himself walking down an expansive wing at the British Museum with Poppy, Natasha, and her dogs. The princess had received special permission to bring the hairy yappers on their tour—in a pram, of all things.

Now Natasha came to a halt in front of a statue of a Greek goddess. "I must ask you to push the corgis now, Nicky," she told him with a lazy yawn. "Only very dear friends are allowed to do so." She cast a sly glance at Poppy, who fortunately was too busy examining the Greek goddess's garments to notice the slight.

Already he'd lifted the pram up a massive set of stairs, which was no small feat with five dogs inside. And now he was to . . . *push* the pram?

Over his dead body.

A quick glance at Poppy showed she'd apparently

heard every word, after all. Her eyes twinkled in amusement.

He gave Natasha a tight smile. "I'm afraid I can't."

She pulled in her chin. "Whyever not?"

It was too late for regrets, but for the umpteenth time, he wished he'd never gotten intimately involved with the princess.

"I can't push *dogs*"—he felt as if he had a pair of stockings stuffed down his throat—"in a *pram*." There was a slight snicker from Poppy. "I never have," he went on, his voice rising, "and I never will!"

Damned dogs in prams.

What was the world coming to?

He refused to be chagrined at his lack of manners—a man could take only so much nonsense—and strode ahead of the two ladies, ignoring Poppy's polite insistence to the princess that she push the pram while Natasha gathered her breath.

If Poppy was trying to make him feel guilty, it wouldn't work.

Nevertheless, he looked straight through several celebrated oil paintings without really seeing them and realized with a start of shock that he wasn't his usual assured self. Poppy was getting to him—far more than Natasha was with her silly attempts to capture his notice.

Yes, Lord Derby's daughter talked too much and she thought she knew everything there was to know, but somehow she was different from all the other ladies of his acquaintance. He thought it might have to do with her total lack of regard for what he thought of her.

That was it. She didn't give a tuppence for his opinion.

It was a refreshing change.

Yet lowering, too.

Not many people had ever been able to work their way under Nicholas's skin, and especially no woman. Yet Poppy's indifference to his masculine charms, the ones he wielded so well over the rest of the female population, was causing him to take notice of her more than he cared to.

Natasha glowered and Poppy beamed when they caught up with him in front of a large canvas by the English painter William Hogarth. It was obvious the princess couldn't bear the fact that a lesser mortal was pushing her corgis about, and Poppy—naughty girl—was apparently enjoying the royal's discomfiture.

"What do you call your primary seat, Drummond?" Natasha demanded to know. "And where is it located?"

He inhaled a silent breath and prayed for patience. He could swear she'd asked twice already. "Seaward Hall's on the North Sea," he replied with an equanimity he didn't feel.

Poppy was so close. He could smell her hair—it had the scent of sunshine and fresh air, mingled with a trace of violets.

"Weren't there Vikings there at one time?" his fiancée contributed to the conversation (what there was of it), her eyes still on the painting, her slender hands gripping the pram.

He couldn't help feeling a rush of pleasure at her interest, as if he were some lovesick boy craving attention from an unattainable female. But he had her, didn't he? Whether she liked it or not, she would soon become his wife.

"Legend has it," he told her in as plain a tone as he'd spoken to Natasha, "there were stashes of Viking treasure buried along the shore. As a boy, I was constantly looking for it."

"You were an adorable, mischievous child," Natasha pronounced as if she'd been witness to his childhood herself. "Let us move on." And she sauntered over to the next painting, her chin in the air.

Poppy glanced at him and giggled. "Yes, you adorable, mischievous duke," she whispered to him, "let us move on."

He narrowed his eyes at her. Not many people could get away with making fun of him.

The remnants of a smile still curved her lips when she pushed the pram forward again and asked, "Did you ever find any Viking treasure?"

"No, I didn't." He couldn't help smiling himself at the memory. "I poked the sand with hundreds of sticks, turned over thousands of rocks. And to this day, I wonder what precious loot I might have missed."

Natasha moved farther down the hall, no doubt drawn by a threesome of fashionable young ladies talking animatedly beneath a painting of a handsome shepherd.

In front of a beautiful scene of a field in Tuscany, Poppy looked from beneath her lashes at Nicholas in the most seductive yet intelligent way. He could barely comprehend how that could be, yet somehow she managed it.

"Natasha's obviously charmed by you." His betrothed had a womanly way of turning her head just so when she was conversing.

"It's all part of being a duke," he said, ignoring the fact that he was drawing up a mental list of things he liked about Poppy. "Rather a bore. What about Natasha's transparent machinations to throw you and Sergei together?"

Poppy shrugged. "I have no doubt it's to get herself alone with you."

"I agree," he replied, "but she must think you'll be receptive to her lead."

Poppy had the grace to blush. "It's in your best interest I go along, Your Grace. A happy prince and princess is our goal, so don't fault me for falling into line."

He chuckled. "I don't—it's the willingness with which you do so that amuses me. Sergei's not nearly your equal, you know."

She opened her mouth to say something—indignant, no doubt, judging from the straight line her delicate brows made over her eyes—but Natasha strode back to them and gave a cursory glance at the painting of the Tuscan fields. "Your English painters are all well and good." She sighed. "But where are the Russians? Levitsky Argunov?"

"Farther down the hall," Nicholas replied. "Shall we head in that direction and stop along the way as it suits us?"

Several gasps in their direction came from the three-some of fashionable young ladies ahead, and no wonder. Sergei had arrived, shining and regal, a smug smile on his lips. He fixed his regal gaze on Poppy alone.

Her cheeks flushed pink, and she bit her lip when the prince bowed low over her hand. Then she cast a quick, nervous glance at Nicholas, as if she regretted teasing him about Natasha.

He arched a brow. Perhaps it would be his turn to laugh now.

Yes, Poppy was anxious to see Sergei again, eager to erase the unfavorable impression he'd left her with at Lady Gastly's literary salon, but she could hardly be thrilled her latest test of him would take place in front of the Duke of Drummond.

She wanted the old prince back—the one she'd known in Russia and had caught a charming glimpse of at the Grangerford ball.

God forbid the prince disappoint her. It would be mortifying if Drummond scorned her taste in men. She didn't like looking the fool in front of him—he already rankled her so.

"We've not missed you, brother," Natasha said airily. "As a matter of fact, you may walk with Lady Poppy. The duke and I are attending to the corgis."

"And it's been a *joy,*" Drummond said seriously, looking between the prince and princess.

Poppy almost giggled. *Did the man have no shame?*

He gave her a dampening look, entirely false, of course—the bounder was as amused by his comment as she was—and took off with the princess and her pram full of panting dogs.

With a bit of relief, Poppy turned to Sergei. "Your Highness, have you seen the bust of Shakespeare? I'm dying to view it myself. It's a few rooms down."

"It will be my pleasure to escort you," Sergei said, wrapping her arm in his. "Of course, you like *Twelfth Night* best of all the Bard's plays. It is *my* favorite, and so it shall be yours."

"No it won't," she said, bristling just a tad. It was early days yet in her assessment of him. "I do like *Twelfth Night,* but I prefer *Macbeth*."

"Oh, but it's important to like the same things, no?" he said with a charming grin. "To be compatible."

She blushed. So he *was* thinking about her in those terms. And then she remembered how different she and Drummond were. She bit her lip. "Well, *friends* can like different things. That's what makes life interesting."

She never felt bored around Drummond.

Sergei gave a short bark of laughter. "Friends?" He leaned closer. "We are more than friends," he whispered. "I have decreed it so."

She cast a nervous glance at the duke. "Remember, I'm engaged," she whispered back, "to the Duke of Drummond."

Finally, she was speaking the truth when she made that claim.

Sergei waved a careless hand. "He is a mere duke. I am a Russian prince. Princes take precedence over dukes."

"But Sergei, the Duke of Drummond is—"

Flirting with a Russian princess, a little imp in her head reminded her, *straight ahead.*

"Who cares about the Duke of Drummond?" Sergei stopped and gave her that smoldering, half-lidded look again. "When may I come to your room?"

Her room?

She couldn't help it. She chuckled. Of course, he'd meant her *drawing* room. English wasn't his first language, so he was bound to make embarrassing mistakes now and then.

"Any time." She patted his arm, feeling vaguely protective of him. "Preferably in the early afternoon. Just say the word."

He gave her a slow grin. "You prefer day to night?"

"Yes. I must say I'm quite fond of the, um, daytime."

Good Lord, she hadn't remembered having such odd conversations with him in St. Petersburg. Perhaps he hadn't spoken English in quite a while.

"You bold girl. What shall you wear?" His voice had a suddenly rough edge to it.

"A—a walking gown, I suppose."

"Splendid." He gave her another heated smile. "I like to take my time."

"That's refreshing." She forced herself to smile back even though his comments were becoming increasingly confusing. "Most men are in such a rush."

Her father every night at dinner, for one. And every man who'd ever come to tea in her drawing room, excepting the Marquess of Stanbury and Lord Tweed, the garrulous suitors who'd droned on so long that she'd had to replace the teapot twice.

The prince looked toward Drummond and his sister, as if he were afraid they'd hear him. "Wear your bonnet, too," he urged her. "Something with feathers. And your parasol. I love a woman who can use a parasol to her advantage."

She had a sudden fear—an illogical, sordid fear that she couldn't name, but it certainly did her no credit.

"Sergei"—she paused—"you *did* mean my drawing room, did you not?"

His eyes cooled a bit. "Why, did you think I meant elsewhere?"

She blinked. He couldn't, wouldn't dare to—

No, she was thinking in an entirely inappropriate direction.

"Of course not," she said primly.

"Prince, Lady Poppy!" It was Drummond, striding toward them. "Did you not see? Boris has escaped."

"Your blasted duke annoys me," Sergei muttered, "and I despise that dog. I hope he goes looking for it and gets lost himself."

"Where did he go?" Poppy asked Drummond, ignoring Sergei's extremely rude remarks.

"I'm not sure." Irritation made Drummond's gray eyes narrow. "He ran down the corridor. Natasha's having a fit of the vapors and is sitting on a chair in the salon straight ahead and to the left. Prince Sergei, please take her home, and Lady Poppy, you come with me." He grabbed her hand.

She felt a great rush of relief. And she also felt a lurch of warmth near her heart at the feel of his firm, masculine grip.

"We'll return Boris to the princess as soon as we find him," the duke called back to the prince.

Poppy was glad her stilted conversation with Sergei was over. And she felt pleasure, unexpected pleasure, that she and Drummond would be alone for a while—without the whining princess's company, either.

Even if the price they must pay for the respite was finding a petulant dog.

CHAPTER 17

Nicholas's mild irritation at being at the beck and call of the princess turned into full-blown resentment. The one-eyed dog was nowhere to be found, despite the fact that he and Poppy had searched through various rooms at the museum for a good half hour.

"The princess says he loves people and will make a beeline for a crowd," he said.

"Then we should try again by the Elgin Marbles," Poppy suggested.

"We've already done so twice."

"How about the Rosetta Stone?"

"All right. Once more."

They turned to the right to the chamber housing the famed stone when Poppy pointed straight ahead. "There he is!"

The squat dog was doing his best to get down a long series of steps to the first floor. They both rushed to him, and Nicholas picked him up. Boris's tongue lolled out of his mouth and he stared defiantly at Poppy with his one eye.

"Your adventure is over, my canine friend," Nicholas muttered.

Poppy stroked Boris's head. "I wonder where he's been hiding?"

Her slender fingers caressing the beast's head, the sweet nothings she murmured, somehow grabbed Nicholas's attention and held it. He was jealous, he realized. Jealous of a dog.

For God's sake, what was he thinking? He didn't need sweet caresses anywhere but where it counted—and even then, it didn't have to be sweet, did it?

A caress was enough.

Not even a caress. A quick swipe or two with a hand would do.

He pulled Boris away, leaving Poppy's hand dangling in midair.

Just because.

"The dog needs no more touching." Nicholas felt a terrible mood coming upon him, and he wasn't sure why.

"Why are you glowering at me?" she asked, her hands on her hips. "What have I done?"

He was saved from answering by the approach of a small woman with a broad face and a frilly cap, who was striding toward them, her hands clenched in fists.

"Blast his furry hide, there he is!" She was followed by a meek maidservant. "That evil dog swallowed the round pearl-and-ruby pendant off my necklace. I picked him up and said, 'Oh, you dear, dear thing,' and next thing I knew, he'd bitten it right off!"

She held up a broken gold chain.

Poppy's eyes were wide. "Um, I'm so sorry, madam.

And I'm sure we'll be able to get the pendant—ahem—after it's gone through him."

The woman pursed her lips. "I can't wait that long. I'm visiting from Surrey, and I must get home. My name is Mrs. Travers. I might be a small lady, but I'm quite important in my village, I'll have you know."

"Please give me your address, madam, and we'll be sure to return the pendant," Nicholas said. "Hopefully within one day. Two at the most."

"I don't know," Mrs. Travers said suspiciously. "What if you decide to keep it? Give me that dog—then I'll know I'll get my piece back. When I do, I'll send you a note and you can come get him."

"We can't very well do that. He's not even our dog," said Poppy. "And we're not thieves. We're not interested in your . . . pilfered pendant."

Mrs. Travers gasped. "You should be. *Your* dog ate it!"

"I'm sorry," said Poppy, her face turning pink. "I simply meant we don't want it."

The woman pursed her lips. "Give me that dog, or I'll—I'll call a constable!"

Nicholas laid a hand on her arm. "Madam, the dog belongs to a Russian princess—"

"I don't care who the dog belongs to." Mrs. Travers burst into tears. "Who ever heard of letting a dog into a museum? He attacked me, the brute! I shall press charges for that, as well."

Poppy tugged on Nicholas's sleeve. "We have to give her the dog," she whispered above Mrs. Travers's ear-piercing wails.

"No, we can't," he said. "Natasha would have a fit."

And blast that Mrs. Travers for shrieking.

"I know," Poppy said, "but we'll get him back in a few days, won't we?"

Nicholas stared at Boris, who merely panted and rolled his one eye. "He's diabolical. I can see him running away at the first opportunity." He turned to Mrs. Travers. "Stop your caterwauling, madam. I'll put you up in fine quarters here in London if you'll stay a day or two."

Her wails ceased abruptly into hiccups and then died away completely, thank God.

"Absolutely not," she said with firm resolve. "I must get back. My maid, as well. And if you have a decent bone in your body, you'll let me take that dog. Consider him on loan."

"Give us but a moment," Nicholas said to her, then turned to Poppy. "She has a point," he said low, Boris still panting contentedly in his arms. "None of this is her fault, and she should be allowed to return home rather than stay here. We'll have to let her take the dog, but he can't go alone. I'll go, as well. If Natasha knows a familiar face is with the brute, she'll be all right. We can't upset the Russian twins, remember?"

Poppy sighed. "I suppose you're right. But how can *I* go? I'll need a chaperone."

"You'll stay here."

"*No.* That's outrageous. We're . . . we're in this together, remember?"

He must admit, her saying so assuaged a portion of his extreme annoyance at the whole situation.

He turned to Mrs. Travers. "Do you know a Lady Caldwell in Surrey?"

The woman put a hand to her breast. "Of course. Lord and Lady Caldwell are one of the finest families in all of Surrey. The altar guild at our church—I'm the presiding officer, you know—was once invited to her home for a delightful tour of her gardens. Their estate is a mere three miles from my village."

"She's my godmother and my father's first cousin," Nicholas said. "We'll stay with her, and I promise we'll return the pendant, in pristine condition, as soon as we're able. In fact, Lady Caldwell would no doubt welcome you and your maid to stay with us until the pendant is, um, made available to us again."

The woman blushed. "I appreciate that, young man." She laid a hand on his arm. "My late husband gave me that bauble. I'm sorry if I was a bit rude. I would dearly love to stay with Lady Caldwell."

"Then it's settled," he said gruffly. "And please don't apologize. I understand your panic." While Mrs. Travers's chins quivered and her maid tried to soothe her, Nicholas turned once more to Poppy. "Your father should have no objections. We've come up with a perfectly proper solution."

"Good." She grinned. "I was beginning to think we were in well over our heads."

Nicholas rolled his eyes. "We'll be much more involved with looking around our feet the next day or two."

"Thanks to Boris." Once more she scratched the little criminal behind his ear.

Yes, thanks to the damned dog, Nicholas thought,

then adjusted his thinking. Perhaps he should be grateful. He'd been in a rut lately, hadn't he? Because of Boris, he'd be leaving London with Poppy. Being with her always promised surprises.

And he must face the fact—he was in desperate lust with his fiancée. Surely he could wrangle an opportunity to be alone with her in Surrey, godmother in residence or no.

Poppy felt rather excited when Nicholas dropped her off at home, along with Mrs. Travers, her maid, and Boris, while he paid a personal visit to Sergei to explain the awkward situation and to send a messenger ahead to Lord and Lady Caldwell to inform them they were coming.

It was amazing how one small dog could create so much fuss—and an opportunity to do something new and different. Yes, Poppy would be with Drummond, but she found herself rather intrigued by the idea of spending more time with him. Not because she had a *tendre* for the irascible duke but because he forced her to keep her wits sharp.

And perhaps because he was an amazing kisser.

Not that they'd get any opportunities to kiss at Lord and Lady Caldwell's.

Would they?

She must admit, that possibility was what had her feeling breathless as she ran upstairs to pack a small, serviceable suitcase Kettle had found for her (as her personal luggage had been disposed of, thanks to Papa).

Mrs. Travers and her maid waited patiently in the

drawing room, comforted by the presence of Cook, who brought in tea, delicious cakes, and idle gossip to share while Poppy packed. Boris waited in the kitchens, where the staff fed him a bowl of slops in hopes it would "push everything along," according to Kettle.

As Poppy folded her best night shift, she explained the whole situation to Aunt Charlotte, who promised to explain everything to Lord Derby when he came home from Whitehall.

"Not a problem, dear," Aunt Charlotte said. "But do remember the Spinster rule to follow when one is a houseguest."

"What's that?"

"A Spinster locks her bedchamber door at night."

Poppy drew in her chin. "That seems rather obvious."

"Yes," Aunt Charlotte said, "but that is only *half* the rule."

"What's the other half?"

"A Spinster locks her bedchamber door at night *only* after she's finished exploring."

"Exploring?"

Aunt Charlotte chuckled. "The beauty of being on one's own is that one may wander about a great house without people always crying, 'Where in devil's name are you going?'"

"I never thought of that," said Poppy.

"Freedom, my dear, is the key to adventure. Guard it well. And no matter how big the adventure or how many demands it places on you, never surrender freedom completely. It keeps one young. And interesting. And alive."

"You're giving me more than one rule, dear aunt." Poppy smiled. "I count five at least."

Aunt Charlotte waved a hand. "Oh, that last bit was something I just made up. But I rather like it. I think I shall add it to the new Spinsters handbook I'm creating. Oh, and don't forget to carry a heavy candlestick and a sharp pin when you explore."

"Very well." Poppy kissed her cheek. "I shall see you in two, no more than three, days."

When she returned to the drawing room ready to depart, Mrs. Travers was overjoyed to see her and even happier to see Nicholas arrive.

"Here you are, Your Grace." Kettle immediately placed Boris in his arms.

Poppy noticed that Drummond looked extremely grim.

"Ladies," he said, "I've news. Both the Russian princess and prince will be accompanying us. They insist. It is their belief that Boris requires his mistress to be happy."

A silence fell over the room, but then Mrs. Travers began clapping.

Poppy's heart sank. She'd been looking forward to getting out of London for a few days. But now that the Russian twins were coming, she was exhausted already just thinking of all the attention they'd require.

She especially didn't want any more odd conversations with Sergei. She was rapidly losing hope he had any of the wonderful qualities she'd thought he'd possessed in abundance in St. Petersburg.

"What a delight!" exclaimed Mrs. Travers. "We shall

be in even more exalted company. You're a duke, so I hear, Your Grace, and your fiancée is the daughter of an earl, which is extremely impressive. But to be traveling in the company of a prince and princess, too? Oh, my. I'm almost glad that beast swallowed my pendant." Her face, which had been lined with smiles, suddenly drooped. "Of course, I will get it back, don't you think?"

"Without a doubt," Nicholas assured her, his voice rather tight. "I shall be overseeing Boris myself."

"Oh, you wonderful man!" Mrs. Travers threw herself at him. "Who ever heard of a duke following after a one-eyed dog to see if he'll, um, produce a pendant? How could anyone say such bad things about you?"

She covered her mouth with her hand, and her maid turned red.

"Oh, dear," she murmured, "my maid and I were in a discussion with Lord Derby's cook."

"About his missing uncle?" Poppy asked.

"Or the octopus?" Nicholas asked, throwing Poppy a look that made her feel as if she were the cause of all this gossip about him, when really—

Oh, dear. She was, wasn't she? Of course, she'd never told her suitors about the octopus, but she'd encouraged Cook to spin her tales. And Poppy had repeated them to Aunt Charlotte and her friends, and now—

Now Cook was telling all of London—and some country folk like Mrs. Travers, too. It seemed everyone was in a tizzy over the duke's supposedly wicked and daring exploits.

Mrs. Travers bit her lip. "We heard about both the octopus and the uncle. But mum's the word."

She turned an invisible key in her mouth.

"That's good of you," Nicholas told her. "But I'm curious. What exactly did Cook say about my missing uncle?"

Mrs. Travers looked to her maid. "You tell him."

The maid couldn't quite look him in the eye. "He was a thin boy with beady eyes. But them beady eyes led him right to Viking gold. It was buried in the sand before your estate facing the sea. But someone in your family killed him for it, poor lad."

She rubbed her nose as if her pronouncement were nothing particularly shocking.

"So you're all cursed," she concluded.

"It seems that way," Drummond said with great cheer. "Off we go, now, ladies. I hear a carriage out front."

Boris licked Nicholas's face and began to whine.

Poppy looked out the window. "It's the Russian twins."

"I've got to ride with the dog," Mrs. Travers said.

"Then you shall ride with the princess," said Nicholas. "Because she won't part from him."

Mrs. Travers clapped her hand over her heart again. "My, how a day can change in a moment! Who ever thought Lily Travers would be riding in a carriage with a Russian princess!"

Yes, and who ever thought Lady Poppy Smith-Barnes, daughter of the Earl of Derby, would be following a one-eyed dog to Surrey?

CHAPTER 18

Nicholas tried not to be disappointed that Poppy rode with Mrs. Travers, her maid, and Natasha. It made sense, of course.

He rode with Sergei.

Another carriage followed behind with a few Russian servants, Poppy's maid, and a number of trunks.

It was the longest ride to Surrey Nicholas had ever taken. The prince talked ceaselessly of his bachelor life in Russia—the women, the wine, the spectacular parties—as if Nicholas hadn't had his own share of wild bachelor moments. And then he rattled on about his interest in cockfighting, a sport Nicholas had never enjoyed. Sergei also boasted about the number of bears he'd shot—nine—and described in minute detail how one goes about skinning one.

Nicholas listened with barely suppressed annoyance. He preferred shooting quail, but it wasn't the lack of mutual interests that caused him to wish himself elsewhere. It was the prince's smug manner that he found so off-putting.

The world, it seemed, revolved around Sergei.

"I'm missing a very good card game right now," the prince said with a bit of temper, and mentioned a well-established London gambling hell where he was quickly becoming a regular player. "Too bad we're traipsing off to Surrey."

Nicholas shrugged. "It seemed the best solution at the time, and the ladies appear excited at the thought of spending time away from Town for a few days. You could have stayed behind, you know."

"Yes, I suppose I could have." The prince shrugged his shoulders and yawned. "But it will be nice to spend time with Lady Poppy."

He was either stupid or extremely vain.

Nicholas gave a short laugh. "Was that really the best thing to say to her fiancé?"

Sergei finally seemed to notice him. "Lady Poppy and I are old friends. Surely you know that."

"Yes, as a matter of fact, I do," Nicholas said coolly. "She told me you're *old* friends. But at the present moment, she's engaged to me. Or had you forgotten?"

The prince arched a brow. "I don't like your manner, Drummond. You're cocky. I even detect a threat in your tone. Against a Russian prince? That's not very diplomatic of you."

Nicholas shrugged. "If you've harmless intentions, you needn't fear any threats."

Sergei made a sulky face. "You take things too seriously, Duke. I'm only a guest in your country seeking to enjoy himself, and one way is by associating with people with whom I'm already acquainted. Surely you would grant a visiting aristocrat that much."

"Do enjoy yourself, Sergei." Nicholas intentionally used his first name. "Just be careful where." He leaned back and pulled out a cheroot. "Care for one?"

Like a spoiled child, Sergei pretended not to hear him. He stared out the window, a steely look of indifference on his face.

But Nicholas knew better. The prince wasn't used to being crossed in any way. In fact, Nicholas's negative impression of him had only deepened after this latest conversation. Sergei was self-absorbed, not particularly bright, nor noble in character.

Nicholas wondered that Poppy had ever had a *tendre* for him, but she'd been only fifteen when she'd met him in St. Petersburg. The prince was handsome—charming, even, when he tried to be. But nothing deeper than that.

Obviously, for a girl in the throes of first love, it had been enough.

When they arrived at their destination in Surrey, Poppy found Lord and Lady Caldwell were nothing but smiles and warm hospitality. After a lovely tea in the drawing room, she repaired to her room, washed her face, and allowed her maid to fix her hair. But then she dismissed the girl to enjoy herself, putting away her own clothes and storing her bag at the foot of her bed.

It was time to do what Aunt Charlotte had suggested. Explore.

The manor house was three stories high and Elizabethan in style, so she had plenty of wings to roam about, her objective being nothing more than to satisfy her curiosity about new places.

It *was* a wonderful thing to be a Spinster.

After a brief chat with the housekeeper, she found herself in the portrait gallery.

"There I am," someone whispered over her shoulder.

She jumped. "Drummond! You scared me!"

He laughed out loud, a hearty laugh that she'd never heard before. "Sorry. I couldn't resist. You were so absorbed in looking for someone. Who?"

"I don't know. The housekeeper told me I'd recognize a familiar face on the left-hand side."

"She must mean me," he said, and pointed to a portrait of a small boy with a twinkle in his eye and a charming half-smile. One of his childish hands lay on top of the head of an adoring dog. The other held a lush, pink rose.

"That *is* you." Poppy instantly recognized the restrained mischief in the boy's stance and expression.

He was adorable. And sweet.

Now she cast a discreet glance at the man he'd become. The boy had grown up to become sinfully handsome, and that childish air of mischief about him had been replaced by a sense that he could be dangerous if provoked.

"Yes," he said. "That is I. My godmother insisted on having me sit for a portrait when I was here one summer."

"The summer you picked all the roses off her prize bush."

"That's right. You heard that story already?"

Poppy chuckled. "She told all of us when we first arrived and you were out seeing to Boris's business."

"Which came up short, not that I'm surprised this early in the watch." He held out his arm. "May I continue the tour with you? We're supposed to appear a happily betrothed couple, after all. And not simply happy—in love. A couple united after three, angst-filled years of being apart."

He sighed, a most over-the-top sigh.

Damn the man. There went her Spinster freedom. And he was rude to keep bringing up the lavish tale of love she used to tell her suitors.

"Very well," she bit out, more than a little dismayed that her plans for wandering about unencumbered had changed. "I've been directed to the east wing, primarily to the second floor to a room where Queen Elizabeth once stayed."

He wrapped her hand in the crook of his arm. "Yes, we'll stop and see that first."

The Queen Room was vast and opulent, not a thing out of place and everything well dusted.

"The room hasn't been used since," said Drummond. "It's rather a shrine. See over there?" He pointed to a beautiful dressing table. "There's a comb on top. The queen either forgot it or left it as a memento of her visit."

Poppy went over and stared at the comb. "That can't be her hair."

"It is," said Drummond. "Can you believe it's still

there? Although for all we know, it could be the maid's hair and they keep replacing it."

Poppy laughed and looked about the room. "I must admit, it's the perfect place for a queen to sleep."

"And the perfect place for a man to steal a kiss," Drummond said. "Especially on the queen's bed."

"No," she said firmly, although her heart picked up its pace. "We can't."

But he pulled her down to the bed anyway, the rogue. She was pinned beneath him, and as indignant as she felt, she couldn't help laughing with him.

Just as suddenly, they stopped.

She felt a sudden rush when she looked into his compelling gray eyes.

He bent low and teased her lips with his own. She let out a sigh and wrapped her arms around his neck. And then he kissed her, slow and sweet, his tongue playing with hers, his mouth hot on her own.

His jaw was pleasingly rough, and she could feel the restraint emanating from his body as he ignited something hot and fierce within her. She arched her back, pressing upward—

And then she remembered. He wasn't kissing her just for the sweet pleasure of it, was he? This was a game to him. This was his way of trying to persuade her to be a docile fiancée, a female madly in love with the Duke of Drummond, and ultimately, a strategy designed to make her give up her Spinsterhood for a man she didn't love. The man had her stocking in his pocket, the better to coerce her into his plans. And his plans were entirely self-serving.

Well, this was one woman who wasn't so easily manipulated.

She pushed him away.

His eyes, which had been smoldering with an appealing heat, became inscrutable gray pools.

"Well," he said dryly, standing up. "That certainly ended *that*."

She stood up herself and smoothed her skirts. "It did, indeed." Her heart was pounding, but she strove for the calm dignity of Queen Elizabeth. "Now, if you would be so good as to show me the rest of the east wing."

Which he did. She saw gorgeous rooms, priceless paintings, statues that could have been in museums, and lovely views of the countryside from massive windows framed in rich velvets and damasks.

But she hardly noticed. She couldn't stop thinking about that kiss on the queen's bed.

Blast Drummond for getting under her skin.

When they walked back, he stopped and showed her a portrait of his parents as a newly married couple.

"Did your parents love each other?" Poppy dared to ask him, even though it was none of her business, she knew.

He nodded. "Very much. After my mother died—I was thirteen—my father was completely lost. But he remarried less than a year later." He paused, his mouth thinning. "To a neighbor who took advantage of his vulnerability. She was a profligate spender and unfaithful, to boot. She also hated me and my brother. Probably because we made it very clear we hated her."

His profile was beautiful, she thought. But there was

an air of sadness about him that made her heart ache for him.

"How awful," was all she knew to say.

He turned to face her. "What about your parents?"

She sighed, just thinking of the old days. "We were a happy family. Mama and Papa were very much in love. And then she died on my sixteenth birthday—of smallpox. We think she got it in our last days in Russia."

He lifted up her chin. "Are you all right? It hasn't been nearly as long for you as it has been for me."

She nodded, even though she felt shaky. "I'm all right. But not Papa. It's as if he died, too. That's why I'm"—she hesitated—"not happy."

Oh, God. She still wasn't, was she?

Being away from her house and her daily life, it was so much easier to see things clearly. How could she be happy when her father was so grief-stricken that he no longer had dinners with her and hardly ever laughed?

Drummond's gaze was concerned. "I'm sorry. And to have that happen on your birthday, of all days."

Poppy swallowed hard. Her heart's steady rhythm increased, became irregular. "Me, too," she whispered.

He pulled her forward. "Time to go," he said, and led her back to the middle wing of the house.

She wouldn't tell him, of course, that today *was* her birthday.

She was twenty-one.

CHAPTER 19

Duty over love. It was as simple as that. Nicholas drank his wine and ate his dinner at Lord and Lady Caldwell's with that simple fact uppermost in his thoughts. It helped assuage the guilt he felt at marrying Poppy for convenience's sake.

Lord and Lady Caldwell had married for love. So had *his* parents.

But they hadn't been in the Service. He was. He'd chosen a different life, and with it came different choices.

Still . . . he couldn't deny the sick feeling he had every time he saw Lady Caldwell observe Poppy at the table with that look—the assessing look families typically give newcomers. Lady Caldwell was imagining Poppy as his future bride, as his beloved mate, and she appeared pleased at the idea.

Nicholas knew he shouldn't feel guilty. But it was difficult to believe he'd made the right choice when he was in the presence of so much love and warmth, which was made most evident when Lord and Lady Caldwell told everyone proudly about their three children and their numerous grandchildren.

Even though he knew he was related to them, he was envious—their original little family was whole and happy and getting bigger every year.

He thought of Frank, his only close relative. And then told himself not to think of him. It was too depressing.

So was the situation with the Russian princess. At the beginning of the meal, Natasha had given Nicholas a meaningful look. "I switched your place card so you'd be seated next to me," she'd whispered in his ear.

"Did you?" He'd tried to keep his tone neutral and his face impassive. Now that he was working on Operation Pink Lady, he couldn't afford to antagonize her or ignore her.

And he'd discreetly moved his knee away from her roving hand, although she'd taken every opportunity during the meal to lean close to him, to place a hand on his arm, to press her hip next to his.

He had no one to blame but himself. He only hoped no one else noticed Natasha's overtures. It seemed rather impossible not to.

But equally as embarrassing was Sergei's extreme attentiveness to Poppy. Nicholas watched as the prince whispered something in Poppy's ear. She gave a light laugh that sounded rather like choking.

"Prince Sergei." Nicholas didn't bother to be overly pleasant. "Do share with us the observation that has caused Lady Poppy some amusement."

The prince lowered his wineglass to the table. "I asked if she were enjoying her birthday."

A wave of shock went through Nicholas. He'd just been talking with Poppy about her birthday—Lady Derby had died on that day. He'd no idea at the time, of course, that today was—

Oh, God. Poor girl.

And she'd simply walked on with him and acted as if nothing were slightly wrong. And sad.

"Birthday?" Mrs. Travers asked. "How old are you, dear?"

"Twenty-one." Poppy smiled, but Nicholas could see she was working very hard to be cheerful.

"You're practically a spinster," said Natasha with a smug smile. "How fortunate Drummond has saved you from such a fate."

"How did you know about her birthday, Prince?" asked Mrs. Travers.

Sergei stared daggers at her.

Poppy cleared her throat. "Before dinner, I was reading a lovely note my aunt had slipped into my reticule. The prince, um, saw it, as well."

Mrs. Travers put a hand on her breast and looked at Sergei. "You looked over her shoulder?"

He arched a brow. "Your point eludes me, madam. I am a Russian prince, you know."

Nicholas wanted to roll his eyes.

Lady Caldwell, ever the hostess, clasped her hands together and smiled. "We have a tradition in our home on birthdays," she said. "Everyone must dance."

Thank God. Nicholas wasn't terribly fond of dancing, but anything to get away from the tension at the table.

Rather than use the ballroom, Lady Caldwell decided they'd do better adjourning to the sitting room, where a few footmen pushed back the furniture and rugs to create a dance floor.

Lady Caldwell sat down to play the pianoforte, but Mrs. Travers insisted on taking her place.

"A waltz, then, Mrs. Travers, to be opened by our newly betrothed couple," Lady Caldwell said with a great deal of affectionate anticipation. Lord Caldwell put his arm around her waist and pulled her close.

When Nicholas spun Poppy about the floor, he held her hand lightly. But he was enchanted by how soft and delicate it was and by how her long, graceful fingers looped confidently over his. And touching her waist was enough to send his thoughts to places they shouldn't go—not with his godmother looking on.

It was refreshing to dance with a girl who had no come-hither expression, who didn't smile seductively and bat her lashes. Poppy's gaze was direct and clear as they met the tempo together with no hesitation.

She was pure grace.

He'd never enjoyed a waltz more.

"Felicitations on your birthday," he said into her ear.

She smiled. "Thank you."

He squeezed her hand. "This day, as happy as it should be, must be difficult for you."

She lifted her shoulders. "It gets a little easier each year."

"I wish you'd told me," he said.

"Why?" Her forehead puckered.

He sighed. "Because you shouldn't go through it alone."

She bit her lip. "Even Aunt Charlotte, as kind as her note was, won't bring up the connection between my mother's death and my birthday. It's a small thing, but yes." She smiled again. "It's much nicer not to bear it alone. Thank you."

"Your mother would like you to dance on your birthday," he said. "Every year, from now on, you should. I'll make sure of it."

She laughed. "I think that's a wonderful idea. I do love to dance. Although—"

"Although what?" He loved having her in his arms and found himself getting lost in her eyes again.

She arched one brow. "Although we shan't be together on my next birthday," she reminded him with a puckish smile. "Or any of them thereafter."

He looked around at the others and then back at her. "That's what *you* think. But let's not worry about that now." He paused in the dance but kept her hand in his. "Is there a fiddler in the house?" he asked the room, and winked at Lady Caldwell.

They both knew the answer to *that* question.

Lord Caldwell's face lit up. "Why didn't you say so before?"

With his wife's blessing, Lord Caldwell abandoned her on the dance floor and went to a cabinet, where he took out a fiddle and, without even shutting the cabinet

door behind him, started playing a lively Scottish reel.
Lady Caldwell urged two footmen to join the party to
make eight.

Nicholas's brain registered no one but Poppy, not
even Natasha, with her plump lips pursed in a sulk, or
Sergei, who elbowed him more than once, nor Mrs.
Travers, so giddy she could barely breathe.

Twice Nicholas and Poppy spun together, hands
locked, and when they did, there was nothing but her
face, bright and happy, set against a colorful, spinning
scene.

At one point the eight of them clasped hands and
turned in a circle. Poppy was across from him, much
too far away, but their gazes locked—and she grinned
at him shyly . . . gratefully.

As if she should be thanking him for anything.

Thank God for you, is what went through his head
at that moment. *Thank God you were born.*

And then he told himself it was much too maudlin a
thought to have on such a merry evening. She was
happy. On her birthday.

That was enough.

In her room two hours later, Poppy sat on her bed and
stared at the words on the pages of the endless novel she
was reading, *Clarissa,* but she didn't really see them.
She was thinking about the night, about the dancing.

About Drummond.

Not Sergei.

Drummond had been so blasted presumptuous, telling her that from now on, he'd insist that she dance on

her birthday—as if they were going to marry—but it was difficult to be angry at him. He was so much more charming than Sergei could ever be, yet . . .

Yet he was the wrong man for her.

Love, she reminded herself. Love, and not mere physical attraction, was what she wanted in her marriage.

And it must run both ways.

Involving herself with an Impossible Bachelor wasn't very sensible.

She sighed and shut her book. Sleep wouldn't come any time soon, she could tell. She swung her legs over the side of the bed.

"Time to explore again," she muttered.

Why not the library?

She knew exactly where it was. She needed time away from Clarissa's travails. Perhaps she'd look for an atlas. She loved looking at maps of other countries.

Quietly, she opened her door and ventured into the corridor with a candlestick, and on silent feet padded down the expansive staircase to the first floor. The library would be on her right.

When she got there, a low fire still flickered on the hearth.

She closed the door firmly behind her, advanced to a bookshelf, and began to peruse the volumes.

"So," she heard a man's low voice from behind her, "you couldn't sleep, either."

She whirled around. Sitting in a chair by the floor-to-ceiling window was Drummond. One booted leg was sprawled over the other, and his chin rested on his fist.

She put her candle on a side table and gave a little laugh. "Why, Drummond. Whatever's the matter? You look as though—"

"As though I'm doing miserably at my job?" He pushed himself out of the chair and came to her. His eyes flared with challenge.

Or perhaps frustration.

Whatever it was, the firelight cast shadows and light on the planes of his face, making him more handsome and mysterious than she'd ever seen him.

She backed up a step, her heart picking up its pace. "I should think you're doing splendidly," she assured him. "We're spending lots of time with—with the subjects we're supposed to spend time with, and—"

"And my diplomatic skills are being stretched to the limit." He raked a hand through his hair and stared at the fire. "How many Service members follow dogs about? Endure petulant Russian princesses? Kowtow to know-it-all Russian princes?"

She blinked. "I—I don't know. But of course you endure what you must endure. It's part of the profession, I suppose."

He gave her a flat look. "You're right, of course. It's just that . . ."

He hesitated.

"What?" she asked him.

He let out a gusty sigh. "It's difficult to focus on my work—on my objectives—with you around. Damn it all, I could put up with Sergei if it were just he and I, but I loathe the way he looks at you. And as for the princess, she's obviously jealous of you and takes pains to put you in your place whenever she can."

He looked at her then, and neither of them said a word. The fire danced and popped, the candle flickered, and everything else was blanketed in darkness and silence.

She knew what he wanted. What he needed.

She stepped forward and pulled the lapels of his coat toward her. "Come here," she whispered.

And she stood up on tiptoe and kissed him. They fit together perfectly. She allowed him to completely encircle her with his body, to devour her lips with his own. Through her thin night rail, she relished feeling every contour of his body, including his masculine hardness thrust up against her lower belly.

And then she pulled back.

"God, Poppy," he said low.

She raised her chin. "It's kind of you to be concerned about me, Your Grace, but I can take care of myself. My presence should in no way deter you from your objectives."

His pupils darkened. "So I should proceed as I always have, with no concern for your well-being."

"Yes," she whispered. "I don't need you, Drummond. And you most certainly have made the point that I get in *your* way."

"Devil take it," he whispered, looking down at her. "Go to your room before I chase you up those stairs and ravish you in your bed."

She picked up her candle, straightened her back, and strode past him.

She would secure her door tonight just as Aunt Charlotte had warned her to do. She only wished she could lock up the new, bewildering feelings welling inside her, all of them centered on the Duke of Drummond.

CHAPTER 20

Thank God for horses. And open fields. And other men who understood that when a man was frustrated with a woman, the best thing to do was to shut up, go with him on a blistering early-morning ride, and hand him a fine cheroot afterward.

"Dear heavens, Max and Nicholas," lamented Lady Caldwell. "It's too early in the morning for those."

"We're outdoors, my love." Lord Caldwell complacently puffed away at his cheroot and patted her hand.

Poppy made a moue of disapproval at Nicholas. "Surely you should eat first."

Underneath a large oak tree, Lady Caldwell had set a beautiful breakfast picnic composed of eggs, meat, hot rolls, Bath buns, pound cake, toast, tea, and cocoa. Liveried servants stood at attention nearby.

"Sorry," Nicholas said, leaning back in his chair and blowing out a plume of smoke. "I promise I'll partake as soon as I'm done savoring this."

"Well, then," said Lady Caldwell. "If you two insist

on being large boys bent on defying the common sense of women who know better, I shall take this opportunity to regale Poppy with a perfectly frivolous tale of romance and heartache."

"Do tell," said Poppy with a captivating grin. She pinched off a piece of pound cake and ate it with relish.

The girl did everything with relish, Nicholas had the unwanted thought, and tamped down the image of her pulling him toward her last night and planting a sensuous kiss on his mouth.

Fortunately, Lady Caldwell distracted him with the sad tale of an unhappy, noble gander who'd lost his gorgeous mate some time ago and was still mourning.

"I visit him every day," she said. "He absolutely refuses to rejoin the flock that lives on the pond. And he won't cheer up. His grief is too great."

"Women know these things," Lord Caldwell whispered to Nicholas, loud enough for his wife to hear.

Lady Caldwell ignored him, of course, much to Nicholas's amusement.

"The poor old thing walks the same path every day," she told Poppy. "It was the last place he saw her."

"How terrible," said Poppy feelingly, her slice of pound cake all but forgotten as she listened to the tale.

"Yes." Lady Caldwell sighed. "I wish there were a happy ending. If only he could find someone else to love."

Nicholas caught Poppy's eye. She stopped chewing and sent him an adorably tragic look. The minx. Just who was this girl who could fall for a story about a silly, lovesick gander and yet have the audacity to tease him the way she had last night?

Without thinking, he leaned over and kissed her mouth. She tasted of cake and sugar.

Her eyes widened at the contact, but he wasn't sorry. They were supposed to be happily betrothed, and he was going to show the world that they were.

Lord Caldwell looked at him assessingly—he'd been kind enough not to ask why Nicholas had been in an ill humor on their ride—then chuckled.

"Young love," he said. "It continues to inspire us old folk." Then he leaned over and kissed Lady Caldwell, as well. "I'm as sick with love for you as that old gander is for his mate. Don't you ever think of running off with the chimney sweep or the footman who danced with you last night."

"Oh, dear," said Lady Caldwell, her cheeks as pink as Poppy's.

The two women exchanged a look, and then the two of them burst into laughter.

"Who knew we were so irresistible?" Lady Caldwell took Poppy's hand and squeezed it.

It was another sign that Poppy was approved of, Nicholas noted with the same mix of pleasure and guilt he'd felt the evening before. But today the guilt was slightly worse. He'd never tell Poppy this, but her little speech last night had definitely reminded him that he wasn't as in control of their situation as he'd assumed. He wasn't as sure that a year from now he wouldn't have to tell Lord and Lady Caldwell that their betrothal had been doomed from the start.

It was a lowering thought.

Lord Caldwell squinted, looking toward the house. "I see the prince is finally awake and about."

It was indeed Sergei, looking every inch the prince, and he was coming their way.

Poppy sat up a bit higher. "I wonder if his sister is still abed. And Mrs. Travers."

"I rather hope so," Lord Caldwell said dryly.

"Max," his wife chided him. "Don't talk ill of our guests."

"Very well, my love," said Lord Caldwell. "If you insist, I'll wait until they depart to debate which one is best to forget—the spoiled royal or the unrelenting jewel-seeker, both of them obsessed with the same dog, albeit for different reasons. I dare say even Boris wishes them to perdition."

Nicholas couldn't help but grin. He was glad to know another man was as fed up with some of the company as he was.

When the prince walked up, he attempted to work his charms on both Lady Caldwell and Poppy, lingering overlong, Nicholas thought, when he kissed Poppy's hand.

"Drummond," the prince said over his shoulder, "you won't mind that I take your future bride on a stroll, would you, before I break my fast? It's a fine morning, and I crave speaking in my own language. She's the only one here who can carry on a conversation in Russian."

Right.

Nicholas forced himself to recall he was supposed to be ingratiating himself to the prince, so he attempted a light tone. "That's a fine idea," he said. "Where shall we walk?"

"Oh, we won't need you," Sergei said. "And I believe I can find my way about the property."

"Yes, Drummond," Poppy said firmly. "You've no need to stir yourself."

She had that look in her eye, the one she'd had last night when she'd told him she could take care of herself. She turned to Lady Caldwell. "I could take Prince Sergei to see the gander."

"I doubt the gander understands Russian," said Lord Caldwell.

"Max." Lady Caldwell made a face at him. "What has gotten into you today?"

"Nothing more than the usual," he said easily, and winked at Nicholas.

He's got it, Nicholas thought. *He knows I despise Sergei, and that Sergei is a rude, obnoxious boor paying overmuch attention to my betrothed.*

Lady Caldwell ignored her husband again and smiled at Poppy. "You can tell the prince the gander's story along the way." And then she directed them to a small pond at the rear of the property.

"Don't be gone long!" Nicholas called testily after the retreating couple, and ripped into a Bath bun.

Lord Caldwell chuckled.

"What's so amusing?" Nicholas asked him crossly while he chewed and swallowed half the bun in one bite.

"What did Erasmus say about women?" asked Lord Caldwell. "Can't live with them—"

"And can't live without them," Nicholas replied, and had the sudden thought that he didn't care for Erasmus. He stuffed the rest of his Bath bun in his pocket. "I'm going after them."

"Good for you," said Lady Caldwell. "That prince is acting awfully possessive. I'm not sure I like his manner."

"Go, Nicholas," said Lord Caldwell. "Show him who Poppy's true love is."

"Right," Nicholas said, in a bad mood again. He certainly wasn't Poppy's true love.

But he *was* going to be her husband, whether she liked it or not.

Poppy was in a substantial quandary, and to solve it, she needed to be alone with Sergei. Which was why she'd insisted on this walk to see the gander without Drummond.

"So," the prince said, his voice velvety soft. "We are alone. Intrigued, aren't you?"

"By what?"

"By me."

She laughed. "What do you mean?"

He shrugged. "My exploits. My charm. I knew the minute I saw you at the Grangerford ball you could be mine."

Good God, she'd been so blinded by her own infatuation, she hadn't seen the obvious—Sergei was a conceited fool.

Now she inhaled a breath. "Oh. Um, about us. You're right. At the ball, I couldn't help thinking of you the way I did when I was fifteen. But those lingering romantic feelings I felt were really just memories, ones I thought we could perhaps relive. But we're both older now, and so much has happened in six years. We're different people. And now I'm engaged to the duke."

"We are not friends any longer?"

She winced at how forlorn he sounded. "Of course we're friends," she reassured him. "But we're nothing more. You live far away. I live here. We had a lovely romantic interlude long ago, but we must move on."

He gazed at her with an intensity that harkened back to her unfortunate interaction with Lord Washburn. But unlike Washburn, at least Sergei was a pleasure to look at. His gorgeous golden locks shone in the sunlight, and his masculine form was surely the envy of any man.

"I can't move on," he said, looking into her eyes. "I find I have a new appetite, and it's for Spinsters."

"Spinsters?" Her heart began to beat harder.

"Yes. I know about your Spinsters Club, Poppy."

She drew in a breath. "How did you—"

"Servants will talk." He chuckled. "All those women who want to marry? They're dull. You, on the other hand, are forbidden fruit. You're a Spinster. Saying the word alone drives me mad with desire. Forget about marrying the duke or any other man. I can buy you great baubles. Give you pleasure like you've never known. And you may remain a Spinster throughout our wild, passionate interlude, which I hope shall span years."

She gasped. "So when you said you wanted to come to my room, you really meant—"

He nodded, a lascivious smile on his face.

So Drummond had been right. Sergei *did* want her because she was unavailable.

"And the parasol? What was I to do with that?" she asked him.

He merely chuckled. "Parasols and naked ladies . . . the combination is delicious."

"Listen closely, Sergei, and listen well." She balled her hands into fists. "I will *not* be your mistress."

"You Spinsters have fire," he whispered.

"No we don't. At least, not for people we—"

Oh, dear. Drummond was heading their way. She took a deep breath and tried to compose herself. With her love for Sergei gone, what was standing in the way of her engagement to the duke anymore? She'd spent more time dwelling on his kisses than on the tenets of the Spinsters Club . . . rules that she'd clung to rotely for so long.

But they were good rules, she reminded herself. Especially the cardinal one: *Don't marry unless you love him and he loves you.*

It seemed such a simple requirement. But it wasn't, was it?

Her relationship with Drummond, she was coming to find out, was like a tangled bundle of yarn. She kept trying to unravel it, smooth out the knots, and understand what she had there, but . . .

It wasn't so easy.

"Prince, Lady Poppy." Already Poppy recognized that stubborn tilt to Drummond's chin that meant he would brook no interference with his plans.

Sergei sighed. "I told you, Duke—"

"You can navigate the property yourself, I know," Drummond said, "but I brought the lady a piece of bread to feed the gander." And he handed Poppy the other half of his Bath bun.

"Thank you." Poppy forged ahead with two men, each of whom was causing her loads of trouble in his own way, and found the gander by a copse of trees. She tossed him the Bath bun, and it landed on the grass near the dirt track he'd made from his constant, insatiable need to find his mate. With a squawk, he waddled quickly over and demolished it, spewing crumbs everywhere.

Sergei walked closer to the bird. He knelt, aimed an invisible rifle, and fired it. *"Ka-pow!"* He grinned back at Poppy and pointed a thumb at his chest. *"I am master of this domain."*

She forced herself to smile. "I believe Lord Caldwell is, but I—I know what you mean. I think."

"Stop talking to that pompous ass a moment and listen to me," Drummond whispered to her.

"I *have* to talk to him," she hissed back. "Groop's orders. Besides, he's from a ruling family, and he thinks he was born to conquer everything he sees."

Drummond arched a brow. "Oh, is that what a royal does? Trods over everything he encounters and says it's his? In my book, a good ruler craves knowledge about an unknown territory and shows a respectful appreciation for what he discovers." He stared down her bodice. "I have a yen to explore—"

"Shush," she whispered, but a slow heat spread through her veins at the look in his eye.

Sergei trudged back to them, his invisible gun forgotten, and the gander at his heels. The bird poked his beak at each of them, presumably for more Bath buns.

"Be gone, silly gander." Sergei waved him off with a hand.

But the gander stayed right next to him, and as they walked back to the picnic area, the large, white bird didn't leave Sergei's side.

"Damn you, waterfowl!" Sergei shouted, stomped his feet, and clapped his hands, but the gander wouldn't go.

"You make a noble pair," Drummond said equably as they trudged on.

"What do you mean?" The prince looked suspiciously at the duke.

Poppy nudged Drummond with a sharp elbow. "He meant you appear quite distinguished," she told Sergei, "with a great bird at your side."

"He will be at my side no longer." Sergei maneuvered behind Poppy in an obvious bid to foist the bird's devoted attention upon her.

Surely a true gentleman wouldn't do that, she had the unwelcome thought, and wondered why she hadn't noticed Sergei's childish side when she'd been fifteen. Then again, she'd been a mere child herself at fifteen.

"The gander can't help himself," she said to Sergei. "I think he's in love with you. Perhaps he thinks you're his wife."

"He doesn't love me," the prince said, drawing in his chin. "He doesn't think I'm his *wife*."

"Well, if he does, it's not your fault," Poppy soothed

him. "She's been gone these two years. He's been searching for her."

"It's a tragic story," Drummond murmured.

Poppy cast him a dark look, which he ignored, the mischief maker. She could see the little boy's gleam of amusement in his eyes every time he stirred up trouble, rather like Lord Caldwell did with Lady Caldwell.

Were all men this way?

Or just the ones who wanted a certain woman's attention?

Could Drummond actually be *jealous*?

She couldn't believe it. And it was easy enough to push the thought aside when they arrived back at the picnic. Sergei demanded the servants restrain the gander and then stalked off in a rage toward the house without addressing his hosts.

Nicholas watched in disbelief as the prince stormed off and the gander started a plaintive honk.

"My goodness," Lady Caldwell said. "I do believe the bird *does* think the prince is his long-lost wife. He's never acted so besotted about a person before."

"I wonder what it is about Sergei that makes him so attractive?" asked Poppy. "His garments? His hair?"

"No, it's because he *is* a goose, the silliest, most self-absorbed Russian prince I've ever met," interjected Lord Caldwell.

"He's the only Russian prince you've ever met," said Lady Caldwell with a chuckle.

"Be that as it may," Lord Caldwell said. "He's still a goose."

Nicholas couldn't agree more. "We should escort Mr. Gander back to the pond," he said. "Poppy? Shall you come?"

For the first time that morning, she gave him an uncomplicated smile. "Of course."

"Too bad Boris is occupied," said Lord Caldwell.

The little dog was being trailed by two footmen around the massive trunk of an oak tree near the house.

"Corgis excel at herding geese, you know," Lord Caldwell pointed out. "But he has more important business to take care of, and woe to him if he either doesn't perform properly or is overtaxed by the burden of responsibility placed on him. He could very well set off an international incident."

"I do believe the gander has already done so," Nicholas replied.

Lady Caldwell chuckled. "Who knew animals could play such pivotal roles in diplomatic affairs?" She handed several Bath buns to Poppy. "Here. Take these with you to coax the gander along."

Long-ago memories of being a carefree boy came back to Nicholas when he twisted off pieces of Bath bun with Poppy and—together, laughing—they lured the gander back to his pond. Eventually, the bird waddled off between two trees, content to be back at his favorite place.

"I enjoyed meeting him." Poppy's mouth was serious as she looked up at Nicholas. "Thanks for cheering me up. When the prince left in such a rude huff, I could hardly believe I had ever held him in such high regard."

Nicholas wanted to soak up every bit of impression

he could about her—her tiny freckles, her ears, so small and trim. Her mouth, with the delicate cleft shaping her upper lip into a beautiful bow. Her hair, curling in tendrils on her forehead and tumbling in fiery color onto her shoulders.

"Don't let it bother you," he said, feeling rather guilty himself. He'd done nothing to make the obnoxious prince feel better. Once again, he'd let personal feelings intrude on his mission. He was jealous—horribly jealous—of the prince and his connection to Poppy.

"I suppose we could have done more to keep him happy," he said. "But who knew he'd get so upset? We'll have to work extra hard to get back into his good graces, which means . . ."

"What?"

"I'll need *you* to coax him out of his bad humor." It went against everything in him to say it. "It's obvious he has little use for me."

Poppy sighed. "You're asking a lot, you know. The man is mad for Spinsters. He found out that I'm one."

"Everyone knows you're a maiden and not a married lady."

"I might as well tell you. It's the name of my secret club—the Spinsters Club. We're all Spinsters with a capital *S*. And now Sergei insists I become"—she looked down a moment, then looked back up, a faint tinge of pink on her cheeks—"his mistress."

"Good God, is that what he was proposing back there?" The blackguard! Nicholas felt a sudden onslaught of deep, unadulterated possessiveness toward Poppy.

She nodded. "I didn't want to tell you because we have to do our duty, remember? You were rather conveniently forgetting during the gander debacle. You were no help at all, as a matter of fact."

Nicholas placed his hands on her shoulders. "I told you last night I forget about duty when you're involved. Which is why we need to get you uninvolved. Go home, and be a good fiancée and let me finish this operation on my own."

"No," she insisted. "That's not fair. I'm the one who found the message in the cane. If I hadn't, you never would have known. And Groop would have given the operation to someone else. I told you at St. Paul's—I intend to be involved. The same way you intend to keep me as your fiancée."

She gave him a small, take-no-prisoners smile.

"Fine." He sighed. "Then prove your mettle. Use that attraction Sergei has for you. Use your Spinster magnetism and hold a dinner party in his honor. That will assuage his pride."

"Me?" Her brows flew up. "Throw a dinner party? I can't do that. Papa wouldn't allow it."

"You said you wanted to stay involved. You say Spinsters are bold and can do anything."

She bit her lip.

God, she looked enchanting when she was worked up and unsure of herself. Then again, she was just as tempting when she was quiet and confident.

Nicholas took her smooth, soft hand in his and pulled her forward, determined that they look like the lovers Lady Caldwell supposed them to be. "Don't be like the gander, going round and round in circles, getting stuck in the same old routines and expectations. Keep your eyes open for Bath buns. For possibilities."

"Perhaps I will," she said stoutly.

"Let's test this theory out right now. I've got a Bath bun of sorts for you."

"You do?"

"Yes. Just take it. Promise?"

She nodded.

He grabbed her hand and hauled her behind a small shed and kissed her. She didn't stop him, either. Instead, she tugged his face closer by threading her fingers in his hair and kissing him back.

All around them, the wind rattled an uneven rhythm through the leaves—nature's song.

His need for her was crazy. Demanding. And highly illogical. There were thousands of girls in London. But the one who'd stumbled into working for the Service, who used to believe she loved a Russian prince, who gave Nicholas every reason to run in the opposite direction—this Spinster—was the girl he wanted to laugh with, to argue with.

To make his own.

CHAPTER 21

Two days had passed since Poppy's eventful visit to the Caldwells. Mrs. Travers had left their estate wreathed in smiles, her pendant recovered. Natasha had happily returned to London, where she had no one else hovering over Boris but herself. And even Prince Sergei had gone back to Town with a modicum of his pride restored, probably because all the London papers wrote articles wondering where he'd gone off to for a few days.

Drummond had unceremoniously dropped Poppy off at her house and told her he'd some work to catch up on for Groop.

So much for our kisses, she'd thought at the time. But she hadn't forgotten what he'd said about Bath buns.

About possibilities.

And about ruts.

The morning sun was casting bright bands of yellow into the drawing room at 17 Clifford Street when Lord Derby walked in and held up a thick, cream-colored card.

"Daughter," he asked in suspicious tones, "what's this?"

Poppy had been waiting for this moment with a mixture of dread and anticipation. She put down her ongoing needlepoint of the Winter Palace—she'd just pulled out one whole section of thread that she'd done in the wrong color—and took the card.

"It's an invitation to come to dinner tomorrow night, Papa." She hoped he wouldn't make up an excuse not to be there. "I've decided to invite the Russian prince and princess—as well as the Count and Countess Lieven."

She'd had the thought that if the Lievens enjoyed the dinner party, they might very well reciprocate and invite her family to their home for an intimate social occasion. Drummond would come along and perhaps they'd catch a glimpse of the Pink Lady portrait before the ball.

"I can read," her father said tersely. "I also see you're sending a similar invitation to Drummond as well as several other acquaintances of mine."

Aunt Charlotte put aside her embroidery. "Perfectly acceptable mix, I believe."

Papa glowered at her. "I'm aware of that, Charlotte. But why a dinner party?"

"Why wouldn't we have a small dinner party?" his older sister asked him.

"Because—" He pressed his lips together.

Poppy stood. "We haven't had one in a great while, Papa. Not since before . . . before Mama died. I felt it was time."

He stared at her, no doubt attempting to intimidate her with his scowl, but she vowed to ignore it.

"Time to do something new," she added a bit weakly. But there, she'd said it. "I do hope you'll be here."

"You should have asked me first."

She knew that. But she also knew if she had, he would have said no.

"Don't allow Cook to make anything I don't like," he said.

Poppy smiled. "I'll do my best."

And then he strode out the front door.

The rest of the morning, she planned the menu with Cook and consulted with the housekeeper until she felt her party was sure to run smoothly and that her guests would be pleased with the fare offered them.

She was discussing seating arrangements with Aunt Charlotte at their noon meal when Kettle came into the dining room with a note.

Aunt Charlotte looked up from reading it. "Princess Natasha has accepted our invitation on one condition. She begs us to patronize a new seamstress on Oxford Street, one of her former lady's maids. It seems she has ready-made gowns the princess believes will be perfect for the dinner party. She'd be delighted if we would seek her out as this woman is not only talented but dear to her heart."

"Why, that's so thoughtful of Natasha! I'm pleasantly surprised to see her thinking of someone other than herself and her dogs." Poppy chuckled. "She does make an excellent suggestion: new gowns for the party. The ready-made ones will do nicely since we don't have time to have any made."

"Very good suggestion." Aunt Charlotte nodded,

well pleased. "I'm glad Drummond has had an invigorating influence on you."

"Has he?" Poppy put her spoon down, rather surprised.

"I believe he has." Aunt Charlotte looked at her assessingly.

Poppy felt herself blush. "I think I'll excuse myself now." She felt suddenly awkward—and no wonder. She'd much to do. Discussing the duke with Aunt Charlotte wasn't a good use of the time she had left before the party, was it? Particularly as she found that subject rather confusing.

Now was the time to focus on details, plans . . . dresses.

An hour later, the seamstress smiled broadly at Poppy's reflection in the full-length looking glass at her shop. "The color matches your eyes and complements your hair," she said with genuine admiration in her voice.

Poppy was a betrothed woman now, the seamstress had reminded her, so she should venture beyond pastels. As a consequence, she'd selected a deep emerald-green satin sheath with shimmering emerald-green beads sewn to the skirt and to the tight, three-quarter-length, sheer lace sleeves.

"And the bodice." Aunt Charlotte stood back to admire her in it. "It sets off your charms to perfection. I like seeing you this way, my dear."

Poppy smiled. It was her first time wearing this magnificent glowing green color, and she loved it. The fit of the gown was superb, the bodice perfectly hugging her breasts, the skirt falling in sleek lines. She felt like a princess, a very grown-up princess. It was ironic that she should be grateful to Natasha for bringing her and this fabulous garment together, but she was. She couldn't wait to tell the princess so at the party.

And another part of her couldn't help thinking about Drummond. She shouldn't care what he thought. She shouldn't care at all. But part of her, no matter how hard she tried to ignore it, couldn't wait to see his reaction when he saw her wearing this gown. She found herself breathless imagining him eyeing her from head to toe, his gaze finally lingering on her bodice.

She looked down and bit her lip. It *was* a daring neckline. But perfect.

The party couldn't come soon enough.

Meanwhile, Aunt Charlotte found a charming dull gold gown. Even though it was nothing like the style she preferred to wear, which was well outdated with panniers and pinched waists, she was happy to carry it home.

"I shan't even wear my wig," she said to Poppy. "In honor of our guests."

The next evening, Poppy donned her gown with high hopes and descended the stairs, her hair perfectly coiffed and her mother's pearl earrings dangling from her ears. She felt beautiful and elegant, ready for her first attempt at being a hostess.

The china on the dining room table sparkled. The extra candles were lit in a candelabra depicting a famous Russian battle scene, and the fresh flowers gifted everyone with their heady fragrance. From the kitchen, delicious smells wafted through the house whenever a servant opened a door to bring in another serving dish or bottle of wine.

The first guests to arrive were Eleanor and Beatrice. Poppy sat with them to enjoy a comfortable coze.

Eleanor wore an exquisite pale blue satin gown with a wide ivory satin sash banded beneath her breasts. Her hair shimmered with little crystal butterflies pinned to her curls. "Your engagement is the talk of London," she told Poppy.

Beatrice was stunning in her white Grecian sheath with gold trim and Grecian braid. "And you're rather a reigning queen."

"Am I?" Poppy laughed. "I hadn't even noticed."

"Well, you are, so enjoy every moment of it." Eleanor hugged her.

Beatrice eyed her thoughtfully. "You already appear to be enjoying yourself. I'm rather intrigued by the spark of liveliness in your eye. I haven't seen that in quite a while."

"You're right," said Eleanor. "I wonder if you don't like your duke, after all."

"Of course not." Poppy huffed.

"Have you kissed him?" Beatrice asked point-blank.

Poppy's mouth fell open. "I—I—" But it was as if she had a piece of bread stuck in her throat.

Eleanor clapped her hands. "You have."

"And apparently he's a marvelous kisser," said Beatrice with a mischievous grin.

Poppy finally recovered. "All right. I *have* kissed him. But that doesn't mean anything."

"It does if it sends tingles to your toes," said Eleanor. "It's one of the requirements of the early dispensation clause, as you know."

"Tingles . . . warm, heady feelings—" Poppy began.

"Warm, heady feelings?" interjected Beatrice.

"Whatever you want to call them," Poppy said dismissively, "they don't mean anything without the other requirements in the early dispensation clause."

"True," said Eleanor. "I can't imagine he respects you the way Sergei must."

"Or that he's as interested as Sergei in what you have to say," Beatrice said. "The prince was most attentive at the Grangerford ball."

"No, I'm sure you're right on both counts." Poppy tried mightily to be annoyed at Drummond for not being a gentleman and for not hanging on her every word, but it was difficult when she couldn't stop thinking about the daring and pleasurable way he'd nudged a knee between her legs and pinned her against the shed wall while he was kissing her after Lady Caldwell's outdoor breakfast.

"But I have something to confess," she told her two best friends. "I made a huge mistake with Sergei. He's nothing like what I thought he was six years ago."

Beatrice and Eleanor both widened their eyes.

"He's not?" asked Eleanor, her strawberry-blond curls shaking.

Beatrice shook her head. "What a shame!"

Poppy bit her lip. "It's worse, girls. He wants me to be his mistress. Can you believe it?"

"I despise him," Eleanor sputtered.

"As do I!" Beatrice's brows became slash marks above her dark almond eyes.

Eleanor drew in her chin. "Why on earth did you invite him tonight when he's such a scoundrel?"

Poppy's mouth fell open. Oh, dear. She couldn't explain that, could she? She couldn't reveal anything about Operation Pink Lady.

She supposed she shouldn't have told her two friends about Sergei's true nature, but they were her closest companions. She couldn't have held that back. She needed their support.

But . . . how to explain his presence tonight?

She gave them a weak smile, hating to lie. "I, um, I invited him and his sister because of old times' sake. I think it will bring Papa a great deal of comfort to have a Russian meal with Russian guests, don't you? St. Petersburg was the last place he had fun with Mama."

Beatrice nodded. "That makes sense."

"It's a tremendous sacrifice for you," Eleanor said, "but very thoughtful."

"And I believe I can handle the prince," Poppy said, assuaging her guilt with a genuine smile of affection for her friends. "Especially with you two in my corner."

"Exactly," said Beatrice. "We're Spinsters. He's asked the *wrong* girl to be his mistress."

"Speaking of which"—Poppy grabbed their hands— "I put you on either side of him at the table. We keep our enemies close. So do take good care of him. But never let him guess what you know."

"Poor Sergei." Eleanor giggled.

And Poppy breathed a sigh of relief. Everything she'd

said about Sergei had been true, hadn't it? She'd simply left out that one small bit about his involvement with the portrait she was trying to help Drummond retrieve.

Fortunately, Aunt Charlotte arrived just then, resplendent in her gold gown, and diverted the talk away from Sergei by passing out her new version of the Spinster bylaws for the ladies to place in their reticules, with a strict reminder that wisdom was imperative in all Spinsters and couldn't always be accrued in sufficient amounts by age twenty-one without some effort at seeking it.

Which led her into a speech about acquiring as much experience as possible as soon as possible—from traveling to studying to flirting with interesting men . . . as long as that flirtation didn't involve . . .

Disrobing.

"It leads to all sorts of complications," their club advisor insisted. "Especially if the man in question is—how shall I say?—endowed with qualities you can't really appreciate until you see them. Or, um, until you see *it*. It could be simply *one* quality. A very nice quality."

Her brow puckered, and she trailed off.

"Do tell us more," Beatrice insisted.

"Yes," Eleanor agreed.

Poppy was highly intrigued, as well. She had a suspicion now what that one intriguing quality might be— after having pressed close to Drummond, she could hardly *not* be aware of it. In fact, the thought of that one quality in Drummond made her a bit weak in the knees.

But the shocking, titillating talk was interrupted by

the arrival in the drawing room of Lord Derby, who greeted the party of ladies cordially. Only Poppy could tell that her papa wasn't used to having guests for dinner. There was a certain endearing awkwardness in his manner that he usually lacked.

The next guests to arrive were Lord Wyatt and several of Papa's old friends from his Cambridge days. Lord Wyatt kept the conversation lively with stories about his expansive castles in Devon and Cornwall, both on vast properties he'd recently acquired. Papa didn't appear to know what to do with his old friends other than talk politics, which Poppy knew he could do in his sleep. Nevertheless, they seemed to enjoy his company, and he theirs.

"Good idea," Aunt Charlotte whispered to her at one point. One of Papa's friends had asked to bring his widowed sister. The woman was pretty and lively, with a tendency to laugh easily, and Papa seemed quite comfortable and jolly himself in her company.

But where was Drummond? And where were Sergei, Natasha, and the Lievens? Poppy could barely stand the suspense. She did her best to be a cheerful hostess, but her stomach was doing flip-flops.

Finally, a carriage was heard arriving out front.

Poppy was terribly excited. She stood, smoothed down her lovely gown, and waited.

Kettle appeared in the drawing room door, announced the party, and she saw—

Drummond and Natasha together.

Whatever for?

But before she could even wonder, she saw that Natasha was wearing *her* gown.

All of the blood in Poppy's face rushed to her feet. She gulped, stung by the depth of her hurt.

How could *she?*

How could Natasha be so cruel?

And then embarrassment spread through Poppy from head to toe, scalding her face red. This was clearly no accident. She'd been played for a fool. And the worst of it was, the princess looked far more compelling a figure than she did. Natasha wore the dress dampened—*dampened*—to a perfectly respectable dinner party. A magnificent emerald necklace dangled between her breasts and glinted in the candlelight, calling every man's attention in the room to her ample bosom.

"I'm sorry we're late." Natasha tossed her elegantly coiffed head. "Nicky here insisted on driving me himself."

Poppy gulped. *Nicky?* She exchanged discreet looks with both Eleanor and Beatrice, both of whom conveyed to her with their eyes that they understood exactly how awful the situation was.

Drummond cleared his throat. "It was what any gentleman would do, Your Highness, when a lady sends an appeal for an escort."

Natasha laughed. "You should give yourself more credit, Nicky. You went above and beyond to make me comfortable"—she drew a hand along his arm and gave a breathy sigh—"for which I thank you."

This was too much. Poppy took a slow, discreet breath. The Duke of Drummond was *her* fiancé—at least for the time being. How dare the Russian princess act as if she were his lover?

She'd little time to fume, however, because Kettle announced the rest of the missing guests, the Lievens and Sergei. Countess Lieven was a supreme hostess herself, and both she and her husband were well acquainted with Lord Derby. Introductions were easy, but they eyed Poppy's gown with faintly bemused expressions.

It was humiliating, to say the least.

Sergei looked back and forth between her and his sister. "Who cares about my sister's gown?" he said in jovial fashion for all the company to hear. "She may have a bigger bosom, but she has only a duke to admire her, while you have a prince, Lady Poppy."

Heavens, was that meant to be a compliment to her? If so, it was the rudest one she'd ever received, and it was an obvious slight to Drummond, as well.

There was an awkward silence.

It was her duty as hostess to cover it up, wasn't it?

"Um, it won't be long before dinner," she said but could think of nothing scintillating to add.

Fortunately, Aunt Charlotte, Beatrice, and Eleanor took over. They began small conversations here and there, so that a few minutes later, it was as if her embarrassment had never happened.

"My little Spinster," the prince murmured for her ears only in a corner of the drawing room, "you do look delectable. Have you thought any more about my proposition?"

"No, I haven't," she whispered back. "Because I'm not interested. I told you already. We're friends *only*."

It was at moments like this that Poppy most missed her mother. Mama would have come up with a sparkling comment about the gowns to make all the company laugh and feel at ease. She wouldn't have needed her aunt and her friends' help. Mama also would have devised a proper set-down for Sergei that would have shamed him and kept him well-behaved.

And later, after everyone had left, she would have wrapped her arms around Poppy and told her she could cry all she liked about having a bosom smaller than Natasha's—there were some things a girl simply didn't have to apologize for.

But Mama wasn't here.

Poppy bent the fingers of her right hand so she could feel her mother's rings squeeze into her palm. She made the decision to focus on her party, to be a superb hostess despite the fact that it had gotten off to a bad start.

So she brushed past Sergei and went straightaway to Natasha, hoping to ease the tension. "What a droll coincidence we've chosen the same gown," she said warmly.

Natasha shrugged. "It's of no consequence to me. But perhaps it should be to *you*."

Poppy's hand itched to slap the smug expression off the princess's face, and her stomach roiled with the new and unexpected crisis of confidence. But she would deal with it as any good hostess would.

"You're entirely correct," she said, then excused herself from the room and hastened to the stairs. But she was stopped from ascending them by a hand on her elbow.

"Just where do you think you're going?"

It was Drummond.

Her heart began to hammer. He'd been instrumental in her choosing to throw a dinner party tonight. And now she wasn't sure she could carry it off.

She schooled her expression into a cool smile and turned. "I'm changing my gown."

Drummond rolled his eyes. "Only women would call wearing identical dresses a disaster, but even so, the damage is already done. Why bother?"

She inhaled a breath. "Because it will diffuse the tension everyone is feeling. Besides, I can't compare—"

"You're right," he interrupted her. "You can't. Which is one reason the princess is so jealous of you and is milking the situation."

"She's hardly jealous. She looks much more—"

"Much more jaded than you, for starters. But enough of her. I'm your guest, too. So what about *my* comfort?"

"What about it?"

"I'd like a kiss. And a glimpse up your skirt. If not that, a squeeze of your bottom."

"Absolutely not." She made a face at him. "Leave me be. I'm going upstairs *now*."

She'd better. Part of her desperately *wanted* him to squeeze her bottom, she realized. She lifted her hem and started walking quickly up the stairs.

"Fine," he called up to her in a low tone. "Just know that if you change your gown, you'll be telling Natasha that you agree she's better than you. And for that, I'll punish you by kissing you in front of all the company. We're engaged, after all."

She stopped climbing. She knew Natasha wasn't

better than she was. But wouldn't a good hostess alleviate her guests' discomfort?

"I'm only being a good hostess," she said, not looking at him.

"Is that so? Then I wish all good hostesses to perdition. We have enough cowards in this world as it is."

She bit her lip. The truth was, she *was* changing her gown because she felt second-best. *Not* because she wanted to be a good hostess.

It was a lowering thought.

"I'm serious," Drummond went on. "Change gowns, and I'll kiss you senseless in front of the countess. Who knows when you'll get into Almack's?"

"I told you—I don't care about Almack's." Poppy gripped the stair railing and closed her eyes. She felt so confused. What would Mama have done about the gown debacle?

The picture came very quickly.

I'd have held my head up high, dear, and not let a rude princess make me feel small, in the bosom or in my character. You're a Derby, and don't ever forget it.

She must face the disconcerting truth. Drummond, rude man that he was, was right. And Mama would have completely agreed with him.

Poppy mustn't let Natasha get to her.

And even though the duke was wise in his own way, Poppy certainly didn't want him stealing any kisses, either. It was all well and good to make Lady Caldwell and Lord Caldwell think they were in love, but not the rest of the world.

She turned back around, descended the stairs, and swept by him.

"You're incorrigible," she muttered, and returned to the drawing room, aware of his low, amused laughter the whole way.

CHAPTER 22

Nicholas sat opposite Poppy in the middle of the table. He was glad she hadn't changed gowns, even if it meant he couldn't carry through on his threat to kiss her in front of all the company.

She tapped a knife on her wine glass, and the table chatter died down. Sergei, who sat between her best friends, gazed at her with a mix of possessiveness and barely disguised lust. Nicholas had seen Natasha attempt to switch place cards and place her brother next to Poppy, but Beatrice and Eleanor had come behind her and, in charming tones, had insisted on keeping the prince between them.

Little did the princess know her strategy to encourage Poppy's interest in her silly brother wouldn't work—at least, not any longer. Poppy appeared completely oblivious to Sergei's charms, what there were of them.

"Tonight's meal," she said, her cheeks a becoming pink, "is composed of Russian dishes, in honor of our Russian guests." She hesitated a moment, then added,

"And in memory of my mother, who spent her last days as a happy wife with my father in St. Petersburg."

Lord Derby sat up as if jolted.

Poppy beamed at him, but his face was stern. Implacable.

Nicholas's heart sank. Poor Poppy. She wasn't having much luck tonight, was she? But at least everyone else made the appropriate murmur of interest at her announcement, except for Natasha. Not that he was surprised at that. If she were a cat, she'd be spitting at her hostess this very moment.

The servants brought in the first course, cabbage soup, or *shchi*.

He sampled it—it was tasty enough.

"A traditional first course in Russia," Poppy said. "Is that not so, Princess?"

Nicholas felt a burst of admiration. Good for her for not shying away from Natasha.

"Yes, you could say that," the princess answered. "Although"—she took one sip from her spoon and laid it down—"if it is not prepared in a Russian oven, it is not true *shchi*."

Nicholas cast a subtle glance at Poppy. Her face was smooth, but her mouth was rather frozen in place. He wished he could take Natasha aside and teach her some manners—by ejecting her from the party. He wished he could do a lot of things . . .

But duty constrained him. Duty to the Service. To his country. To his family name.

He drained a glass of wine too quickly to forget his discontent, which was easy enough, as course after course followed, all authentic Russian dishes. He found them delicious and robust, cleverly prepared, and presented by Poppy with a touchingly sincere appreciation for Russian culture and cuisine.

"Count, Countess," he said at one point, "I understand you have many Russian treasures at your home."

"Yes, we do have amazing treasures," Count Lieven said. "And when Prince Sergei chooses to share it with us, we shall soon be watching over the portrait by Revnik."

"How delightful." Poppy smiled. "All of London can't wait to see it."

"The night of the ball, the portrait shall be revealed in all its glory," said the countess. "You and the rest of London may bask in it then."

"And not a moment before," said Natasha, sending a steely glance Poppy's way.

Nicholas detected a faint bit of disappointment in Poppy's eyes, so he raised a glass in her direction. "Splendid meal," he said.

There was a chorus of assents and compliments made to the cook, although none came from Lord Derby—Nicholas hoped no one else noticed—or Natasha, who made her displeasure clear.

"Of course," the princess said with a sniff, "we prefer to use a French chef at home. His chicken Kiev and veal Orloff have no compare."

"Ch-chicken Kiev? Veal Orloff?" Poppy said, her hand fingering the beads at her neck.

"Franco-Russian cuisine," Natasha explained. "The *preferred* cuisine of the Russian elite."

"Although rustic Russian dishes do have their charm," Sergei said, sucking on a bone and grinning.

Rustic.

Nicholas saw Poppy try not to wince at the word.

"I adore *rustic*," Lady Charlotte piped up.

"So do I," said Beatrice.

Eleanor, Lord Derby's Cambridge friends, Lord Wyatt, and the Lievens agreed, as well.

But Nicholas could tell Poppy was bereft. The twins—and her father—had taken away her fun.

He felt enraged on her behalf. But there was nothing he could do.

He *hated* that feeling. He burned, *yearned,* to do something to make her feel better.

Perhaps to diffuse the tension, Lady Charlotte hit the side of her wine glass with a knife, and the table went quiet. "And now," she said, "I'd like to conclude the meal by asking the newly betrothed couple, Nicholas and Poppy, to share a kiss for their adoring family and friends."

Poppy looked at her aunt as if she'd been asked to jump off a cliff.

Lady Charlotte merely smiled. And then she locked eyes with Nicholas. *What was the old girl up to?* he wondered. Surely she was aware her niece didn't want to marry him.

Poppy cleared her throat. "It's probably not a good idea." She flicked her eyes at the Countess Lieven.

"Oh, yes it is," the countess said with a sweet smile, looking back and forth between him and Poppy. "Go right ahead."

Nicholas was surprised at her amenable reaction, considering how stuffy she was at Almack's. Perhaps it was Poppy's affinity for Russia that had softened the countess's usually strict rules about propriety.

"Very well," he said with a grin, and stood. But inside, as he walked around the table, he felt anything but lighthearted. Lady Charlotte had set before him a task that he didn't think he could accomplish. Poppy got no comfort from him. He rubbed her the wrong way. He'd forced her into an engagement, after all.

He couldn't make her happy.

She almost cowered when he approached but then must have thought better of it. He took her hand and pulled her up from her chair.

The tension in the air was palpable.

She looked into his eyes—hers were full of confusion and definite reluctance—but what could he do?

He would kiss her.

And when he did, he would try, to the best of his ability, to make her feel happy and relaxed, even though the circumstances of the kiss were awkward and she felt anything but.

He pulled her close and touched his lips to hers.

It's just me, he tried to convey.

Nicholas.

Forget everything else. Forget your father's stern face, and Natasha's rude comments. Forget Sergei's leers and remember . . .

Remember that you're beautiful. And kind. And fun. And . . .

The most interesting girl I've ever known.

Miraculously, she softened and relaxed, and then . . .

She was kissing him back. Kissing him as if she needed him somehow.

He needed her, too.

God, did he need her!

The kiss was fairly chaste, however, to those who watched. He was sure of it. But the jolt of connection he'd felt with her had been real.

An intimate message between the two of them.

Too bad it was in a code he couldn't fully understand.

As if by mutual agreement, they parted.

Her face was flushed. His hands were sweating.

She sank back into her chair, and there was the sound of one pair of hands clapping. He glanced around and saw that it was Lady Charlotte, who was grinning ear to ear. And then the others clapped, too.

Nicholas looked around the table. Sergei's enthusiasm was obviously feigned, as was Natasha's, but everyone else's was genuine.

He felt drained somehow—confused—and was glad to find his seat.

He and Poppy avoided looking at each other for the rest of the meal, but he was very aware of her presence. The meal ended with fruit, nuts, and cheese, as well as a delicious Russian dessert and a spirited discussion about the latest play at Drury Lane from almost everyone but Natasha.

"Didn't you and Drummond see that play?" Lord Derby asked Poppy.

God, that was the night they'd gone to the top of St. Paul's.

Poppy smiled. "Yes, indeed."

Nicholas kept his fingers crossed.

"What did you think of it, Lady Poppy?" Lord Wyatt seemed anxious to hear her opinion.

Poppy touched the edge of her bodice and cleared her throat. "It was delightful."

Count Lieven drew in his chin. "Even with that sad ending? And the murder scene?"

Poppy gave a little laugh. "Oh, *those*." She waved a hand. "The rest was a lark, and the ending was apropos, so I consider it delightful to have a sad ending if it *works*. Don't you agree?"

Nicholas restrained a grin. He looked at Eleanor and Beatrice and saw they appeared very confused by Poppy's answer, too. But then in the next instant, Beatrice flung her elbow out when she raised her wine glass and knocked Sergei's arm, which shoved the apple he'd raised to his lips against his teeth.

"Ow," he exclaimed, staring at her. Then he rubbed his gums.

"Oh, dear," Beatrice murmured. "I'm so sorry."

Sergei puckered his brow. "All right."

He picked up the apple again, and then from the other side, Eleanor knocked an entire glass of wine into his lap.

"What the devil?" He stood, his brows lowered and his face reddening. "You two are dangerous."

A footman rushed over with a serving cloth. Sergei vigorously wiped himself down, threw the cloth back at the footman, and in a great sulk, sat back down.

"I'm so sorry," Eleanor said to him, her hand to her gaping mouth.

Funny, her eyes didn't look sorry. Nicholas cast a glance at Beatrice and then Poppy. Neither of them looked sorry, either. In fact, Poppy had her wine glass to her lips, but he could detect the barest twinkle in her eye.

She was in on this somehow.

The minx.

In the midst of the tension, Kettle came in with a message for Lord Derby and Lord Wyatt. They'd been called away to another important late-night meeting.

"We shall all depart," Sergei declared. "Everyone, rise. Sitting in wet breeches is not comfortable, and if I must depart—"

"So shall everyone else," finished Natasha with a toss of her head.

Sergei directed a dark look at Eleanor and Beatrice, both of whom murmured their apologies once more.

At the door, Lord Wyatt thanked Poppy for a delightful evening, made a gracious bow, and said he'd go ahead to the meeting and see Lord Derby there shortly. The Cambridge contingent were also perfectly proper in their thanks.

Behind them, Count Lieven said, "I hope we do this again."

"We shall also have you for tea very soon," the countess assured Poppy. "Can you come?"

"Your duke, too," added the count with a chuckle.

"I'd be *thrilled*," said Poppy, smiling a real smile

for the first time in an hour. She looked up at Nicholas with a genuine gleam of satisfaction in her eye.

She'd done well, very well, to have received such an invitation.

But he merely nodded graciously at the Lievens. "I look forward to it. Thank you very much."

Natasha had become even more sullen than usual since he'd kissed Poppy. Now she kept her thanks to a minimum and swept by Nicholas without a word.

Good.

He needn't put up with her flirtations anymore. He'd been invited to the Lievens' home, and the twins dared not take that portrait when they knew the Lievens were so looking forward to showing it off.

Sergei, on the other hand, apparently had forgotten his momentary pique and fervently raised Poppy's hand to his mouth to kiss it. "Next time I insist on being here before everyone else arrives," he said, "to sample the most delicious morsels first."

Nicholas clenched his jaw.

Delicious morsels.

He knew what delicious morsels Sergei was talking about. He was staring at them—Poppy's breasts, which were exposed to perfection in her gown, just enough creamy white skin to get a man wanting to see the rest.

Deuce take it, the prince deserved a beating, and if Nicholas weren't surrounded by lovely people with delicate sensibilities, he'd have pounded him right then and there.

When every last guest was gone, except for him—

and he wasn't really a guest, he was practically a member of the family, wasn't he?—Poppy shut the front door and turned to her father and Lady Charlotte.

"I hope you enjoyed yourselves," she said, her brow furrowed with concern.

Her aunt hugged her. "Of course I did. You were a splendid hostess. Although Princess Natasha is a churlish sort." She turned to Nicholas. "She appeared quite fond of you, Drummond."

Was he supposed to answer that somehow?

His cravat felt suddenly tight. "Did she?" was all he replied. "I hadn't noticed."

His answer apparently satisfied because no one pursued the subject.

"Papa." Poppy tugged on Lord Derby's arm like a little girl. "Did *you* enjoy yourself?"

"The meal was serviceable," he granted, vaguely patting her arm, "although you know I prefer English dishes." He hesitated. "I need no reminders of our time in Russia, daughter. They pain me."

Poppy visibly deflated. "I'm so sorry. I didn't know they caused you hurt, Papa."

He cleared his throat. "Don't waste time worrying about *me*."

"Of course I worry about you! Did—did you not enjoy seeing your friends?" she stumbled on. "And meeting that lovely widow?"

His lips thinned. "I don't need to meet any widows, but as for my friends, yes, it was good to see them. Thank you for arranging it. Perhaps we can do that again. Someday."

"Really?" Nicholas saw a tiny glimmer of hope in Poppy's eyes.

"Yes, really," her father said, his voice softening just a tad. "I know you mean well, so no regrets about tonight."

He chucked her chin, and Poppy nodded, a small, genuine smile on her lips.

Lord Derby then turned to Nicholas. "I'm off to that meeting with Wyatt now. Kettle will see you out, or you may stay a few moments if you'd like. There's brandy in the library. Poppy can show you my new atlas."

Nicholas inclined his head. "Thank you, sir."

The privileges of the betrothed. He must be in good standing with Lord Derby. Must have been that political talk they'd had the other night. It could be, too, that Lord Derby realized his daughter wasn't the sort of young lady that made a man's life . . . easier.

"I think I shall head upstairs with Aunt Charlotte." Poppy yawned behind her hand. "I'm rather tired. Sorry, Drummond."

"Not quite yet, daughter," Lord Derby chided her. "You've given three hours tonight to your Russian guests—let your English betrothed have five minutes."

Nicholas was tempted to smirk, but he knew it would only rile Poppy.

Lady Charlotte kissed his cheek. "Who needs Russian princes with you around?" she whispered in his ear.

Gad. If only Poppy had heard *that*. She'd have been none too pleased.

Of course, he himself was. He enjoyed Lady Charlotte's company and felt almost proud that he was gaining acceptance amid the other members of the household—with the exception of Kettle and Cook, and, um, his own fiancée.

True to form, after Lady Charlotte and Lord Derby said good night, Kettle made it very clear with a quelling glance that he'd stay within calling distance of Poppy should she need him.

Kettle was a very intelligent butler.

When Nicholas and Poppy entered the library, he poured himself a brandy, and for her, a small glass of ratafia.

"You did splendidly," he said.

"Thank you." She gave him a brilliant smile. "We succeeded in some ways. All right, perhaps not with the food—and the gown was a disaster—"

"And Sergei seemed to run into some very unfortunate problems," he interrupted her.

She had the grace to blush.

"But we'll get to see the Lievens' home," she said. "And even Papa said he managed to have a good time, in his own fashion. Although he's still very touchy, isn't he? About Mama." She sank into a chair and stared at the small fire burning in the grate, the glass dangling from her hand. "Overall, however, I'm pleased."

"You should be." Nicholas knelt before her and took her hand. "Neither the food nor the conversation nor your gown mattered tonight as much as your intent. Your goal was to make your guests feel at home, and that can never be criticized. I'm sure your mother would have been very proud for how well you succeeded."

She gave him a pensive smile. "Thank you." She squeezed his hand. "But if you don't mind, I really *am* tired. I'd like to go to bed."

He backed up only enough to give her room to stand. When she stood, they locked gazes.

"Did you think that kiss Lady Charlotte demanded of us a disaster—or a success?" he asked her.

She looked down for a moment, then back up. "I don't know," she said quietly. "It's the only part of the evening that I can't peg as either one."

"Before you go up," he said, "I'd like to show you something that might help you decide."

"What is it?"

He pulled a lock of hair off her face. "The real meaning of *thrilled*."

CHAPTER 23

Nicholas pulled Poppy close. The fire was at his back, heating his calves. But he had another fire inside, one that had been banked all night until he could get her alone, and it was now burning high.

He held still a moment and listened for Kettle on the other side of the half-closed library door. The butler was whistling through his teeth at his station near the front door.

Good.

As long as Nicholas knew Kettle's whereabouts, he could do what he so wanted to do. He leaned down and kissed Poppy's neck right below her ear.

She let out a sigh.

He kissed her once, a playful, openmouthed kiss that she responded to by melting into him. When he pulled back, he smiled inwardly. She obviously wasn't as tired as she thought she was. Her eyes flickered and heated with want.

"I need you to trust me," he said. "Will you?"

She looked at him with wide eyes and nodded.

Silently, he crouched on his haunches and pulled up her gown, exposing her jeweled slippers. He inched the gown's slithery, beaded smoothness slowly up her legs. All the while, his hands held her close, and he dropped little kisses on her calves, then her knees, and finally her thighs.

Her breathing was jagged, which pleased him. He looked up, hoped his eyes told her he was enjoying himself immensely, and put an index finger to his mouth.

She swallowed, nodded, then bit her lip.

Gently, he pushed her legs farther apart, which—wonder of wonders—exposed her fully to him. Already hardened with desire, his need went up another notch, but he would ignore it.

Tonight was for her alone.

Lost in the sweet scent of her and the soft miracle of her skin, he kissed the insides of her thighs, going slowly higher, until he reached her most tender spot. He nuzzled it—she whimpered—and then he flicked it with his tongue.

She let out a gasp.

He stopped moving.

Kettle was still whistling.

Nicholas pulled back and motioned for Poppy to put her hand over her mouth. With a shaky hand, she did just that, and he went back to what was becoming his greatest delight—pleasuring her.

He blew on her first.

She moaned again. Softly.

And then he probed her with his tongue, going deeper.

And deeper.

Her legs began to buckle, so he stopped, listened for Kettle, who was now whistling a sea ditty, and took the opportunity to stand and move Poppy gently back to the chair. "You'll need to be very, *very* quiet," he whispered to her.

She nodded, and he pushed her legs wide apart.

Her cheeks flushed and her eyes bright, she kept that hand clamped over her mouth.

He couldn't help grinning at her obedience—she so rarely listened to him. But he had little time to gloat. She chuckled behind her hand.

"Sssh." He stared sternly at her and she resumed her quiet posture, although her eyes were full of mischief.

The minx.

With only the whisper of the fire, the ticking of the clock on the mantel, and Kettle's occasional whistling as a backdrop, Nicholas gave the sensual game all he was worth.

Within seconds, Poppy had her free hand in his hair. Thirty more seconds of well-timed teasing with his tongue, and he could only tell he'd brought her to pleasure by the way she arched her back and held herself suspended, which brought her sweetest flesh even closer to his mouth.

He gave one last plunge of his tongue into her womanly depths at the same time she was peaking, and only wished it were the length of him inside her.

But that would come another time. He felt determined it would be so.

She might not think she was marrying him, but

blast it, if he had to marry to keep his job, there was only one woman who interested him whatsoever.

Poppy.

He might not love her, but she fascinated him. And he wouldn't give up trying to win her until he had her lying naked on a rug somewhere in front of a fire and they were coming to completion together.

For now, he'd have to be satisfied with teaching her the art of love without his full participation.

She sank back down and let out one long, slow breath.

Gently, carefully, he pulled down her skirt and stood.

"*That,* my dear, is *thrilled,*" he said. "Every time you tell Sergei or his sister you're thrilled to see them, please remember what *thrilled* really is, and remember you experienced it with me."

As he spoke, she stared at him as if she'd never seen him before. She was gorgeous, her lips deep red and her cheeks rosy. He'd satisfied her. He'd removed that awful, bleak look from her eyes, as well as that stiff, worried posture.

He felt good about that.

"I'll go now," he said, and kissed the top of her head. "Good night."

"Good night, Nicholas," she said softly.

Nicholas, he thought, happy to hear it. *Not Drummond.*

"Nicholas?" she called after him.

There was a heated silence between them.

"Don't forget your cane," she whispered.

"I won't," he said, his voice gruff. He was loath to leave her.

If Kettle were the nosy man she'd claimed he was, he would have already found the five-pound note and message Nicholas had left him inside the cane, with strict instructions that if he ever planned on serving as butler when Nicholas was a permanent member of the household, he'd best not question his integrity ever again. Although he could keep checking the cane whenever he felt like it, as it was an amusing temptation that might yield occasional rewards.

At the front door, Kettle handed him his hat, which Nicholas donned.

For a brief second, they both had their hands on the cane. Their eyes met in mutual understanding, and Kettle's, he noted, even held a smidgeon of respect.

"Thank you, Kettle." Nicholas slung the cane under his arm.

"Have a good night, Your Grace."

"I'll do my best." It wouldn't be easy, however. He'd be dreaming about Poppy's trusting, vulnerable gaze all night.

CHAPTER 24

The day after her dinner party, Poppy woke up thinking about Nicholas, about his mouth—about what he'd done to her with his mouth. And then she thought of his eyes, their mysterious gray depths—their warm, sympathetic, and sometimes *heated* depths.

No wonder he was called an Impossible Bachelor.

He was too, too delicious a man to ever be thrown into a category as bland and all-encompassing as the list of eligible, unmarried gentlemen she presumed the patronesses at Almack's kept at the door of that esteemed establishment to screen out lesser mortals.

He was far more interesting than the terms *eligible* and *unmarried* could convey.

Nicholas had encouraged her to believe in herself last night. Indeed, all evening he'd been a bulwark of support, lighting a fire beneath her unsurety so that she felt confident, a true hostess. Afterward in the library, he'd shown her a tender, considerate side that fascinated her . . . and made her want him even more.

Padding over to her window, she looked out at the

London morning and sighed. Her legs wobbled again at the memory of what they'd done together. She pressed her mouth, her breasts, her belly against the window-pane. It was cold and hard—in sharp contrast to Nicholas's mouth and hands.

She had an obsession with his mouth now. And his hands.

By God, and everything else about him, too.

She pulled back from the window and ran both her hands over her breasts, lingering over her nipples, and then ran her hands down her belly to that point between her legs where she'd found such pleasure with him.

And wished . . .

Wished.

She threw back her head and gave a soft moan of frustration. Nicholas had started a craving in her, a craving she needed *him* to fulfill.

She was to see him tonight. They were attending a rout at the Merriweathers'. All the furniture would be removed, the windows thrown open. London society would squeeze itself inside the house to make merry.

Surrounded by hundreds of people, she'd be squashed next to him, her breasts brushing his chest, her belly up against his belly. His mouth would be close to hers. He'd lean down, whisper, and perhaps at one point, they'd kiss, and while they did, he'd caress her hip, her back, and her breasts.

She'd—why, she'd be tempted to cup his hardness in her hand.

Would anyone even notice if she did?

It was a daring, thoroughly naughty thought that left her breathless and excited.

She watched with curiosity as a young messenger boy carrying a large, wrapped parcel crossed the street and headed to the front door of her home.

A moment later, a maid knocked on her bedchamber door.

"Something from Prince Sergei, miss," she said and held out the parcel.

"Really," she said, almost reluctant to take it.

But she did and shut the door behind her. She sat at her desk, tore open the note on top of it immediately, and read it.

Then reread it.

She let out a short laugh and clasped the note to her breast, amazed at how differently she saw the world now. This was the prince she remembered from St. Petersburg . . . but she was no longer the same girl.

The note was charming. Even romantic. He asked her forgiveness for insisting she involve herself with him in an illicit relationship—and for a chance to start over.

But it was also false. Oh, so false.

She wanted to be excited, and moved, and in love with him again, but she wasn't. She could never be again. She was no longer in the bud of her youth, and she definitely wasn't a fool.

The prince was all talk and no substance.

She didn't trust him.

But she *would* accept his invitation.

He wanted her to attend a special gathering at his

rented apartments. It was to be a masked dinner with a special surprise event to follow, culminating in the unveiling of the Revnik portrait at its conclusion, which he would reveal in her honor since she so wished to see it.

"Please come," he wrote. "It is the only way I know to make up for my ungentlemanly actions."

She made a face. Did he think her completely naïve?

Nevertheless, she would go. She had to see the portrait. It was reason enough for going.

But would she tell Nicholas?

She looked down at the tissue paper in the box. She still hadn't opened it, but Sergei had asked her to wear the gown and mask he'd sent with his compliments. It was supposed to be a romantic gesture, but it did nothing but annoy her. It suggested he felt a sense of possession over her she'd already told him he had no right to have.

Now if Nicholas had sent her a gown, she would have loved it.

Why?

Was it because she enjoyed being possessed by him?

Yes, she had last night. But at the same time, with Nicholas, she sensed he respected her, had waited for the right time to assume that possession—he'd waited until he sensed she was ready, and wanted it.

Sergei, on the other hand, hadn't taken her feelings into account at all.

She folded back the tissue paper and looked upon

the dress with nothing beyond an objective admiration
for the seamstress who'd sewn it. The gown was well
made, a bit low in the bodice, but she wasn't surprised.
It was Sergei, after all, who'd ordered it.

He wasn't that bright. His choice of gown revealed
his intentions clearly.

He still wanted her.

She was glad for one thing—when she held the
mask up to her face, she did feel mysterious and adventurous. And she'd be anonymous, which was a good
thing.

But wait—

She read the note again. The ball was this evening,
and she couldn't very well—

She bit her lip. She'd have to go to *both* events. She
could do it. She'd go to both, and Nicholas, when she
eventually told him, would be amazed at her devotion
to duty.

But should she tell him now, before the fact? He'd
be so intrigued to know she'd be getting a glance at the
Pink Lady.

She decided against it. He didn't like Sergei. Who
knew what would happen? She couldn't risk his interfering and her not getting to see the portrait, after all.

It was going to be an even more exciting evening
than she'd thought, but first she had some planning
to do.

She flew down the stairs in search of one of the new
stableboys. The Merriweathers lived only two blocks
from Sergei's apartments, but she'd need an escort.

Going back and forth in a carriage wouldn't be practical. There'd be an abundance of them outside the rout all night long.

No, the best thing to do would be walk between the two places with a stableboy armed with a pistol to protect her and hope for the best.

It could be done. She was sure of it. But before she did anything, it was imperative that she talk to her aunt.

Fifteen minutes later, Poppy was rolling out one of her father's favorite pastries, one she regretted she hadn't made in a good long while—a traditional English apple tart. And she'd invited her aunt to help her.

Aunt Charlotte sprinkled flour on the dough as Poppy rolled.

"I think things went well last night," Aunt Charlotte said.

Poppy laid the dough in a pan. "Overall, they did, but"—she turned to look at her aunt—"why did you insist on that kiss between the duke and me?"

Aunt Charlotte blinked several times.

Her guilty look.

Poppy's heart beat harder. "What is it?"

Aunt Charlotte bit her lip. "I'm afraid I might be giving you bad advice, my dear. I don't know that I should be mentor to the Spinsters Club."

Poppy's hands grew clammy cutting up the apples, so she wiped her fingers on her apron. "Are you jesting?"

Aunt Charlotte shook her head. "I'm coming to the

conclusion that I don't want you to become *me,* you see."

There was a long, dark silence. A sleek tabby kitchen cat meandered in and out of Poppy's ankles. Her chin wobbled. "But I thought you were happy. It's the whole point of the Spinsters Club, that it's better to be alone than to be with someone you don't love."

"I *am* happy," Aunt Charlotte said. "Yet years ago, when I was a young woman, there were romantic opportunities I neglected to pursue. I was too boxed in. I had a certain vision of what love was, and Poppy"—she shook her head—"I think I was wrong. Shortsighted. Too proud and too committed to a plan *I* had—instead of letting go and letting life lead me. I wasn't open to the possibilities."

Open to the possibilities!

Poppy felt her face pale. Those were the words that had come to her at the Golden Gallery and when she'd heard Keats's poem. Nicholas, too, had used that phrase when they'd watched the gander at Lady Caldwell's.

She didn't know what to say.

"There was one man named Gerald Goodpenny," Aunt Charlotte continued gently. "His ears stuck out and he didn't like horse racing—which I loved—so I wouldn't consider him as a beau. Yet he was funny and sweet and had quite a brilliant mind. He married my friend Dora, and now they have fifteen grandchildren. He's gotten so much handsomer with age." She chuckled. "It could be I think he's handsome because— because he's a good man with a sassy mouth. I saw him at a wedding recently, and he spanked me on the bottom, right in front of Dora, for being so silly as to never kiss him when he'd asked me."

"And his wife didn't object?"

Aunt Charlotte smiled. "Of course she did, but it was all in fun. Dora and I are good friends. She punched Gerald's shoulder, and he kissed her and told her he loved her more than all the tea in China."

"How lovely for them," Poppy whispered.

Aunt Charlotte gave a little chuckle. "Yes, it is. He's a good man, and Dora knows it." She paused for a moment and began to cut up another apple. "There's nothing more attractive than a good man," she said, slicing through the fruit's flesh and laying out a line of apple wedges for Poppy to place into the pastry shell. "Behind closed doors, good men are often more mischievous and exasperating than the truly bad ones. The difference is they're naughty because they're happy—boys at heart, no matter how many responsibilities they bear or how old they become." Her eyes were dreamy. "I didn't see that when I was young and rather wild."

Poppy shook her head. "But Aunt, you know I intend to break my engagement as soon as possible. You embarrassed me in front of all the dinner party when you asked me to kiss Drummond."

"I know." Aunt Charlotte blew out a breath. "The thing is, Poppy, I can't bear to see you leading a false life."

"It's only for the nonce."

"Is it?" Aunt Charlotte laid down her knife and let

out a weary sigh. "Are you sure you're not letting your devotion to the Spinster bylaws blind you to what's right in front of your eyes? Last night I had the sudden urge to see you wake up. I had this feeling the duke would be able to do that—quite the way the prince in the fairy tale woke up Sleeping Beauty."

"I can't believe in fairy tales anymore," Poppy insisted. "Look what happened when I daydreamed away six years, all for Sergei."

For too long she'd let her unfounded hopes about Sergei rule her reason, hadn't she?

Never again. She wouldn't allow fantasy back into her life. She would quit listening to Cook's stories. She would be full of common sense and say, "Pooh," if anyone even attempted to ignite her imagination in any way.

She was done with dreams.

Finished with fancy.

"Are you sure you don't believe in fairy tales anymore?" Aunt Charlotte smiled knowingly. "Because I could swear, last night, Drummond *did* wake you up."

Poppy felt herself blush—*did he* ever *wake me up!* she longed to exclaim—but she continued sprinkling sugar and cinnamon on the apples. "I don't know what to say. I—I'm surprised, nay, shocked, at your change of heart. At everything you're saying."

"Are you angry?"

"Yes," said Poppy, her vision suddenly blurring. "Because I'm afraid. I'm afraid to be fanciful. To go back to daydreaming."

She looked down at the pastry.

Aunt Charlotte lifted her chin and pulled a curl off her face. "There's no need to be afraid. The Spinster rules are an excellent guide. But a guide only . . . to keep your courage up, to give you support as you travel the road to womanhood. Your heart is the true guide. Let that lead you, above all."

Poppy couldn't help the tiny smile that tugged at her mouth. "That's actually quite good advice. I suggest we keep you as the mentor of the Spinsters Club."

Aunt Charlotte smiled back. "I withdraw my resignation."

They worked for another five minutes, spooning the apples into the crust, pinching the sides into a pleasing scalloped pattern.

"He's demanding," Poppy said quietly, out of the blue, "occasionally irascible, and he doesn't have half the charm of Eversly or his set."

Aunt Charlotte nodded. "But he's such a substantial presence. He's making charm seem a rather flimsy virtue these days."

He.

They were talking of the Duke of Drummond, of course.

But they were also talking about the man she was falling in love with, weren't they? She wasn't quite there yet. But it was a distinct possibility.

Poppy surveyed their apple-and-crust creation and then popped it into Cook's already warm oven. Nicholas was far from the typical polished London gentleman, but who cared?

He was substantial.

CHAPTER 25

The morning after the dinner party at Poppy's, Nicholas left Groop's office rather stunned.

Groop had heard rumors—someone was trying to interfere with Nicholas's engagement, but the spymaster hadn't been able to give him any more details than that.

"Rumor has it that someone is annoyed," he murmured over his spectacles. "Someone would love to see you two apart. And I have no idea how far they're willing to go."

That someone could be anyone from Frank, who would likely cast aspersions on Nicholas's character and curse him in pubs around London, to someone plotting to kill him—or Poppy.

That was the rub. Poppy was involved now.

Working in the Service, one tended to develop enemies. Nicholas was used to living with a certain element of danger on a regular basis. He'd always been able to take it in stride.

But now Poppy's safety could be in jeopardy.

He wished he'd considered that possibility more when he'd become engaged to her. But he'd been too bent on getting the job done. And he'd focused on the future—moving her out of London to Seaward Hall most of the year. He'd acted as if she were a pawn in a giant chess game, and she still was, in a way, but now he knew that pawn personally, had worshiped her body with his mouth, had laughed with her and argued with her, and—

He wanted to keep her safe.

In the carriage on the way to the Merriweathers', there was a strange silence between them. Considering what they'd done together in her father's library the night before, it was interesting.

"Are you all right?" he asked her.

She flung a shawl over her daringly low bodice. "Yes," she said. "Are you?"

"Fine." He felt a bit awkward. He wasn't sure why, except that she looked extremely beautiful.

She gave him a tight smile. "We should have fun tonight. I enjoy the Merriweathers' routs. Every year someone falls out a window into their bushes."

"Different person each time?" he asked, jiggling his leg.

Why, he was like a nervous schoolboy. That kiss last night, followed by what they'd done in the library . . . he must admit it was getting more difficult to keep her at arm's length.

She giggled. "Yes. Haven't you been to one of their routs before?"

He shook his head. "I'm not big on parties. I find most of them a crashing bore."

"Oh." She nodded sagely. "That's why most everyone in Town has no idea who you are."

"Exactly. I have a small estate in Sussex, I frequently go north to check on Seaward Hall, and when I'm in London, I tend to hole up at my bachelor pad at the Albany or visit close friends, like the Traemores."

He leaned forward suddenly and put a hand on her knee. "I must confess something," he said. "I enjoyed last night. Very much."

Her eyes widened. "I did, too." Her grin was wide and bright. "I'm glad you mentioned it."

He couldn't help but laugh. "I think we're feeling better now, aren't we?"

"I think so." She looked down and back up at him.

But it wasn't true. His confession had made things worse. Neither one of them said a word. There was too much tension between them, and now they were at the Merriweathers'. He got out and lifted her down, and when her feet touched the pavement, their lips were so close he could have kissed her.

But he didn't.

He was afraid if he did, he wouldn't be able to stop, and he had a job to do—to keep her safe in a place with hundreds of people and convince the world that he was about to marry her.

He grabbed her hand—she was silent again—and brought her into the crush that was the party. He loved feeling her fingers grasped in his and her body brushing up against him. She was his fiancée, and he wasn't going to let her go. Not tonight, to any thugs intent on hurting her, nor later, when she tried to break off the engagement.

He was going to fight for her, convince her they should be married. The idea of the marital bed was no longer something he dreaded but looked forward to with great pleasure.

They also laughed together often.

What more could a man want in a wife or a wife in a husband than an ideal sexual partner and an abundance of laughter?

He wasn't sure yet how or where the test between them would take place, but it would, and he vowed to be ready.

A half hour later, they'd walked through several rooms inch by inch. The noise was deafening. Many people stopped and grabbed them and begged for a few minutes' conversation.

Nicholas noticed Poppy began to appear distracted.

"Let me get you a refreshment," he suggested.

It would be her third. The first lemonade had been knocked out of her hand by a random stranger. The second she'd already downed.

"Actually," she said, "I—I think I need a few minutes."

"Oh? What's wrong? A fallen hem? A curl out of place? I think you look lovely." And she did, all peachy skin and dampened brow.

She blushed. "I haven't talked to Eleanor or Beatrice today, and I'd like to. Would you mind?"

He shook his head. "Not at all. I'll keep an eye out for you."

He wouldn't tell her he'd be keeping a *very* close eye out, thanks to Groop's alert.

"Fine," she said. "I'll see you in a little while."

He put a hand on her waist and squeezed lightly. "Be good," he said, even though he longed to be bad with her, to wrap his arms around her, kiss her madly, and caress her plump breasts and curvaceous bottom.

"I will," she said.

And she began to squeeze through the crowd to get to another room, presumably one where her friends were.

Nicholas watched her go, feeling lonely of a sudden. It was all right, though. He enjoyed being able to see her from afar. He could observe the slender nape of her neck, her abundant, shining hair reflecting the candle-light. And when she looked to the side, he admired her delicate profile.

He followed her from a distance, feeling pulled as if by a magnet.

And then Natasha stepped in front of him.

CHAPTER 26

At the rout Poppy found Eleanor in a corner in a small crowd watching a mime pretend to crawl up a ladder. Where he came from, no one knew, but odd things like that tended to happen at routs.

Poppy had gone to see her best friends earlier in the day to explain to them what she was doing this evening. She couldn't tell them about the painting called Pink Lady—that was a Service secret—but she did tell them she needed further closure with Sergei and required their help to get it.

"He doesn't seem to comprehend I'm not interested in him," Poppy had told them.

"That's obvious," both of them had said.

As usual, the Spinsters stuck together. Beatrice and Eleanor endorsed her plan wholeheartedly. They were well over lamenting the fact that the only man for Poppy no longer suited—that he was, in fact, a roué. They couldn't wait to hear what the special event was that he had planned and only asked her to be careful.

Now Poppy tugged on Eleanor's sleeve. "You promise you and Beatrice will stay in separate rooms and on separate floors until I get back?"

"Yes," Eleanor replied, patting her hand. "If Nicholas finds me, I'll chat with him for as long as I can, and when he gets antsy and asks after you, I'll say I just saw you but that now you must be talking to Beatrice. And then when he goes looking for *her,* she'll say you just left her and came back to me. It should work for at least a half hour. And it should take another half hour before he becomes desperate enough to seek us out. Which gives you an entire hour to go see Sergei. Good luck."

Eleanor kissed her cheek.

"Thank you!" And Poppy scurried off, or tried to. The crush was getting bigger, and she had to avoid Nicholas, which would involve a lot of luck. Her hair was like a beacon, and she had no idea what rooms he'd travel through.

But the crowd served as a good cover, and although leaving was difficult, three minutes later, she was finally out the front door and down the steps.

Her young stableboy waited a little ways down the street, beyond the long row of carriages pulling up to the Merriweathers' or departing.

She grinned when she saw him, relieved not to be alone. London had its dangers, especially at night, and only a foolish girl would allow herself to be alone in the darkness.

"We must hurry," she whispered when she saw him.

"Right, mum," he whispered back with a grin.

"Do you have your pistol? And the slippers and mask?"

"I do." He handed her the slippers—sturdy and comfortable—and she quickly donned them.

"Very good," she said. "Off we go."

Together they covered the two blocks to Sergei's apartments in record time, racing beneath gas lamps, in and out of shadows the whole way. Once at Sergei's door, she handed the stableboy back the sturdy slippers and her shawl and put on the delicate slippers he gave her. The last thing she did was don the mask he'd been holding for her.

"Right," she said with a nervous smile. "See you in forty minutes."

"I'll be standing here waiting, miss." He threw her a little salute.

She knocked on the door and was shy and anxious when she saw the stern face of the Russian guard appear.

"You've arrived just in time for dinner," he said. "Everyone has gathered in the drawing room."

He took her down a long, gloomy hall lit only by a few sconces, each holding only one miserable candle, to a room at the far end emanating light.

It was like being in one of Cook's stories . . .

Poppy's hands began to sweat. When she turned into the drawing room, she saw a colorful tableau—masked women in bright gowns and feathers sitting on several sofas with masked men in fabulous waistcoats and intricate cravats lounging between them.

Something inside her recoiled. She didn't like the masks. They lent a faint air of menace to the atmosphere. And the whole scene appeared . . . too informal.

Sergei was bending over one of the men, filling his glass with an amber liquid. A woman next to that man laughed loudly, leaned over, and whispered something in his ear. He laughed back, grabbed her knee, and caressed it with his hand.

Goodness.

That was awfully familiar of him. She wasn't sure if they were married, but even husbands and wives, at proper dinner parties, didn't show such obvious physical affection to each other. It was ill-mannered. Such touching was to be kept private.

She had a strong recollection of the extremely private moment she and Nicholas had shared in the library.

"H-hello, Prince." She forced herself to smile.

He looked up, the crystal decanter still in his hand. She could see his eyes widen behind his mask.

"It's *you*!" he said loudly, and chuckled. "Lady X!"

One of the men put a quizzing glass up to his mask. "This is your Lady X?"

"Yes," said Sergei, approaching her and kissing her hand. "And isn't she a beauty?"

"She's got amazing eyes," a woman with wild hair cackled. "She'd make a lovely Cleopatra."

"I'd be her Antony," said one man with burnished curls. "We'd complement each other perfectly."

No, you most certainly would not, she longed to tell him.

"Where's my dagger?" said yet another man.

One of the women giggled. "By the bottle of sow's blood, you idiot."

Sow's blood?

Poppy felt herself freeze in place even as her heart thumped harder. Why on earth were these people talking about sow's blood and daggers? And even though she knew Sergei called her Lady X to preserve her anonymity, it felt disrespectful, rude, and even frightening to be in a place where people's actions weren't connected to their names.

Who *was* Sergei, really?

And why had she ever thought that spending one week with him when she was fifteen meant she knew him?

The prince lifted her chin with a finger. "No need to worry. Tonight is to be a pure romp. Enjoy yourself behind that mask, and no one will be the wiser tomorrow."

"But Sergei—" She shook her head. "You said—"

He'd said in his note he was sorry for being boorish. He'd written her a lovely apology.

"Yes, Lady X?"

She clenched her fists at her sides. "I—I can't—"

She couldn't stay. That's what she was trying to say. The room grew quiet. Everyone stared at her. Sergei's brow furrowed, and Poppy felt alone.

Very alone.

She wished she could turn around and march out, but she couldn't, not when everyone's attention was focused on her. She had a horrible suspicion the prince or his bodyguards would come after her—make her stay.

Those gloomy candles in the hallway were no help. She was beginning to panic.

Yet she pulled herself together and smiled—a small, uneasy smile. "I can't ... wait to see the portrait. When shall we?"

Sergei seemed to relax. "We'll eat first," he said. "I've had my cook prepare an eight-course meal. We'll wine and dine and make merry, and then we shall have a surprise. Later, when the clock has struck midnight, we'll view the portrait."

Midnight?

Poppy's heart sank. There was no way they'd finish an eight-course meal in an hour, and she certainly couldn't stay to make merry and have a surprise—she'd no desire to find out what it was—and then stay until midnight.

What should she do? Could she leave and come back again? How could she explain that to Sergei?

Oh, bother, she was a terrible liar. He'd never believe her if she said she had to go home to get a draught for a headache and that she would return.

The truth, of course, was that she wouldn't return.

"To the dining room," he said, and held out his arm to her.

Numbly, she laid her hand on his forearm and allowed him to lead her there, down that gloomy hall again.

The dining room was cramped. She'd never be able to hang back and hope not to be noticed. When Sergei seated her on a corner of the table, in the chair to his right, she was elbow to elbow with the fellow who'd been looking for his dagger. Across from her was the wild-haired woman who'd commented on her eyes.

And Sergei himself was so close at the top of the table, his knee touched hers.

She wished she'd told Nicholas where she'd been going. At least Eleanor and Beatrice knew. And the stableboy. Perhaps he'd knock on the door after forty minutes and rescue her. But she doubted it. He'd be too afraid to knock. He'd wait for her for hours if he had to.

Poppy's chest tightened, but then she reminded herself that Eleanor and Beatrice would tell Nicholas where she'd gone, sooner rather than later. Although knowing them, she was sure they would do their very best—ironically, on her behalf—to keep Nicholas ignorant of her whereabouts as long as possible.

She was stuck. She'd simply have to see what happened . . . and vow never to be so foolish again as to trust someone she barely knew, someone who'd shown her very clearly in recent days that he wasn't the man she'd thought he was.

Sergei's foot brushed against her slipper once. And then he trod on her toes so hard she winced.

Was he trying to get her attention? To flirt?

"I find a have a new appetite, and it's for Spinsters," he'd told her at Lady Caldwell's.

And a thing for naked ladies with parasols.

She'd been foolish to come. But it was too late. She cleared her throat, looked down at her plate, afraid to meet his eyes, and had a momentary pang of intense regret. She'd forgotten her pin, the one she usually kept in her sleeve in case of emergencies. She'd like nothing better than to stick that pin in his hand if he played with her foot again.

But she couldn't. She'd have to use wilier tactics to escape his attentions. And while she sipped a glass of ratafia, she tried to imagine what those tactics would be.

"No, Natasha." Nicholas was firm when he pushed her hands off his chest. He saw Lady Eleanor on the far side of the room chatting with some women. Poppy was nowhere near.

Perhaps that meant she was with Beatrice instead.

Natasha sulked. "But why do you stay away? I don't care that you're to marry. Come back to me."

He shook his head. "As I've already told you, it was a mistake. You've plenty of admirers, so you won't be alone."

He left her abruptly. It was the only way. She was entirely too possessive, and he regretted ever spending time with her, much less getting into bed with her.

Let it be a lesson, he told himself. *You can only gamble so often before you lose.*

His gambling days were over, at least with women. And he was glad of it. It was an unanticipated benefit of marrying Poppy that he'd never considered.

But where was his fiancée?

It had been a good twenty minutes since he'd seen her. He battled his way through the crowds to find Beatrice and looked for Poppy along the way. No luck. Ten minutes later, he found Beatrice, laughing and talking with several admiring gentlemen on the next floor.

"I'm so sorry, Your Grace," she yelled in his ear. "I just saw Poppy, and she left. I think she was looking for you. Or maybe Eleanor."

"She's not with Lady Eleanor," he yelled back.

"Perhaps now she is." Beatrice grinned at him and shrugged her shoulders.

They both knew how it went. It was a rout. Leave someone and it might be the next day before you found them.

Heaving a sigh, he got back into the crowd and searched again.

He didn't feel concerned until he'd found Eleanor again and she'd said she hadn't seen Poppy in some time.

"Wait. How long?" His instincts told him something was off.

Eleanor's eyes widened only slightly. "Um, ten minutes, no more. I'm sure she's around here somewhere. Probably with Beatrice."

He cocked his head. "Lady Eleanor, are you not telling me something?"

Her mouth dropped open, but from behind him, a large gong sounded, effectively blocking any further conversation.

"Here ye, here ye!" cried a drunken fellow at the top of the room. Nicholas recognized him as an old school friend. "It's time for toasts, and the first one shall be in honor of two marvelous people, who are—amazingly enough, considering the lady's record of spurning suitors—betrothed to be married. Where are you, Drummond?"

Oh, good Lord.

Nicholas felt all the embarrassment of someone who had unwittingly become the center of attention. He raised his hand in the air. "Here," he called in restrained tones.

The drunken toastmaster nodded. "Very good. Now where's Lady Poppy?"

Blast. Nicholas had no idea.

"Drummond? Your lady love?" called the toastmaster.

"She's here . . . somewhere," Nicholas said, knowing full well how pathetic that sounded. He was at the rout to show the world he was settling down, preparing to become a dull married man—and yet, his future wife was nowhere near.

Not only that, the flirty Russian princess somehow found her way to him again. "If she doesn't show soon, some of us will take it to mean he's *free,*" she cooed to the crowd.

Everyone roared with laughter.

The toastmaster raised his eyebrows. "Are you sure Lady Poppy hasn't changed her mind about you, Drummond?"

Damn it, Poppy's voice hadn't rung out from any corner. Where was she?

The crowd laughed even harder.

And suddenly, he knew. Poppy wasn't even at the rout. He felt it in his gut. And Eleanor knew. The way she'd stumbled over her words and gotten flustered . . . probably Beatrice knew, as well.

Where had Poppy gone?

"What say you, Your Grace? Are you sure you still have a fiancée?" called the toastmaster.

"Yes, I'm sure," Nicholas replied testily, but no one could hear him.

They were still laughing.

CHAPTER 27

Her forty minutes inside Sergei's apartment were almost up. Poppy had to do *something*. But what? They were only on their third course, stuffed eel, which she despised, and there was no end in sight.

A lady had few acceptable reasons to leave the table. The only one she could think of was illness.

"Dear heavens," she said in a whisper, and put the back of her hand to her brow.

"What is it?" Sergei asked her.

"I feel a bit faint."

The woman across from her looked skeptical. "Do you?"

Poppy drew herself up. "Yes, I do!" she said indignantly, then remembered she should sound weak—and sighed. "If you don't mind, I'll need to excuse myself from the table. I'll need only a few minutes, of course."

Sergei's brow creased. "My footman will escort you to a room where you may recover yourself."

At least he was being kind enough to allow that.

She gave him a hasty smile and stood.

"Lady Poppy shall return," Sergei told the company.

They were getting awfully drunk.

A footman brought her into the hallway—she looked longingly at the front door—and up the stairs to the next floor, where he deposited her in a bedchamber.

"I'll wait outside the door," he said gruffly, as if she were a prisoner.

He pulled the door shut, and she immediately went to the windows and looked out. There was no balcony, no possible way out. She'd have to outwit the footman and get back down the stairs and out the front door.

But what about the painting? God knows, after tonight, she'd probably never see Sergei again. She should try to see the painting if at all possible.

Inhaling a deep breath, she opened the door again. "Excuse me."

The footman looked terribly bored. "Yes?"

Not even a *yes, milady,* she noticed.

"I forgot to ask what room the portrait is in. The one to be unveiled."

The footman raised a brow. "That's not to concern you until midnight."

She gave a little laugh. "I know. But I'm one of those curious types."

"Are you?" He looked a bit more interested.

"I simply want a peek," she said, "before the others. I like the thrill it gives me, to do things without other people knowing. Do you know what I mean?"

She had another flashback to that sensual encounter in the library with Nicholas. She *would* choose the unlikely word *thrill* when she was scared witless. Nicholas was nowhere near, but thinking of him gave her a small boost of courage.

"I think I do know what you mean," the footman said, and came closer, his mouth curving in a hopeful smile, his eyes roaming over her in a brazen manner.

Oh, dear. She didn't want to go in *that* direction.

Quickly, she pulled a ring off her finger, being careful not to take one of her mother's. "If you show me the portrait, I'll give this to you." She held the ring up for his inspection.

He reached for it, and she snatched it back.

"Not yet," she whispered. "Hurry. Let's look quickly, and then I'll give you the ring."

"You swear?"

"Yes, I swear."

It would be a small price to pay.

So he led her to another chamber on the same corridor.

"Right," he whispered. "Don't make a sound. In a moment, you'll see Revnik's final masterpiece. Prepare yourself. Your peek shall end in ten seconds."

He swept off the red silk drape.

Poppy sucked in a breath.

Goodness.

The painting!

Why, it was—

It was stunning.

Poppy tried to keep her head about her as she gazed at a full-length scene of a beautiful woman in a pink gown.

She was looking up with something akin to adoration at her dancing partner, whose back was to the viewer.

It was the Pink Lady, the painting the Service had been hoping for. Somewhere on the canvas was the key to the identity of the mole in Parliament.

Poppy forced herself to breathe in. Then out.

It was an extraordinary work. Revnik had managed to pay homage to a shining moment in both a couple's personal history and Russia's cultural history. And on a deeper level, the painting was a timeless tribute to lovers everywhere.

"Time's up," the footman said, and replaced the drape.

"Wait!" Poppy swallowed. "Please. One more look."

"Absolutely not." The footman then beckoned her to follow him out of the room. "I want that ring now."

She handed it to him with trembling fingers.

"Let's get you back to the dining room," he said.

"No," she replied. "Take me to the front door instead. Tell the prince I was too ill to stay."

"You do seem a bit off at the moment."

"Believe me, I *do* feel ill."

"But the prince will be angry at me for letting you go."

"You've got the ring for compensation if he fires you. And here's another one." She twisted off a second ring and handed it to him. This one *was* her mother's, but she knew Lady Derby would have understood her giving it away. "Would you really care if you leave his employ? It's awfully gloomy here."

"It's not always that way—"

"Please," she interrupted him. "I simply need your help to leave."

He shrugged. "All right, although you're going to be missing the best part."

"I already saw the painting."

"Not that. The special event."

"Please," she said. "I don't care about a special event. I simply want to leave without anyone hearing us. Perhaps we should go out the back way."

"Fine." He took her down the servant stairs and out the back door.

She ran down the alley and around to the street, feeling like she'd made a narrow escape. But it wasn't the only feeling she had. She was even more overcome by shock.

The stableboy was waiting on the corner. "Only a little late, miss!" He attempted to hand her the sturdy slippers.

"No time," she said, and they went racing down the street, back to the rout.

She must stay calm. She mustn't let anyone know what she'd seen—

Her own mother waltzing with Papa in that portrait.

"You let her *go*?" Nicholas said to Eleanor and Beatrice.

Eleanor bit her lip and nodded. "She's with a stableboy. He's got a pistol."

"She's perfectly safe," Beatrice said.

"I'm not so sure about that," said Nicholas, "but I've no time to talk. I must find her *now*."

"We'll come, too," the girls said together.

With Nicholas leading the way, the three of them hastened down the front steps of the Merriweather mansion and onto the pavement.

"It's not the streets of London I'm worried about so much as Prince Sergei and what he's planning," Nicholas said, striding fast.

Eleanor and Beatrice looked at each other, then back at him.

"Poppy knows he's not the man for her." Eleanor scurried to keep up with him.

"She's only going to say good-bye," said Beatrice. "And she always carries a pin in her sleeve. She won't put up with any nonsense from Sergei."

Nicholas decided to share what Groop had told him. "I've heard rumors today there are people who don't want us to marry and might try to prevent it."

"Oh, my!" said Eleanor.

"I wouldn't be surprised." Beatrice swung her arms in time with his. "Plots are my specialty. Tell me more— I'll figure out who's behind it."

"I know nothing more," he assured the two girls. "It could be mere rumor. But I've concerns about her safety, nonetheless."

"We'll be sure to keep an eye on her," said Beatrice, "and thank you for telling us."

"You're her closest friends. I know you have her best interests at heart."

Beatrice got closer to him. "The question is, Your Grace, do *you*?"

"I'd like to know, as well," said Eleanor, her voice a

little breathy. "This marriage proposal of yours doesn't make much sense."

"And do you think her using my name for three years to fob off her suitors made any more sense?" he asked them.

"Yes, it kept them at bay," said Eleanor.

"So she could indulge in a fantasy about Sergei," Nicholas replied dryly.

"So?" Beatrice said, arching a brow. "It's better to be a Spinster with lovely daydreams than wife to a man you don't love."

"Point taken. Men have the same concerns, of course. I myself have no intention of marrying a nag, a spoiled brat, or a weak-kneed fainter."

Eleanor giggled. "Poppy is none of those things."

"I'm already aware," Nicholas said, grinning back. "Rest assured, I've perfectly logical reasons for marrying her."

"Logic isn't good enough." Beatrice threw him a stern look.

"We Spinsters want men who are willing to make fools of themselves for love," said Eleanor.

Beatrice nodded. "Men who've seen us at our worst and are still devoted to us."

Nicholas restrained himself from rolling his eyes.

Eleanor patted his arm. "Just know that we'll do everything we can to help Poppy get out of the betrothal if we think you're not the man for her."

"Thank you. I now consider myself educated—and warned." He took both their elbows and led them across the street.

Beatrice leaned into him. "I forgot to mention, if you prove yourself to be the *right* man for Poppy, we're very easy to get along with."

"And if *she* doesn't know yet that you're the right man for her, we'll help you. Just say the word." Eleanor winked.

"That's good to know, ladies. Not that I need help from interfering females."

Beatrice gasped and hit him on the shoulder.

He chuckled. "You two are almost as unmanageable as Poppy."

"Yes, we are," Eleanor said. "And there she is!"

Straight ahead, pointing a pistol at a large Russian thug Nicholas recognized as one of Sergei's bodyguards, was Poppy.

The bodyguard held the stableboy by the scruff of the neck.

"Put him down *now,*" Poppy was saying in a threatening voice. "Before I shoot you in the knees."

"See? I told you she could take care of herself," whispered Beatrice to Nicholas.

He wouldn't call being caught in a conflict with a large thug at night an appropriate situation for a young lady to be in, but yes, he granted that Poppy appeared to be taking care of herself.

"I'm holding on to him until you drop that pistol," the bodyguard cried. "He's already kicked me in the privates twice!"

The stableboy's legs flailed and he punched the air. "Put me down, you big lout!"

"Poppy!" cried Eleanor.

She threw them a brief glance. "What are *you* doing here?"

"Looking for you," Nicholas said mildly. "Hand me the gun."

"No, not until he puts the boy down." She thrust the gun barrel toward the thug.

He sighed and dropped the stableboy, who promptly turned around and kicked him in the knee.

Poppy kept the barrel trained on the bodyguard as she transferred the gun to Nicholas. "This man," she said in furious tones, "followed us from Prince Sergei's demanding that I return, even though I'm clearly ill"—Nicholas thought she looked healthy as a horse—"and said if I didn't go back posthaste, he was going to carry me back. Whereupon he picked up my dear stableboy, who was only defending me with those kicks, and who thankfully had the wherewithal to toss me the pistol before the thug got it."

Nicholas had an odd feeling. That bodyguard didn't exude menace to him. He appeared confused. Even frightened.

Nicholas put the pistol in his breeches and looked sternly at him. "Go home and tell your master that he'd best send a note of apology to the lady for the extreme distress you've caused her and her servant. Kidnapping will get you both deported."

"My master didn't want me to kidnap Lady Poppy," the thug said in a heavy Russian accent, "just give her a ride home in a proper carriage. The footman said she was terribly ill. Prince Sergei might be a vain oaf, but he's not evil."

"Then why did he have all those . . . those awful people at the dinner party?" Poppy asked. She looked at Nicholas and her two best friends. "They were talking about daggers and sow's blood. And they were much too familiar with me and each other—why, one woman had hair hanging in her face, and a man said he'd be the Antony to my Cleopatra! The corridor was wickedly gloomy, hardly any candles at all, and Prince Sergei kept trodding on my toes and nudging me with his knee."

The brute drew in his chin. "The prince is a large man and the table was small. He was worried about fitting you and the entire theater troupe around it."

"Theater troupe?" Poppy's brows arched high.

"Yes," said the bodyguard, "he hired them to entertain you. They were going to do a skit for you from *Macbeth*. That was to be the surprise. He had the corridor darkened to create the appropriate atmosphere."

"Oh, my God," Poppy whispered. "I told Sergei *Macbeth* is my favorite Shakespearean play."

Eleanor and Beatrice both giggled, but Nicholas restrained himself from laughing. Poppy deserved the scare, he thought, going off and frightening him like that.

"It was all a great misunderstanding," he said to the bodyguard. "Say nothing to Sergei about Lady Poppy's concerns, and please thank him for his hospitality. I'll make sure she gets home."

CHAPTER 28

Her mother was the Pink Lady.

Poppy had had only ten seconds to look at the painting, but she would have recognized her mother in one second, much less ten.

Lady Derby was front and center in Revnik's last portrait, dancing with Poppy's father. She recognized the back of his head. She thought she might even have recognized his cuff links.

Viewing her parents' romantic history forever captured on canvas was astounding . . . and gratifying. Seeing her mother's face again—well, that alone was quite a shock. And a lovely, lovely surprise. So sweet, in fact, that she'd felt as if she'd had another moment with her mother, a fact she would cherish forever.

But then on top of all that deep emotion, she realized the painting she already adored was somehow involved in a Service operation.

The worst of it was she couldn't speak of any of it with Eleanor and Beatrice or her father or Aunt Charlotte. She was dying to—but Nicholas had told her at

the top of St. Paul's that she couldn't tell her friends
and family about any Service activities.

How she longed to tell them!

She so wanted them to see the painting, too, but if
Nicholas retrieved it from the Lievens' ball, when
would they ever see it? And what would happen to the
painting? Over whose mantel would it eventually re-
side?

When they returned to the rout, Poppy decided she
must leave her two best friends there and go home with
the stableboy. Otherwise, she would simply burst with
all the emotions and thoughts jostling for space inside
her, and confess all. That wouldn't make Nicholas,
Groop, or the Service happy.

"You're not going home with the stableboy," Nicholas told her. "Your *fiancé*"—he emphasized the word—
"shall escort you both in my carriage. The boy can
ride with the coachman, and you'll tell me about your
evening—an evening, by the way, which you saw fit
not to inform me about."

She was so agitated, she allowed his censure to flow
right by without becoming embarrassed at being caught
out. "True," she said, "but that was for your own good."

"Why was it for my own good?"

"Because I was involved in a Service activity. You
yourself said I should tell no one."

Nicholas helped her into the carriage and followed
her inside. "I didn't mean not tell *me*. We're working
together. What the bloody hell were you doing besides
telling Sergei to forget his romantic aspirations toward
you?"

Poppy thought about how much *more* she'd been doing and inhaled a deep breath. "I suppose the girls told you he invited me to a masked dinner. He even sent me this gown."

The details seemed fairly unimportant at the moment.

"Yes, they told me," Nicholas said, his mouth a thin, dangerous line. "Let me make one thing clear . . . you can't disappear like that again. Now that you're involved with me, you must be more careful about being alone." He took her by the shoulders. "Groop told me someone might be trying to break us up. Who knows what lengths they'll go to? When one is a Service employee, enemies abound, and sometimes you're not sure who they are."

She bit her lip. "Oh, dear. With that in mind, then, what I have to tell you is so important and secret, we'll have to drop the stableboy off and go back to the top of St. Paul's."

"Very well." Nicholas was wearing his serious Service expression, which she found extremely attractive. "But I've another safe place we can go to that's much closer and won't involve traipsing up five hundred thirty steps."

Which was how they wound up at a small but plain sturdy sailing craft tied to a dock on the Thames.

"It's mine," said Nicholas, "but I don't get to use it often." He helped her aboard. "This will take a few minutes. Sit tight in the cockpit and enjoy seeing London at night from the river. We're lucky we have a light wind and a big moon tonight, perfect for a sail."

So she sat and watched him untie the rope holding them to the dock and hoist the sail. Then in a silence broken only by the occasional luff of the sail and the sounds of London in the background, he steered the boat to the middle of the Thames and took another few minutes to anchor it.

"Let's go below," he said eventually.

He opened the hatch and beckoned her down. She climbed down the ladder, well aware of his warm hand at her waist. Once below, she looked around at the cozy interior of the craft and sighed. "As safe places go, this is perfect."

"Thanks. I think so, too." Nicholas left the hatch open so the moonlight could stream in. "Take a seat, please, and tell me what happened."

She sat on a cushioned berth, and he joined her.

The gentle rocking of the boat was just what she needed to soothe her agitated nerves. Nicholas didn't say a word. He waited patiently, which she appreciated.

"I saw the Pink Lady painting," she said eventually.

"You did?" She sensed excitement in his tone, even though, as usual, he was controlled. "I thought it was at the Lievens'."

"Not yet. Of course, it could be that Sergei brought it back to his apartments for a showing tonight. That's why I went. He issued me a special invitation to see it."

"Well? What did you discover?"

Poppy looked directly into his eyes, which were black pools in the darkness of night. "My mother was in the painting," she said. "She's the Pink Lady."

Nicholas gave a short laugh. "You're joking."

"No." She inhaled a deep breath.

"Are you sure it's your mother in the painting?"

"Yes. I admit I thought perhaps I was seeing things. But it was Mama. And that gown she wore . . . it's still in a press in a spare room at home." She pressed a hand to her mouth for a moment and couldn't help blinking back a tear. "I was so happy to see her again. With Papa."

It was an image seared onto her memory forever.

Nicholas squeezed her hand. "It must have been a shock for you, as well."

She nodded. "Yes, it was. But it was also a gift. A huge one."

"I can see that it would be." His voice was gentle.

She gave a little sniff. "Right now I don't want to think about why my parents are in a painting sought after by the Service. It's too upsetting." She sat up, the words bursting to be said. "Right now, I want *you,* Nicholas."

"Come here," he said.

She flung herself into his arms and he held her tight. But the hug quickly turned into a kiss. He was warmer than toast, his masculine form more finely sculpted than any thoroughbred stallion's. And he was handsomer than any man she'd ever known.

She had to admit that encircled in Nicholas's arms, she didn't feel confused and upset. She felt safe and happy.

He stopped kissing her for a moment and looked grievously worried.

"Why did you stop?" she asked him, her lower belly heavy and warm, her breasts aching to be touched.

"Because we need to be careful. This is a very tempting situation. We could do anything we want. Which means—"

"We could do *whatever* we want with *whom* we want *when* we want," she said breathlessly. "We could . . . disrobe."

"Exactly." He shook his head. "Wait a minute. What did you say?"

All right, she shouldn't have said it, but it was Nicholas and he'd never tell. "We could—"

"Never mind," he said, his mouth curved in amusement. "I heard."

She bit her lip and stared at him.

"Poppy." He took her by the shoulders. "We can't do that."

"But you must admit, we could."

He sighed. "Don't you understand how women become with child?"

Of course she did. She'd seen dogs mating on the street. And she'd once seen a bull and a cow.

"Yes," she said. "But we've no fear of *that* happening."

He gave a short laugh. "To the contrary. A man and a woman naked together can easily make a baby."

"Not if we don't get into one of those strange positions. They should be easy enough to avoid, shouldn't they?" She laughed, thinking of that poor cow. "I'd feel awfully silly."

Nicholas narrowed his eyes at her. "Despite what we did in your father's library, you're still unversed in the art of lovemaking, and you're never making it more obvious than now."

"I only want to see you"—she smiled shyly—"in your natural form. And maybe kiss you naked, as well." She reached out and ran her hand over his shirt. "You said no one would catch us. And I promise not to tell if you don't."

He groaned and captured her hand. "You're killing me, Poppy." He pulled her closer. "And you're beautiful, you know. I want to take all your clothes off, too. But you'd regret this later."

She thought of Sergei. And she thought about all her other suitors. She had no desire to see any of them naked. She would have closed her eyes (she actually did when Lord Washburn lost his breeches in that fountain during his proposal to her), but with Nicholas—

There was something about him that made a girl want to keep her eyes open.

"*Please,* Nicholas," she begged him.

He was silent, brooding, staring into her eyes.

She could see the indecision there. "You told me nothing with you would be boring anymore. Remember?"

He gave a short laugh, and his expression relaxed. "All right, then. But we must be careful. *Very* careful."

She couldn't help it. She was so delighted, she kissed his chest, right over his heart. He smelled of man, a potent scent that made her heady with something—

Desire, she knew now. It happened when you could barely breathe and be sensible because you could think only about kissing and touching someone else.

"All we're doing is disrobing." She said it firmly and vowed to forget what Aunt Charlotte had said about the matter. "Hardly anything to worry about, particularly as it's you and me. Think of all we've been through together already."

She couldn't help a little giggle as she removed her shoes and stockings. He did the same, and she marveled at the breadth of his shoulders when he removed his tailcoat.

He raised an eyebrow. "Are you suggesting we're *friends*?"

"Yes." She looked away a moment. He was so very handsome, she felt suddenly shy. "It's quite something to think I'm friends with the wicked Duke of Drummond, isn't it? But we're friends only for the nonce. As soon as we get our clothes back on, we'll go back to our usual arrangement."

"Which is your vowing to get out of our betrothal, and my refusing to let you. And your insistence on helping with Operation Pink Lady, or else you'll take matters into your own hands, which would no doubt spell disaster for me and the Service.'"

"Exactly," she said. "We're bound together by mutual blackmail."

And a hearty appreciation for each other's bodies.

She wouldn't think about how much she appreciated

his substantial qualities, the ones she and Aunt Charlotte had referenced in that talk they'd had over Papa's apple tart.

Disrobing was actually quite a simple thing, Poppy convinced herself, and carefully undid a button on his waistcoat.

CHAPTER 29

"I'm not so sure your trust in my self-control is merited," Nicholas said. He untied Poppy's laces while she began work on his neckcloth.

They'd hardly anything to worry about, she'd said moments earlier.

Right?

Wrong.

Seeing her gown fall like a whisper at her feet brought home to him how deeply he was out of his element. For him, at least, this was suddenly about far more than sexual attraction. Her stays were next, and when she was released from them, completely nude, he was in awe of her beauty, of her vulnerability, of who she *was*—in a way he'd never been before with any other woman.

He ran a finger between her breasts and up to her chin, which she lifted proudly to him. Her eyes were filled with excitement and serenity—both at the same time. She grabbed his finger and kissed it softly.

Slowly.

That kiss reverberated deep within him. Somehow, feeling her lips on his skin was like connecting with himself again. He was home. For the first time in decades.

With her, he'd found a place to be.

Just be.

The wonder of it all left him speechless.

Naked as Eve, Poppy diligently worked to remove his shirt. Without a word, he helped her pull it over his head, enjoying the sight of her, flushed and pretty and so determined.

He crossed his arms over his chest and let her work on his trousers. She gave a little huff as she pulled down on both sides.

He chuckled.

She looked up, a bright gleam in her eyes, and laughed back. "They're so *tight*."

"Indeed. Tighter now than they were mere minutes ago."

She paused in her efforts and blushed. "I noticed."

He was glad she had. It satisfied a deep craving in him to have her admire him—in any way.

"I'm looking forward to this part," she whispered.

"Good. So am I."

In about fifteen seconds flat, they were both naked and kissing and most definitely in trouble. But Nicholas was too wrapped up in squeezing Poppy's delicious bottom to care.

And she was sighing and pressed up close to him. He ran a hand down her flank, and she pulled back and looked at him with a resolute gaze. "From now on,

I'm going to want to see you naked—and touch you naked—every time we're together."

She touched him shyly with her fingertips.

"Oh, God." He groaned, and leaned his forehead on hers. "That's impossible, but you're quite adorable to say so."

She reached up for another kiss, wrapping both her hands around his neck. Thank God those soft, feminine hands were away from the danger zone, he mused, and gave her a deep, sensuous kiss.

"Would you like to go on deck?" he asked her when they came up for air. "The ceiling's a bit close in here. And we've got a moon out."

"But what if someone sees?" she asked, brushing a curl off his forehead.

"No one will," he said, somehow touched by the gesture. "We'll look like a shadow from the shore."

"I think it sounds like a marvelous idea." She clambered up before him as if she climbed ladders naked every day, which only whetted his appetite for her further.

He'd seen plenty of naked women. Why did this one in particular drive him mad with lust and occupy his thoughts when he wasn't with her?

He had no idea, and he wasn't one for thinking deeply about the opposite sex.

Women, he knew, were trouble.

Best to keep things simple.

On deck he spied the jib sail hastily folded and squashed between the mast and the hatch cover. He spread it out on the cabin top, and they lay down together, folding the edges of the jib over their exposed flesh.

It was a cozy yet tantalizing shelter. He put his arm behind her head, and she pressed her hip tightly against him. Together, they looked up, beyond the gently swaying boom with its loosely furled sail, to the stars.

"Tonight is different from any other night I've ever had," Poppy murmured. "When I saw my mother in that painting, it was like I woke up from a dream. Everything's crisper now. Bolder."

She looked at him and smiled.

It was hard for him to remember to breathe. She was gorgeous. Her hair, a dark, coppery forest, fell about her creamy shoulders and breasts. Her hip was an alabaster hill that sloped away to long, slender legs.

He leaned over her and kissed her, and while he did, he explored the soft depths of her most feminine flesh with his fingers, reveling in the sighs of pleasure she was making into his own mouth.

"*Nicholas,*" she murmured, and he continued his finger play.

In the next few seconds, he switched positions, not a small feat on top of the small boat. He was back at his favorite spot, in between her legs, his mouth on the sweet core of her femininity.

"Oh, thank heavens," she said breathily, arching her back. "I haven't been able to stop thinking about this since you—"

He lifted his head. "This time you don't have to be

silent," he said into the soft mound of curls between her thighs. Then he went back to playing with her flesh with his tongue, sipping and kissing and taking his fill.

"This is bliss," she whispered, and wrapped her hands around his head, grabbing for him, pressing him closer. In an ancient motion echoed by the gently rocking boat, her hips lifted to meet his probing tongue.

"Nicholas," she cried, and at the right moment, he brought her to pleasure, two fingers of one hand sliding deep into her, his other hand gripping her bottom, her femininity drawn up to his mouth. Her fingers were tangled in his hair, and her chin pointed heavenward, toward the stars. Her slender neck and taut breasts reflected the moonlight.

She was beautiful.

Beautiful.

"You're . . . beautiful," he said, feeling rather drunk with the word.

When she was fully spent, he laid her down and lay next to her, scooping her into the circle of his arms. Her body quivered, and she gave a languid sigh. For a few moments, she was quiet, and together they looked up at the night sky again.

"Look," she said, pointing.

"I see it," he said, and had a sudden feeling of completeness.

Naked girl.

Shooting star.

Rocking boat.

It didn't get better than this, did it?

* * *

After a few more minutes of listening to the creaking sounds of the boat tackle and the slap of water against the hull, Poppy sat up.

"Where are you going?" Nicholas asked her.

"Nowhere." She looked down the length of him, and pressed her hand over his shaft. Instantly, it hardened into rock again.

Her touch was exquisite.

She bit her lip and smiled. And then slowly, she began to run her hand up and down him. "Do you like this?" she asked shyly.

"God, yes." What else *could* he say? He was hers. All hers. She could do anything she wanted with his body, as far as he was concerned.

She applied herself more vigorously. "I like it, too."

He pulled himself up, leaned back on his elbows, and watched her. Just seeing her this way, kneeling over him, intensely focused on pleasing him, was enough to send him over the edge. But he didn't want that to happen. Not quite yet.

"Watch the boom," he warned her as it swung dangerously close to both their heads.

She laughed.

"I'm serious," he said.

She lowered her head, but she also laughed again. "You and your lectures," she told him.

In retaliation, he caressed her bottom. She moaned with pleasure. And then he put his hand between her legs and began to stroke her.

She dropped her head, and her hair fell over his torso, tantalizing him with the sensation.

"You're wicked," she whispered, and made those whimpers of delight that he knew would come to haunt his nights.

"Just a warning," he said, as his climax came nearer. "It can be quite messy."

"I don't care." She sucked in shorter breaths.

"I want you to come, too."

"Come?"

"To pleasure," he said. "With me. What you did before."

She didn't have time to reply because a few seconds later, they did just that.

Together.

Afterward, they lay side by side on their backs, arms and legs outstretched, the boat bobbing a bit more forcefully.

"The wind's picking up." Nicholas wished Mother Nature weren't working against him at the moment. But he supposed they must eventually leave this lovely little boat—how could he ever have thought it plain?

Poppy rolled over on one elbow and looked at him. "I suppose this time we've had together—being naked and kissing . . . and all those other wonderful things—is over, then."

He rolled up, too, and pulled her hair from her face. "You're right," he said. "And I hope you enjoyed it. Because"—he hesitated—"it can't happen again, especially if you don't intend to marry me."

He wondered, and not for the first time, why she found him so unsuitable.

She cast her eyes down. "I know it can't happen

again," she whispered, and looked back up at him. "I see the danger now."

He pressed his lips together. "Yes. You see how—"

"How now I can't think of anything else," she said rather passionately, almost angrily. She pressed her lips together.

"Don't be upset," he said. "Of course you'll be able to think of other things. But it takes time to . . . recover. And if you stay busy, you can manage without this, um, sort of experience. Until you marry. And then you can do it all the time, and it's even better when—"

She brightened. "When what?"

"When the man and the woman can have a real coupling." Did she not care that they never would, if she had her way?

The waves rocked the little sailboat, and all was quiet. Snug. In their intimate little world, he felt he could ask her something he'd wondered about—but hadn't had the courage to ask until now.

"Poppy." He heard a faint edge of unsurety in his voice. "What exactly are you looking for in a mate?"

He was unfamiliar with rejection from women, but his curiosity went deeper than that. He wanted to understand her, what she thought about, who and what made her happy. Or sad. Or angry.

For the first time in his adult life, he was interested in forging a connection, a bridge, to another person.

"Someone who understands me," she said instantly.

"And I don't?" he responded, quick as lightning.

"Do you?" she challenged him with a saucy grin.

He pulled a piece of hair off her face. "We certainly

have fun together," he said, and thought hard. "I think you like adventure. You're restless, searching for something, but perhaps you're not sure what."

She bit her lip. "You're right, actually."

He chuckled. "I'm the same way. Yes, I'm a duke, a position many might envy, but I want adventure, as well. I think it's in my blood. Uncle Tradd must have had this same restlessness. A large part of me would like to drop everything and travel the world."

"Then why don't you?"

"Mainly because of Frank. But also because of the other responsibilities I have as the Duke of Drummond—keeping up Seaward Hall and my other estates, for one. It's why I work for Groop. At least I can experience a little adventure without leaving home."

"So you're saying . . . you're sad."

He shrugged. "Not sad, exactly. But not happy, either. Caught between the life I have . . . and the life I want."

"Funny," she said. "I feel the same way."

"So you can have no objections to our betrothal. I understand you, don't I?"

She narrowed her eyes at him. "But there are other things on the list, too."

"What list?"

"The Spinsters Club list. A girl can't resign her membership unless a potential mate meets all qualifications."

"Which are?"

"I can't tell you. They're confidential."

A covetous, predatory look came into his eye. He

never appeared more dangerous, Poppy thought, than when he was after a secret.

"Hmmm," he muttered, "said like a real clandestine agent. Although your friends let me know about a couple of your requirements. They both involve love. Is that what you're seeking?"

There was a beat of silence.

"Of course." She felt out of breath when she said it. "Which is why I won't marry *you*. I must love my husband, and he must love me."

Nicholas looked down at the deck of the boat, and her heart sank.

When he met her gaze again, his was shrouded. "It's time to go back."

No fairy tales, she told herself, and hardened her heart. "You don't want to discuss frivolous things like love," she said evenly. "You think I'm foolish."

He shook his head. "Not foolish. I think you're fanciful, yes."

She huffed. "You believe love isn't possible."

"No." He stood and began unraveling a line. "I told you my parents loved each other. So it can happen."

"Then why are you so against the idea?"

"I never said I was."

"You could have fooled me." She hesitated. "You're afraid of it, aren't you? Because you saw what happened to your father when he lost your mother. You saw how changed he became after she died. He was weak. Easily led. You don't want that to happen to you."

He didn't say a word.

She sighed. "I'm in a similar situation. I can't say my father has recovered from his loss, but you know what? I've decided I'd rather have one day of what he had with my mother than never have it at all. And if I marry a man I don't love, I ruin all my chances. Which is why I'm willing to risk being a Spinster for the rest of my life. I refuse to settle."

Nicholas stared at her a moment. "I think we should marry. We'll make a great team. But I won't lie and spout romantic notions about love to coerce you. We understand each other. We'll protect each other. Isn't that enough? Do we have to add potential hurt to the mix?"

Poppy couldn't say another word. She was too disappointed. And angry.

She watched Nicholas put up the mainsail and sail the little boat back to shore, back to a world where young ladies and gentlemen danced and flirted . . . and then put their secret passions aside and married wisely.

Her heart clenched.

Didn't love matter at all?

CHAPTER 30

Nicholas felt it was as if last night's difficult conversation on the sailboat had never happened.

As if the highly sensual encounter they'd had before that conversation had never happened.

As if the intimate laughter, the feeling that they were comfortable—even happy—together, had never happened.

In the afternoon, he'd taken Poppy to the Lievens', where they'd enjoyed tea and a pleasant conversation in which the Russian ambassador had inadvertently revealed that the Pink Lady portrait would be kept in an alcove in a corridor above the ballroom during the ball. Countess Lieven also told them Revnik's masterpiece would be brought down and unveiled near the ball's conclusion.

Good information to have.

Afterward, when Nicholas took Poppy for their afternoon ride through Hyde Park, they were back to being nothing more than two people working on the same Service project.

"I agree that a mole in Parliament is a bad thing," Poppy said crisply, "but couldn't Revnik have written Groop a letter? Or gone to visit him? Instead, he had to paint a portrait of my parents and ruin it with some sort of spy gobbledygook?"

"*Ssshh.*" Nicholas looked around and saw no one nearby. But they couldn't take chances.

"I'll tell you," she whispered, "I think my mother bought it as a surprise for my father. She probably paid good money for it. Revnik had no right to use it for his own purposes. He died unexpectedly, probably of the same smallpox epidemic Mama did, and years later, Sergei found the portrait. He made a claim to it because no one came forward. Well, no wonder. Mama, poor lady, was dead and buried."

That scenario sounded very likely.

"But it contains something of value to England," Nicholas said. "Don't you think your mother would have approved, had she known?"

"I suppose. But it would have been nice of Revnik to ask her permission first."

"When it comes to national security, you can't very well ask permission."

Poppy stared down her nose at him. "Whatever the circumstances were, this painting belongs with my family. Now more than ever, we have to retrieve it."

"*I* have to retrieve it. And I've every intention of doing just that. Not for your family, I'm sorry to say. The needs of the Service come first. It's the way things have to be."

"But what will they do with it?"

"I've no idea."

Poppy looked up at him with flashing emerald eyes. "If they think it belongs to England, Prinny could take it. Or one of his cronies. That's not right."

"Life's not fair." Nicholas squeezed her hand. "I understand your frustration."

"Good. Because I'll need your help. I'm going to prove Mama purchased that painting."

"I told you—the Service commissioned it."

Poppy huffed. "Mama was duped. She commissioned it. I'm getting that portrait back, and it's going over the mantel in Papa's library. I won't say a word to my father or my aunt until it happens. It will be a great surprise."

"Not to mention you're not supposed to talk to them about anything Service-related, remember?"

"Yes."

He thought for a minute. "I'm only going to help you look for proof of ownership," he said, "if I'm still able to proceed on my mission as planned. If you make any moves toward Sergei before the Lievens' ball, claiming the painting is yours, you'll compromise OPL. If that happens, probably neither one of us will ever see the painting again. And if you find your proof, you'll have to wait until I turn the painting over to the authorities to stake your claim. Agreed?"

"Very well." She glowered at him. "England can get a first look. But it had better be quick."

"You're a good citizen," he said. "I know you're anxious. If you really want to find out more about the Pink Lady painting, the best way would be to start at home.

If your mother commissioned it, there might be a receipt or correspondence in her desk that might prove your claim."

"I've already thought of that." Poppy beamed. "When I left you last night, I couldn't sleep." A becoming blush spread up her face. "I crept into my father's library and looked through his desk drawers. There was a big, fat file with Mama's old appointment books, some correspondence from friends, and whatnot. He must have emptied her desk and kept everything, the poor dear. I found her appointment book from St. Petersburg."

"Good work. Did you see anything interesting?"

"I don't know. I brought it with me. I wanted to look through it with *you*. We're partners, through thick and thin."

"That's quite considerate of you," he said, rather touched.

"No matter what happens in our personal lives," she said in neutral tones.

"Oh. Right."

That conversation at the conclusion of their interlude on the boat *had* been uncomfortable.

While Poppy flipped through the slender volume, Nicholas watched over her shoulder. Her mother's handwriting seemed to leap from the page, so energetic yet elegant—like Poppy.

She looked up. "Mama mentions many times that she has a sitting with R."

"Revnik."

"I think so." Her face brightened. "Perhaps this might

be of interest. She mentions a monetary amount—quite a substantial one—to be given to R." She grinned. "She did buy the portrait, then. For Papa!"

"It seems like it," Nicholas said. "But we still have no proof. Cryptic notes, which we all jot down in appointment books, are not enough to establish provenance."

"What a shame." Disappointment clouded her eyes. "This seems like proof to me."

"It wouldn't hold a bit of water in any legal battle," he said gently.

She sighed. "It doesn't seem right that Sergei has our painting."

"Go through the book one more time," he encouraged her. "Only this time, from back to front. You might have missed something."

A tense minute passed.

"I see nothing else," Poppy whispered. "Except perhaps"—she stared at one page—"here's one line—it looks like an address, 15 Vine Street."

"No name with it?"

"No."

"Nor city?"

"No, unfortunately."

"Then we'll assume it's London."

"But my mother had this book in St. Petersburg."

"Yes, but she might have written that address down as a place to mail something. If it were a St. Petersburg address, it would have a Russian name."

"But 15 Vine Street could be an address anywhere in England!"

"I know," said Nicholas. "But she lived here, in London. And I know of a Vine Street near Spitalfields Market, in the East End. Sometimes you simply have to go with—"

"Intuition." She smiled.

"Exactly," he replied.

CHAPTER 31

Poppy had never been in this part of London's East
End, and now she was navigating narrow, unfamiliar
streets with Nicholas in an unmarked carriage.

Only a few days before, she'd promised to give up
indulging in whimsy, but here she was, dressed like a
milkmaid. "I can't believe you have things like this in
your possession," she marveled.

He'd even given her a small wooden pail to carry.

He laughed. "I usually don't keep disguises for
women. But after our meeting at St. Paul's, I decided
I'd best be prepared with you involved."

She rather admired how quickly he'd developed a
five o'clock shadow on his jawline. "Burned cork can
do wonders. You look rather roguish."

"My intent."

Poppy couldn't help being amazed at the transfor-
mation in him, from London gentleman to rough workman. His broadcloth shirt gaped to his muscled belly.
His pantaloons were tucked into a sturdy pair of boots.
He had a broad piece of canvas rolled tight and tied

with a worn rope—it looked as though he used it as a sleep roll and traveled from job to job with it.

She had a sudden urge to jump in his lap and run her hands all over his broad chest. She remembered what it had looked like when they'd been completely naked together atop the sailboat.

She looked up and caught him looking down her bodice. It *was* rather tight.

"I know what you're thinking," he said dangerously.

"Yes, but guess what? I've been around you long enough now to know what *you're* thinking, too."

"You knew from the very beginning when you saw me on the stairs at the Grangerford ball."

"Not the *very* beginning."

"Are you sure?" He gave her a devilish smile. "I think you knew well."

She pressed her lips together. "What a thing to say to a lady."

But he was right. She *had* known.

The carriage turned onto Vine Street.

"There it is," she said. "Number fifteen."

It was a plain, modest row house with clean windows and a freshly painted blue front door. No smoke rose from the chimney. A small tree out front rattled its leaves in the stiff breeze.

She smelled that peppery smell that comes before a storm.

The hired driver took the horses by the house at a slow walk.

"It appears no one's home." She craned her neck to see into the house, but it was nearly impossible from where she was in a moving vehicle. "Shall we knock anyway?"

Nicholas shook his head. "I instructed the driver to make a slow inspection of the street and to come back around in fifteen minutes. See if there are any changes."

"I don't see any neighbors about."

"Let's hope it stays that way," he said. "We don't want to attract any attention."

"You mean, you don't want to talk to the neighbors?"

He shook his head. "Not if we can help it. We don't want them going to the man who lives here and telling him someone's snooping about his business."

"How do you know it's a man?"

"No curtains."

Aha. Poppy felt a dash of admiration for Nicholas's skills of observation. "He must not have anything to hide, then. Which is a good thing. My mother wouldn't have a sinister man's address in her appointment book."

"You'd think not. But having no curtains could also be his cover. Hiding out in the open, so to speak."

"Why would Mama have his address? She wouldn't know anyone in this neighborhood."

"It could be 15 Vine Street from another city or village," Nicholas reminded her, and called to the driver to go to the opposite end of the street.

"We'll walk back to the house on foot," he said. "And don't worry. Just stay with me."

She let out a nervous breath. "Of course I'm worried. It's not every day a girl breaks into someone else's home."

"We're going straight to the front door. I've got my

bundle of wood, so if someone answers, I'll offer to sell it. What will you do if we're discovered?"

"Run to the designated meeting place on Pearl Street," she said. "If you don't appear within fifteen minutes, I'll have the driver take me home."

"Good."

Poppy's chest tightened when they strode up the pavement toward 15 Vine Street.

And then five children came scampering down the street, laughing and chasing each other. They lingered beneath the tree in front of 15 Vine, swinging from its branches.

"What bad luck," she whispered.

"Happens all the time," Nicholas said. "Turn here."

Exactly ten houses down from their target, they turned right and came up a dirt alley to what Nicholas counted out as the back door of 15 Vine Street. The chickens in the coop behind it greeted them with nervous clucks, their feathers lifted by the increasing wind.

Poppy waited nervously, her hair flying about her face, as he knocked on the back door.

No one was home.

Nicholas worked the door with a small tool and managed to twist the knob. But the door stayed shut.

"Bolted," he whispered, strong gusts moving snatches of his hair as well.

He looked above them. And then behind them. There was no way in from the roof, Poppy could see. And behind them all she saw was the coop with a small shed inside. A sound came from it, a slight creaking.

"What's that noise?" she asked.

"Let's go see."

She entered the coop with Nicholas, and he peered inside the shed, chickens scattering at his feet. "There's a false wall in here," he said. "Keep the chickens back, please."

Oh, God. How did one keep chickens back?

She did her best, pushing chickens away from the shed with her feet and even her hands while Nicholas examined the wall. But the birds were making so much noise.

Too much noise, but what could she do?

When Nicholas was finally done moving something about—she had no idea what—he left the coop and tossed his canvas roll and the logs behind some empty barrels. "Hide your bucket there," he said. "And wait by the back door. I'll see you in a minute."

Poppy was aghast when he entered the coop again and disappeared into the small shed. She hid her bucket behind the barrels, and was much relieved when she saw him appear a few minutes later at the back door.

He slid the bolt back and drew her in.

She fell into his arms. "It was a *tunnel*?"

"Yes. Behind the false wall. There's a ladder propped in it. That noise you heard was the wind catching at a lantern swinging from one of its rungs. Someone needs to repair the shed walls to make it airtight."

The sounds of the children out front had faded away. Nicholas took her hand and they walked into a pristine room with an oak table, two mismatched chairs, a smoothly made bed, and a fireplace with a large black pot swinging from it.

"Come quickly," he said. "We've only a few minutes."

He led her behind a hung blanket, where they discovered a serviceable desk with neatly arranged stacks of paper on it, a small signet ring, a quill and inkpot, a set of keys, a scarf, and on the floor, several crates of papers. A colorful braided rug was the only adornment to the space.

"Oh, dear," she said. "We can't look through all that in a few minutes."

Nicholas was already on the floor. "He'll have a system." He was scanning the tops of the files in one of the crates.

For a moment, he sat back on his haunches, apparently surprised by something.

"What is it?" she asked.

He shook his head. "No time. I'll tell you later."

"Nicholas."

"I promise." He was sifting through the files again. "They're not alphabetized or organized by year."

She looked over his shoulder at the contents of the crate. "What a strange way to file things. A number in the top right-hand corner. They're in sequential order but with big gaps in between them. And a few have identical numbers. There seems to be no rhyme or reason."

"That's because he doesn't want anyone to understand his filing system." Nicholas paused for a moment, then sifted quickly through the files and pulled one out. He put it back, thought some more, and pulled out another file. Opening it, he lingered a few seconds on the first page.

His eyes glowed with satisfaction. "I've got it," he said. "What year was your mother born, what month, and what day?"

Poppy told him.

He sat quietly for a moment. "Look for the number thirty in the second crate while I look here," he said, then went to work sifting through the first box.

"Nothing in the second crate," she told him a minute later.

"Nor in mine."

They were both at work on the third box when they heard a few men talking loudly and occasionally guffawing out front.

"They're coming home from the pub after a hard day's work," Nicholas said. "They won't notice anything amiss."

"Are you sure?"

"No, actually," he said. "You're never sure in this business."

"Don't tell me that."

"It's part of the fun." He chuckled.

"You call *this* fun?" Her fingers stumbled from file to file.

"It makes for a good story later." He pulled out a file and scanned it. "Damn. I thought I had it. But it's the wrong number thirty."

They searched another fifteen seconds.

"Another thirty." Poppy yanked a file out and thrust it at him.

He threw it open. "Is your mother's name Marianna?"

"*Yes,*" she cried, her voice cracking. But then her heart nearly stopped—she heard shouts outside.

"*Mr. Harlow. How are you this evening?*"

"*Harlow, you need to get out more.*"

Several other male voices in the street echoed the raucous greeting.

From the front of the house, a Yorkshire accent called back, "Off with ye, lads. Go piss on someone else's tree. I'll nowt have ye drinkin' o'er here."

From behind the house, the chickens started cackling. Poppy grabbed Nicholas's arm. She couldn't speak. Calmly, he scooped up the papers and handed them to her.

"Hide these as best you can," he whispered.

She did as she was told, shoving the papers into her bodice. Her heart was hammering, and her breath caught in her throat.

The man who lived here was coming down the front walk. She heard his shoes crunching the gritty pavement.

Nicholas moved like silk, silently and smoothly, putting the file back in the crate and returning everything to its place. Without another word, he moved the small braided rug and pulled up a ring on the floor.

"Down," he ordered her.

Poppy stuck her leg down the dark hole, fumbling for a ladder with her foot, and finally found one.

"Keep going," he hissed.

When she heard the front doorknob rattle and then the front door swing open on squeaky hinges, she had to suppress a little cry. She stumbled through the dark and hit the bottom of the tunnel. Behind her, she felt a whoosh of air as the trapdoor shut silently above her head.

She sensed Nicholas's presence rather than saw him.

Yes. They were going to be all right.

She threw her hand out and felt nothing but air to her left, so she blindly moved that way. The tunnel smelled of damp earth and decay, like a tomb.

One step at a time, she told herself. She moved forward and was astounded to realize she wasn't afraid. The truth was, she'd never felt so exhilarated in her life.

As he descended the ladder, Nicholas was mentally reeling. And not from their near miss with the house's occupant. He'd had such close calls before. This was his second time in the tunnel, so he navigated it a bit easier going out than he had coming in. When he caught up with Poppy, he grabbed her hand.

"We're all right," he whispered, and gathered her close.

She clung to his neck like a drowning sailor, the papers in her bodice a small, stiff wall between them.

"You're very brave," he murmured in her ear.

She was still clinging, but she was also nuzzling—his ear, to be specific. "I *love* breaking into houses," she whispered.

"You do?" It was another shock. He gave in to temptation and caressed her backside.

"Mm-hmm."

He pulled her hard against him, and they kissed in the pitch-black darkness—kissed as if they were both starving and this kiss were their last meal.

Finally, reluctantly, he pulled back.

"Why do you make me feel so wanton, Your Grace?" she whispered. "We're underground. We're in someone else's *tunnel*. And you're the most exasperating man I know. I should be running from you, but instead, I—"

"You what?"

"I crave your kisses," she said simply.

Somehow that humble admission touched him like nothing she'd ever said before. She was so brave. And true to her feelings.

He pulled her to him for one more kiss. "I want you, too. Actually, I'm desperate for you. You're the most maddening woman *I* know, and I wouldn't have you any other way."

"Really?" She placed little kisses along his jawline.

"Really," he said, caressing her waist. "But—"

"But back to business." She pulled away, her tone firm and Service-like. "I'm ready for my orders."

He led her to the portion of the tunnel leading upward. Rain was falling hard now, and droplets of cold water dripped down on their heads.

"This Mr. Harlow can see out his back windows," he said. "We can't leave until we know he's not looking,"

"How can we do that?" she asked.

"There's a peephole at the top. We're lucky, really, for the rain. It's gotten darker and he'll probably light a lantern. We'll be able to see him more readily, and hopefully, he'll retreat to his office behind the blanket."

"I hope so." Her whisper was thin.

"We'll stand together on the ladder because we have to leave together. And we obviously have to leave fast. You'll go first. Head to the barrels and pick up your milkmaid's pail before you go."

He heard her stifle something that sounded rather like a snort. "We've got chickens to get around," she said. "They're all huddled in the shed."

"You're supposed to be terrified."

"I am. But it's still funny."

He chuckled, too. "You're right. It is. But meanwhile, I need you to be our lookout. Leave as soon as the coast is clear. I need to slide that false wall back into place, and I've got to do it quickly."

It was a good ten minutes before Poppy moved. But when she did, Nicholas was right behind her. She did a marvelous job of tiptoeing around the chickens without disturbing them. Then she clambered over the side of the coop and ran to the barrels.

The rain was falling in sheets, disguising any noise they might make. Nicholas took three seconds to replace the wall and sprang over the coop for the barrels, where he picked up the logs and the canvas roll.

He caught up with his partner in crime, who was already walking rapidly back up the alley to the north.

When they reached the corner, they slowed their pace. She was breathing hard, she had rivulets of water running down her cheeks and nose, and her hair was a god-awful mess.

But he thought she'd never looked so beautiful.

CHAPTER 32

When Poppy arrived with Nicholas back at the hackney on Pearl Street, the driver barely spared her a glance. Nicholas had assured her he'd paid the man well not to ask questions. On trembling legs, she clambered in first with her little bucket, Nicholas not far behind with his logs and canvas roll.

Only when the vehicle lurched forward did she let herself fall apart . . . just a little. She fell against Nicholas's equally wet shoulder and began to laugh.

"I can't believe—" She giggled. "I mean, I really can't believe—" She sat up ramrod straight and stared at him. "Did we just *do* that?"

Nicholas, even rougher-looking now than he was earlier, arched a brow. "Yes, we did, and the papers bulging out of your bodice are proof."

Dear God. She'd forgotten about the papers in all the excitement. She pulled them out—luckily, they were mostly dry—and tossed them on the opposite seat.

"I don't know if I can look at them quite yet. I need to recover."

"I do, too," he said. "And not just from breaking into that house. From *you*. You're delicious as a sodden milkmaid."

There was a beat of silence, and she let out a breathy sigh. "You're appallingly good-looking in your workman's disguise. Especially when wet."

"Am I?"

"Yes." She splayed her hands against his chest and stared into his eyes.

He tugged on one of her bodice laces and stopped, the lace taut in his hand.

She looked up at him.

And stopped breathing.

Something in his eyes melted her heart. He leaned forward . . . she met him. And they kissed. In the middle of it, Poppy realized it was the best kiss she'd ever had. Because that kiss told her everything her heart already knew.

She was in love.

With Nicholas.

A few seconds after the most riveting kiss he'd ever had, Nicholas admitted to himself that doing Service work with Poppy was much more exciting—and yes, more risky—than working alone.

But the risk seemed worth it.

She was becoming rather an addiction, and he'd have to be careful. After they married—a future he refused to consider wouldn't come to pass—he was to deposit her at Seaward Hall. But he was already asking himself how he could go back to work in London knowing she was sleeping in *his* bed, having *his* children, arranging flowers from *his* garden, and having adventures in *his* castle.

Because he was sure she would. Life at Seaward Hall would never be dull with her in residence.

"I'm ready," she said, her lips cherry red from their kissing. She moved back to the other seat. "Tell me what surprised you at that house. Something did."

"I'll say." Nicholas was still trying to take it in. "The house belongs to Mr. Groop. I immediately recognized his handwriting on the files. And on his desk, I saw a scarf he often wears to his office."

Poppy held her hand to her mouth. "Heavens, what was it like, knowing you'd burgled your own employer's home?"

"Like entering the Prince Regent's bedchamber," he said, "something completely off limits and, quite frankly, a place you never want to see."

"How did you find my mother's file when all you had was those cryptic numbers to go by?"

He enjoyed seeing her eyes sparkle with excitement.

"Part luck," he said. "Part knowing Groop and his quirks. His hobby is learning everyone's birthdays, and he enjoys playing with numbers. So I did some mental arithmetic with my own birthday to see if I could find my file. I tried a few different combinations, and one worked. It turns out he adds the digits comprising the year, month, and day to come up with that mysterious number. It was easy enough to get your mother's number using the same formula."

Poppy leaned toward him, her eyes sparkling. "Did you see your own file?"

He hesitated. "Yes. But I didn't have time to read it."

"I'll bet you wanted to." She chuckled.

"I'm not so sure."

"You were completely focused on helping me, and for that I thank you."

The grateful, overlong look she cast him warmed him at the center of his being. "You're welcome," he said gruffly.

She smiled, and there was an easy silence between them. He wasn't used to enjoying being with a woman so much. She put on no airs. Yet she was always a lady to him.

Even at her most wanton.

"He goes by Mr. Harlow at home, apparently," she said.

"And puts on a broad Yorkshire accent."

Poppy's brow furrowed. "Why would my mother have anything to do with Mr. Groop?"

"Let's look at the papers and find out. But I must warn you"—he pulled her across to his seat and looked deep into her emerald eyes—"it appears as if Revnik wasn't the only one working for the English government."

Poppy's mouth dropped open. "You're jesting, aren't you?"

"No. Your mother had Groop's address. Not many people do. I never have."

Poppy shook her head. "Let's look through the papers," she whispered.

Together they did just that.

"Twenty years in the Service," Nicholas said, scanning one page. "She was known as the Pink Lady."

Poppy's lips were a round O as she read another page. "*My* mother. A spy for the English." She put the papers down and stared at Nicholas. "But she never acted like a spy. She acted like a mother. And a wife. And a friend." Her eyes got a little shiny. "I—I didn't even know she loved pink so much that she'd choose it as her spy name."

"She might not have. She might have chosen it because she *never* wore pink. To throw off anyone who got hold of the name."

Poppy sniffed. "You're right, actually. She never did wear pink. Except in the portrait. And that was probably a clever little thing she did for the Service, in honor of her spy name."

It was one thing Nicholas loved about the Service. The people who worked for it were resourceful. Brave. And clever.

"Remember," Nicholas attempted to reassure her, "even though she was employed by Groop, she was still your mother. And a wife. And a friend."

Poppy shook her head. "But I still feel hurt. It's as if . . . I didn't know her."

The atmosphere in the carriage grew decidedly gloomy, like the weather outside.

"Of course you knew her," Nicholas insisted. "You

know me, don't you? And I happen to do secret things. It doesn't change who I am. You can trust me."

"That's true." Poppy bit her lip thoughtfully.

He was flattered she agreed.

"And how about you?" He grinned. "You're in the clandestine business at the moment. Are you any different? Or are you still . . . Poppy?"

She gave a little shrug. "I suppose I am. I wonder if Papa knew?"

"That's hard to say."

"But when you love someone . . . shouldn't you tell them *everything*?"

He had an unbidden, brief recollection of that entire night he'd spent with Natasha at the Howells' residence.

"Sometimes," he said carefully, "to protect that person from harm, you don't tell them everything. It's not because you don't love them. It's because you *do*."

Not that he loved *her,* but he hated to disappoint her. And he knew of many Service people who shielded their loved ones from harm by keeping secrets close to their chests.

"If Mama took her secret to the grave," Poppy said, "then I suppose it's not mine to reveal to Papa."

"I tend to agree. But I've also learned, never say never about anything."

They resumed their perusal of the papers. Poppy took her time, seeming to cherish each page. Once she was through reviewing one sheet, she'd pass it carefully on to Nicholas.

"This is my mother, after all." Her eyes glowed with

quiet pride. "I want to read everything carefully. Apparently, she was an expert at her job."

A moment later, she held a paper aloft and grinned. "*Ta-da!* The receipt we've been searching for."

She thrust it at Nicholas, and he read it carefully. "It does appear Lady Derby commissioned the painting," he said. "But . . . I hate to tell you—"

"What?" Poppy placed a hand on his arm, her eyes wide.

He spoke as gently as possible. "Now that we know your mother worked for the Service, this receipt could be a falsified document she carried in St. Petersburg. It would validate to anyone questioning her activities that she was a legitimate client of Revnik's. In other words"—he paused, hating to disappoint her after all their hard work—"the painting probably belongs to the Service. I'm very sorry, Poppy, if that's the case."

She stared at the receipt. "I hate the Service," she whispered. Then she looked at him, her mouth determined. "I know this receipt is real. Mama mailed it to Groop for safekeeping."

"I'm not saying she didn't, but—"

Poppy put out a palm to stop him. "She knew Revnik would use the portrait to convey a message about the mole, but Mama paid for it. And she wanted to give it to Papa."

She had a bold, clear light in her eye. "If you're right, Nicholas—and Mama was still Mama when she was doing things in secret—that's how she would have worked. She'd have selflessly allowed the government its bit, but she would have been thinking of Papa more."

She folded the receipt and put it back in her bodice. "In fact, I'm sure Mama's the genius who came up with the idea of painting the mole's identity into the portrait. Who was to know Revnik would die of the smallpox, and she shortly thereafter?"

She had both hands on her hips, her eyes flashing green fire now.

What was she, Nicholas wondered, Athena come to life?

He wanted her more than ever.

And he respected her more than ever.

"I wouldn't dare to disagree with a person showing such conviction," he said softly. "You've already proven to me that your gut instincts are good, so I'm not at all disheartened by these new revelations, are you?"

"Absolutely not." She threw back her shoulders. "It simply means I have more work to do before I can get Mama's portrait back."

"Which I still have to retrieve, you know."

"*Steal* is the right word, actually." She gave him a cool glance. "It's mine. Not the government's. But I'll stay true to Mama's wishes and allow the government a first look."

He grabbed her upper arms and pulled her close, his heart gripped by her passion. "You're bloody marvelous, do you know that?"

She laughed. "It's Mama's influence."

It was hard to kiss and grin at the same time, but they managed. And they managed a lot more than that. The carriage rolled up to 17 Clifford Street at the exact moment he put his mouth over her bared breast and ran his tongue around her puckered nipple.

"We're getting much too brazen," she whispered, and pulled her bodice up hastily.

"And you love it," he said.

"I do, actually." Her tone was cheeky.

Perhaps one day they could take a trip to Sussex to his small property there. They'd bring Aunt Charlotte to chaperone and feed her a large meal with lots of brandy-laced trifle, and then he'd take Poppy on a small picnic by a stream, but it would be a feast of a different kind . . .

"Nicholas?" She had her hand on the carriage door.

For the first time, he felt vulnerable letting her go. To the point that—

Well, he just hated to see her go. No use delving into his feelings more than that.

"I want to thank you for today," she said almost shyly. "I'll never forget it. Remember how we both said on the sailboat that sometimes you feel like you're living the wrong life? Today . . . today I felt like I was living the right one."

God, she was lovely.

And too good for him.

He took her hand again and kissed it. "You say the most impossible things."

She gave a little laugh. "Yes, and you're an Impossible Bachelor. Put us both together and we're . . ."

"We're what?" he asked her.

"Why, it's obvious."

"It *is*?"

Something shimmered in the air between them, but he wasn't sure what it was.

Poppy almost looked as though she felt sorry for him. "Good-bye, Nicholas," she said with a restrained little smile.

And before he could help her out, she opened the carriage door and left.

CHAPTER 33

Possible, that's what Poppy thought she and Nicholas were. But if he couldn't see it for himself, then she wasn't going to bother explaining. Nor would she marry him. The only man a Spinster would marry was someone who knew as well as she did they were meant to be together.

She shouldn't have to convince a man to love her, should she?

And the same went for her relationship with Papa. The next afternoon, she gathered her courage and stood before his closed library door. Aunt Charlotte had left that very morning for their country home in Kent to visit a dear old friend. She'd be gone a week, and Papa would be home more to watch over Poppy. It was as good a time as ever for her to approach him.

She lifted her hand, bit her lip, and knocked at the library door.

"Come in," Papa called, ever stern.

When she entered, he looked up, his eyes etched

with his usual worries about the state of the country and his role in Parliament.

"This is a welcome diversion." He paused in his writing.

"Am I, Papa?"

He sighed. "Of course you are."

She bit her lip. "I'm sorry. It's just that—"

"Yes?"

She sank into a chair. "You're gone all the time. And I never see you. And I wonder sometimes if you wish Mama had never had me. Often when you look at me, you appear angry."

Lord Derby laid down his quill. "I'm not angry at you. I do what I do for love of you. To make you proud. And to leave this country in a better way for you and your children after I'm gone."

Poppy studied his dear, lined face. "I'm thankful. And proud of you. But sometimes I wish you were here with me, laughing with me, *talking* to me. Sometimes I think that would help me more than you doing your duty. How can I tell my children funny little stories of their grandfather if you're not here? They'll learn all the grand things, of course, about your time in Parliament. But I want them to know *you*. That you like three lumps of sugar in your tea. And very shiny black boots. And singing. Not that you've done that in ages, not since before Mama died." She swallowed. "But sweet, special things like that."

Lord Derby hesitated. "I—I don't know what to say. Other than I'm sorry you feel ignored."

Her throat tightened. "I know you're doing your

best. But I wish we talked more about Mama. Since she's been gone, we never do."

Lord Derby frowned. "You're asking a great deal this morning. Why now?"

She shrugged her shoulders, feeling sheepish. "Only because I'm growing up, I think. I'm trying to be brave and live in the present, rather than the past. And the present includes *you*. I want to be part of your life, Papa. I want *more* from you than a frown and a lecture. I want my old father back. It might mean we have to start in the past and work our way to the present moment, but please. I'd like us to try. We've missed so much that we could have shared together."

He stared at her, his brows arched and his eyes no longer exuding authority and sternness. His gaze was concerned and sad.

Even lonely.

"I'll give your words much consideration, dear," he said.

"Thank you. And Papa, now I have another favor to ask."

"What's that?" he asked over his spectacles, back to his old House of Lords self.

She smiled. "Nothing so weighty as the first favor. Although it's related. I simply want permission to go through Mama's things. It's time we kept the special things and . . . and cleared out the others."

Lord Derby's brow furrowed. "All right. You and I shall go through her things together. Tonight. After dinner. At eight o'clock sharp."

Poppy gave him a little curtsy. "I'll be there, Papa."

She leaned over and kissed his cheek. "And thank you. I know this will be difficult, but I'm sure it's what Mama would have wanted."

"On with you now. You're just like your mother. Nosy and bossy and"—he paused—"and you've got me wrapped around your little finger."

"I do?" Her eyes filled with tears.

"Of course you do. Now go. I've got a speech to write."

She looked back at him from the door and felt a burst of hope. Perhaps she would be starting a new relationship with Papa.

It would be a fresh start for both of them.

CHAPTER 34

Nicholas was adjusting his cravat in the mirror of his bedchamber, preparing for a night of card playing with Harry, Lumley, and Arrow—Poppy was staying in with her father—when a series of rude knocks came at his door.

He opened it to Frank, who stepped into his quarters and laughed. "I got you now, brother."

Nicholas shut the door behind him. "How so?"

"I know about you and Natasha. You've been sleeping with her."

"I'm frightened," Nicholas said in his drollest manner and went back to his mirror. He wasn't sure what to think, actually. Perhaps he should be concerned.

But he'd never show Frank.

Frank cackled. "My source is impeccable."

"Oh? Who is it?"

"Natasha."

"Why would she tell you?"

"She wants to marry you, old boy, and she's paying me lots of money to help spread the word that she's having a baby Staunton. Nick, if it's a boy. Or Nichola, if it's a girl."

"What?"

"She sent me to see her diplomatic host while she's in Town—what's his name?"

"Lord Howell. He's to look after her until she leaves England."

"Right, well, I told the old codger you and the Russian princess carried on while he and his missus were in the country. I gave him a lock of Natasha's hair that I supposedly found at your apartment, and I demanded payment to keep quiet about the baby."

He snorted with amusement.

Nicholas threw down his neckcloth. "Why couldn't Natasha tell Lord and Lady Howell her lies all by herself?"

Frank laughed. "Because then she looks like a conniving widow. This way, she comes across as fairly innocent, lured into bad behavior by an Impossible Bachelor. And just to make sure the Howells don't believe the princess and I are in on this together, she gave me Boris. I told them I'd stolen the beast and would return him only if they pay me a fine sum of money. Both Lord and Lady Howell would never dream she'd give away her precious dog, even for a moment."

"So the Howells will speak to her," Nicholas said. "She'll be suitably agitated, denying everything, at least in the short run, and begging for her dog back. Which means they'll believe you really are a blackmailer, brother. They'll also believe I fathered her child. It's a clever ruse."

"But it *is* true," said Frank, "at least the part about you sleeping with her."

"She's a widow, not a virgin, and I never slept with her. We had a few titillating romps between the sheets, nothing more."

Frank crossed his arms over his chest and chortled. "Your quibbling doesn't matter, and you know it. It's a matter of diplomatic protocol. Lord Howell was assigned to look after Natasha, and he'll be in massive trouble at Whitehall if it gets out that you had an affair with her, especially if she's with child. Marriage, on the other hand, is a respectable outcome."

"Look, Frank. I'm sure I'm not the only man in London who's found himself in the princess's bed. A widow taking lovers is hardly unheard of, and I certainly took care that she wouldn't be with child."

"How do you know—if you were drugged?"

A small part of Nicholas was alarmed that Frank knew those details of his liaison, but he quickly brushed it off. "A man knows."

But he must admit, he didn't know one hundred percent, did he? He'd never been drugged. What if—

No. It couldn't be.

Nevertheless, he was uneasy. "And why should you care whom I marry anyway, Frank? Isn't one girl the same as the next to you? Why the preference for the princess over Lady Poppy?"

"Revenge, of course." Frank scratched his ear, quite as if he were speaking about the weather. "For you always being the good brother and having the title and all the money."

"How is my marrying Natasha allowing you to get revenge?"

"You lust after that Poppy woman, and I can't wait to see her throw you over. She'll call you a scoundrel. An utter disgrace. But even better, you'll have to live with Natasha—and her dogs—the rest of your life. Sergei's already out buying a proper dueling pistol with which to kill you if you don't marry her, and Natasha's being comforted by the Howells as we speak."

Nicholas didn't deign to reply.

Frank turned purple. "You think you're always going to win, don't you? Well, not this time." He slammed the door behind him.

It bounced back open.

"Don't forget to walk Boris if you know what's good for you!" Nicholas called after him.

Sure enough, a mere ten minutes later, Lord Howell sent Nicholas a note demanding his presence at his home immediately.

Dear God. He'd have to cancel his card game and find a way out of the mess with Natasha. But how could he do so without making her look like an idiot?

And was it possible that he had fathered a child with her while he was drugged?

He deserved the scare, he realized now. He'd run wild with no stops on his behavior for far too long.

But, no. He couldn't have fathered Natasha's child. He wouldn't let blind panic rule his sense of logic. What man would be able to forget the pleasure involved in making a baby? And how could a man even *have* a fertile sexual response if he'd been so drugged that the next day he'd had trouble waking up well after the sun had risen?

He was sure, absolutely sure, someone else had fathered Natasha's baby. Either that, or she wasn't with child at all.

She'd have to confess, that's what. He'd get her to see the light.

But when he arrived at the Howell residence, Natasha wouldn't budge.

"You compromised me," she said, blubbering in front of Lord and Lady Howell. Her corgis were draped over every sofa arm, and a few were sleeping on the rug. "I'm having your baby."

Nicholas inhaled a deep breath and instantly regretted it. The smell of dog, which he usually didn't object to, was rather overwhelming.

"Natasha." His tone demanded she look at him. Finally, she met his gaze. "Tell the Howells you're making this up."

She burst into false tears again and collapsed on the sofa, somehow finding a spot between two of her pets.

"You're making things worse, Your Grace," Lady Howell cried. "She's already feeling poorly, thanks to you and your—"

She fixed her beady eyes on his crotch.

"Bettina," Lord Howell chastised her.

Lady Howell puffed up like a dandelion. "So? Am I to mince words? This so-called gentleman bedded our Russian charge. And now she's with child. He must do the right thing this instant and marry her."

Lord Howell stood. "Of course he shall. Won't you

come up to scratch, Your Grace? You're from an old and proud line."

Lady Howell drew in her chin. "But we'd never heard of it, dear, until—"

"It's an old and proud line, Bettina." The tips of Lord Howell's ears were turning bright pink.

"*Duke?* Will you do the right thing?" Lady Howell's assertiveness was all but forgotten as she stared at him with wide, worried eyes.

Nicholas felt the weight of his noble family tree bearing down on him. They may never have heard of the Drummond line, but it *was* old and proud. And he wasn't a blackguard. "Of course I would do the right thing *if*—"

"See?" Lord Howell whirled on his wife. "He'll do it."

"Lord Howell—" Nicholas objected. "I never said—"

Lord Howell put up his palm. "You'll do the right thing. And by tomorrow we expect your other engagement shall be called off. We'll keep Natasha inside till that's done. Then you'll take her to Gretna."

"We'll put it about that you two were irresistibly in love and ran off together," said Lady Howell.

Nicholas's fists curled at his sides as he took in the conniving miss who never seemed to run out of crocodile tears.

"Natasha." His voice was icy. "When you can think more clearly, you'll do the right thing and tell your hosts the truth."

She put a trembling hand to her breast. "I—I don't know what you mean. Your own brother saw you leaving here the morning the Howells were away. If your own brother would turn you in, how could you *not* be guilty?"

He was extremely tempted to take his pistol and shoot a vase off the mantel simply because he was livid. But he knew dramatics would get him nowhere. This family was convinced he was to marry Natasha.

He bowed to Lord and Lady Howell. "I will *not* be returning. The princess will have something important to tell you, so please urge her to confess."

But nobody said anything. Lord Howell merely stared right through him, Lady Howell patted Natasha on the head, and Natasha's face contorted and turned red.

"I love you, *Niccckky,*" she bawled.

The dogs began to bark at her. One of them howled. It was a veritable canine chorus, except for one fat corgi who gave a leisurely scratch to his ear with his hind leg and then sank to the rug and closed his eyes.

He was probably as sick of the whole business as Nicholas was. The worst part about it was—

It was his own fault. He'd refused to grow up when he should have. And now he was paying the price. On that bitter note, he stepped over a particularly shrill yapping corgi and departed without another word.

CHAPTER 35

That same evening, in a small sitting room off his bed-chamber, Lord Derby patted Poppy's hand. She could feel a new beginning flower between them already, like the pretty daisies painted on Mama's box of treasures. Together, they'd spent the last thirty minutes sorting through most of it.

Poppy had laughed, and she'd cried, examining the items her mother had valued.

She was seeing many of her mother's things for the first time in years . . . her favorite brush. Her crystal atomizer with the cobalt-blue tassel. Her squashy red felt pin cushion Poppy had made as a young girl and which her mother brought out at every opportunity, especially when her friends were over.

And a miniature of Mama holding Poppy as a baby. She and her father both cried the longest over that one. But they were having a wonderful time, despite all the emotion.

"Despite your rough beginning, are you pleased with your choice of fiancé?" Papa asked her now. His voice had a whole new quality—not new, actually, but old. It sounded the way it had before Mama had died.

Poppy girded herself to pretend she wasn't planning on leaving the Duke of Drummond behind. She couldn't tell Papa of her plans, even with this new closeness. Not yet. It would ruin things between them.

"Of course," she answered. "Although I worry about what will happen to you when I'm married and gone."

And she was. If she ever met a man she wanted to marry, what *would* happen to Papa?

Lord Derby chuckled. "I'm flattered, but a lady's first allegiance should be to her husband. *Not* to her father."

"Oh, dear." She felt a bit choked up again. "I don't like to hear that."

"But it's the truth." Papa's tone was gentle. "When a woman finds the right man, she must cleave to him, putting the marriage first and all else second."

"But—"

He hugged her close, and Poppy was happy, but she couldn't help noticing what Papa had said.

Marry the right *man.*

He'd qualified his statement.

Had she misjudged him? She'd lied to all her suitors the past three years, but perhaps if she'd only explained to Papa what sort of man was the right man for her, she never would have had to go to such lengths.

She took his hand. "Papa, did you *really* believe Lord Eversly was the right man for me?"

He made a wry face. "I'd no idea. But it's a bit late for that, isn't it? Perhaps I should have asked you."

He searched her eyes, concerned.

"I should have told you," she said simply.

"Will Drummond suit, do you think?"

She gave a small nod.

"Good." Papa patted her hand. "I like him. I think you'll suit very well."

She felt a surge of emotion close her throat. She thought . . . nay, she *knew* she and Nicholas would suit very well, too. Pity that he didn't seem to be aware of that. She tried to fend off the sense that a black cloud was forming around her, one that would bring her pain.

Papa scratched his ear, which he was wont to do when he was embarrassed. "I have a small box, too," he said. "If you don't mind, I'd rather go through it with you while I'm alive. I—I wish your mother had had that chance."

"I'd love that." Poppy grinned at him, and her heart felt lighter at his enthusiasm.

He had a pack of old playing cards that had belonged to her grandfather, and a fine cheroot he'd received the day Poppy had been born. "I received two," he said, "and smoked one. I wanted to save it, you see. It's not often a man is blessed with two beautiful women in his life. The first time I saw you, you looked at me with your mother's eyes and gave a lusty cry with her same rosebud mouth."

"Oh, Papa." Poppy wiped away a tear again.

With slightly shaky hands, he unwrapped the final small tissue bundle.

Poppy inhaled a sharp breath. There they were, the

cuff links from the portrait. They gleamed black and gold in the candlelight.

"These are my special cuff links," he said. "I wore these the day I proposed to your mother and I wore them to our wedding. I wore them to your baptism. And I wore them to a wonderful ball we attended in St. Petersburg at the Winter Palace." He hesitated. "Your mother had never looked so beautiful. And we had never been so much in love. We had less than a few months together after that."

Poppy swallowed. "They're wonderful, Papa."

"Her death was so sudden," he said quietly. "I believe I never got over the shock of it. I'm sorry, my dear. I should have reached out to you."

"I did feel lonely," she admitted. "But I'm sure for you it was even worse."

Now that she knew what it felt like to love Nicholas, she could understand the depth of her father's grief a little more.

He kissed her cheek. "When you gave that dinner party, you were so like your mother."

"Was I?" That made her happy. "But—" She paused. "You didn't like the meal. You were very quiet."

He looked down at his hands and then up at her. "It wasn't the meal. I was sulking. Afraid to move forward. Since your mother's death, I haven't been able to touch those Russian memories without flinching. And look at you, you've been working on that blasted needlepoint of the Winter Palace for years." He chuckled.

She had to laugh at that, too. "I have, haven't I?"

"You were also able to produce Russian dishes for

the party," Papa said, "and still have a smile on your face. That night I learned something. I learned my own daughter was braver than I am."

"Oh, Papa!" She hugged him. "Don't say that. You asked me to make English dishes and I ignored you. I'm so sorry."

He shook his head. "Don't be. You woke me up that night. Made me see I need to . . . to move on. Part of that is remembering the past, but not the sad times so much as focusing on the good."

"And we had many good times," Poppy reminded him.

"Indeed, we did." Lord Derby smiled. "Let's not waste any more time on blame or regret. Just remember this. I love you."

"And I love you."

She clasped his hand. But their happy moment was interrupted when an urgent knock came at their front door.

"Who could that be this late?" Lord Derby stood, listening.

"I've no idea." Poppy stood as well, feeling vaguely fearful. It was awfully late for a knock at the front door.

They walked down the corridor together to the top of the stairs. Poppy was surprised to see the prince and princess below. Kettle was busy taking Prince Sergei's hat and cape. Natasha stood by his side, dogless, and when she looked up and saw Poppy, her expression was, oddly enough—

Triumphant.

CHAPTER 36

Nicholas was miserable. And all because of a woman.

Not Natasha. She was merely a pest—a very bad pest who had wrangled her way too far into his life. Somehow he'd escape her.

But he saw no way to evade the inevitably wretched depression he would soon be floundering in . . . all because a certain bossy, emerald-eyed miss would no doubt despise him when she heard the news.

He could see the headline in the papers now: "Duke Fathers Russian Princess's Baby Out of Wedlock."

It was absurd. But that was exactly the situation he found himself in.

If Poppy had any regard for him, surely she would lose it after word got out. Somewhere deep inside him, he couldn't bear that thought. But he knew what to do—what he'd always done when unwanted feelings attempted to surface: bury them under layers of busyness. Accomplishments.

Attention to duty.

After the debacle at the Howells', he went straight to

Groop, who practically lived at his office. Nicholas must admit he was glad the old fellow was still there, candles burning at his desk. He could use a bit of paternal advice.

Groop wore a closed half-smile. "So you're looking for a way out. Even though you might be the father."

"I'm *not* the father." He was almost certain of it. "She could be making the whole thing up, as far as I know."

"You'll simply have to go along with it."

"You mean *marry* her?"

"You could be of use to us in St. Petersburg. It could mean a promotion."

Nicholas scoffed. "Not possible."

"It's either marry her, or devise a means to get out of it *after* you retrieve the painting. We can't afford to upset the twins so much that they pack their bags and leave England with the portrait before the ball."

"Are you sure we can't go in any earlier than the ball to get it?"

"No. That night affords us the least risk. Large crowds and many distractions suit this sort of operation. Which reminds me, we'll have to call a high-level meeting to ensure Lord Derby stays away that evening. He could raise a public stink and interfere with our plans. You've abandoned his daughter, after all."

Nicholas raked a hand through his hair. "Can we not tell Lord Derby and Lady Poppy the new betrothal is a sham? That it won't stand much longer because I won't allow it?"

"They have no need to know. We can't afford to let any word get back to the princess."

"But . . . but Lady Poppy will think I'm a scoundrel!"

"Well, aren't you?" It was the closest Groop had ever come to looking amused.

Nicholas flinched. He *had* been a dissolute fool. "It's too late, isn't it? To shed my wastrel reputation."

Groop almost scoffed. "You know what that would require."

"Yes, either dying or keeping my breeches on. A year ago I wouldn't have been able to tell you which one was worse. But now—"

"Now you've matured. It happens to the best of us, Your Grace. And since you're in quite a quandary, I'd say yes. It *is* too late."

So it was settled. Nicholas's engagement with Natasha was *on*. No more trying to get out of it, at least until after the painting was safely in his hands.

And by then, Poppy—at least her tender feelings for him—would be long gone.

"Don't go yet, Your Grace."

Nicholas paused at the door, sensing bad news by the way Groop hesitated before he spoke.

"It seems rather a shame," the spymaster said, "but the higher-ups have recently decided to destroy the painting after they get their look at it. They claim we can't very well have a portrait stay in circulation with a picture of a mole on it. Our modus operandi must be protected."

Nicholas's heart sank. "No," he whispered.

She'd never forgive him.

Ever.

It was the final nail in the coffin of his plan to make her his wife. Even he wasn't willing to marry someone who hated him. Up until now, he'd had hope. He'd made progress with her—true progress, from total un-acceptance of him to the point that they'd become friends—but now . . . now all those efforts might as well never have occurred.

"It can't be helped." Groop was implacable. "You have to seize the portrait on behalf of the Service and resign yourself to never seeing it again. Duty above all, Your Grace. And Lady Poppy has no need to know. You're the one charged with destroying the painting after our analysis is complete. The MR is contingent upon this action. Dispose of it completely in a timely, untraceable manner which calls—"

"No suspicion upon me or the Service." Nicholas hardened his heart. "I know the drill."

Duty first.

Duty first.

He swallowed back the myriad emotions clamoring within him. Sometimes it paid in unexpected ways to work for the Service.

And sometimes it was a living hell.

CHAPTER 37

Poppy felt the oddest butterflies in her stomach. Neither the prince nor princess gave Papa a cordial social greeting in response to his own gracious welcome. Sergei's apology for bothering them at the late hour was terse at best, and he made no effort to kiss her hand.

Instead, he inclined his head. "I've a matter of grave import to discuss with you, Lord Derby and Lady Poppy."

"Please come in." Lord Derby gestured toward the drawing room.

Once their guests were seated, she offered brandy for Sergei and ratafia for Natasha.

"Nothing for me," Natasha said shortly, her rudeness coming as no surprise.

"Thank you, no," Sergei responded, his eyes giving nothing away. But he was more formal than she'd ever seen him.

Poppy tried to remain calm. But something was terribly wrong, and it had to be about the portrait. Did they know the painting was of her mother? Was that a complication that somehow interfered with their plans for it?

She looked at her father, whose expression was rather concerned, as well.

Sergei drew in a deep breath. "I must involve you in a conversation that you might find distasteful."

Natasha's eyes glinted. "*I* will tell her."

"No." Sergei was curt. "*I'll* tell her."

"May I remind you there are two of us here," Lord Derby said. "You shall have to tell us both."

While the twins glared at each other, there came another urgent knock on the front door.

"Open up!" a masculine voice cried.

Poppy sat up straighter. It sounded vaguely like Nicholas. But not like the Nicholas she'd come to know. This voice sounded rude. Obnoxious.

There was a small ruckus in the hall—Kettle's voice could be heard murmuring a hasty greeting—and a few seconds later, Nicholas pushed past the butler before he could announce him and strode into the room.

He looked wilder than she'd ever seen him.

"Why, it's Lady Poppy Smith-Barnes and her noble father," he said, his thumbs in the top of his breeches. "As well as her very good Russian friends."

He bowed and sent a defiant smirk around the company. Then he pulled a flask out of his pocket and took a long draught.

Poppy was mortified. And confused. *Very* confused.

Lord Derby put up his quizzing glass. "Is that *you*, Drummond? In your cups?"

Sergei stood. "Perhaps you should come back another time, Drummond," he said testily.

"You'd like that, wouldn't you?" Nicholas arched a rude brow at him. "I suggest you sit and be quiet. Or leave. Both you and your sister. We've had enough of your ridiculous spats, haven't we?"

Poppy jumped up. "What is *wrong* with you, Drummond?"

She threw him a desperate look. *Don't you remember you're supposed to keep our Russian friends happy?*

They could leave the country with their uncle's painting.

He *must* remember.

But Nicholas didn't seem to comprehend her meaning. He merely stared at her beneath lowered brows, his gray eyes stormier than she'd ever seen them.

"Yes, Drummond." Lord Derby stood in a huff. "You don't speak that way in my house to my guests. Now behave yourself, or leave."

Natasha put her nose in the air. "I completely agree with Lord Derby. That's no way to speak to—"

Sergei put a hand on her arm in a signal that she be quiet. Natasha scowled, but she did, thankfully, shut her mouth.

"We will stay." Sergei's whole manner was stiff when he sat back down. "But you must not forget—I am a Russian prince."

"And *I* am a princess," said Natasha, her chin in the air.

For goodness' sake, Poppy thought. How many times were they going to remind everyone?

"I am master of this household," Lord Derby said, "and I expect decorum on all sides." He tossed a quelling glance at all their visitors, none of whom seemed intimidated in the least, especially Drummond, who leaned arrogantly against the pianoforte without permission.

Sergei began again. "I was about to inform Lady Poppy and her esteemed father that—"

"*I'll* tell them," Nicholas interrupted, and scratched his jaw rudely in front of the company. "Brace yourselves. You and all of London, actually. The princess and I are to marry."

CHAPTER 38

A strong sensation of shock and fury coursed through Poppy's frame even though she'd insisted from the very first time she'd met the duke that she wouldn't marry him. In fact, she'd planned to end the betrothal in less than a week. Nevertheless, in the eyes of the world, they were betrothed, and from the looks of it, she'd just been royally cast off.

"What could you possibly mean, Drummond?" she demanded. "*We're* engaged."

"Yes, what's this about, Your Grace?" Lord Derby, his face reddening, was on his feet again.

"I regret to inform you my first obligation is to the princess," the duke said coolly. "She's with child, and her guardian, Lord Howell, has made the claim"—he took another swig from his flask—"that I am the father."

"You *are* the father, and you will pay." Sergei jumped up again, his eyes flashing fire.

Poppy's heart fell to her feet.

Lord Derby's face was like granite. "I'd call you

out, Drummond, if I thought I could kill you." Poppy had never heard him so menacing.

"Don't, Papa." She put a hand on his arm. *"Please."*

He took her hand and squeezed it. "I won't, daughter. But it's only because I know what he can do with a pistol. I don't want you an orphan so young."

Poppy's thoughts were jumbled, and she felt hot and cold at the same time. She wished she could faint, but apparently she was too stoic to faint.

She'd been a fool. A complete and utter fool. But she wouldn't dare show the world she was—

Brokenhearted.

Oh, God.

Was she really? Was this what a broken heart felt like? She'd trusted Nicholas with her body and allowed him to see into her soul and—

Become friends with him. *More* than friends.

She released Papa's hand, stood, walked to the pianoforte, and slapped the Duke of Drummond across the cheek.

"Ouch," he muttered, rubbing his jaw.

"I despise you, Nicholas Staunton," she said between gritted teeth. "And I never want to see you again."

Natasha said nothing, but Poppy saw her eyes light with amusement.

Nicholas shrugged and looked around the company. "What's done is done." He returned his gaze to Poppy. "I'll go now. It's obvious you're not terribly . . . *thrilled* to have me here."

She felt a stillness inside. For a split second, the veil lifted from his gaze. It became clear. Steady. She imagined she could see the old Nicholas. The true Nicholas. The one she'd come to care for.

"Demmed right we're not thrilled!" Lord Derby pointed to the door. "Out with you, Drummond. I believe everyone should go, as a matter of fact." He looked pointedly at Natasha and Sergei.

Natasha threw a smug look at Poppy, then went to Nicholas and tried to cling to his arm. But he dodged the maneuver by pushing off the pianoforte and taking another swig from his flask.

"Come, sister," Sergei said. "And you, Drummond, if you know what's good for you."

Poppy blinked back tears. But before anyone could leave ahead of her, she turned on her heel and marched out.

Departing the drawing room before her uninvited guests seemed a paltry statement to make.

Tomorrow morning, she would leave Town instead.

CHAPTER 39

Nicholas sent word round to his three best friends, Lord Harry Traemore, Captain Arrow, and Viscount Lumley, to meet him at their club.

"So there's no hope for you and Lady Poppy?" asked Captain Arrow, who was in Town for a fortnight's shore leave.

"How could there be?" Nicholas shrugged. "She certainly doesn't want me anymore. I'm a scoundrel."

No one disagreed, he noticed.

But Lumley patted his back. "I'd hope for the best, old boy. Perhaps this Russian princess will be just as suited for you as Molly is for Harry. Even if she drugged you."

"And claims you seduced her," added Arrow.

"And has too many dogs," muttered Harry.

Nicholas looked miserably into his tumbler of brandy. "I certainly was no angel." He drained his glass and stared at his friends. "But she's not, either. I don't believe for a minute I fathered her child. I don't believe there even *is* a child. She's mad. And for some reason, she's chosen me to be her favored suitor. I think it was because I was kind to her dogs. I told her they could become ill from whatever substance she used to drug me."

"Well, we should make you her *un*favorite suitor," said Lumley with a twinkle in his eye. "I've loads of practice with that."

"Good point." Arrow chuckled. "Although why a handsome devil like you has trouble with women, I've no idea, Lumley. What should Nicholas do to have her call it off? Because telling a woman you have another love interest sometimes only makes her dig her claws in harder."

"You should know," said Harry, "with your women in every port."

Arrow threw him a dirty look. "I'd claim you were jealous, but I can't, can I? You're happy as a clam with your Molly."

"You know it," said Harry, with a wink and a smile.

"Right." Lumley sat up. "Here's what you should do, Drummond. Be attentive. Kind. Bring the princess flowers. Tell her you worship the ground she walks on. And then—"

"I need something that works fast. That's guaranteed."

"Oh, in that case"—Lumley nodded and pulled a sheet of paper out of his pocket—"just show her this." He handed the sheet to Nicholas and told him what to say.

Nicholas felt a glimmer of hope. "Thanks." He tucked the paper in his coat. "Leave it to the Impossible

Bachelors to help get me out of this mess. I hope it works."

"It'll work, old boy," Lumley assured him.

"After you rid yourself of Natasha, what will you do about Lady Poppy?" asked Arrow.

Nicholas shrugged. "Nothing. She told me she never wants to see me again."

He couldn't tell them about the portrait, about how his job required he choose duty over all else. And that Poppy would never forgive him for letting her mother's portrait be destroyed.

"You don't love her?" Lumley asked. "She's a gorgeous thing, and I'm tempted to pursue her if you won't. She seems the type who'd appreciate a decent fellow like me."

"Yes, she would," Nicholas said miserably, then cast Lumley a dark look. "But don't even think about it."

Arrow chuckled. "Oh-ho, so you have feelings for her, after all? I assumed you were succumbing to the parson's mousetrap for money. It's the only good reason I can think of for any fellow with a brain to get married." He angled a grin Harry's way. "Pardon me, Harry. You're the exception, of course. We know you're whip-smart and married Molly for love."

Harry chuckled. "Someday you'll smarten up, too, lads, never fear. I only hope it's not too late for Nicholas. One has to fight for the right woman. Not sit about being soft and letting wily Russian princesses take over."

He directed a careless grin Nicholas's way, but his gaze was serious.

Nicholas felt the barb.

"I don't *have* a right woman," he said testily. "And I certainly don't plan to wed Natasha. I intend to stay a bachelor as long as I can."

How long would that be?

Marriage was a requirement of his job at the Service. And Prinny might soon be breathing down his neck again to make him participate in another Impossible Bachelors wager.

Soon he'd have to find a milk-and-water miss to marry. A boring girl with a bland expression and nothing but duty in her expression when they'd make love in their marital bed.

Duty.

When someone applied the concept to life with *him*, he certainly didn't like it.

He didn't want duty in a marriage. He wanted fun. And spontaneity.

He wanted Poppy.

But it was too late.

He took a large swallow of brandy. The burning sensation in his stomach masked the emptiness he felt inside.

"So you'll stay a bachelor as long as you can, eh?" Harry appraised him sharply. "Lucky you."

There was a pause, a brief awkwardness in the air, then Arrow laughed. So did Lumley.

Nicholas decided to take Harry's remark at face value. "Yes, lucky me," he said, and everyone—even Harry, the only legshackled man among them—raised their snifters in a toast to his future.

CHAPTER 40

Poppy knew she'd fallen in love with Nicholas. She just didn't know how much until she'd left London immediately the morning after their broken engagement, kissing her distressed father good-bye and journeying forth only with her maid and a manservant, for the countryside of Kent, where Aunt Charlotte already waited.

There'd be nothing to *do* in Kent, Poppy mused as she passed by miles of pasture and small villages. Nothing to do but read and do needlepoint and have tea with the vicar's wife.

She hoped that would be a good thing. She longed to put the embarrassment of her broken engagement behind her, as well as the humiliating scene in front of Sergei and Natasha.

But unfortunately, with only a quiet maid and somber manservant to keep her company, her thoughts went constantly back to her time in London, to all the wonderful moments she'd had with Nicholas. And she realized in an appalling moment of clarity—

She realized it would be no small task getting over the wicked Duke of Drummond.

Emphasis on *wicked*.

She'd known because of the way her body had reacted when they'd locked eyes at his *thrilled* comment and they'd had a flash of connection—despite everything that had gone wrong.

Much had, of course. He'd had an intimate history with the princess, one that Poppy had known nothing about. He'd fathered her baby.

But there was nothing Poppy could do but put the scoundrel behind her and move on, more a Spinster than ever before . . . because now she had a broken heart.

She was only miles from the village in Kent when a large carriage passed her own. It was painted with an impressive shield that immediately told her Sergei must be inside it.

Her own carriage rolled to a stop, and she braced herself.

What could Sergei want?

She sighed and wished him gone already.

He came striding up and opened her carriage door. "Lady Poppy," he said, "please alight." He held out his hand. "I've something of great importance to ask you."

She shook her head. "Your Highness, I already told you—"

He chuckled. "It's not what you think. I insist. Please step down."

So with an importuning glance at her maid and man-servant (hopefully, they would come to her aid if she needed them), she descended.

Sergei escorted her to a nearby tree stump. "Please," he said. "Sit."

Which she did with a great deal of trepidation.

He placed a lingering kiss on her hand. "You are as beautiful as ever. Perhaps more beautiful than you were last time I saw you."

Goodness. He was certainly laying it on thick. And it had been less than one day since their awkward meeting at her house. She found it hard to believe she'd looked beautiful then. She imagined her eyes had been popping out of her head at all the wretched goings-on, and her face must have been beet red, as well.

He got down on one knee. "Lady Poppy, I come to bestow upon you the magnificent honor of being my bride. I see it is the only way I can have you."

Good God.

She had to restrain a giggle. He was the most conceited man she'd ever met. Once again, she wondered how she'd ever thought he was the only man who could ever tempt her to drop her membership in the Spinsters Club.

This was the moment she'd hoped for, the one that she'd thought would make her life perfect.

He *was* a Russian prince. Some might tell her she should instantly say yes. But the old pat excuse went running through her head . . .

Thank you, but I must decline. I love the Duke of Drummond.

Only this time, her explanation wasn't some made-up story based on Cook's outlandish tales. This time, her reason was genuine. Even in her misery, she recognized the irony of her situation, that the lie that had conveniently extricated her from so many unwanted betrothals now inflicted pain on her in its truth.

Sergei sniffed, a long, drawn-out sniff. "I can promise we'll see very little of my eccentric sister and her husband. They'll stay in England. We'll make our home in Russia. I will enjoy making many babies with you, but you will pretend to be a Spinster every Saturday evening, no? It will be our game."

And then his perfectly sculpted mouth stretched in a lecherous grin.

She slid off the stump. "Your Highness, thank you, but no, thank you. I really must be on my way."

He grabbed her arm. "But Lady Poppy. I am a Russian prince!"

"Yes." She smiled at him. "But you are a *pompous* Russian prince. You hum in the most awful manner when you should be quiet. You asked me to be your mistress and parade about naked with a parasol, and then you invited me to a terrifying party where all your guests got drunk and I was treated like a prisoner by your footman. Now you have the temerity to come after me on the road, as if I'll fall at your feet and be grateful for your attentions. Spare me. I don't want them."

He angled his head. "You don't?"

She exhaled a breath. "I'm in love with someone else."

"Who?" He wore a babyish pout.

"The man marrying your sister. The Duke of Drummond, my former fiancé."

Sergei scoffed. "He is but a duke."

"I know," she said, patting his arm. "But as you are selfish and vain, this should make you feel better—I can't have him. So I shall continue being a Spinster. Probably forever."

The prince kissed her hand. "If I can't have you, I like knowing you'll be a Spinster forever."

"Ohhhh!" she cried, and stalked off.

"But Poppy! I love you!" he called after her.

"Not as much as you love yourself!" she cried over her shoulder, and clambered back into her carriage.

"Please leave right away," she told the driver, her heart beating hard with fury *and* satisfaction.

The driver did just that, although it took some expert maneuvering to get around the prince's coach-and-four. It was another hour to the cottage, long enough to muse on how much she'd changed since she'd met Nicholas. She was braver. More adventurous. And she certainly didn't suffer fools lightly.

And now she was lonelier than she'd ever been in her life.

Aunt Charlotte was surprised to see her, of course, and then terribly concerned when Poppy relayed the entire story about Nicholas and Natasha. She also told her about Sergei's rather indecent proposal of marriage.

Her aunt listened, and at the tawdry tale's conclusion, patted her hand. "You came to the right place. We'll be secluded here. I'll make you tea and cakes and—"

"No Bath buns, please." Poppy was adamant on that point.

They'd remind her too much of Nicholas and that walk they'd taken trying to lure the gander back to his pond, as well as the impromptu "Bath bun" Nicholas had given her afterward.

Too many things reminded her of him.

Late that afternoon Aunt Charlotte quietly netted a bag while Poppy attempted to immerse herself in *Clarissa*. She was failing miserably, so when a knock sounded at their door, she was happy for the diversion.

A moment later, a manservant came to the sitting room. "Lord Eversly to see you, ladies. Shall I allow him in?"

"Certainly," said Aunt Charlotte.

Poppy was a bit stunned.

Lord Eversly, carrying two large bouquets of flowers, strode into their small sitting room, exuding good cheer.

Poppy laid her book aside on a low table and stood. "Lord Eversly. This is a surprise."

He smiled warmly, which was a balm to her sad heart. "I hope a good surprise." He handed her a bouquet full of red roses.

"Thank you," she said, entirely flummoxed.

"My pleasure," he said, and handed the other bouquet, filled with daisies and other charming flowers, to Aunt Charlotte.

Aunt Charlotte beamed. "We're thrilled to see you, Eversly. Welcome to the countryside of Kent."

Thrilled.

Of course, Poppy had to think of Nicholas at that moment.

Lord Eversly bowed low over Aunt Charlotte's hand. "Such a pleasure to see you, my good lady. Your brother sends his compliments."

Poppy froze. Lord Eversly had gone to see her father?

There was an awkward silence.

"Tea?" she asked him.

"Later, perhaps," he said politely, then turned to Aunt Charlotte. "Would you mind if your niece took me on a tour of the garden?"

Aunt Charlotte shot Poppy a meaningful look, which Poppy ignored. There was absolutely no possibility the earl had romantic intentions toward her. She'd already declined him. Surely he wouldn't try to win her again.

"Lady Poppy?" Lord Eversly eyed her hopefully. "Would you care to go with me?"

"Certainly," she said, a trifle hesitant, although she wasn't sure why.

Outside they wandered through rows of rosebushes.

Lord Eversly stopped near a charming fountain of an angel. "Lady Poppy, I shall get right to the heart of the matter. As I have expressed to your father in a visit to him this morning, I care for you very much. When I heard Drummond is to marry the Russian princess, my heart told me that perhaps it was not too late . . . for me."

He gave her a meaningful look.

She inhaled a breath. She'd no idea what to say, so she thought hard for a moment.

"Lord Eversly," she said eventually, "I'm flattered by your offer. And I'll be happy to give you my answer at the Lievens' ball . . . if you can wait that long."

For a brief second, he appeared taken aback, but then he recovered. "Of course," he said warmly. "I'll be happy to wait until the first waltz. But until that time, I'd like to leave you with a memory I hope shall sway you."

He took her in his arms and kissed her. The kiss wasn't particularly chaste, either. He kissed her thoroughly and well.

When he pulled back, he searched her face.

She forced herself to give him a little smile.

"Think about it," he said. "I'll make you a good husband. We can be happy together."

"Yes," Poppy whispered. "I'll think about it."

She'd felt nothing when he'd kissed her, nothing but an awareness of his sweet nature. But having a kind husband was a good thing, was it not?

The rest of his visit passed pleasantly enough. He stayed for dinner and told them he had plans to spend the night at the village inn. He would leave early the next morning for a meeting in London.

Throughout dinner and their short conversation afterward, Poppy was anxious to tell Aunt Charlotte what had transpired in the garden, and she sensed her aunt was anxious, as well. So when they finally shut the front door behind the earl, Aunt Charlotte didn't even wait to walk back to the sitting room.

"Do tell," she said in the cozy entryway.

"He asked me to marry him. Again."

"My heavens." Aunt Charlotte bit her lip. "Well, we both already know you don't love him. If you don't love him, you won't marry him, correct?"

"Yes, I know." Poppy sighed. "According to the Spinsters Club. But I'm not sure about those rules anymore."

She wandered listlessly back to the sitting room and sank onto a settee.

Aunt Charlotte sat next to her. "Why, dear?"

"Because look where love has gotten me."

"You love Drummond, don't you?" Aunt Charlotte's tone was sober.

Poppy nodded slowly. It hurt to acknowledge the fact.

Aunt Charlotte sighed.

"Drummond is to marry Natasha." Poppy forced herself to say the words. "And according to the Spinsters Club, I should remain a Spinster because I can't have the man I love. But all those rules are based upon the idea that true love is the only reason to marry. You yourself told me to stay open to the possibilities."

And so had Nicholas, Poppy recalled bitterly.

"I did, didn't I?" Aunt Charlotte said, her bright blue eyes troubled.

Poppy hesitated. "Quite frankly, I don't know if I can live alone the rest of my life thinking about Drummond. I'd rather stay busy—with a good husband, many children, and a new life. I'd like to start over. Who's to say I can't fall in love with Lord Eversly? And even if I can't, we can become good friends."

"You're being very practical," Aunt Charlotte said. "And I must admit, I've found solace in other things, too." She grasped Poppy's hand. "But you misread my intentions, dear, about staying open to romantic possibilities. You must believe true happiness is possible with Eversly. You can't marry him simply to run away. Or to cover your hurt."

"I'm not sure yet what I'll do," said Poppy, squeezing her hand back. "So please be patient with me while I think about it this week."

"Of course. We'll have a peaceful few days."

But the next morning, several village women came to visit.

"The Russian prince was seen on the road to our village," said the squire's wife, her cheeks pink with excitement. "Someone said he intercepted your carriage, brought you out of it, and got down on a knee and proposed. And then another man, an earl, came here with a massive bouquet of roses yesterday. You're a popular young lady."

"When is the wedding?" said another woman.

"And whom shall you choose?" asked a third. "We heard the awful news about your other fiancé. Drummond. He's to marry the Russian princess."

"Yes, he is." Poppy smiled awkwardly. "I'm sorry to disappoint you, but as of now, there is to be no wedding for me."

The faces of the ladies all registered disappointment.

"Poppy's still thinking," said Aunt Charlotte.

"So the earl, too, proposed yesterday?" the squire's wife asked hopefully.

Poppy sighed. "It's a private matter, ladies. That's all I can say."

"We understand." The ladies departed with many friendly wishes for a good day. But the rest of the afternoon, other villagers gathered nearby in little clusters and were staring at the house.

At dinner that evening, the squire himself knocked on the door.

"I'm going to stop this right now," Poppy said, and opened the door, Aunt Charlotte at her side.

"It's my understanding," the squire intoned, "that Lady Poppy is to be married to the Russian prince."

Aunt Charlotte opened her mouth to say something, but Poppy cut her off. "I'm sorry, sir, but your information is incorrect. Lady Charlotte and I are departing in the morning for London."

And she tried to shut the door.

But the squire stopped it with his hand. "Of course, you'll have many parties to attend in London before the big event. But do let us know when the nuptial feast will occur. If it's to be in Town, my wife and I would be honored to represent the village."

"Thank you," Poppy answered, and managed to shut the door. "Tomorrow morning," she said grimly, leaning against it, "we're leaving this place and going back to London to get some peace."

"I told you once before, village life is as grueling as Town life, if not more." Aunt Charlotte chuckled.

But Poppy wasn't amused. She packed her bags and went to bed that night with much to contemplate. The adventures of *Clarissa* called, however, and she was dying to forget her own troubles. So she opened the novel and read about Clarissa's until her candle burned low.

CHAPTER 41

Nicholas wasn't happy. Every night he dreamed about that wretched scene at Lord Derby's, where Poppy told him she never wanted to see him again. And every morning he'd wake up and hear in his head the cryptic comment Harry had made at their club:

Lucky you.

Was he really lucky?

Or wasn't he?

He stared at the small oil painting above his desk—a drawing room scene of him and Frank as boys—and came to a decision. He had nothing to lose.

Absolutely nothing.

His properties and title were in a state of decay, his brother was a wastrel, and Poppy rightfully despised him. The sting of her dismissive slap on his jaw had brought home to him the realization that every good thing in his life had slipped away. He wasn't sure how he'd come to this point, why he'd neglected to respect the age-old adage that nothing worthwhile comes easily.

But looking into Poppy's scornful eyes the night

they'd ended their betrothal, he'd understood as never before that good things came at a price, a price he'd been unwilling to pay—

Until now.

He couldn't fix everything, but he could do one thing right.

He was going to work on his relationship with Frank. He'd held his sibling at arm's length all these years because Frank had gone from being a brother to a burden. Yet it certainly hadn't been Frank's fault that Nicholas had been charged by familial duty to nurture him to manhood in the absence of his parents.

Nicholas had chosen not to accept the responsibility gracefully. He'd been standoffish, all the while pretending Frank had been the one driving him away with his rude manners.

It wasn't true, and Nicholas would have to rectify the situation immediately.

He found Frank in the same cheap hotel. His room was tiny and dim, and the wall was lined with stacks of small, empty kegs. There were a few more now than the last time.

He nudged Frank in the arm, and his brother jerked awake, bleary-eyed, roundly cursing Nicholas.

"You didn't really drink all these, did you?" Nicholas pointed to the kegs.

"None of your business, you rotter. Go away." Frank's waistcoat was stained, and he smelled like he belonged in a barn.

Nicholas hauled him up. "Let's go. We've got some talking to do."

Frank grumbled, of course, but a few minutes later, Nicholas managed to get him outside. "We're going on a walk," he said. "And to get something to eat and drink. But not brandy."

Frank cursed him roundly again, but he stumbled alongside him.

Nicholas took a sideways glance at him. "I've been a bad brother," he said low. "And I've come to apologize."

Frank stopped in his tracks. "Wha'?"

"I've neglected you," Nicholas said simply. "And I'm sorry."

Frank blinked and looked around. "Am I dreaming?"

"Hey, Frankie!" a rough voice called out from across the street. "Here's another!"

Nicholas turned and saw a swarthy cooper in his open-air shop, holding aloft a small keg. "She's a beauty, ain't she?" A bright fire burned merrily behind him.

Frank's face lit up. "She sure is! How much?"

The cooper grinned. "A few more shillings than you have in your pocket, lad. Ask your rich brother for some more money."

Nicholas squinted at the cooper, then looked back at Frank. Was there something special about that barrel? Why was his brother so excited by it?

And why would he want to own it?

"I'm not sure what's going on," he said to Frank. Now that he thought about it, there were no alcohol fumes emanating from the small kegs in Frank's room.

Frank made an ugly face. "It's none of your business."

Nicholas grabbed his arm. "Listen to me, brother. I don't want to hurt you. I want to *understand* you."

"Sure you do. Dummy."

Nicholas prayed for more patience. "Are you . . . are you saving barrels for a reason?"

Frank looked down and bit his lip. "I like them, is all," he muttered. He wouldn't look Nicholas in the eye.

"You like barrels." Nicholas made it a statement.

Frank's forehead was furrowed deeply, but he nodded. Once. Quickly.

This was all very odd, Nicholas thought. But interesting.

"Let's get a couple of meat pies," he said. "And we'll talk about the barrels."

"Hey, governor!" called the cooper. "What's your decision about this keg here?"

"I'll check back with you later," Nicholas called to him, and made a motion with his chin for Frank to keep up. "I want to hear about barrels first."

"All right," Frank said in a surly tone, but at least the pucker in his forehead was gone. And his eyebrows weren't two slash marks, either.

Progress, thought Nicholas, and for the first time in years, he felt a smidgeon of tenderness for his sibling well up in his heart. Just a smidgeon, though. Nothing more.

But still, it was something.

An hour later in a quiet inn, after the two of them had shared a simple meal of steak-and-kidney pie, ale, and a small pudding, Nicholas felt as if he'd just met a person he'd never known. Frank mumbled on and on about barrels. Their different sizes. The various woods used to make them. The great fire always going at the cooper's shop.

He even chuckled when he told the story about how the cooper's cheeks blew out every time he had to squeeze the metal hoops around the staves.

My God, thought Nicholas. The man wanted to be a cooper. He was probably born to be a cooper!

But who'd ever have considered it a possible future for the son of a duke?

No one.

Frank was a tradesman at heart.

"How would you like to learn the coopering trade?" Nicholas asked him.

Frank drew in his chin. "Me?"

Nicholas nodded.

"But I—I can't learn to be a cooper."

"Why not?"

"It's hard work. I don't know how to *do* hard work. I *hate* hard work."

"Here's the secret." Nicholas leaned forward. "It's not hard work when you enjoy it. Then it's called fun. You might work long hours and get tired at the end of the day, but you'll go to bed happy."

"Happy?" Frank scowled.

"It can happen to you," Nicholas said. "You can become happy."

"Really?" Frank's eyes cleared, and Nicholas saw something more than a surly wastrel looking out. "But what would Mother and Father think?"

"Why, they'd want you to be happy. And productive. You want it, too."

"I do?"

"Yes. You've just been too angry to see it. I'm going

to take you back to that cooper. We're going to arrange an apprenticeship. If he says no, we'll find another cooper. We're not going to give up until *you,* Frank Staunton, are making barrels. You've got the brawn *and* you've got the brains. Someday, everyone will be buying Staunton barrels."

Frank grimaced.

But then Nicholas realized it was actually a small, real smile. He couldn't remember the last time he'd seen one on Frank's face.

"But you'll need to stop drinking so much," Nicholas said, "and stealing spoons from White's—"

"Oh, I'll stop. I'll be busy shaping staves," Frank interrupted him.

"Good." Nicholas grinned, happy to see Frank had barely touched his ale, he'd been so excited talking about barrels. "I can't wait to see your progress. I'll visit every week."

"Will the princess come, too?"

"No." Nicholas was firm. "I'm not going to marry her."

Frank's face fell. "But you have to. She paid me good money."

"Where is it now?"

Frank shrugged. "I drank it away. And bought a fine, tall cask."

"I didn't see it in your room."

Frank's eyes bugged out. "That's because . . ."

"What? Spit it out, brother."

Frank sank low in his chair. "That's because I bought it for the princess. She told me I'd better get her one to put Lady Poppy in and then send it on a wagon to the sea, where someone was going to place it on a packet to Australia and release her when the boat set sail. I have it in a special place, where no one can find it, in a small shed behind Lord Howell's residence."

"You're joking."

Frank shook his head.

"You were willing to *kidnap* Lady Poppy?"

Frank blew out a gusty breath. "No." He had the grace to look ashamed. "I was going to tell you sometime. But the princess is scary. Like a witch."

Nicholas knew exactly what he meant. "All right, then. Tell me the rest."

Frank groaned. "The princess said if I didn't do what she said, she wouldn't sleep with me anymore."

"She's sleeping with you?"

"Only once, and it wasn't very good. We were at your apartments—"

"My apartments?"

"Yes. Reading your correspondence. Going through your desk."

"Bloody hell." Nicholas stood up. "You got in my apartments?"

"I told the doorman I was your brother, and she said she was a Russian princess, and then she stuck her hand between his legs and twisted until he screamed, and he opened the door."

"Good God. Why were you there?"

"She wanted to know if you had a new mistress and was looking for signs of one. That, plus she wanted to go through your things and sniff your coats, especially."

"And you went along with all this?"

Frank shrugged. "She's pretty. And then she threw me on the floor and told me to get the cask and instructed me what to do with it, and we rolled about a bit, and I *think* I ravished her."

"You don't remember?"

"No. Next thing I knew, I woke up and she was gone."

"So she drugged you, too."

"I suppose. And then this old man came in and saw me, and I told him almost everything. Not about the cask. Just that I'd heard from the friend of a friend that someone was after ruining your engagement to Lady Poppy and that the princess told me."

"An old man walked into my apartments?"

"Yeah. Ugly bugger. Long face, beady eyes."

Groop.

It had to have been.

"Did he explain why he was there?"

"No, just said he'd been following me and the princess and was concerned when she came out all red-faced and crazed-looking, and I didn't. He said he knew you and I didn't get along, but then told me we should. We're brothers, after all, he said, and he picked me up and bought me a hot meal and gave me some money."

Nicholas wondered why Groop would care about Frank. He wasn't the type to go about being a Good Samaritan or showing himself at all. He usually left the secret trailing of persons of interest to his underlings.

Odd.

But nice somehow, even though Nicholas was furious all this had taken place in his apartments and he'd never known.

And he was even more enraged to think that the princess intended to put Poppy in a barrel and send her to Australia, using his brother to do her dirty work.

His brother.

He simply had to stop thinking about it, or he'd go to the princess now and put *her* in the cask and ship her home.

It was the opposite of what the Service wanted him to do.

CHAPTER 42

Much to Poppy's dismay, when she returned to London, rumors were flying there, too. The newspaper even carried a small article about Sergei's madcap proposal on the road and referred to her as having been lately engaged to the Duke of Drummond.

Poppy didn't go out. Instead, she kept reading *Clarissa*. She was extremely grateful to the author Samuel Richardson for giving her an idea . . .

A dangerous, outrageous idea. Clarissa had been caught up in unseemly events—some of which took place in a brothel—and remained virtuous despite it all, hadn't she?

Poppy's virtue, on the other hand, was hanging on by a thread—she'd thoroughly enjoyed being almost ravished by Drummond—but like Clarissa, she wasn't going to sit and watch the world go by. She was going to put herself on the line.

She was going to *do* something.

Something that even the wicked Duke of Drummond of Cook's tales might do. Something that the real Duke of Drummond thought he was going to do (but wasn't because *she* was).

She was going to retrieve the painting for her family. All by herself.

Hiding out in the open. Isn't that what Lady Derby had done by commissioning that portrait and by being in the Service in the first place?

Poppy was going to hide out in the open, too. She'd be brazen like her mother and Clarissa and hope for the best. She'd retrieve the portrait, and if she got caught, she'd show the world her mother's receipt signed by Revnik and dare anyone to deny its veracity.

It was a gamble. But she was sure the Service wouldn't step forward and make a claim. Hadn't Nicholas told her that the clandestine agency would no more acknowledge its role in anything than a small child would admit to stealing a sweet from his nurse's apron?

And what need would the Service have of the painting, anyway—after they'd seen it and uncovered their precious mole? Which she'd let them do while she was holding on to it—and only in the sanctuary of her own home.

But she needed the Spinsters to help her.

She called on Eleanor and Beatrice at one of their favorite emergency meeting places, the Ribbon Emporium, where no one would ever guess they were talking about anything more substantial than ribbons.

They all shared one big hug.

"We're so glad you're back in Town," said Eleanor.

"And so sorry about Drummond," Beatrice murmured.

"I don't believe the princess's story," said Eleanor.

"Neither do I." Beatrice's eyes were lit with speculation. "She's after Drummond, and she'll get him any way she can."

Poppy gripped both their hands. "The irony is, these last few weeks I've been tasked to keep her happy."

Beatrice drew in her chin. "By whom?"

Poppy bit her lip. "I can't say. But it's possibly a matter of"—she looked around to make sure no one was listening—"*national security*," she whispered.

Eleanor gave a nervous giggle. "You sound as if you're working for the government on a secret mission."

Poppy let her eyes go very wide and said nothing.

Beatrice let out a little squeak. "You are, aren't you?"

"I can't say."

"Pick a pink ribbon if *yes,* and a green ribbon if *no,*" Eleanor urged her.

Poppy picked up a pink ribbon.

"I can't believe it," cried Beatrice.

"This is amazing!" Eleanor clapped her hands.

"I've been dying to tell you about this latest . . . pink ribbon," Poppy said with a grin, "but you really didn't have a need to know. That's some kind of rule the duke must abide by, the need-to-know principle."

"*Drummond?*" Eleanor hastily picked up a yellow ribbon and pretended to examine it. "Is he working on this with you?"

"Oh, dear," said Poppy, totally flustered. "I really can't say, but—"

She held up a pink ribbon.

"He's in on it, too!" Beatrice crowed.

Eleanor's brows flew up. "Goodness, Poppy, what's going on?"

She flushed. "All I can tell you, girls, is that—much as I was dying to tell you before and couldn't—you *do* need to know what I'm up to now. Because this is much more than a simple matter of national security. This has become a Spinsters problem—and we must solve it together."

All three of them exchanged grave looks.

"Tell us what we have to do," Eleanor said.

Beatrice had a noble look in her eye. "We're up to the task."

So Poppy told them about the painting and her plans for it. It would mean Nicholas wouldn't get his M.R. But he was a duke and an intelligent man, she reminded herself, and there were always opportunities for other M.R.'s in the Service.

He'd land on his feet, she had no doubt.

"I have no solid proof Mama commissioned it," she said, "except the receipt Nicholas and I managed to get our hands on—which he says may be fake."

"Why would it be fake?" Eleanor asked.

Poppy drew in a deep breath. "Because my mother . . ." She held up another pink ribbon. "Can you guess?"

Beatrice put her hand to her throat. "Your mother worked for the government? This is getting to be a bit overwhelming."

"Isn't it shocking?" Poppy agreed. "But I know Mama, and I trust my own intuition. She and Revnik both might have colluded to put a message in the painting, but if she's the mother I know, she got that idea after she'd already asked Revnik to paint the portrait as a gift for Papa."

"We believe you," Eleanor said.

"And we're going to help you get it back," said Beatrice.

Poppy was so pleased. "Here's the other part of what I wanted to tell you. I found the man who seems perfect for me."

Eleanor's mouth split into a wide grin. "You have?"

"Who?" Beatrice's eyes widened.

Poppy tried to say who it was, but his name got stuck in her throat. She was angry. And hurt. She felt the veriest stooge.

"Oh, dear." Beatrice sighed. "It's the Duke of Drummond, isn't it?"

Poppy nodded. "You know he's marrying Natasha. And even if he weren't, I wouldn't want him. He—he's not to be trusted."

"He's an Impossible Bachelor," Eleanor said. "You knew that from the start."

"I never meant to fall for him," Poppy said. "In fact, Sergei proposed."

Both her best friends were in a tizzy.

"It's what you wanted," Beatrice said.

"This is—*was*—your dream come true." Eleanor giggled.

"Yes, it used to be." Poppy gave a quick shrug. "But then Eversly proposed." She paused. "And I might accept him."

Beatrice squeezed her arm. "But you don't *love* him.

A true Spinster would never marry a man she doesn't love."

"I know." Poppy couldn't help it. She felt a lump in her throat. "Remember I said this isn't just a national security problem but a Spinsters problem?"

"Yes, as a matter of fact," said Eleanor in a soothing voice. "And we never really went over that."

"I simply assumed you meant that Spinsters stick together, even when one of us is stealing—I mean, *retrieving*—a painting," Beatrice clarified.

"I did mean that," said Poppy. "But I also meant that I'm afraid I'm calling into question our basic bylaws. I've informed Aunt Charlotte of my concerns."

"Exactly what are these concerns?" Eleanor asked.

Beatrice led them to a park bench not far from their waiting carriages, and they all sat.

Poppy smoothed out her skirts. "I fell in love with the wrong person. Yet he fits every single requirement for giving up my membership. My situation reveals a basic flaw in our bylaws."

Beatrice and Eleanor stared at her.

Beatrice bit her lip. "So you're saying, according to our bylaws, Drummond's your perfect match—but he's not."

"Exactly," said Poppy. "How could he be, when he's . . . already broken my heart?" Her voice cracked a little. "A man like Eversly wouldn't do that. He's too kind. And thoughtful. I'd be much better off renouncing my Spinsterhood for *him*."

"I see what you mean," said Eleanor. "If *much better off* means your heart is never at risk."

Beatrice sighed. "That's what it comes down to. You'd be safe with Eversly. But with Drummond, there's the chance you'd be hurt."

They sat for a moment in silence.

"Spinsters are brave," said Eleanor eventually. "We're not supposed to give in to fear."

Beatrice smoothed Poppy's hair. "If we love someone, we have to be willing to put ourselves at risk."

"I think the bylaws stand," Eleanor insisted. "You shouldn't marry anyone who doesn't meet the requirements. Drummond does, and you have to be willing to risk everything for him."

Poppy closed her eyes. "It's too late."

"Has he been to the altar yet with Natasha?" Beatrice raised a brow.

"No," Poppy said, "but he fathered her baby."

She couldn't bear to think of their intimacies in her father's library and on Nicholas's sailboat and then imagine that he'd done all that and more with that scheming witch!

Eleanor scoffed. "And you believe Natasha?"

"Over the man you love?" Beatrice eyed her disbelievingly.

"He never denied it," Poppy said, a little embarrassed. "But he never admitted it, either. In fact, he was acting quite unlike his usual self."

"He's a man with secrets, isn't he?" Eleanor waggled her brows.

"Yes," whispered Poppy.

He was a man with secrets. And she suddenly remembered that moment when he'd said *thrilled*. He hadn't looked drunk then. Perhaps he'd been trying to tell her something—and couldn't.

Thrilled was their special word.

One might even say it was their code word.

A small flame of hope surged in her breast. She reached out and grabbed both her friends' hands. "I knew I loved you for a reason."

Beatrice grinned. "And we love you, too."

"We no longer have a crisis with the Spinsters Club," Eleanor declared. "You're going to be shrewd about it, but you're not going to give up on Drummond just yet. Of course, we still have that matter of the portrait to deal with."

"We've no time to waste." Beatrice stood and popped up her parasol. "Ladies?"

Poppy pulled Eleanor up by the hand.

And they formed a small huddle, their hands resting over each other's.

"Hell will freeze over," they recited in whispers, "before we—"

"Give up our passions," said Beatrice.

"And give in to our parents," murmured Poppy.

"To marry men we don't love," added Eleanor.

They released their hands and said as one, "The Spinsters Club? Never heard of it." Then Beatrice twirled her parasol, Eleanor adjusted her bonnet, and Poppy yawned to cover a happy grin.

She said her good-byes and walked to her carriage, feeling so much better now that she'd spoken to her friends.

But her grin faded when she opened the door and

saw a strange elderly man with a pale face and high shirtpoints waiting for her inside.

"Hello, Lady Poppy," he said in a thin, grim voice. "Do get in. I am Mr. Groop, and I have something very important to tell you about the Duke of Drummond."

CHAPTER 43

Nicholas stood next to a table laden with bowls of caviar at the Lievens' ball, Natasha hanging on his elbow. Finally, it was time to retrieve the painting. He'd endured several days of misery being cast into the role of Natasha's beloved. He'd also spent several frustrating days of speculation, wondering about Groop and his odd behavior. He dared not ask the spymaster what he'd been up to, following his brother like that. He needed time to gather more information, and he must be subtle about it.

One way he'd tried was by casually mentioning Frank's name to Groop. Just once. Interesting how the old man never acknowledged they'd met.

But why? What had Groop to hide?

"I'm so hungry," Natasha whispered up to him with an alluring smile that did nothing but aggravate him. "Would you fix me a plate as I'm eating for two?"

Nicholas really hadn't wanted to hear that at the moment. But what could he do other than endure? So he gritted his teeth and handed her a plate of caviar and toast points.

"Here you are"—he inhaled a deep breath—"my dearest darling."

Natasha jerked her gaze back to his, her eyes alight with something fervent. "So," she said breathlessly, "you *do* love me."

He put on his best besotted look. "I worship the ground you walk on. And I look forward to all the children you'll bear me. I want to have ten."

"Ten?" Natasha made a face.

"Oh, yes," he said. "Let me show you where we'll live with our happy brood."

And he pulled out the map of Lumley's new estate. "The Orkney Islands, above Scotland. We shall be on the northernmost isle. I've already dubbed the house 'Castle Natasha.' It's not a castle, really, more a humble abode, but we don't need anything but love to survive, do we, my dear?"

Natasha sucked in a breath. "Over my dead body shall I move there."

Nicholas chuckled. "Of course you shall." He folded the map and put it back in his pocket. "It's heaven on earth, even if it is a bit cold."

He sniffed and looked about the room.

Natasha was staring at him as if she'd seen a ghost. "What about Seaward Hall?"

"I sold it," he said. "I want to carry you even farther away, where I can have you all to myself. Oh, and did I tell you about the sheep? The corgis will herd them every day."

"My corgis do not herd anything," she said. "They're too delicate, and they know nothing of herding."

"It's in their blood," Nicholas said. "They'll be outside, mucking about. No time for walks in prams."

"I tell you—" Her voice had a dangerous edge to it.

Nicholas placed a finger over her mouth. "You're simply gorgeous when you speak of your dogs," he whispered. "In fact, I wrote you a poem. Shall I recite it?"

"Shut up," Natasha said through gritted teeth. "I abhor your obsequious manner. You are the Duke of Drummond. You're cold and haughty, like me."

He shook his head. "That was a façade, my dear. All a façade. It came crumbling down"—he looked deep into her flat, dark eyes and felt his first bit of acting nerves—"when I, um, met you."

The princess's lip curled up in a sneer. "This is a massive joke," she said. "You're trying to rid yourself of me. Well, it shall never happen. You are mine. *Forever.*"

And she flounced off.

Blast.

What was he to do now? He had a vision of the future—in it, he was buried up to the neck in corgis.

A bleak weariness settled over him.

"Hello, Duke."

He turned around.

Poppy.

It was like sunshine had come out and blown away all the gray clouds. She was stunning tonight in a Grecian-style gown that made her look like Artemis, goddess of the hunt. She was also more beautiful—and intimidating—than he'd ever seen her.

He bowed. "Good evening, Lady Poppy." He realized his tone was cold, but how else was he to act around the only woman in the world who'd made him think twice about staying a dangerous, aloof bachelor?

"Congratulations on your betrothal," she said. "I wish you many years of happiness with the princess . . . and her dogs."

Nicholas merely scowled. He could think of no reply suitable for her ears.

Poppy lifted her chin and moved past him, and he caught a whiff of her familiar, intoxicating scent.

He couldn't think of her right now. He had to focus on his plan.

On his duty.

The dancing began, and Natasha returned to his side and insisted they participate. He'd never been more glum. Duty couldn't be this. It couldn't be dancing with a Russian princess who was glowering at you and stepping on your feet. Could it?

If it was, why was it sitting so heavily on his shoulders? Why could he not embrace it the way he always had before?

At one point, he was paired in a quadrille with Lady Beatrice.

She smiled at him. "Remember what I said, Drummond? If you're worthy of Poppy, we'll help you. The best way we can do that is to assure her you're made of stern stuff and not Natasha's toy. Prove us right."

And then she was whisked away.

Natasha's toy.

Ha.

He'd prove to the world he wasn't Natasha's toy, all right.

The next moment, he was joined in the dance by Lady Eleanor.

"Poppy's a woman who knows her mind," she said. "She's loyal and steadfast and brave. I trust you'll show her you're the same."

And then she was twirled into another man's arms.

Nicholas wasn't happy. He didn't like his integrity questioned. But he must admit that Ladies Eleanor and Beatrice had a point. Tonight was the night he must take charge of his fate and not let it rest in the hands of Natasha or Groop.

He danced with his traitorous fiancée next.

Nicholas cleared his throat. "You've used my brother grievously to entrap me."

Her eyes widened. "How can you believe anything Frank says?"

"And you're a threat to Lady Poppy. What were you going to do once you put her in that barrel? Kill her?"

"That's outrageous," she sputtered.

"It doesn't matter. I'll play your game tonight, but no more. We're not engaged nor shall we ever be."

She opened her mouth to say something more, but then he spun her away . . . out of his arms.

And if he had anything to do with it, out of his life.

He watched Poppy now talking to someone on the other side of the ballroom. She knew he was to retrieve the painting tonight for the Service. Yet she didn't appear to be bothered. She'd always wanted to assist him—she'd begged him, as a matter of fact.

He must find out the reason for her nonchalance.

Interrupting her conversation with an elderly widow, he said, "Lady Poppy, might I have a word?"

The elderly widow's jaw dropped. "But aren't you *not speaking* to each other?"

"You're correct," said Poppy, "but unlike some people I know who simply *talk* about taking risks, I believe in actually taking them"—she cast a challenging look his way—"so I shall speak to him, after all."

"What was that about?" he asked, dragging her away. "I take risks. All the time."

"Is that so," she said coolly, and wouldn't look at him.

He felt himself getting angry. "Yes, it's so."

She shrugged. "You could have fooled me."

"I'm taking a massive risk this evening," he said, "and you no longer care?"

"Why should I?"

"Because you wanted to help me take it."

She put a delicate hand on her hip. "Why should you be concerned what I think? You threw me over, so the way I see it, I'm no longer your fiancée. My life is none of your business."

"You're right to be angry about Natasha. But all that happened before I met you."

Her emerald eyes blazed. "You told me to trust you. I did. I trusted you with my heart. I told you I was a Spinster. That I deserved respect. That I would settle for nothing less than love. Yet love doesn't interest you, does it, Drummond? You used me, the same way you apparently used Natasha."

And she strode off.

"Wait a bloody minute," he called after her. "I didn't throw you over. I told you I'd marry you. *You* were the one who said you were going to get out of our arrangement, no matter what."

But she ignored him.

The scamp.

She looked luscious in that gown. He was angry with her and mesmerized by her all at the same time. He wanted her.

Dammit, he didn't only want her. He *loved* Lady Poppy Smith-Barnes—every annoying, charming, delicious inch of her.

Why had it taken him so long to figure that out?

He caught up with her again. She yanked her arm back and tried to get away, but he wouldn't let her. Instead, he looked her up and down, soaking in her beauty, but, even more, her strong spirit. "I'm not going to marry Natasha. I couldn't possibly have fathered her child. Whatever you hear tonight, don't believe it."

"That's your concern, not mine," she said stoutly.

The little spitfire. How he craved her good opinion again!

She pushed an index finger on his chest. "Lord Eversly has asked me to marry him." Her tone was defiant. "And I'm to give him my answer before the first waltz."

Everything seemed to stop.

"Don't marry him," Nicholas said right away. "Remain a spinster—a luscious, fiery Spinster—and wait for a man who's worthy of you. However long it takes."

It wasn't he. Not yet.

But it would be.

He would prove himself worthy.

He had no choice but to trust her to wait and believe he was the only man for her. It was the hardest thing he'd ever done, but he turned and walked away again, and all the while he was thinking of her, not of his duty.

He must think of her. He *would* think of her right now. In fact, he intended to think about her—and eat with her and sleep with her and frolic with her—for the rest of their lives.

Because they'd be together.

Happily married.

His duty to the Service and his obligation to Operation Pink Lady were important, yes. They had their place in the great scheme of things. But he had a higher duty to live the life he was meant to live. And an even greater duty to his heart. He was still going to retrieve the painting, but now he'd do it for Poppy. Forget the MR and to hell with Groop's orders.

Operation Get Poppy Back was officially under way.

CHAPTER 44

"Nicholas!" Poppy called after him. She could hardly breathe.

He turned around for a split second and they locked eyes.

"I want to remind you of something you once told me." Her hands trembled, so she grabbed bunches of her gown. "You said taking chances is part of the fun—what makes life exciting. You like surprises, don't you?"

"Of course." His mouth curved up. "They keep one on one's toes."

"Don't forget that," she advised him.

"Don't *you* forget, either." He gave her a mock bow and disappeared into the crowd.

"Oh, I won't!" she yelled, and hopped on her toes to get a last look at him in his normal state of utterly confident complacency.

Because he was going to get quite a surprise. He had no idea how big, but it was huge.

Huge!

She couldn't wait to tell him the whole thing, but she'd decided to tell him the first part tonight and save the rest for later—if there was a later.

A later that involved disrobing, especially.

She hoped there'd be a later, but how could there be?

He hadn't asked her to marry him when she'd told him about Eversly's proposal.

He'd simply told her to wait.

For what?

For *him*?

If so, why hadn't he asked her to wait for him outright?

She bit the tip of her finger. Perhaps she was supposed to read between the lines. He was a secret agent, after all, and she was a brilliant decoder.

Or *could* it have been her overactive, fanciful imagination attributing all sorts of lovely thoughts to him that simply didn't exist?

No more fairy tales, she'd told herself. And here she was indulging in them again.

Natasha came up to her and raked her with a scornful glance. "You told me long ago you'd be here with your future husband. And that you would kiss him in front of all the company. But you certainly look all alone and invisible to me."

"I don't think so," said Poppy, "or you wouldn't be so concerned about putting me in my place."

The princess gasped. "I have your so-called future husband. He's *mine*, and my brother is about to make the official announcement. You might want to leave."

She gave a simpering little laugh.

"I refuse to give you the satisfaction," Poppy replied with a toss of her head. "In fact, I plan to be front and center when that announcement is made."

She turned her back on the princess, only to see Lord Eversly approaching, a hopeful light in his eyes. "Lady Poppy! How good it is to see you."

She forced herself to smile. "Hello, Eversly."

He took her elbow and, in the kindest, gentlest manner possible, led her to a corner. "I must know your answer *now*. We're about to have the first waltz, and of course, I want to dance it with you. And then soon we shall have our own ball to make our betrothal announcement."

She looked at him, her heart beating hard, and shook her head. "I'm so sorry," she said. "My answer has to be no. You're a wonderful man, and I do hope you'll find a woman who appreciates you. But I'm sorry—I can't be the one."

His sweet expression dissolved into disappointment, which tore at her heart.

"It's still the Duke of Drummond you love, isn't it?" he whispered.

She nodded. "I know it's impossible."

"It's all right." He gave her a kiss on the cheek. "I believe in true love, too."

She took his hand and squeezed it. "You're so kind."

And he left her.

She followed him with her eyes and saw several young debutantes eyeing him as if he were a tremendous catch. And then a matron stopped and spoke to him, gesticulating to a pretty miss to come forward. She did just that, giving him a sweet curtsy. He held out his arm and she took it, her face beaming. And as fast as that, Eversly was swept back into the social whirl.

Natasha was right. Poppy was alone, without even Eleanor and Beatrice for company. They'd left the ball and were hiding in the bushes below the terrace leading to the rear gardens, waiting until just the right moment to enter the ball again.

It was all part of her plan to steal the painting back for Papa and herself.

"It's time," Sergei said from a small stage near the musicians. "Time for the first waltz and an official announcement." His eyes roamed around the room and alighted on Nicholas, who looked more cold and intimidating than she'd ever seen him. Natasha clung to his elbow, her dark, scheming eyes alight with triumph. "Come forward, you two."

Nicholas strode forward with Natasha, looking as if he were about to go to the guillotine. They both stepped on the stage.

Poppy pushed her way to the front of the crowd.

Nicholas refused to look at her. But Natasha did, and her mouth was pursed in a satisfied smile.

Poppy did her best to remain calm, ignoring her increasingly shallow breaths.

"You can do it," someone said in her ear. She flinched, looked behind her, and saw a long-faced, beady-eyed footman just disappearing between two matrons.

Mr. Groop was right. She could. And she would.

She looked up at Nicholas, her heart in her throat.

Sergei smiled at the crowd. "It gives me great pleasure to announce the betrothal of my sister, the Russian princess Natasha, to—"

"Stop!" Poppy interrupted him.

A hush fell over the crowd, and she pointed to Nicholas. "That man is not the Duke of Drummond. I have proof that his missing uncle—the one everyone thought had been murdered—is still alive. *He's* the Duke of Drummond, not Nicholas."

"She's lying." Natasha stared daggers at her.

Sergei scowled. "What's this about, Lady Poppy? Duke?"

"I've no idea," Nicholas said low.

"I have his uncle's signet ring here." Poppy held it up. "It even has his initials. It was given to me by Tradd Staunton himself. He's kept his identity hidden all these years because he works for the Service."

"The Service?" was the general outcry, except for a few debutantes who exclaimed, "What's *that*?" and one ancient gentleman who insisted the Service had been disbanded years before.

"He goes by the code name Mr. Groop," Poppy went on, and saw Nicholas's face blanch. "But a document signed by Prinny himself proves Groop's claim and his right to the Drummond title and properties. So I'm afraid, Nicholas Staunton, you're back to being Lord Maxwell. You'll inherit someday, but your uncle is so busy with the Service, the Drummond title, properties, and coffers are his very last priority."

Everyone gasped.

"Show me that ring," Nicholas demanded, and looked at her as if she were mad. "And where's that document?"

"Here's your ring!" She tossed it into the air. There was a collective gasp when it landed in the crowd. "Groop was here just one minute ago, dressed in livery, but you'll never discover him. He's a master of disguise. One of the servants has the document on a tray. Have fun finding it *and* the ring."

People burst into talk and many held up quizzing glasses to see where the ring might have gone and where this document might be and if Groop were still lurking somewhere in the vicinity.

"I despise you, Nicholas Staunton!" cried Natasha. "I marry no less than dukes."

"But what about the baby?" someone called from the crowd.

It was Lord Howell.

"What baby?" Natasha crossed her arms over her chest and pouted.

"You mean . . . you *lied*?" Lord Howell's face was purple.

"I am a Russian princess," Natasha answered, and strode off, calling for her attendants.

Was that the best excuse she could give for her bad behavior? Poppy huffed, but no one noticed—no one except Countess Lieven.

"Portrait or not," she said in Poppy's ear, "that girl is not representing our country at all well. I will send her packing in the morning, back to St. Petersburg. Her mother will put her in the convent for sure this time. Strike up a lively tune!" she called to the small string orchestra, and she strode toward Natasha.

The band dutifully began a Viennese waltz. At the same time, a strange honking noise arose from the back of the room, near the doors to the garden, which were now flung open.

And much yapping.

Followed by several high-pitched screams.

Poppy's mouth dropped open. *Nicholas Staunton,* she thought, *this is the distraction you created to retrieve the painting?*

She was in shock, yet she wasn't. The man was cheeky.

Finding their flat-footed way amid a forest of silks, satins, muslins, and crisp cotton was a gaggle of geese— waddling, nipping, honking, demanding attention. But their noise wasn't nearly as bad as the yapping from the corgis.

Poppy sucked in a breath when she saw Boris. He and the rest of the dogs were enthusiastically trying to herd the geese, one of which looked very familiar.

"My beloved dogs!" Natasha could be heard screeching. "Save them!"

There were loud shouts and several crashes of presumably precious china and crystal. The musicians continued stumbling through a waltz. Count Lieven stood near them, his face sweating as he desperately called for order.

"I am a Russian prince!" Poppy heard Sergei yell. "Get this blasted gander away from me!"

She felt as if she were in a dream.

She also knew one thing—she loved Nicholas. But neither he nor anyone else was going to decide where her mother's painting was going except *her*.

Her hands began to sweat. She had to go. *Now.* And retrieve the painting before Nicholas did. It was all right. He wouldn't need the M.R. anyway. No, indeed.

She wished she could be there when Nicholas heard the reason why.

A quick glance at Eleanor and Beatrice satisfied her that they were doing their jobs. They were scurrying about, dressed in livery and powdered wigs and holding their trays aloft with documents glued to them (the real one was safe at home), while guests chased them. Groop had long ago disappeared. A large crowd followed Beatrice right out the door to the gardens.

Eleanor sped in big circles around the ballroom, or tried to. The geese and corgis got in her and everyone's way.

Aunt Charlotte, her hand to her breast, caught up with Poppy. "What's going on, dear?"

"I have to take the painting," she said calmly, striding toward the stairs.

"No," Aunt Charlotte gasped.

"It's quite all right, Aunt. It's *my* painting, and I can—"

"No, dear. Not that. A large goose is following Prince Sergei as if it's besotted with him. It's quite a charming sight."

And she left her.

Nicholas was a mischief-maker. But Poppy couldn't afford to be amused by him *or* the presence of Lady Caldwell's gander—not yet. She was almost to the stairs, at the top of which was a corridor, an alcove, and the painting. If she could just get through this crowd of people, geese, and dogs, she'd be home-free.

Out of the corner of her eye, she caught Nicholas ignoring the servants with trays and heading toward the stairs himself.

She must beat him.

She kept walking—faster.

It's now or never, she told herself when she reached the lowest stair, and sprinted up them. Silently, she sped down the corridor. The footmen had left their posts and were attempting to restore order in the ballroom.

Just as Count Lieven had said over tea, the painting was positioned in an alcove under a window. It rested on an easel and was draped in a red silk cloth.

She'd have to take it down the servants' stairs and out the back way.

When she picked up the frame, Poppy had never been more nervous or excited. Goodness, it was heavy! Heavier than she'd thought it would be. And the blasted drape was sliding off and catching under her feet.

"Stop right there," a low, menacing voice said behind her.

But it didn't scare her. How could it? It was only Nicholas.

She stole a quick glance at him. "No," she insisted. "I've no time, and you had best go away and look for that document. Don't you care that Groop's your uncle?"

But he didn't, the bounder. At least not at the moment.

Instead, he grabbed the painting from her arms. "What do you think you're doing?"

She tried to rip it out of his hands, but he was too strong for her. And then he held the large rectangle over his head.

"I'm stealing it," she whispered loudly, and leaped to get it.

He held it higher. "You can't steal this."

"Most certainly I can. It's *mine*."

"*I'm* stealing it," he said, and moved toward the stairs. "For you, you minx, not the Service, so please get out of my way."

"Oh, no, you're not." She gave one more mighty leap and still fell short of the painting's edge. "Wait. What did you say?"

"I quit the Service. I'm stealing this for *you*."

"You did? You *are*?"

"Yes. And I don't give a rat's arse at the moment that Groop's my uncle, although you were quite clever to try to throw me off like that. You're all that matters to me, you saucy Spinster, you."

"Really?" It felt as if her whole world lit up.

They both heard a movement on the stairs and locked gazes.

"Hurry," he said. "To the curtains."

Quickly, he put the painting back on the easel. Poppy adjusted the red silk drape over the portrait, and they ran to the curtains.

She pressed against Nicholas's body and closed her eyes, not because she was afraid—but because she was so glad to be near him again, to be inhaling his man scent, to be leaning on his strong chest.

"What do you think we should do?" whined one footman, clomping up the stairs.

"I dunno," said another. "It's pandemonium. If we bring it out now, we might drop it."

"Or a damned goose will nip it."

Poppy looked up into Nicholas's eyes. They were full of mirth. She stifled a giggle with her hand.

But just as suddenly, his mysterious gray eyes—which she'd come to adore—softened.

"I love you," he mouthed.

The two footmen went back and forth, discussing the merits of taking the portrait to the ballroom now versus taking it later, when things had calmed down.

Poppy tried to convey hope in her gaze to Nicholas. She hoped the footmen would leave. She hoped she and Nicholas could grab the painting and leave themselves.

She hoped . . .

They could have a happy ending.

Was it too much to ask?

He leaned down and kissed her. A quick kiss, but it said much. He knew her. He knew her better than anyone, and when she kissed him back, she was saying she knew him better than anyone, too.

And they were meant to be together.

Forever.

"I love you, too," she mouthed silently.

Nicholas held her close and pressed a lingering kiss on top of her head. She took comfort in the beating of his heart.

The footmen decided to leave the painting for the time being and return to the chaos in the ballroom.

Thank God, Nicholas thought.

As the thunk of footsteps disappeared, he squeezed Poppy's elbow. "Let's be quick about it," he whispered.

"Right," said Poppy.

They'd steal the painting together. Neither one said so out loud, but that moment behind the curtains clearly sealed the bond he'd been denying.

Love wasn't exactly a convenient thing to have happen at the moment, Nicholas realized. But it was there, big, warm, and new—but a fact of his being, as natural a part of him as breathing.

Not that he could think about love right now. Or the shocking news about Groop. Or his own unexpected reduction in title back to Lord Maxwell (which didn't bother him in the slightest).

There was a painting to be stolen.

Recovered, he amended.

Poppy ran to the servants' stairs. "Over here," she called softly.

They began the descent and went only five steps before they heard two voices from below—maids who were in hysterics, being yelled at by someone to get brooms—and were coming upstairs.

The rightness of their purpose gave Nicholas an

extra boost of resolution. "We'll simply take it out the front door."

Poppy's eyes grew wide. "We have no choice, do we?"

"Who'd even notice?"

He turned the draped portrait sideways and grabbed the upper front corner. Poppy took the lower rear corner.

And they walked down the front stairs with it.

No one seemed to care. Or notice. The geese and dogs were causing too much disruption. Sergei and Natasha were red-faced and upset. Eleanor and Beatrice were nowhere to be seen, but a large crowd was still looking for the ring, their heads bent to scan the ballroom floor.

The orchestra played another waltz to which only one couple danced, Eversly and the sweet girl Poppy had seen him with earlier.

No one stood at the front door of the ballroom to see Nicholas and Poppy out. It was flung open, and an elderly couple were taking their leave, talking loudly of the geese's honking. Nicholas allowed them to go first, and he and Poppy were right behind them when Nicholas felt a jerk on the painting.

"Heavens," said Poppy from behind him. "*Do* let go of my gown, Boris!"

And then Boris saw Nicholas. He yapped and bounded up to him, hugged him on the leg, and refused to let go.

"This dog is evil," Nicholas said, three feet from the front door.

"He's in love with you." Poppy couldn't help giggling. "The way the gander is with Sergei."

"Very funny," Nicholas said dryly.

Into complete silence.

He looked behind him. Poppy's pale, slender neck turned, as well.

Everyone in the ballroom was staring at them.

"Where are you going with our painting?" asked Countess Lieven into the silence.

"Um, I—I was taking it home," said Poppy.

There was a stirring of the crowd. But then a group of gentlemen strode through the front door, Lord Derby and Lord Wyatt among them.

The tension in Poppy's expression eased a fraction. She was obviously relieved to see her father.

Lord Derby looked around with great concern. "We were called from a useless meeting by a beady-eyed, long-faced man in livery who said a small riot is being waged here. How can we be of help, Count? Countess?"

The count glowered at him and then pointed a finger at Poppy. "Your own daughter is stealing a very valuable Russian painting, right from beneath our noses. Does she think we're *stupid*?"

Lord Derby opened his mouth to say something, but nothing came out.

"Lady Poppy doesn't think you're stupid," Nicholas intervened. "The painting actually belongs to her, Count, Countess. The provenance can be verified—you'll understand that we may take it back without asking permission and restore it to its rightful owners, the family of Lord Derby."

The count's brow furrowed. "Improperly handled provenance? Are you suggesting this great Russian masterpiece doesn't belong to Revnik's niece and nephew and is not ours to celebrate as a grand piece of Russian culture here, tonight, at this ball?"

Nicholas smiled politely. "Yes, Count, Countess. I say that with all due respect."

"But you're wrong, Drummond." Sergei stepped forward. "My uncle Revnik painted this portrait, and we found it under his bed. It *is* ours. My sister and I inherited our uncle's estate."

Lord Derby had found his voice, and now he looked at his daughter with a great deal of worry. "We don't want to make any mistakes here, Poppy. This could affect relations between our two countries. Until now, I had no idea this painting existed."

The count's face turned beet red. "Lord Derby says he doesn't even know of the painting? What's going on here?"

The countess put her hand up. "You must prove the painting belongs to you, Lady Poppy."

"I must agree," Lord Derby said.

"All agreed, say *aye*," piped up one of his Parliamentary colleagues.

A fair number of people in the ballroom raised their hands.

Poppy's cheeks bloomed pink. "I have proof, Papa. Here's the receipt." She pulled yet another paper from her bodice. "It proves Mama commissioned this painting from Revnik, and she paid for it."

She held it out to her father. He and his colleagues peered at it.

Lord Wyatt cleared his throat. "That's a fake," he said calmly to the company. "I'm not free to say more, but this portrait belongs to England, and I hereby confiscate it on behalf of His Royal Highness's government."

CHAPTER 45

"You can't take it!" Sergei cried.

"I agree. That's outrageous!" Count Lieven crossed his arms and stuck out his chin.

The crowd began talking madly.

Please, Poppy begged the universe, *please make sure we get Mama's painting back in the family. It belongs with* us.

The countess raised her hand. "Stop everything," she said. "Let us show the company the painting first. It is why we held the ball."

Nicholas unveiled the portrait, and there was a collective sigh of admiration from the crowd in the ballroom.

Poppy could look at the painting all day if she had to. It was that wonderful.

"It's lovely, no?" said the countess. "Revnik was a master."

"Indeed he was," said Poppy, echoing the murmurings of approval from the ballroom floor. She yearned to put that portrait in her father's library above the mantel so he could see it every time he looked up from writing one of his speeches.

Nicholas and Lord Derby were both staring, transfixed, at the canvas.

"Th-that's my wife," said Lord Derby.

"It is, Papa." Poppy had tears in her eyes. "And that's you, facing her. See your special cuff links?"

He peered closer. "I do."

Nicholas met Poppy's eyes. His were full of something glad and determined.

Could he have uncovered the identity of the mole? She hoped so, but from what she could see, it was simply a painting . . . of her parents on an extraordinary night.

Papa cleared his throat and addressed the company. "My wife must have commissioned the painting when we lived in St. Petersburg. We went to a magnificent ball at the Winter Palace."

Poppy laid a hand on his arm. "Mama wanted to remember that night with you."

Lord Wyatt stepped forward. "Nevertheless, the portrait is now in the custody of the Prince Regent's government, and I will take it."

"No, you won't," Nicholas intervened, his voice steely and his expression intimidating. "Who are you to say Lady Poppy's receipt is faked?"

Lord Wyatt's mouth thinned. He had no answer.

Nicholas held up the receipt. "It's perfectly proper. I have no doubt we can compare this signature of Revnik's to another genuine one and it will be a clear match. Now get out of our way. The painting belongs to a private party. England will have to negotiate with Lord Derby and his daughter Poppy for access to it."

"You're mad!" Sergei stood before Nicholas. "May I remind you the painting belongs to me and my sister? And I'm determined we should depart with it right now."

"No, Sergei," Poppy cried. "My intuition is very good—like my mother's. And I'm sure she commissioned this painting."

"Dear Lady Poppy," Count Lieven said kindly, "both you and the English government still have offered no real proof that the painting belongs to either of you. The government says your receipt is fake. You deny it. Who are we supposed to believe? At the very least, an inquiry will have to be made into this painting's provenance."

Lord Derby put his hand on Poppy's shoulder. "My dear, he's right. We have no proof beyond your receipt, which is in dispute. I suggest the painting remain in the possession of the Lievens, who will guard it until the matter is settled fairly."

Poppy couldn't bear to part with the painting.

But it was slipping away. She just knew it! Lord Wyatt had an almost fanatical look in his eye. He was determined to get it. And so was Sergei. He was flexing his hands as if at the first opportunity he would grab it and run.

She looked at Nicholas.

His eyes were warm, loving, and . . . and—

She looked at the portrait. She wanted it, yes. For Papa and for her.

But . . .

She didn't need it. She needed to cling to the people in her life that she still had. She needed to love them, and let them love her. She needed to immerse herself in life.

With Nicholas.

We're not going to get it, are we? she said with her eyes.

He took her hand and squeezed it. *Don't give up hope,* his gaze said back.

But then Aunt Charlotte appeared at the edge of the crowd. "I believe *I* can prove who the portrait belongs to," she said, her voice ringing throughout the room.

Aunt Charlotte?

Everyone turned to her beloved chaperone.

"What gives you the right to say *that*?" the countess demanded.

Poppy's heart lurched. Her aunt looked so serious, so afraid, yet so determined when she gazed around the room, her white wig slightly askew on her head.

"A Spinster," Aunt Charlotte began in her most confident voice, "*never* reveals details of her private life if she can help it. You see"—she smiled knowingly—"it's usually much more interesting than other people's, which can lead to a fair amount of jealousy. But tonight—luckily for you—must be the exception to that rule."

"Go on, then, sister," said Lord Derby, who'd walked to Aunt Charlotte's side and held her hand.

Aunt Charlotte took a deep breath. "As much as I've tried these past weeks—amid all the hoopla about his art—to forget Revnik ever existed, I must admit that he was one of my great loves." She looked up at her little brother. "I met him in St. Petersburg, Archie, when I came to stay with you for a month. In fact, I met him when I was with Marianna the day she commissioned the painting. She told him she wanted it painted for *you*. I accompanied her on many sittings to Revnik's studio, which is how our affair developed. But it ended abruptly, as love affairs are wont to do."

Poppy moved next to her father and held his hand tightly.

Aunt Charlotte gave them both a sad smile. "He saw you together that night at the ball at the Winter Palace. He told me he wanted to capture that moment, when Marianna looked up at you and . . . love shone from her eyes. Those were his exact words."

Papa was silent, struggling under the weight of strong emotion. Poppy squeezed his hand harder.

Aunt Charlotte perked up. "I went back to London. My life was there, and I was determined to put Revnik behind me. Marianna wrote me and told me he was almost finished painting her portrait—for *you*, Archie, she told me once more—but I never saw it. I assumed he'd never finished it and that it was lost to us."

Poppy's heart filled with more hope. "Do you have her letters, aunt?"

Aunt Charlotte nodded, tears in her eyes. "I most certainly do, dear. And I'll share them with whoever needs to see them, if it will help establish the Derby claim to the painting."

The crowd started talking again, loudly, about who owned the painting.

Aunt Charlotte raised her hand.

"You may speak," said another of Lord Derby's Parliamentary friends, who nodded in her direction.

"*I* tell people when they can speak," asserted Countess Lieven.

"I was only adjusting my wig," Aunt Charlotte said. "*No one* tells me when I may speak."

And she glared at both Lord Derby's Parliamentary crowd and at the countess.

Poppy was so proud of her.

"I believe my letters from Marianna are enough," Aunt Charlotte went on, as blithely as if she hadn't cut down Very Important People mere seconds before, "but there's one more possibility." She paused. "While Revnik and I were lovers, he told me something he claimed he'd told no one else: he sometimes left a message somewhere on his paintings, usually in a mirror."

Everyone gasped. There was a small mirror in the background of the portrait.

Poppy looked at Nicholas. Was his instinct telling him the same thing hers was?

She was sure that painted mirror held an important message.

CHAPTER 46

Nicholas was intrigued. He already knew Lord Wyatt was their mole. The little figure in the background of the painting, the one exchanging documents with a Russian envoy, was his very image.

No wonder Wyatt was desperate to claim the painting on behalf of the government.

Later, Nicholas would wonder if Lord Wyatt's grand new estates in Cornwall and Devon were bought with money he'd obtained selling secrets. He'd also be there to support Lord Derby when he found out the disturbing news that someone he admired and respected was working against England.

But right now Nicholas could only think of Poppy and her mother's portrait. He gave Lady Charlotte his full attention.

"Revnik told me what look like shadows and reflections in the mirror are words written backward," she explained. "But one must hold a looking glass up to the image to see what it says."

Poppy's strawberry lips were parted. Nicholas could

see the questions in her eyes. Could Revnik have left a message? And to whom would it be addressed?

Nicholas could also see in Lord Derby's face a desperate desire to have another chance, in any form, to connect with his long-departed wife through Revnik's masterpiece.

"Quickly," called the countess to a footman. "Bring us a looking glass."

A moment later, the countess had one. She approached the painting carefully and held the looking glass to the small, painted mirror.

"A gift," the countess read slowly, carefully, "to a devoted mother and wife, Marianna, who honors her husband Archibald with her undying devotion and love . . . from Revnik."

Thank God.

Poppy looked at her father. Both of them had tears in their eyes. "It most clearly *is* our painting, isn't it?" Derby said to her.

Poppy nodded her head, and this time, Captain Arrow came to her with a handkerchief and wiped her eyes for her.

Where had *he* come from?

Poppy couldn't wipe her own tears because she was holding on to the painting again, as well as her father's hand, and Nicholas was behind her, still squeezing her shoulder.

"Thank you," she whispered to Arrow.

"My pleasure." He smiled, and Nicholas swore half the ladies in the room sighed aloud.

"I have *faith*," Arrow said very deliberately to her

and Nicholas, "that I shall see you more often, Lady Poppy."

"Oh, you will," said Lord Harry, who was suddenly nearby. He gave Nicholas a meaningful look.

Harry was proud of him, Nicholas could tell.

"I look forward to getting to know you, too, Lady Poppy," said Lumley, ever cheerful. "As a matter of fact, we showed up a few minutes ago to do just that. You and Nicholas were walking down the stairs with the painting, and I said to Harry, 'She's the one. She's as dangerous as Drummond—but much prettier.'"

"Thanks." Nicholas was ready to pummel his friend. All in fun, of course.

Poppy blushed and gifted Lumley with a lovely smile that made Nicholas's heart beat faster.

Lord Derby cleared his throat and leveled his gaze at him. "I'm glad we have that settled, Drummond, but why is it, exactly, that you're accompanying my daughter out the front door of the Lievens' residence?"

Nicholas stood tall. "Because I love her, sir."

There were gasps all around.

Lord Derby stared at him as if he were a lunatic. "I'm supposed to believe this, after you abandoned the engagement you entered into with her?"

"I wouldn't let him marry me, Papa," Poppy blurted out. "I refused him. I told him I would find a way out, no matter what he did. Even when he threatened to carry me to Gretna."

There were more gasps.

Poppy moved closer to Nicholas, who put down the painting and squeezed her tight.

The girl was being entirely too brave and honest. Which, come to think of it, was probably why she always seemed to wind up in trouble. But Nicholas wouldn't have her any other way.

"Why, Poppy," her father asked her, "have you evaded marriage for three long years?"

She drew in a deep breath and looked at Nicholas. "Because I never met the right man, Papa. I was content—*happy*—to be a Spinster. I wanted to marry for love and love alone. Or not marry at all."

Nicholas watched as she looked then at Beatrice, Eleanor, and Lady Charlotte. All of them seemed to share a secret smile.

The crowd shifted almost noiselessly. Two women sat on the floor, plopping grapes in their mouths, as if this were a fabulous Greek play and they were the audience.

Nicholas hugged his true love close. "I'd like to ask Poppy to marry me, Lord Derby. With your permission."

Lord Derby looked thoughtfully at him.

"*Please,* Papa. I love him."

Nicholas could sense Lord Derby was troubled. After a tentative moment—after the earl had shared a good, long silent moment with his daughter and then with Nicholas—his mouth curved up.

"You have my permission, young man," he said.

Nicholas grinned. "Thank you, sir."

Poppy threw her arms about her father's neck and kissed him. "Thank you—you and Mama both," she whispered. "I swear it almost feels as if she's stepped out of the painting and is standing next to me right now."

And then she went to Nicholas.

Their eyes locked, and he knew he was exactly where he was supposed to be. She was more beautiful than he'd ever seen her, all because her expression was more tender and fierce and loving than he'd ever seen it before.

He held tight to both her hands.

"Poppy?" Her father's voice was thin. "Are you sure marriage to Drummond is what you want?"

"More than anything," she said, her voice carrying strong and true throughout the room.

"Life will be one great adventure with your daughter, sir," Nicholas told Lord Derby.

"I know exactly what you mean, son." Lord Derby chuckled, then looked at his child. "I believe you've chosen the right man, my dear, and actually"—he looked back at his Parliament friends—"it's time for me to retire. I'll have grandchildren to get to know."

"But what about Prinny's next blunder?" cried one of his colleagues.

"And reforming the demmed corn laws," shouted another.

"Shut up," Lord Derby replied, his eyes back on Poppy.

She smiled up at him, then looked at Nicholas.

And he saw the whole world in her eyes.

EPILOGUE

"I can't believe we're married," Poppy said, looking down at Nicholas. She was bursting with love for him. And desire for him. *All* the time. Which made it terribly hard to remember to put her clothes on.

He laughed up at her. "You'd better be glad we *are* married. Minx." He caressed her arms, sending a warm surge of happiness through her. "You're enjoying the marriage bed, aren't you?"

"Of course." She loved the new sensation of having him inside her. And she especially loved making him groan with pleasure. He was a marvel, her man—and she was absolutely addicted to him.

She stretched her hands above her head and felt like a cat with a bowl of cream. "We've done this well into the dozens of times."

"Yes, *this*," he said with an adorably crooked smile. "I love *this*. And we've only been married—"

"Seven days and—"

"Eight hours," Nicholas finished for her. "It's even

more remarkable when you consider two of those days we spent careening north in a mail coach."

"And I loved every minute of it," she assured him.

"Did you?" His eyes lit up like a boy's.

"Of course." She smiled and ran a finger along his jaw, remembering how avid he'd been to hold the blunderbuss and how disappointed he'd been when he hadn't had to fend off any highwaymen.

Now that he wasn't in the Service, he had to find adventure somewhere, and he'd always wanted to ride on the mail coach.

"But darling"—the word was new and splendiferous to her—"is it possible to stay in bed too long? I mean, could we become ill?"

"The only effect I can think of occurring from loving your wife over and over is—and it's not an illness—is the lady becoming with child."

Poppy's eyes widened. "Thank God *that's* all."

She really had been worried. Except for a daily walk to the beach, they'd hardly been out of bed since they'd arrived at Seaward Hall, three days after marrying at St. Paul's in London. Papa, Aunt Charlotte—and all of Poppy and Nicholas's friends—had waved them off.

They'd had the castle to themselves. The servants had welcomed Poppy as if she were their duchess, even though she wouldn't be for years. But she would be mistress of the house in the meantime—Lady Maxwell, wife to Lord Maxwell, who was heir to the Duke of Drummond.

Groop was still Groop. Even though he was also Uncle Tradd, the proper duke. The Service was his life, and he would remain in London, behind the scenes as always.

Poppy looked out the window at the cliffs, the long stretch of shoreline with that massive rock jutting from it, the one where Nicholas used to play, and the expansive, ever-restless sea. "It's certainly a lovely view," she murmured.

"Yes?"

"And the castle is majestic." She brushed a lock of hair out of his eyes and smiled. "If in a bit of disrepair."

He grinned. "Ah, well. The massive dowry you've brought me will help with restoring it. Although"—he sat up on an elbow—"I told your father to hold off. I have plans for this place. And I'm clever enough to re-store it in limited fashion on my own. Groop—"

"You mean Uncle Tradd—"

Nicholas sighed. "I will never call him Uncle Tradd."

"Yes, you will."

"I won't."

"Oh, but you will. He's coming to stay for two weeks next month."

"*What?*"

"You're no longer in the Service, so he is now Uncle Tradd."

She ignored the dark look he threw her.

"Let's get back to the subject," he said dryly. "I was saying that Groop, or *Uncle Tradd,* as I shall call him simply to make you happy, gave me the M.R. for all my years of service. I'm going to invest in some new farm equipment and sheep. Lumley has loads of them to get us started."

"Excellent idea," she said. "I'm sure you won't need Papa's money. Especially as we have the Viking treasure to call our own."

Nicholas made a face. "Very funny."

She clapped her hands. "I've been dying to tell you! I was waiting for the right moment. A moment when we wouldn't be naked, and we'd be serious-minded. But so far that hasn't happened, so I might as well choose *now*."

He sat up, his elbows locked behind him, his pupils large and dark. "What is this? One of your jokes?"

He was so handsome sometimes, she couldn't look at him without wanting to kiss him. So she did.

"Absolutely not," she said a moment later.

"Tell me. *Now*." A moment before, in the middle of their kiss, he'd been so . . . *sweet*. But now he looked the sternest she'd ever seen him.

"Very well." She couldn't help a smug smile. "Dear Uncle Tradd—the man you used to refer to as Groop— appeared in my carriage one day and said that it didn't seem right that you'd have to act as duke when he was the real Duke of Drummond. And he thought it would be a fair trade to give you the Viking treasure he'd found in return for your being his heir and taking care of the properties while he had all the fun in the Service."

"Devil take it, what Viking treasure?"

Poppy bit her lip and hoped she would tell the story exactly as Uncle Tradd had.

"Well, when he was thirteen, he found a cache on the beach, buried beneath a rock. He confided in a footman he trusted, someone he'd apparently looked up to as a friend, and the footman kidnapped him to try to force the location out of him. When Tradd wouldn't reveal it, the thug dumped him in the worst part of London, figuring he'd never make it back."

"So that's what happened." Nicholas's brow smoothed out as if the weight of the world had fallen off his shoulders. "Family mystery. Solved." He paused. "I suppose we ought to be grateful the footman couldn't bring himself to outright kill him."

"Indeed," Poppy said. "Tradd grew up as a thief to survive, which is how he got into the Service. He never went back to reclaim the treasure or his title. He said he was too busy trying to stay alive, and when he was old enough to make it out of London, too ashamed. He'd done all sorts of nasty things to avoid dying, and he was afraid to come home. But he told me where the treasure is. I dug it up—with Cook's help—"

"Not Cook! She's probably told everyone by now!"

Poppy waved a hand. "She swore she'd never tell."

Nicholas rolled his eyes.

"At any rate," Poppy went on, "the treasure is somewhere in this house. And let me tell you—it's enough treasure to build ten more amazing, grand Seaward Halls. We'll be so rich, we'll be able to travel the world together, too."

"Really?" His eyes sparkled.

"Yes," she said with a grin, "and we'll bring Frank up here to Seaward Hall to set up his own cooper shop!"

Nicholas blew out a breath. "Poppy, my love, *where—is—the treasure?*"

She laughed and ran a hand down his chest. "I won't tell you. Not until you tell me what an IF is."

"You must be joking."

"No. I'm not." She blinked once, slowly.

At first, his mouth drew into a thin line, and his eyes—oh, but they were the stormiest gray she'd ever seen them.

"I refuse to be intimidated," she said. "I'm not afraid of you. I don't care how many octopi you've wrestled."

His mouth curled up. "I see what you're up to," he said warmly.

"You do?" He was making her breathless again.

"Yes, I do. You want *me* to want *you* more than I want that Viking treasure!"

She grinned. "I never thought of that, but perhaps you're right."

He nuzzled her neck and pulled her underneath him. "Well, I do, Lady Maxwell. In fact, don't tell me where the treasure is."

She lifted her head. "Oh, dear."

He laughed aloud. "You can't keep a secret, can you? It's killing you!"

She felt a moment's pique. "Yes, it is killing me, so I demand you tell me—what is an IF? So I can reveal the location of the treasure. *Please.*"

He kissed her mouth, a lovely, slow kiss, then pulled back. "An IF," he said softly, "is your inevitable fate. I knew you were mine as soon as I saw you at the Grangerford ball, gazing up at me as if I were an ax murderer."

She giggled. "And I knew you were my IF when you

said in that highbrow manner, 'I'll be glad to take you where you want to go, Lady Poppy.'"

"Oh, really?" He kissed the tip of her nose.

"Do that now," she whispered. "Take me where I want to go, Nicholas. Before I show you the treasure."

"You *are* my treasure," he said, wrapping her in his arms. "The rest can wait."

Coming soon...

Don't miss the next novel in Kieran Kramer's
Impossible Bachelors series

CLOUDY WITH A CHANCE OF MARRIAGE
ISBN: 978-0-312-37403-7

Available in May 2011 from St. Martin's Paperbacks

"Delectable."
—Julia Quinn, *New York Times* bestselling author

Be sure to check out the companion blog to

WHEN HARRY MET MOLLY

at

www.musingsofthemistresses.blogspot.com

The musings of Athena, Bunny, Hildur, and Joan—the four mistresses who befriend Molly—are amusing indeed. Visit them now!

…and don't miss the blog belonging to Poppy's Aunt Charlotte of

DUKES TO THE LEFT OF ME, PRINCES TO THE RIGHT

www.thespinstersclub.blogspot.com

You'll love spending time in her splendiferous Spinster world!